A SECRET BIRTHRIGHT

BY
OLIVIA GATES

MILLS
BOON

Published in Great Britain 2012
by Mills & Boon, an imprint of Harlequin (UK) Limited,
Eton House, 18-24 Paradise Road, Richmond, Surrey TW9 1SR

© Olivia Gates 2012

ISBN: 978 0 263 89198 0
ebook ISBN: 978 1 408 97774 3

51-0712

Harlequin (UK) policy is to use papers that are natural, renewable and recyclable products and made from wood grown in sustainable forests. The logging and manufacturing processes conform to the legal environmental regulations of the country of origin.

Printed and bound in Spain
by Blackprint CPI, Barcelona

"Do you have any idea about the extent of my craving for you?

"How long it has gone unfulfilled? How much it has cost me to suppress it, to stay away from you?"

Each beat of her heart rocked her as a shadow detached itself from the darkness engulfing the upper floor, taking his form. His body materialized. Then his face emerged from the shadows and she gasped.

Even from this distance, there was no mistake.

The ultra-efficient surgeon, the indulgent benefactor, the teasing, patient playmate was gone. A man of tempestuous passions had emerged in his place.

And she had no right to his passion. She'd lose even the bittersweet torment of his nearness tomorrow. She'd never again feel this alive.

Dear Reader,

I didn't set out to do it, but when I was halfway through writing *A Secret Birthright,* I realized that in it I'd gathered almost all of my most loved themes in writing for Desire! A sheikh, a medical theme, a secret baby, family drama, royal intrigue, love at first sight and a seemingly impossible love.

Is it any wonder the result was one of my most enjoyable books to write, ever?

As I wrote, unraveling the mysteries in the book, I loved being inside Fareed's mind as he finds out the secrets only as the reader does. I also loved being privy to Gwen's conflicted and anguished thoughts and emotions, which give us glimpses of the complex, high-stakes situation and let us wonder right along with her if, when it all comes to light, she will lose everything she's ever loved.

I hope you enjoy discovering the story's many secrets and accompanying Fareed and Gwen on their bumpy road to happy-ever-after as much as I enjoyed writing it all!

I love to hear from readers, so please feel free to contact me at oliviagates@gmail.com. I'd also love it if you "Like" my Olivia Gates author page on Facebook and follow me on Twitter @OliviaGates.

To find out about my latest releases, read excerpts and enter my contests, please visit me on the web at oliviagates.com.

Enjoy, and thanks for reading.

Olivia Gates

Olivia Gates has always pursued creative passions like singing and handicrafts. She still does, but only one of her passions grew gratifying enough, consuming enough, to become an ongoing career—writing.

She is most fulfilled when she is creating worlds and conflicts for her characters, then exploring and untangling them bit by bit, sharing her protagonists' every heart-wrenching heartache and hope, their every heart-pounding doubt and trial, until she leads them to an indisputably earned and gloriously satisfying happy ending.

When she's not writing, she is a doctor, a wife to her own alpha male and a mother to one brilliant girl and one demanding Angora cat. Visit Olivia at www.oliviagates.com.

To all my Romance World friends.
Authors, editors, fans and reviewers.

I don't have enough words to thank you for being
who you are, and for being there for me
when I most needed friends.

One

"I don't want to see another woman. Ever again."

A long moment of silence greeted the fed-up finality of Sheikh Fareed Aal Zaafer's declaration. His companion's empathy and exasperation hung heavy in the stillness.

Then Emad ibn Elkaateb sighed. "I *am* almost resigned a woman isn't in the cards for you. But because this isn't about you or your inexplicable personal choices, I have to insist."

Fareed's laugh was one of incredulous fury. "What *is* this? *You,* who brought me damning proof on each imposter? You're now asking me to suffer another one? To grit my teeth through more pathetic, disgusting lies? Just who are you and what have you done with Emad?"

Suddenly the decorum Emad maintained dissolved. Fareed blinked. Emad rarely budged in giving him the "dues of his birthright," insisted it was an integral part of *his* honor as Fareed's right-hand man to observe Fareed's position as his prince.

Now Emad's expression softened with the indulgence of twenty-five years of being closer to Fareed than his family, friends and staff in his medical center combined. "Anticipating your disappointment was the only reason I objected to the…scheme that brought upon you all of those opportunists. On any other account, I can't begin to fault your methods. My own haven't produced results either. Hesham hid too well."

Fareed gritted his teeth on the upsurge of frustration and futility. Of grief.

Hesham. The sensitive soul and exceptional artist. And out of Fareed's nine siblings, the youngest brother and the most beloved.

It was their father and king's fault that Hesham had hidden. Over three years ago, Hesham had returned from a long stay in the States to announce that he was getting married. He'd made the mistake of believing their father might be persuaded to give him his blessing. Instead, the king had flared into an unprecedented rage. He'd forbidden Hesham to contact his fiancée again, or to consider wedding anyone not chosen by their royal house.

When Hesham refused to obey him, the king's fury had escalated. He'd ranted that he'd find the American hussy who'd tried to insinuate herself into the royal line and make her wish she'd never plotted to ensnare his son. As for Hesham, he wasn't letting him dabble in his pointless artistic pursuits and shirk his royal duties anymore. This was no longer about what or whom Hesham chose to amuse himself with. This was about heritage. He wouldn't let him taint their bloodline with an inferior union. Hesham *would* obey, or there would be hell to pay.

Fareed and his brothers and sisters had intervened on

their brother's behalf, then had worked together to release him when their father had placed Hesham under house arrest.

Hesham had wept as he'd hugged them and told them he had to disappear, to escape their father's injustice and to protect his beloved. He'd begged for their word that they'd never look for him, to consider him dead, for all of their sakes.

None of them had been able to give that word.

But even though each had tried to keep track of him, with Fareed the one who'd gone to the greatest lengths, Hesham had all but erased himself from existence.

A new wave of rage against their father scorched his blood.

If it hadn't been for the oath he'd taken to serve his people, he would have left Jizaan, too. But that wouldn't have been a punishment for their father. He wouldn't have cared about losing another son. All he'd said after Hesham's disappearance had been that he cared only that Hesham did nothing to disgrace their family and kingdom. Fareed believed that their father would have preferred to see Hesham and any of his future children dead before that came to pass.

What had come to pass had been even worse.

After years of Fareed yearning for any contact with him, Hesham's call came from an E.R. in the States. Hesham had called him only to use his last breaths to beg for a favor. Not for himself, but for the woman for whom he'd left his world, who'd *become* his world.

Take care of Lyn, Fareed...and my child...protect them...tell her she's everything...tell her...I'm sorry I couldn't give her what she deserves, that I'll leave her alone with...

There'd been no more words. He'd almost bloodied his

throat roaring for Hesham to tell him more, to wait for him to come save him. He'd heard only an alien voice, telling him his brother had been taken to surgery.

He'd flown out immediately, dread warring with the hope that he'd be in time to save him. He'd arrived to find him long dead.

Learning that Hesham had been in no way responsible for the accident had deepened his anguish. An eighteen-wheeler had lost control and decimated eleven cars, killing many and injuring more. Grief had compromised his sanity, yet he'd fought it to offer his services. As an internationally recognized surgeon and one of the leading experts in his field, he had been gratefully accepted, and he'd operated on the most serious neurological injuries, had saved other victims as he hadn't been able to save Hesham.

It had been too late by the time he'd learned that a woman had been with Hesham in the car. She'd had no injuries, no identification, and had left the hospital as soon as Hesham had died. Descriptions had varied wildly in the wake of the mass casualties.

With a bleeding heart, he'd taken Hesham's body back to Jizaan. After a heart-wrenching funeral, which the king hadn't attended, Fareed had launched a search for Lyn and the child.

But Hesham *had* hidden too well. It seemed he'd been erasing each step as he'd taken it. Investigations into the new identity he'd assumed had revealed no wife or child. Even the car he'd died in had been a rental under yet another name.

After a month of dead ends, Fareed had taken the only option left. If he couldn't find Hesham's woman, he'd let *her* find *him*.

He'd returned to where Hesham had died, placed appeals in all the media for the woman to contact him. He'd kept his message cryptic so only the right person would approach him. Or so he'd intended...

Women had *swamped* him.

Emad had weeded out the most blatant liars, like those with teenaged children or with none, and still advised Fareed not to waste his time on the rest. He'd been certain they'd all turn out to be fortune hunters. Being a billionaire surgeon and desert prince, Fareed had always been a target for gold diggers. And he'd invited them by the drove.

Fareed couldn't comply, couldn't let anyone who remotely answered the criteria go without an audience.

He'd felt antipathy toward every candidate before she'd opened her mouth. But he'd forced himself to see each performance to its exasperating end. He believed Hesham, the lover and creator of beauty, would have fallen in love only with someone flawless inside and out, someone refined, worthy and trustworthy. But what if Hesham hadn't been as discerning as he'd thought?

But after a month of agonizing letdowns, Fareed had gone home admitting his method's failure. He'd known any new attempt would fail without new information to use. For two more months, he'd been driven to the brink on a daily basis thinking his brother's flesh and blood was out there and might be in need.

He'd groped for a sanity-saving measure, answered a plea from a teaching hospital in the States to perform charity surgeries. A part of his schedule was always dedicated to charity work, but he'd never tackled so many within such a tight time frame. And his work at his own medical center was too organized to provide solace. For the last four weeks he'd lost himself in the grueling endeavor that had managed to anesthetize his pain.

Today was the last day. And after the distraction provided by the crushing schedule, he dreaded the impending release like an imminent jump off a cliff...

"Somow'wak?"

Emad's prodding "Your Highness" brought him out of his lapse into memories and frustration.

Fareed heaved to his feet. "I'm *not* seeing any more women, Emad. You were right all along. Don't go soft on me now."

"I assure you I'm not. I've been sending the women who've come asking for an interview with you away."

Fareed blinked. "There's been more?"

"Dozens more. But I interviewed them in your stead without inflicting even a mention of them on you."

Fareed shook his head. Seemed his desperate measure would haunt him for Ullah only knew how long. "So what's new now? Don't tell me you're suddenly hoping that my 'grief-blinded gamble' might, 'against all rationality and odds,' bear fruit?"

Emad's lips twitched at Fareed's reminder of his reprimands. *"Somow'wak* has an impeccable memory."

"Aih, it's a curse." A suspicion suddenly struck him. "Are you telling me you want me to start this...*farce* all over again?"

"I want you to see this one woman."

Fareed winced at the look that entered his eyes. Emad wouldn't look at a lion with more caution.

Jameel. Great. He was losing it. He huffed in disgust at his wavering stamina. "Why this one? Why is she special?"

Emad sighed, clearly not appreciating needing to explain his conviction. "Her approach was unlike any other. She didn't use the contact number you specified in the ad but has been trying to reserve an appointment with you through the hospital from the day we arrived. Today they told her that you were leaving and she started weeping. ..."

Fareed slammed down the dossier he'd picked up. "So she's even more cunning than the rest, realized that the others' approach hadn't borne fruit and tried to get past your screening by conning her way to me through my work. And when *that* didn't work, she made a scene. Is that why you want me to see her? Damage control? To stop compounding the 'scandal I created for myself and my family'?"

Emad's dark eyes emptied of expression. "I wouldn't want to resurrect that mess after I managed to contain it. But that's not why. The people in reception today are new. They only heard the story of her waiting around for the past four weeks in case you had an opening in your schedule from her disjointed accounts. When they couldn't deal with her, they sent for me, and I...saw her, heard what little she'd been able to say. She...*feels* different from the rest. Feels truly distraught."

Fareed snorted. "An even more superlative actress, eh?"

"Or maybe the real thing."

His heart boomed with hope, once, before it plummeted again into despondence. "You don't believe that."

Emad leveled his gaze on him. "The real thing *does* exist."

"And she doesn't want to be found," Fareed growled. "She must know I've turned the world upside down to find her and she didn't come forward. Why would she decide to show up when nothing has changed?"

"Maybe nothing we know of."

Fareed closed his eyes. Emad's calm logic was maddening him. He was in a far worse condition than he'd realized if anything Emad, of all people, said or did had him within a hair's breadth of going berserk. It seemed he'd distracted himself at the cost of pushing himself to a breakdown.

Emad's deep tones, so carefully neutral, felt like discordant nails against his restraint. "But what we do know is that Hesham's Lyn is still out there."

And what if that woman down there was her?

He closed his eyes against hope's insidious prodding. But it was too late. It had already eaten through his resistance.

This woman most probably wasn't; but really, what was one more performance to suffer? He'd better get this over with.

He opened his eyes as Emad opened his mouth to deliver another argument. He raised his hand, aborting it. "Send her up. I'm giving her ten minutes, not a second more. Tell her that. Then I'm walking out and I'm never coming back to this country."

Emad gave a curt nod, turned on his heels.

He watched him exit the ultramodern space the hospital had given him as his consultation room, before he sagged in the luxury of the leather swiveling chair. It felt as if he'd sunk into thorns.

If more fake, stomach-turning stories about his brother were flung in his face, he would not be responsible for his actions.

He glowered at the door. He'd seen all kinds. From the sniveling to the simpering to the seductive. He had an idea which type this one would be. The hysterical. Maybe even the delusional.

He steeled himself for another ugly confrontation as the door was pushed open. Emad preceded the woman into the room.

But he barely saw him. He didn't hear what Emad said before he left, or notice when he did.

All he saw was the golden vision approaching until only the wide desk stood between them.

He found himself on his feet without realizing he'd moved, only one thought reverberating in his mind.

Please, don't be Hesham's Lyn!

The thought stuttered to a standstill.

B'Ellahi, what was he thinking? He should be wishing that she was, that his search was over.

It shouldn't make a difference that her drowned sky-at-dawn eyes dissolved his coherence and the sunlight silk that cascaded over her bosom made his hands ache to twist in it. It didn't matter that the trembling of her lush lips shook his resolve and her graceful litheness gripped his guts in a snare of instant hunger. If she turned out to be Hesham's Lyn…

His thoughts convulsed to a halt again.

He wanted her to be anything *but* that. Even another imposter.

B'Ellahi, why?

The answer churned inside him with that desire that had surged out of nowhere at her sight.

Because Hesham's Lyn would be off-limits to him. And he wanted this woman for himself. He wanted her…

As he'd wanted her the first and only time he'd seen her.

He *remembered* her now!

It was the total unexpectedness of seeing her again, let alone here, that had thrown him at first. That, and the changes in her.

That time he'd seen her, her luminous hair had been scraped back in a severe bun. She'd been wearing makeup that he now realized had obscured her true coloring and downplayed her features. A dark suit of masculine severity had attempted to mask her screaming femininity.

She'd been younger, far more curvaceous, yet somehow less ripe. Her vibe had been cool, professional…until she'd seen him.

One thing remained the same. Her impact on him. It was as all-consuming as it had been when he'd walked into that conference room.

He vaguely remembered people scurrying to empty a place for him at the front row. She'd been at the podium. It wasn't until the stunning effect she'd had on him ebbed slightly that he realized what she'd been doing there.

She'd been delivering the very presentation he'd gone to that conference to attend, about a drug that helped regenerate nerves after pathological degeneration or trauma. He'd heard so much about the outstanding young researcher, the head of the R & D team. He'd had a mental image to go with her prodigious achievements, one that had collapsed under its own inaccuracy at the sight of her.

He'd held her gaze captive as he'd sat grappling with impatience for the presentation to be over so he could approach her, claim her. Only his knowledge that the sight of him had been as disruptive to her had mitigated his tension. His pleasure had mounted at seeing her poise shaken. She'd managed to continue, but her crisp efficiency had become colored by the self-consciousness he'd evoked. Every move of her elegant body and eloquent hands, every inflection of her cultured delivery, *everything* about her had made focusing on the data she'd been conveying a challenge. But her work had been even more impressive than he'd anticipated, only deepening his delight with her….

"Is it all a lie? Are *you* a lie?"

He almost flinched. That red wine-and-velvet voice.

It had taken hearing it to know it had never stopped

echoing in his mind. Now it was made even more potent
by the raggedness of emotion entwined in it.

But had she said...?

The next second her agitation cascaded over him, silencing questions and bringing every thought to a shocked
halt.

"Is your reputation all propaganda? Just hype to pave
the way to more reverence in the medical field and adulation in the media? Are you what your rare detractors say
you are? Just a prince with too much money, genius and
power, who makes a career of playing god?"

Two

Gwen McNeal heard the choking accusations as if they came from a disembodied voice. One that sounded like hers.

It seemed the past weeks had damaged what had been left of her sanity. She'd made her initial request for a meeting with it already strained. But as time had ticked by and her chances of meeting him had diminished, her stamina had dwindled right along.

She'd thought she'd be a mass of incoherence when she was finally in his presence.

Then she was there, and the sight of him had jolted through her like a lightning bolt. The intensity of his gaze, of his impact, had slashed the last tethers of her restraint.

She'd just accused him of being an over-endowed sadist who lived to make lesser beings beg for his intervention.

At least the unchecked flow had stopped. All she could

do now was stare in horror at him as he stared back at her in stupefaction. And realize.

He *was* what she remembered. Description-defying. Or there had to be new adjectives coined to describe his brand of virility and grandeur. Seeing him felt like being catapulted into the past. A past when she'd known where her life was heading. A life that had been derailed since she'd laid eyes on him.

Ever since, she'd told herself she'd exaggerated her memories of him, had built him up into what no one could possibly be.

But he was all that. It was all there, and more. The imposing physicality, the inborn grace and power, the sheer influence. She had no doubt time would continue to magnify his assets until he did become godlike.

One thing time hadn't enhanced, though. His effect on her. How could it when that had been shattering to start with?

Then he moved. The move itself was almost imperceptible, but the intention behind it, to come closer, when that would engulf her even deeper into his aura, intensify his effect, went off inside her like a clap of thunder.

Desperation burst from her in a new rush of resentment. *"Five minutes?* That's what you allow people in your presence? Then you walk away without looking back? Do you smirk in satisfaction as they run after you begging for a few more moments of your priceless time? Do you enjoy making them grovel? That's how much regard the world's leading philanthropist surgeon really has for others?"

A slow blink swept his sinful lashes down, before they lifted to level his smoldering gaze on her.

"I actually said ten minutes."

She'd thought his voice had been hard-hitting in the videos she'd seen of his interviews, lectures and educational surgeries. In reality, the depth and richness of his tones, the potency of his accent, the beauty of his every inflection made the words he uttered an invocation.

"And when I said that…"

She cut him off, unable to hear more of that spell. "So you granted me *ten* minutes instead of five. I can see how your reputation was founded, on such magnanimous offers. But I've already wasted most of those ten minutes. Do I start counting down the rest before you walk away as if I'm not here?"

He shook his head as if it would help him make sense of her words, and L.A.'s winter afternoon sun slanting through the windows glinted off his raven mane. "I won't do any such thing, Ms. McNeal."

Her heart gave one detonation. He…he…he *remembered* her?

The world receded into a gray vortex. A terrible whoosh yawned in her ears. Everything faded away as she plunged in a freefall of nothingness.

Something immovable broke her plummet, and she found herself struggling within the living cables that encompassed her, reaching back to the reprieve that oblivion offered.

"*B'Ellahi*…don't fight me."

The dark melody poured into her brain as she lost all connection with gravity, was swathed in hot hardness and dizzying fragrance. She opened her eyes at the sensation and that face she'd long told herself she'd forgotten filled her vision. She hadn't forgotten one line of symmetry or strength, one angle or slash or groove of nobility and character and uniqueness. Sheikh Fareed Aal Zaafer would be unforgettable after one fleeting look. Secondhand exposure would have been enough. But that firsthand encounter had been indelible.

But if she'd thought his effect from a distance the most disruptive force she'd ever encountered, now that she filled his arms, he filled her senses, conquered what remained of her resistance.

A violent shudder shook her. He gathered her tighter.

"Put me down, please." Her voice broke on the last word.

His eyes moved to her lips as soon as she spoke, following their movements. Blood thundered in her head at his fascination. His hands only tightened their hold, branding her through her clothing.

"You fainted." His gaze dragged from her lips, raking every raw nerve in her face on its way back up to her eyes.

She fidgeted, trying to recoup her scattered coordination. "I just got dizzy for a second."

"You *fainted*." His insistence was soft like gossamer, unbending as steel. "A dead faint. I had to vault over the desk to catch you before you fell face down over that table."

Her eyes panned to where she'd been standing by a large, square, steel-and-glass table. Articles were flung all over the floor around it.

Even though she'd never fainted in her life, no doubt formed in her mind. She had. And he'd saved her.

The bitterness that had united with tension to hold her together disintegrated in the heat of shame at her behavior so far. All she wanted was to burrow into his power and weep.

She couldn't. For every reason there was. She had to keep her distance at all costs.

He was walking to the sitting area by the windows as if afraid she'd come apart if he jarred her. What did was the solicitude radiating from him.

She pulled herself rigid in his hold. "I'm fine now...
please."

He stopped. She raised a wavering gaze to his, found it
filled with something...turbulent. Then it grew assessing,
as if weighing the pros and cons of granting her plea.

Then he loosened his arms by degrees, let her slide
in nerve-abrading slowness down his body. She swayed
back a step as soon as her feet found the ground, and her
legs wobbled under her weight, as if she'd long depended
on him to support it. His hand shot out to steady her. She
shook her head. He took his hand away, gestured for her
to sit down, command and courtesy made flesh and bone.

She almost fell onto the couch, shot him a wary glance
as soon as she'd sought its far end. "Thank you."

He came to tower over her. "Nothing to thank me for."

"Just for saving me from being rushed to the E.R., probably with severe facial fractures, or worse."

His spectacular eyebrows snapped together as if in pain,
the smoldering coals he had for eyes turning almost black.
"Tell me why you fainted."

She huffed. "If I knew that, I wouldn't have."

His eyes drilled into hers, clearly unsatisfied with her
answer. "You're not alarmed that you did faint, at least
you're not surprised. So you have a very good idea why.
Tell me."

"It was probably agitation."

His painstakingly sculpted lips twisted. "You might
be a renowned pharmaceutical researcher, Ms. McNeal,
but I'm the doctor among us and the one qualified to pass
medical opinions. Agitation makes you more alert, not
prone to collapse."

He wouldn't budge, would he? She had to give him
something to satisfy his investigative appetite so she could

move on to the one subject that mattered. "It—it was probably the long wait."

He still shook his head. "Eight hours of waiting, though
long, wouldn't cause you to be so exhausted you'd faint.
Not without an underlying cause."

"I've been here since 4:00 a.m…" His eyebrows shot up
in surprise. And that was before she added, "yesterday."

His incredulity shot higher, his frown grew darker.
"You've been sitting down there for thirty-six hours?"

He suddenly came down beside her, with a movement that should have been impossible for someone of
his height, his thigh whisper-touching hers as those long,
powerful fingers, his virtuoso surgeon's tools, wrapped
around her wrist to take her pulse. Her heartbeats piled
up in her heart before drenching her arteries in a torrent.

He raised probing eyes to her. "Have you slept or even
eaten during that time?" She didn't remember. She started
to nod and he overrode her evasion. "It's clear you did
neither. You haven't been doing either properly for a long
time. You're tachycardic as if you've been running a mile."
Was he even wondering why, with him so near? "You
must be hypoglycemic, and your weak pulse indicates your
blood pressure is barely adequate to keep you conscious. I
wouldn't even need any of those signs to guide me about
your condition. You look—depleted."

From meeting her haggard face in the mirror, she knew
she made a good simulation of the undead. But having him
corroborate her opinion twisted mortification inside her.

Which was the height of stupidity. What did it matter if
he thought she looked like hell? What mattered was that
she fixed her mistake, got on with her all-important purpose.

"I was too anxious to sleep or eat, but it's not a big deal.

What I said to you is, though. I'm sorry for…for my outbursts."

Something flared in his eyes, making her skin where he still held her hand feel as if it would burst into flame. "Don't be. Not if I've done anything to deserve this…antipathy. And I'm extremely curious, to put it mildly, to find out what that was. Do you think I left you waiting this long out of malice? You believe I enjoy making people beg for my time, offer it only after they've broken down, only to allow them inadequate minutes before walking away?"

"No— I—I mean…no…your reputation says the very opposite."

"But your personal experience says my reputation might be so much manufactured hype."

Her throat tightened with a renewed surge of misery. "It's just you…you announced you'd be available to be approached, but I was told the opposite, and I no longer knew what to believe."

She felt him stiffen, the fire in his eyes doused in something…bleak. She'd somehow offended him with her attempts at apology and explanation more than she had with her insults.

But even if she deserved that he walked away from her, she couldn't afford to let him. She had to beg him to hear her out.

"Please, forget everything I said and let me start over. Just give me those ten minutes all over again. If afterward you think you're not interested in hearing more, walk away."

Fareed crashed down to earth.

He'd forgotten. As she'd lambasted him, as he'd lost himself in the memory of his one exposure to her, in his delight in finding her miraculously here, then in his anxiety when she'd collapsed, he'd totally forgotten.

Why he'd walked away from her that first time.

As she'd concluded her presentation and applause had risen, so had everyone. He'd realized it had been the end of the session when people had deluged him, from colleagues to grant seekers to the press. He'd wanted to push them all away, his impatience rising with his satisfaction as her gaze had kept seeking him, before darting away when she'd found him focused on her.

And then a man had swooped out of nowhere, swept her off her feet and kissed her soundly on the lips. He'd frozen as the man had hugged her to his side with the entitlement of long intimacy, turned her to pose for photos and shouted triumphant statements to reporters about the new era "their" drug would herald in pharmaceuticals.

He'd grabbed the first person near him, asked, "Who's that?"

He'd gotten the answer he'd dreaded. *That,* a Kyle Langstrom, had been her fiancé and partner in research.

As the letdown had mushroomed inside him, he'd heard Kyle announcing that with the major hurdle in their work overcome, there'd soon be news of equal importance: a wedding date.

The knowledge of her engagement had doused his blaze of elation at finding her, buried all his intentions. His gaze had still clung to her receding figure as if he could alter reality, make her free to return his interest, to receive his passion.

Just before the tide of companions had swept her out of sight, she'd looked back. Their eyes had met for a moment.

It had felt like a lifetime when the world had ceased to exist and only they had remained. Then she'd been gone.

He'd seen her again during the following end-of-conference party. The perverse desire to see her again even when it oppressed him had made him attend it. He'd stood there unable to take his eyes off her. She'd kept her gaze averted. But he'd known she'd been struggling not to look back. He'd finally felt bad enough about standing there coveting another man's woman that he'd left with the party at full swing.

He hadn't returned to the States again until Hesham.

He'd replayed that last glance for months afterward. Each time seeing his own longing and regret reflected in her eyes. And each time he'd told himself he'd imagined it.

He'd long convinced himself he had imagined everything. Most of all, her unprecedented effect on him.

It had taken him one look today to realize he'd completely downplayed it. To realize why he'd been unable to muster interest in other women ever since. He might not have consciously thought it, but he'd found no point in wasting time on a woman who didn't inspire the white-hot recognition and attraction this woman had.

Now she'd appeared here, out of the blue, had been waiting to see him for a month, her last vigil lasting a day and a half of sleepless starvation. She'd just said she was here because he'd "announced he'd be available to be approached."

Had she meant his ad? Could it be, of all women, this one he'd wanted on sight, hadn't only been some stranger's once, but Hesham's, too?

If she had been, *he* must have done something far worse than what she'd accused him of in her agitation. What else would that be but some unimaginably cruel punishment of fate?

He hissed, "Just *tell* me and be done with it."

She lurched as if he'd backhanded her. No wonder. He'd sounded like a beast, seconds away from an attack.

Before he could form an apology, she spoke, her voice muffled with tears, "I lied—" She had? About what? "—when I said ten minutes would do. I *did* keep asking reception for any moments you could spare when they said full appointments were reserved for patients on your list. I now realize they couldn't have acted on your orders, must have done the same with the endless people who came seeking your services. But I was told you're leaving in an hour, and that long might not do now either and…"

He raised his hands to stem the flow of her agitation, his previous suspicions crashing in a domino effect.

"You're here for a *consultation*?"

She raised eyes brimming with tears and…wariness? Nodded.

Relief stormed through him. She wasn't here about the ad, about Hesham. She was here seeking his surgical services.

Next moment relief scattered as another suspicion detonated.

"You're sick?"

Three

She *was* sick.

That explained everything. The only thing that made sense. Terrible sense. Her desperation. Her mood swings. Her fainting.

She had a neurological condition. According to her symptoms, maybe…a brain tumor. And if she'd sought him out, it had to be advanced. No one sought him specifically except in conditions deemed beyond the most experienced surgeons' skills. In neurosurgery, he *was* one of three on earth who'd made a vocation of tackling the inoperable, resolving the incurable.

But a month had passed since she'd first tried to reach him. Her condition could have progressed from minimal hope to none.

Could it be he'd found her, only to lose her again?

No, he wouldn't. In the past, he'd walked away from her, respecting the commitment she'd made. But disease,

even what others termed terminal, *especially* that, was
what he'd dedicated his life to defeating. If he could never
have her, at least he would give the world back that vibrant
being who'd made giving hope to the hopeless her life's
work. ...

"I'm not sick."

The tremulous words hit him with the force of a bullet.

He stared at her, convictions and fears crashing, burning.

Had she said...? Yes, she had. But that could mean
nothing. She'd already denied knowledge of why she'd
fainted. She could still be undiagnosed, or in denial over
the diagnosis she'd gotten, hoping he'd have a different
verdict. ...

"It's my baby."

This time, only one thing echoed inside his head. *Why?*

Why did he keep getting shocked by each new verifi-
cation that this woman had a life that had nothing to do
with him? That she'd planned and lived her life without
his being the major part of it?

Often he'd found himself overwhelmed by bitterness
without apparent reason. He now admitted to himself what
that reason had been. That he still couldn't believe she
hadn't waited to find him, had accepted a deficient connection with someone else.

But that sense of betrayal was ridiculous, had nothing
to do with reality. Her marriage *had* been imminent when
he'd seen her. So why did it shock him so much that she
had a baby, the normal outcome of a years-old union?

And that baby was sick. Enough to need his surgical
skills.

His heart compressed as he realized the reason, the
emotions behind her every word and tear so far. The same

desperation he'd once felt, to save someone whose life he valued above his own.

How ironic was it that her intensely personal need for his purely professional services had made her finally seek him out?

He'd long given in to fate that had deemed that their paths diverged before they'd had the chance to converge. But to have her enter his life this way *was* a punishment, an injury. And he wasn't in any condition to take more of either.

If it had only meant his own suffering, he would have taken any measure of both. But he held his patients' lives under the steadiness of his hand, their futures subject to the clarity of his decisions. He couldn't compromise that.

Now he had to deal her the blow of refusing her baby's case. He would make sure her baby got the very best care. Just not his.

He inhaled a burning breath. "Ms. McNeal…"

As if feeling he'd let her down, she sat up, eyes blazing with entreaty. "I have Ryan's investigations with me, so maybe minutes will do. Will you take a look, tell me what you think?"

She only wanted his opinion? Didn't want him to operate on her baby? If so…

Again, as if she felt him relenting, she scrambled up. He noticed for the first time the briefcase and purse she'd dropped. All he'd seen had been her. In spite of everything, his eyes still clung to her every move, every nuance, and his every cell ached with long-denied impulses.

He saw himself striding after her, catching her back, plastering her body against his, burying his fingers in the luxury of her golden cascade of hair, sweeping it aside to open his lips over her warm, satin flesh. What he'd give for only one taste, one kiss…

She was returning, holding the briefcase as if it contained her world, her dawn-sky eyes full of brittle hope.

Ya Ullah, how was beauty like that even possible?

He'd never been attracted to blondes, never preferred Western beauty. But to him, she was the embodiment of everything that aroused his wonder and lust. And it was only partially physical. The connection he felt between them, that which needed no knowledge or experience, just *was,* was everything he wanted. When he couldn't have her.

She started fumbling with the briefcase's zipper as she neared him, and another idea occurred to him.

If this would be only a consultation, he owed her a full one after all the suffering she'd endured for the mere hope of it.

He should also give himself a dose of shock therapy. Seeing her with her baby, with her whole *family,* might cure him of this insidious malady he'd been struck with at her sight.

He stayed her hand with a touch, withdrew his as if contact with her burned him, and before he tugged her against him.

"I won't be able to give you an opinion based on those investigations. I don't rely on any except those done to my specifications." Alarm flared in her eyes. He couldn't believe the effect her distress had on him. It...physically hurt. He rushed to add, "Anyway, my preferred and indispensable diagnostic method is a clinical exam. Is your baby downstairs with his father?"

Her gaze blipped, and she barely suppressed a start.

Before he could analyze her reaction, she murmured, her voice deeper, huskier, "Ryan is with his nanny at our hotel. They both got too tired and Ryan was crying nonstop and disturbing everyone, I had to send them away."

Agitation spread across her features like a shadow. "I thought I'd bring them back as soon as I got an appointment with you. But the hotel's near the airport, and at this time of day, even if I'd told Rose to come as soon as I knew you'd see me, it would have taken her too long to get here. I didn't even tell her, because Mr. Elkaateb said you had only minutes to spare. That's why I said an hour won't do...."

He raised a hand, stopped her anxiety in its tracks. "I'm going home on my private jet, so the timing of my departure is up to me. Call your nanny and have her bring Ryan over."

Her eyes widened. "Oh, God, thank you…"

A hand wave again stopped her. He hated the vulnerability and helplessness gratitude engendered in others, was loathe to be on its receiving end. Hers took his usual discomfort to new levels.

She nodded, accepting that he wanted none of it, dived into her purse for her phone.

In moments, with her eyes fixed on him, she said, "Rose…" She paused as the woman on the other side burst out talking. Realizing he must hear the woman, Gwen shot him an apologetic, even…shy glance. "Yes, I did. Get Ryan here ASAP."

He barely stopped himself at a touch of her forearm. "Tell her to take her time. I'll wait."

The look she gave him then, the beauty of her tremulous smile, twisted another red-hot poker in his gut. He had to get away from her before he did something they'd both regret.

He turned away, headed back to the desk and blindly started gathering the files he'd scattered.

When she ended her phone call, without looking up he asked the question burning a hole in his chest, trying to sound nonchalant, "Isn't your husband coming? Or is he back home?"

He *needed* to see her with her husband. He had to have that image of her with her man burned into his mind, to erase the one he had of her with *him*.

She didn't answer him for what felt like an eternity. His perception sharpened and time warped with her near.

He forced himself to keep rearranging the desk, didn't raise his eyes to read on her face the proof of her involvement with another. He should, to sever his own inexplicable and ongoing one. He couldn't. It would be bad enough to hear it in her voice as she mentioned her husband, the father of her child.

When her answer finally came, it was subdued, almost inaudible. He almost missed it. Almost.

His heart kicked his ribs so hard that he felt both would be bruised. His eyes jerked up to her.

She'd said, "I don't have a husband."

He didn't know when or how he'd crossed the distance back to her. He found himself standing before her again, the revelation reverberating in his head, in his whole being.

He heard himself rasp, "You're divorced?"

She escaped his eyes, the slanting rays of sunset turning hers into bottomless aquamarines. "I was never married."

He could only stare at her.

A long moment later, he voiced his bewilderment. "I thought you were engaged when I saw you at that conference."

He thought, indeed. He'd thought of nothing else until he'd forced himself into self-inflicted amnesia.

Color rushed back into her cheeks, making his lips itch to taste that tide of peach. "I was We...split up soon afterward." She snatched a look back at him, her lips lifting with a faint twist of humor. "Sort of on the grounds of irreconcilable scientific differences."

Suddenly he felt like putting his fist through the nearest wall.

B'haggej' jaheem…in the name of *hell!* He'd walked away because he'd believed she would marry that Kyle Langstrom. And she *hadn't.*

Frustration charred his blood as realizations swamped him, of what he'd wasted when he hadn't pursued her, hadn't at least followed up on her news. He would have found out she hadn't married that…that *person.* But that didn't necessarily mean that…

"He's not the father of your child?"

She ended that suspicion with a simple, "No."

Before delight overtook him, another realization quashed it.

She might not have married Langstrom, but she had a man in her life. He *had* to know. "Then who is your child's father?"

She shrugged, unease thickening her voice. "Is this about Ryan's condition? Do you think knowing his father is important for managing it or for his prognosis?"

He was tempted to say yes, to make it imperative for her to answer him. The temptation passed, and integrity, damn it to hell, took over. He exhaled his frustration with the code he could never break. "No, knowing the source of a congenital malformation has no bearing on the course of treatment or prognosis."

"Then I don't see how bringing up his father is relevant."

She didn't want to talk about this. She was right not to. He'd never dreamed of pursuing private information from anyone, let alone the parent of a prospective patient. But this was *her,* the one woman he had to know everything about.

He already knew everything that was relevant to him. From her work, he'd formed a thorough knowledge of her intellect and capabilities. Instinct provided the rest, about her nature and character and their compatibility to his. What remained was the status of any personal relationship she might have.

And yet, there *was* a legitimate reason for him to ask about the father. "It's relevant because the father of your child should be here, especially if your child's condition is as serious as you believe. As his father, he has equal right to decide his course of treatment, if there is any, and an equal stake in his future."

Concession crept in her eyes. It was still a long moment later when she spoke, making him feel as if the words caused her internal damage on their way out. "Ryan... doesn't have a father."

And all he could ask himself now was when? When would that woman stop slamming him with shocks? When would she stop giving him fragments of answers that only raise more maddening questions?

"You mean he's not a part of your lives? Is he gone? Dead?"

What? the shout rang inside his head. *Just tell me.*

Her eyes shot up to his. She must be as attuned to him as he was to her. He'd kept his tone even, his demeanor neutral. But she must have sensed the vehemence of his frustration.

She finally exhaled. "I had Ryan from a donor."

This time he did stagger back a step.

There *was* no end to her surprises.

But he was beyond surprised. He was flabbergasted. He would have never even considered this a possibility.

Even though he knew this would mean something huge when he let it sink in, and he couldn't understand why she'd been so averse to disclosing this fact, it only raised more questions. "Why would someone so young resort to a sperm donor?"

She kept her eyes anywhere but at him, her color now dangerous. "Age is just one factor why women go the donor route. And it's been a while since I left the designation 'so young' behind. Thirty-two is hardly spring chick territory."

His lips twitched at this, yet another trace of wit. "With forty being the new thirty even where child bearing is concerned, you are firmly in that territory. If I'd just met you, I wouldn't give you more than twenty-two."

Her shoulders jerked on a disbelieving huff as she gave him one of those glances that made his blood pressure shoot up. "I've looked in a mirror lately, you know. You yourself said I look terrible. But anyway, thanks for the... chivalry."

"I only ever say what I mean. You have proof of that from my unsweetened interrogation." One corner of her lips lifted. "And my exact word was *depleted*. It's clear you're neglecting yourself in your anxiety over your child. It doesn't make you any less...breathtaking."

It was her own breath that stalled now. The sound it made catching in her throat made him dizzy with desire.

He intended to hear that sound, and many, many others, as he compromised her breathing with too much pleasure. For now he pressed on. "And I'll keep it up until you tell me the whole story, so how about you volunteer it?"

Her shoulders rose and dropped helplessly. "Maybe you should keep it up and I'll answer what I can because I don't know what constitutes a whole story to you."

"I want to know why a woman like you, who will be

pursued by men when you're *seventy*-two, chose to have a child without one. Was it because of your ex-fiancé? Was there more to your breakup than you let on? What did he do to put you off relationships?"

The hesitant humor playing on her lips reached her eyes. He couldn't wait until he could see it fully unleashed. "I did ask for it. But you can't be further from the truth in Kyle's case. I'm the villain of the piece in that story. It was because of me that even working together became counterproductive."

Zain. That was succinct and unequivocal. And still deficient.

He persisted, "Then why?"

She looked away again. "Not everything has to have a huge or complex reason. I just wanted a baby."

He knew she was hiding something. The conviction burned in his gut with its intensity. "And you couldn't wait to have one the usual way? When another suitable man came along?"

"I wasn't interested in having another man, suitable or not."

She fell silent. He knew she'd say no more on that issue.

He had more to say, to ask, to think, and everything to feel. It all roiled inside him, old frustrations and new questions. But one thing crystallized until it outshone everything else.

Not only didn't she have a man in her life, but she also hadn't wanted one. After she'd seen him. He *knew* it. Just like he hadn't wanted another woman after he'd seen her.

Elation swept him. Changed the face of his existence.

He didn't know how he stopped from doing what he'd wanted to do since that first moment—sweep her in his arms and kiss her until she begged for him. But he couldn't do it now.

Not having her now was still torment, only sweet instead of bitter, and the wait would only make having her in time that much more transfiguring.

For now, she needed his expertise, not his passion. He would give her everything she needed.

Her eyes were focused on him in such appeal that he could swear he felt his bones liquefying. "Won't you look at the investigations anyway, just to get an idea, while we wait?"

Eyes like these, influence like this, should be outlawed. He'd tell her that. Soon.

He smiled at her, took her elbow, guided her back to the couch. "I'd rather form an uninfluenced opinion."

She slid him a sideways glance, and the tinge of teasing there almost made him send everything to hell and unleash four years' worth of hunger on her. "Is anyone even capable of influencing your opinion?"

He laughed. For the first time…since he didn't remember when. After endless months of gloom, with her here, with her free, he felt a weight had lifted. If it weren't for Hesham, for his unfound woman and child, he would have said he was on the verge of experiencing joy.

"All this because of my interrogation?" He gently prodded her to sit down, got out his cell phone, called Emad and asked him to bring in a meal. When she insisted she'd settle for a hot drink, he overrode her with a gentle "Doctor's orders."

He came down beside her, close enough to feel imbued by the fragrant warmth of her body, but leaving enough space for her attempt to observe a semblance of formality.

She looked at him now, not enraged or wary or imploring, but with fascination, unable to stop studying him as he studied her, and the openness of her face, the clarity of her spirit…amazing.

He sighed his pleasure. "I would be a very poor scientist and a terrible surgeon if I wasn't open to new influences. I should be making the crack about you. After half an hour of my premium persistence all I got out of you was a half-dozen sentences."

She looked away, making him want to kick himself for whatever he'd done to make her deprive him of her gaze. "Your judgment *has* served you, and endless others, unbelievably well. You're one surgeon who deserves to have omnipotent notions."

"You mean my rare detractors aren't right and I'm not just a highborn lowlife suffering from advanced narcissistic sadism laced with a terminal god complex?"

She buried her face in her hands as he paraphrased her opening salvo, before looking back up at him, embarrassment and humor a heady mix in her eyes. "Do you think there's any chance you can pretend I never said that?"

He quirked his lips, reveling in taking her in degrees from desperation to ease. "Why would I? Because you were wrong? Are you sure you were? Maybe I behaved because you handed me my head."

A chuckle cracked out of her. "I doubt anyone can do that."

"You'd be really, really surprised what you can do."

He let *to me* go unspoken, yet understood.

Before he could analyze the effect this declaration had on her, Emad entered with the waitstaff.

Fareed saw the question, the hope in his eyes as Emad took in the situation. Fareed gave a slight headshake letting him know she wasn't the woman they'd been looking for.

But she was the woman *he'd* been looking for.

After preparing the table in front of them, and with disappointment and curiosity filling his eyes, Emad left.

For the next hour Fareed discovered new pleasures. Coddling Gwen—to her chagrin, before she succumbed, ate and drank what he served her, delighting in her re-surfacing steadiness, in the banter that flowed between them, the fluency of appreciation.

Then Emad knocked again. This time he ushered in a woman carrying a child. Gwen's child.

Fareed couldn't focus on either. He only had eyes for Gwen as she sprung to her feet, her face gripped with emotions, their range breathtaking in scope and depth. Anxiety, relief, welcome, love, protection and so much more, every one fierce, total.

He heard the child squeal as he threw himself into her eager embrace. He registered the elegant, classically pretty redhead in her late forties, who Gwen introduced as Rose Maher, a distant maternal relative and Ryan's nanny. He welcomed her with all the cordiality he could access, filed everything about her for later analysis. Then he turned to Gwen's child.

And the world stopped in its tracks.

Four

Fareed hadn't thought about Gwen's child until this moment. Not in any terms other than his being hers.

He hadn't had the presence of mind to formulate expectations, of the child, of his own reactions when he saw him. Had he had any mental faculties to devote to either, he would have thought he'd feel what he felt for any sick child in his care.

Now he knew anything he could have imagined would have been way off base.

She'd said Ryan didn't have a father. He could almost believe that declaration literally now. It was as if he was hers, and hers alone. Even the discrepancy in age and gender, the almost-bald head, did nothing to dilute the reality that he was a pure part of her, body and soul.

But that absolute kinship and similarity between child and mother wasn't why the sight of Ryan shook him to his core. Ryan, even though no more than nine or ten months old, was his own person. His effect wasn't an echo of his mother's, but all his own.

Ryan looked at him with eyes that were the same heavenly blue as his mother's but reflecting his own nature and character, inquisitive, intrepid, enthusiastic. His dewy lips were rounded on his same breath-bating fascination as he probed him as if asking if he was a friend. Then he seemed to decide he was, his eyes crinkling and his lips spreading.

"Say hello to Dr. Aal Zaafer, Ryan."

Fareed blinked as Gwen's indulgent tone cascaded over his nerves, such a different melody from any he'd heard from her.

It had an equal effect on Ryan, who smiled delightedly up at her. Next moment, his every synapse fired as the child turned back to him, encompassed him in the same unbridled smile. Then he extended his arms to him.

He stared at the chubby hands closing and opening, beckoning for him to hurry and pick him up.

Gwen moved Ryan out of reach. "Darling, the adorable act works only on me and Rose." Fareed's eyes moved from Ryan's crestfallen face to her apologetic one. "I didn't think he would ask you for a ride. He doesn't like to be held much, even by me. Too independent."

She thought his hesitation meant he didn't want to hold Ryan? She didn't realize he was just…paralyzed? Everything inside him wanted to reach back for Ryan, but the urge was so strong, so…unknown that it overwhelmed him.

He had to correct that assumption. He couldn't bear that she thought she'd imposed on him, couldn't stand seeing Ryan's chin quiver at being apparently rebuffed.

"I'm—" he cleared his throat "—I'm honored he thinks

I'm worthy of being his ride. He probably fancies one from a higher altitude."

A chuckle came from his left. His gaze moved with great effort from the captivating sight mother and son made to Rose.

She was still eyeing him with that almost-awed expression in her green eyes, but humor and shrewdness were taking over. "Ryan is a genius, and he knows a good proposition when he sees it. And you're as good as it gets."

A strangled gasp issued from Gwen. He didn't need to look at her to know that her eyes were shooting daggers at Rose.

His lips spread in his widest smile in years. "Ms. Maher, I knew you were a discerning woman the moment I saw you."

Rose let out a tinkling laugh. "Call me Rose, please. And oh, yes, I've been around long enough to know premium stuff when I see it, too."

He almost felt the heat of mortification blasting off Gwen. And he loved it. Rose was saying the exact things to dissolve the tension, to set him free of the immobility that had struck him.

"I am honored you think I belong on the premium shelf, Rose, almost as much as I was to be considered a desirable ride by Ryan." He shared another smile with the woman he already felt would be his ally, before he turned to Gwen and held out his arms.

His heart revved at what flared in her eyes. Momentary belief that his arms where inviting *her* into their depths. And a stifled urge to rush into them.

He let her know he'd seen it with a lingering glance before he transferred his smile to the baby who was already bobbing in her arms, demanding to be released. "Shall we, young sir?"

Ryan squealed his eagerness, reached back to him. Fareed noted his movements, already assessing his condition. He received him with as much care as he would a priceless statue that might shatter if he breathed hard. He looked down on the angelic face that was regarding him in such open wonder and something fierce again shuddered behind his breastbone.

Ya Ullah. That baby boy wielded magic as potent as his mother, and both their brands of spells had his name on them.

"You won't dent him, you know?" Rose said.

He swept his gaze to her, his lips twisting. "It's that clear I'm scared witless of holding him?"

Rose let out another good-natured laugh. "Your petrified expression did give me a clue or two that your experience in handling tiny humans *is* nonexistent."

"You don't have kids?"

Gwen's soft question swept his gaze back to her. She looked…horrified that she'd asked it.

Satisfaction surged inside him. She needed to know his private details as much as he'd needed to know hers. Even though she was clearly kicking herself for asking, she *was* dying to know. If he had children, and therefore, a wife.

He'd thought his life wasn't conducive to raising a family, that he didn't have that innate drive to become a father. Now he knew the real reason why he'd never thought of having children. Because he'd never found a woman he wanted to have them with.

Now looking at her, holding her child in his arms, he did.

He looked down at Ryan, who was industriously trying to undo his shirt's top buttons, before he looked back at her, giving her a glimpse of what he felt, if not too much of it. She wasn't ready for the full power of his intentions.

Then he murmured, "I don't."

Her lashes fluttered down. But he felt it. Her relief.

Elation spread through him. "But I am an uncle many times over, through two of my sisters and many first cousins, to an assortment of boys and girls from ages one to fifteen."

Gwen raised her eyes back to his, and...*ya Ullah.* Although still guarded and trying to obscure her feelings, the change that had come over them since she'd walked in here, the warmth she couldn't fully neutralize, singed him. "I bet you're their favorite uncle."

He grinned at her. "You honor me with your willingness to waste money betting on me. But a waste it would be. 'Favorite Uncle' is a title unquestioningly reserved for Jawad, my second-eldest brother. We call him the Child Whisperer. All I can lay claim to is that I think they don't detest me. I've been too preoccupied for the span of their lives to develop any real relationship with them. I would have liked to, but I have to admit, when I'm around them, I wonder how their parents put up with their demands and distraction and still function. I wonder how they made the decision to have them in the first place."

Wisps of mischief sparked in her eyes. "So that's why you kept asking me why I had Ryan? Because you think your nephews and nieces are a noisy, messy time-suck, and that an otherwise sane adult can have a child only by throwing away logic and disregarding all cautionary tales?"

He raised one eyebrow at her. "You know you've just called me Uncle Scrooge, don't you?"

Rose burst out chuckling. "Busted."

Gwen spluttered qualifications, shooting reproach at Rose, and he aborted her protests with a smile, showing her he was offense-proof, especially by anything coming from her. "Don't take it back when you're probably right. Interacting with children has never been one of my skills."

The only child he'd loved having around and taking care of had been Hesham. But he'd been only eight years older. He hadn't had any relevant experience with children outside his professional sphere.

She made an eloquent gesture indicating how he was holding Ryan with growing confidence, picking up various articles for his inspection. "If it has never been, then you're capable of acquiring new skills on the fly."

He'd always been uncomfortable receiving compliments, feeling the element of self-serving exaggeration in each. But her good opinion felt free of ulterior motives, *and* was clearly expressed against the dictates of her good sense. To *him* it felt…necessary.

He transferred his smile from her to Ryan. "It's this little man who's making me look like a quick study. He's the one doing the driving here."

Rose nodded. "Ryan does that. Just one look and a smile and the world is his to command. Very much like his mother."

Gwen's eyes darkened on something that gripped his heart in a tight fist. Something like…anguish. *Ya Ullah,* why?

Next second, he wanted to kick himself. How could he have forgotten the reason she was here? Ryan's condition.

But he had forgotten, during the lifetime since she'd walked in and turned his life upside down all over again. But from holding Ryan, he had a firm idea what his condition was. It was time he did everything he could to put her mind to rest about it.

He adjusted his grip on Ryan, feeling as if he'd always held him, turned his face up with a finger beneath the dimpled chin that was a replica of Gwen's. "Just so I don't look like a total marionette, Ryan, how about we pretend I have a say here? How about you let me examine you now?"

"How about I leave you to your new game and go find me some food?" Rose said, clearly to give them privacy.

Fareed produced his cell phone, called Emad back. Emad appeared in under ten seconds, as if he'd been standing behind the door, which he probably had been. Eavesdropping?

He was resigned that Emad would go to any lengths to ascertain his safety. But what was there to worry about here? Getting ambushed by lethal doses of charisma and cuteness?

He gave him a mocking glance that Emad refused to rise to. "Will you please escort Rose to an early dinner, Emad? And do make it somewhere where they serve something better than the food simulations you got us from the hospital's restaurant."

He expected Emad to obey with his usual decorum, which never showed if he appreciated the chore or not. But wonder of wonders, after nodding to him with that maddening deference, he turned to Rose with interest almost eagerness—sparking in his eyes. Fareed hadn't seen anything like that in the man's eyes since his late wife.

The gregarious Rose eyed him back with open appreciation and murmured to Gwen for all to hear, "So incredible things *do* come to those who wait, eh, sweetie?" She didn't wait for Gwen's reaction and turned to Fareed. "It's been a treat meeting you, Sheikh Aal Zaafer. Take care of my lovelies, hmm?"

He bowed his head. "Fareed, please. And we'll be meeting again. *And* you can count on it."

She grinned at him, gave Gwen's hand a bolstering squeeze, caressed Ryan's cheek then gave *his* an affectionate pat before turning to Emad. "Shall we, Mr. Dark Knight?"

Emad gaped at her, clearly unable to believe this woman had just petted his prince. And that she'd called *him* that.

Then his eyes narrowed on a flare of challenge and approval as he gave her his arm. "By all means, Ms. Maher."

"Can't come up with a slogan for me, huh?" Rose beamed up at Emad. "But we have time. You'll think of something."

Before the door closed behind them, he heard Emad saying, "I don't need time, Ms. Wild Rose."

Fareed shook his head as the door closed behind them. He looked at Ryan, who was testing his stubble. "Can you believe this, Ryan? Emad teasing? Seems the power to change the laws of nature runs in your family."

Ryan squeaked as if in agreement and Fareed turned his gaze to Gwen, offered her his hand.

She stared at it for moments, her lower lip caught in her teeth, the very sight of conflicted temptation.

Before he gave in and reached for her hand, she gave it to him. He almost groaned and barely kept from bringing her nestling into him. He would make her give in, fully, irreversibly. In good time.

First, he would see to her peace of mind.

He made it a pledge. "Now I'll see to Ryan, Gwen."

Gwen's heart gave another boom before resuming its gallop.

But it wasn't only hearing her name on his lips that caused this latest disturbance. It was that he pronounced it *Gwaihn,* the breathy sound as he prolonged it a scorching sigh, making an intimacy of it, a promise...of so many things she couldn't even contemplate.

As if having her hand engulfed in his wasn't enough.

But she had herself to blame for this. She'd given her hand to him when she should have shown him she'd allow only formal interaction.

But she hadn't been able to withhold it. He was offering her what she'd been starving for. Support, strength other than her own to draw on, an infinite well of it. And whatever the consequences, she hadn't been able to stop from reaching for it.

He took them to the other end of the room, behind an opaque glass partition, to what turned out to be a fully fitted exam room.

"Gwen…" She started again. He cocked his head at her. "May I call you Gwen?"

She almost cried out, *No, you may not. Please, don't.*

Out loud she reluctantly said, "If you like, Dr. Aal Zaafer."

"I like, very much. And it's Fareed."

This was getting worse by the second. "Er…all right, Dr. Fareed…or, uh, do you prefer Sheikh?"

"Just Fareed."

And wasn't that the truth. He *was* unique, as his name proclaimed him to be. She'd looked up its meaning long before…

She shook her head, trying not to let the memories deluge her. "I can't call you just…that."

"Rose did, without a second's hesitation."

"Rose, as you noticed, is…is…"

"Blessedly unreserved. You should follow her example because I won't be called anything else by you. We're not only colleagues—" before she could contest *that,* he pressed on "—working in complementary fields, but I owe a lot of my most positive results to your breakthrough. The drug you developed has been my most reliable postoperative adjuvant therapy for years."

She gaped at him, her heart flapping inside her chest with a mixture of disbelief and pride. "I didn't realize... didn't know..."

He gave her one of those earth-shaking smiles of his. "Now you do. And even though I'm getting impatient with your slowness in developing the other drug that should shrink tumors before surgery, I'll forgive you on the strength of the first one. So we have far more than enough grounds for at least a first-name basis."

His lips listed those acceptable reasons, but his eyes told her the truth. He *wanted* this intimacy, would have it.

But she *needed* formality to hide behind, to keep things in perspective. Otherwise...

No. No otherwise. If anyone was off-limits to her, it was Fareed Aal Zaafer. She'd better never forget that.

"How about that game? It's super-easy and a lot of fun."

The indulgent drawl, which he only produced while talking to Ryan, snatched her out of her latest plunge into turmoil.

She watched him lay Ryan down on the exam bed and hand him a reflex hammer and penlight to play with. He moved around, turning on machines, gathering instruments, all the time explaining what he was doing and naming everything and what they were for.

He was talking to Ryan because he must know she knew all that. And that he was explaining to a ten-month-old, without the least condescension, as if he believed it was never too early for Ryan to learn, as if he hoped Ryan would at least understand the consideration in his attitude, choked her up again.

When he returned to Ryan's side, she asked, "Won't you call your assistants?"

He cocked one eyebrow at her, teasing sparking the

fiery brown of his eyes. "You think I can't handle examining one highly cooperative tyke on my own?"

"Actually, I'm worried this is the calm before the storm. In previous visits, Ryan acted as if the doctors were torturing him."

His eyebrows shot up before he looked at Ryan. "But you won't do that to your obedient ride, will you? And I won't make it such a cheerless endeavor that you'll be driven to tears. You can even assist me, hold instruments, test and taste them to your heart's content. Between us, we'll make this a great game, Ryan."

His thoughtfulness, then the way he said *Rye-aan,* Ryan's similar-sounding Arabic name, lanced through her.

After receiving Ryan's gleeful endorsement, he moved to start prepping him. She moved, too, bumped into him.

Feeling his steadying hands on her shoulders made her jump back. "I—I'll just undress him."

He gave her a tiny squeeze before setting her free and turning to Ryan. "As Ryan's designated driver this afternoon, I think he'd want me to do the honors, right, Ryan?"

Sure enough, Ryan let out a squeal of agreement.

She stood back, every nerve buzzing as he undid Ryan's snap-button jumpsuit with great care and dexterity, although it was clear he'd never performed the task before. Instead of fidgeting as he usually did, Ryan stunned her by chewing on a chart and offering Fareed every cooperation in stripping him down to his diapers.

"You're an extremely well-cared-for little prince, eh, Ryan?"

Her heart gave another painful thud, which was stupid. It was just a figure of speech.

"Now, let's start the game."

She stood mesmerized, watching Fareed's beautiful hands probe Ryan's muscles for power, pushing and pulling on his feet and legs, making Ryan an eager participant. He turned to sensation, walking his fingers along nerve paths, before pouncing with tickles and eliciting Ryan's shrieking giggles.

Next came recording muscle contraction and nerve conduction and he made Ryan help him fit in plugs and place leads over his body, all the time explaining everything. Ryan hung on his every word, his eyes rapt as he watched this larger-than-life entity who'd entered and filled his limited world. Fareed warned him that the tests were a bit uncomfortable, but would be over in no time, and Gwen braced herself for the end of the honeymoon.

But as he started the tests, instead of the dreaded wails, Ryan seemed to only notice Fareed's banter, awarded him with a steady stream of corroborating gurgles.

She shouldn't be surprised. Fareed's darkest silk voice made *her* forget a world outside existed, or a past or a future....

What was she *thinking?* She should only be thinking of running away once this exam ended, forgetting she'd ever seen him again.

She'd only sought him as a last resort, had hoped to slip in among his appointments undistinguished. But she'd ended up having his attention in its most undiluted form. Then it had gotten worse and he'd remembered her, had been treating her since as if he...

Her thoughts piled up as he dressed Ryan then caught her eye. "I'll see those investigations now."

She pounced on the briefcase, but he gently stopped her fumbling, took over. He studied the X-rays and MRIs briefly, set aside the reports without reading them before putting everything back in the briefcase. Then he turned to Ryan, who was demanding to be picked up—by him.

He complied at once. "So how was that? Fun as I promised, eh?" Ryan whooped an agreement. "But you know what? We had all this fun together, and I haven't even introduced myself. My name is Fareed." He pointed to himself, said his name a few time.

Ryan's eyes twinkled before he echoed triumphantly, "Aa-eed."

"Ma azkaak men subbi!" Fareed exclaimed. "What a clever boy you are." Ryan seemed delighted by Fareed's approval, and continued to say Aa-eed over and over. Fareed guffawed. "We'll work on the *F* and *R* later. I bet you'll get it right in a couple of months, being a genius, like Rose said—" he turned to her "—and like your mother is."

Gwen felt about to faint again.

It's dreading his still-unvoiced verdict, she told herself.

But it wasn't. She *was* terrified of having her worst fears validated, but that lightheadedness, as if she'd been hungry all her life, was the effect he had on her. Anything he did, every move and look and breath induced pure emotional and erotic tumult....

What was happening to her? What was it about him that made her someone she didn't know? Someone who couldn't complete a thought without it turning into something...licentious?

He was guiding her back into the room, stopping by the desk for a computer tablet. At the sitting area, he set Ryan on the ground, gave him every safe article around to play with. Ryan instead made it clear he wanted to nap. She produced a blanket from the bag Rose had left behind and Fareed spread it in front of the couch, where Ryan crawled and promptly feel asleep facedown.

Once they sat down, Fareed said, "Tell me about Ryan, Gwen."

Don't call me that, she wanted to cry out. She needed to

regain her balance and there was no hope she would when he kept calling her *Gwaihn* in that lion's purr of his.

Instead she nodded her shaky assent. Over the next minutes, he obtained an exhaustive history of Ryan's pre- and postnatal periods and developmental milestones, his fingers flying over the glossy tablet's surface documenting it all.

Finally, he put the tablet down, turned to face her. "You do know he has *spina bifida occulta?*"

His question/declaration felt like a direct blow to her heart. She'd known, but had still been hoping against hope....

Tears surged again as she nodded. "As a researcher of drugs targeting the nervous system, I knew the basics of the condition." Incomplete closure of vertebrae around the spinal cord, which instead of hanging loose in the spinal canal was tethered to the bone, potentially causing varying degrees of nerve damage and disability. "I studied it extensively because I suspected Ryan of having it. But every pediatrician and neurologist told me not to worry, that ten percent of people have it and are asymptomatic, something they discover as adults during X-rays for unrelated complaints. I persisted, and a couple conceded that he has minor neurological deficits, which might or might not mean future disability but that there was no treatment anyway. But I couldn't just wait until Ryan grew up and couldn't walk or never developed bowel or urinary continence. I had to know for sure that there was nothing to be done, and only you...only your opinion will do..."

The sobs that had been banked broke loose.

He was down on his haunches in front of her in a blink, his hands squeezing her shoulders. "It was amazing that you noticed the mild weakness in his legs and clawing in his toes. He's sitting and crawling, and with him far away from being toilet-trained and without previous experience with children, I'm beyond impressed that you discerned his condition even after the repeated dismissal of your worries. But I can excuse the doctors who examined him. It would take someone as extensively versed in the rare as I am to form an opinion on so irregular a condition."

Her sobs had been subsiding gradually, at his soothing and under the urge to swamp him with questions.

The paramount one burst from her. "And you've formed one?"

He nodded. "You were absolutely right. Without surgery, he may develop increasing disability in lower limb motor function and bowel and urinary control."

She sank her fingers into his sinew and muscle. "So there is a surgery? To prevent further damage? What about any that already exists? *Is* there damage? What about bowel and urinary problems? My sources say even when surgery successfully closes the defect and releases the cord, those usually never go away...." She faltered on the last question, what she of all people knew was a long shot. "And if there's a residual handicap, would my drug help?"

He rose, came down beside her. This time, she sank into his solicitude gratefully, only the last vestiges of her willpower stopping her from physically seeking it.

"Most, if not all, surgeons wouldn't touch a case like Ryan's. They'd say their findings are too ephemeral to warrant a surgery that wouldn't offer much, if any, improvement. But I say different."

Hope surged so hard inside her that she choked with its agonizing expansion. "You—you mean you're not telling me to give up?"

He shook his head. "Of course, any surgery comes with risks." The world darkened again. He caught her hand, squeezed it. "I have to mention risks because it's unethical to promise you a risk-free procedure, not because I expect problems. But I can and do promise you and Ryan the best result possible."

Her tears faltered. "Y-you mean *you* want to operate on him?"

He nodded. "He'll be safe with me, Gwen."

She stifled another heart-wrenching sob. Fareed's arm slid around her. "And yes, your drug will regenerate the nerve damage. I know it's not approved for use on children, but because I believed the delay in approval was built on bureaucracy and not medical facts, I have obtained permission from the region's drug administration under my personal responsibility and have used it on even younger patients than Ryan with adjusted doses and certain precautions to astonishing results. Together, we'll cure Ryan, Gwen."

And she had to ask the rest, everything, now, before this turned out to be a deranged dream, before she fainted again. "How long will it take? The surgery? The recuperation? How soon can he have it? How much will it all cost?"

"The surgery itself is from four to six hours, and the recuperation is from four to six weeks. He can have it as soon as I prepare everything. And it won't cost a thing."

That stopped the churning world. Her tears. Her heart.

"You must have misunderstood," she finally whispered. "I'm not here seeking charity. I didn't even think of asking you to perform the surgery, only hoped you'd write me a report stating that it's a surgical case, so no surgeon could tell me it isn't."

He pursed his lips. "First, there's no charity involved—"

She struggled to detach herself from the circle of his support. "Of course there is. You're here performing pro bono surgeries. But I can pay. Just tell me how much, and I will."

"*You* will pay? Not that it's an issue here, but why wouldn't your insurance cover your child's medical expenses?"

She should be more careful what she said. He noticed everything. Now she had to satisfy him with an explanation or he'd corner her with demands for more information she couldn't give. "I insisted on costly investigations the doctors said weren't needed, moving me to an unfavorable insurance category, so the coverage would be only partial now. But that doesn't matter. I'm very well paid and I have a lot of money."

He leveled patient eyes on her. "Of course you are and you do. And there is *still* no cost involved."

She shook her head. "I can't accept a waiver of your fee. And then there are many other expenses besides that."

His lips quirked, teasing, indulgent. "First, I'm a big boy, if you haven't noticed, and I can waive my fee if I want to, which I mostly do. My 'reputation' isn't *totally* hype, you know. Second, there won't be any other expenses back home."

She gaped at him. For a full minute.

She finally heard a strangled echo. "Back home?"

He rose to his feet with a smile. "Yes. You, Ryan and Rose are coming with me to Jizaan."

Five

Gwen stared at the overwhelming force that was Fareed Aal Zaafer, and was certain of one of two things.

Either she'd finally lost her mind, or he was out of his.

She squeezed her eyes shut, as if that would stop the disintegration of this situation, set it back in the land of the acceptable. She opened her eyes again hoping she'd see on his face what should have been there from the start, polite forbearance with a patient's hysterical mother.

But he was looking at her with that indulgent intensity that singed her. Worse, a new excitement was entering his gaze, as if he was realizing more benefits to his decision by the second.

"As soon as Rose and Emad return, we'll go to your hotel and collect your luggage on our way to the airport. We'll be in Jizaan in under twenty-four hours."

He'd said it again. This Jizaan thing. She hadn't imagined it the first time. This was real. He meant it.

But he *couldn't* mean it. He had to be joking. He did have a wicked sense of humor. . . .

No. His humor, while unpredictable and lightning-fast, was not in any way mean, at least, not in any of the lectures and interviews she'd seen. It would be beyond cruel to joke now and he was the very opposite of that: magnanimous, compassionate, protective.

But he was also single-minded and autocratic and she had to stop him before this crazy idea became a solid intention.

He detailed said intention. "We'll go to dinner first, or we can have it on board the jet." He got out his cell phone, cocked his head at her. "What would you like to have? Real food this time, I promise. I can either reserve seats in a restaurant, or have your choice ready on the jet."

"I can't go to your kingdom!"

The shaky statement managed to do the job. It stopped him short.

For about a second. Then he smiled. "Of course, you can."

She raised her hands. "Please, let's not start another 'I can't' 'No, you can' match. We just finished one about payment."

"Yes, let's not. You do remember how you fared in that last match? No point in repeating the same method and expecting different results, hmm?"

The definition of insanity, which also described this situation. She did feel her sanity slipping another notch. "You know what you're proposing is impossible."

"I know no such thing."

She shook her head, disbelief deepening, dread taking root. "You're asking me to just haul everyone halfway across the world. . . ."

"I'll do the 'hauling,' so cross that out on your no-doubt

alphabetized list of worries. I'm sure you have your affairs sorted out for as long as you thought would see Ryan's medical situation resolved. But in case you're not fully covered, and fear repercussions for prolonged or unexcused absence from work, one phone call from me should get you an open-ended leave, with pay."

Her breathing had gone awry by the time he finished. "It's not just my work, it's...*everything.*"

He crossed his arms over his chest, someone who would not be denied, who had an answer to everything. "Like what?"

She groped for something, anything, latched on the first logical thing that occurred to her. "Like passports. We didn't bring them on a trip we couldn't have dreamed would take us outside the States."

His daunting shoulder rose and fell. "You won't need them to enter my kingdom."

"But we'd need visas...."

He intercepted that, too. "Not when you're entering the kingdom with me, you don't. And I'll bring you back with me, so you won't need more than your American IDs to re-enter the States."

Her eyes darted around, as if looking for a way out. There was none. He kept neutralizing possible objections in advance. "And anyway, to make you feel better, once in Jizaan, I'll have the American embassy there issue new passports for you and I'll have visas stamped on them."

She knew he could do that with a flick of a finger. Any country would bend over backward to accommodate him.

"And if you're worried about your family, I'll call them right now, give them all my contact info, so they'd be in touch with you at all times. I can even take any of them who wish to come along, too."

Her heart emptied at his mention of her family. A subject she had to close before he probed it open. "Rose is my closest relative."

And probe he did. "You said she was a maternal relative. So what happened to your mother?"

She could feel the familiar pain and loss expanding all over inside her. She had to get this over with, dissuade him from broaching the subject ever again. "She died from surgical complications just after I entered college. I have no one else."

He looked thoughtful. "And that must have factored in your decision to have Ryan after your engagement fell through, so you'd form your own family."

She let her silence convince him his deduction was right, when it was anything but.

"I'm very sorry to hear you were all alone in the world for so long. Coming from such an extensive family, I can't imagine how it must have been for you."

"I'm no longer alone."

"Yes." After a long moment when sympathy seemed to radiate off him, he smiled. "So we checked off passports, visas, fees and responsibility to family as reasons to resist my plans."

"But these are not the only..." She stopped, panting now as if she'd been trying to outrun an out-of-control car. She *was* trying to escape his inexorable intentions. "What am I saying? I'm not debating the feasibility of something that's not even an option. And the only thing that will make me feel better is that you drop this and...and..." She stopped again, feeling herself being backed into a trap her own capitulation would close shut. And he was standing there, waiting for her to succumb, knowing that she would. She groaned with helplessness, "Why even suggest this? Why not perform the surgery here? If it's because you're worried I'd be saddled with hospital expenses,.."

He waved that majestic hand of his. "I could have had the hospital waive them by adding Ryan to the cases I was here for."

"Then why?" That came out a desperate moan.

He gave her such a look, that of someone willing to spend days cajoling and happy to do it. "You want reasons in descending or ascending order of importance?"

"Oh, please!" She tried to rise, failed to inject any co-ordination in her jellified legs. "Just…just…"

He sat down, put a soothing hand on her shoulder. "Breathe, Gwen. Everything will be fine, I promise. As for why, one main reason is that I can't stay away from my medical center any longer. And I certainly won't operate on Ryan, then leave him to someone else's follow-up. The other major reason is that I can only guarantee my results in a case as delicate when I'm in my medium, among the medical team I put together and the system I constructed."

Those *were* major reasons. "But still…"

"No 'but stills.' You're coming with me and…"

She interrupted him this time. "Even if we have to come, we don't have to right away. We can go back home, prepare ourselves, and when you have a surgery date arranged, we'd fly over."

He was the epitome of accommodation, yet of determination. "Why go to the trouble and expense when you have a free and convenient ride now? At absolutely no extra cost or effort on my part? And there's nothing to arrange. Once in Jizaan, I'll take Ryan for the mandatory pre-op tests, then do the surgery at once."

Her heart punched her ribs. "Th-that fast?"

"There's every reason to do it as soon as possible. But don't worry about a thing, I'll take care of everything."

"But I *can't* just let you do everything, pay for everything. If we have to go to Jizaan, then I'll at least pay our way."

He leaned back, folded his arms across his expansive chest. "So what do you propose to do? Give my pilot and cabin crew your credit card? Or will you want to stop by an ATM to get cash?"

"Please, don't joke! The most I can consent to not paying is your own fee. *If* you really waive it on a regular basis."

His face lost any lightness. "After all the things you implied I was, are you now calling me a liar?"

"Oh, God, *no!*" she blurted out. "I meant…"

His serious expression dissolved on a smile that could have powered a small city. She must be in even worse condition than she'd thought if she hadn't realized he *had* been joking.

"I know what you meant." His fingers gently probed her pulse. "Your heart is in hyperdrive. It's physically distressing thinking you'd be in someone's debt, isn't it?" *It's more your nearness, your touch,* she almost confessed. "But rest easy, Gwen, there's no debt. I will always owe many surgical successes to your expertise. Let me try to repay it with mine. As for me, on a professional level, adding the success of Ryan's surgery to my achievements will be more than payment enough for me." Suddenly the eyes that had become serious for real, crinkled on bedeviling. "But if you have money you can't bear having, I'll give you a list of causes in Jizaan and you can donate it in lieu of payment."

She had no answer now but more tears.

They welled up, filling her whole being. It was beyond incredible. To have his incomparable skills and support. It was also beyond terrible. To have to go with him, be near

him, for weeks, be exposed to his influence and subjected
to her weakness.

Beyond the tragedies that had sheared through her life
and heart, that was the worst thing that could have happened to her. She would have gone to hell and wouldn't
have bothered coming back to see Ryan healthy and happy.
Now she would go to the one place she considered worse
than hell. And she could never explain her feelings to
Fareed.

She finally whispered, "I—I don't know what to say."

He sat back, his imposing frame sprawling in the contentment of someone who'd fulfilled his purpose. "You do.
A three-letter word. Beginning with a *Y* and ending with
an *S*."

A thousand fears screeched in the darkness of her mind.
And she closed her eyes and prayed. That when she said
it, it would only mean Ryan's salvation, and not her dam-
nation.

She opened her eyes, stepped off the bleak, yet familiar, cliff of resignation into the abyss of the unknown.

And whispered the dreaded, "Yes."

The trip to Jizaan passed in a blur of distress.

Fareed, with Emad and the flight crew, orchestrated
a symphony of such lavish luxury that it almost snapped
her frayed nerves. She was so unused to being waited on,
so uncomfortable at being on the receiving end of such
indulgence, when she was unable to repay it, too, that it
exhausted her.

After the first three hours, she'd escaped by sleeping the
remaining eight hours to their refueling layover in London.
She'd taken refuge in sleep again in the second leg of the
journey, leaving Rose and Ryan to plumb the jet's inhab-
itants' ceaseless desire to spoil them.

She was floating somewhere gray and oppressive when she felt a caress on her hand.

She jerked out of the coma-like sleep knowing it was Fareed. Only his touch had ever felt like a thousand volts of disruption.

"I apologize for disturbing your slumber, but we're about to land." His eyes glowed like embers even in the jet's atrocious lighting, his magnificent voice soaked in gentle teasing. "I hope fourteen hours of sleep managed to provide a measure of rest."

She would have told him they sure hadn't if her throat didn't feel lined with sandpaper. She rose from the comfort of the plane bed, returning it to its upright position, feeling as if she'd been in a knock-down drag-out fight.

Apart from everything that disturbed her past, present and future, she knew why she felt wrecked. She might have been hiding in unawareness, but she'd felt him as she'd slept, and his thoughts, the demand, the promise in them and her struggle against them, had worn her out.

Rose waited until he left to approach her with Ryan, eyeing her in sarcastic censure. "That was sure record-breaking."

"You mean you and Ryan staying awake for that long?" Rose huffed. "Oh, we slept, around an hour on each leg. *We* were savvy enough to take advantage of that once-in-a-lifetime experience. While *you* are either stupid, or stupid not to grab at all that…God offers."

From the proof of undeniable experience, Gwen knew that Rose, the only "aunt" she'd ever had, had only her best interest at heart. She'd always counted on her outspokenness to make her face the truth when she shied away from it. But now that smack of reality only made her sink deeper into despair.

Rose had no idea how impossible everything was.

She was almost thankful when Fareed returned, bringing with him another dose of disturbance. She wasn't up to more evasive maneuvers with the other unstoppable force in her life.

She was unequivocally thankful when Rose engaged Fareed in conversation during landing. It left her able to pretend to look outside her window when she saw nothing but her internal turmoil.

They were really in Jizaan.

After touchdown, Fareed got up and took Ryan from Rose.

Gwen jumped up, tried to take him. Fareed looked down at Ryan. "Which ride do you want, *ya sugheeri?*"

Thorns sprouted in her stomach at the loving way Fareed called Ryan his little one.

Ryan, who seemingly understood anything Fareed said in either English or Arabic, looked back at her with dimples at full blast. Then he bobbed in his arms, spurring him to move.

There. She'd gotten her answer.

As Rose preceded them out of the plane with Emad, Fareed kept a step behind her.

His bass purr hit her back. "I'm not competing with you for his favor."

She slanted him a glance over her shoulder, almost winced at the incredible sight of him, as immaculate and fresh as if he hadn't been up for the past twenty-four hours, after a month of grueling surgeries, too. He towered over her, his shoulders broad enough to blot out the whole world, virility and gorgeousness radiating off him in shock waves.

Looking ahead before she stumbled, she murmured, "It never occurred to me that you were."

"And he's not choosing me over you."

A mocking huff broke from her. "Could have fooled me."

His deep chuckle resonated in her bones. "He's not. I'm just the new toy."

She would have chuckled, too, if she'd been able to draw more air than that which kept her on her feet and conscious.

And that was before he took her elbow, offered the support he must have felt she needed, smiled down at her. "You really should be happy we're enjoying each other's company so much." Her knees almost lost their solidity as seriousness tinged his gaze. "But I can't be more relieved that he likes and seeks me. The coming time isn't going to be easy, and trusting me is going to make everything so much better for him."

He was *that* thoughtful? She'd only ever known one other person with that kindness....

Memories lodged into her heart like an ax. She clamped down on the pain. She couldn't afford to let those overwhelm her now. She needed to be at her strongest, her most resolute. For Ryan. And for her own struggle.

She passed by a time zones clock, blinked at its verdict. Four-thirty in the afternoon in L.A., 5:30 a.m. in Jizaan. Exactly twenty-four hours from the moment she'd staggered into his orbit.

She felt as if her life before those hours had been someone else's, someone whose memories were sloughing off to be replaced by this new reality that had no rhyme or reason.

Then she stepped out of the jet and into another realm.

Her career had taken her all over the world, other desert kingdoms included, but Jizaan felt...alien, unprecedented.

The least of it was the airport itself, what she'd caught glimpses of from the air, what had the design, ambition and otherworldliness of a horizon-dominating space colony.

Everything else was painted with a brush of hyperreality. The star-sprinkled sky midway between the blue of eternity and the indigo of dawn had the vibrancy of another dimension, the stars the sharpness and abundance of another galaxy. The desert winter breeze that kissed her face and ran insistent fingers through her hair, even when jets' exhaust should have tainted it, felt cleansing, resuscitating. The whole atmosphere was permeated by echoes of a history rife with towering passions, unquenchable feuds and undying honor. She felt it all tug at her through her awareness of Fareed, whose blood ran thick with this land's legacy.

She stole a look at him, found him looking down at Ryan, his expression laced with fondness. Ryan, secure in Fareed's powerful grasp, was looking around, his face rapt as he inhaled deep, as if to breathe in the new place, make it a part of him.

Her heart constricted. If only...

"Ahlann wa sahlann bekom fi daari-wa daarakom."

Fareed's deep tones caressed every one of her nerves— until she translated what he'd said.

He was welcoming them to his home. And theirs.

She knew this was simply the ultragenerosity the region was known for, where they offered guests their homes as theirs. She still felt as if a wrecking ball had swung into her. She swayed with the force of the phantom sensation.

Fareed grabbed her tight against his side.

He'd probably saved her, this time from a plunge down a flight of steel stairs. But being ensconced in his heat and hardness, his concern was unendurable.

She groped for the railing, quickened her descent, pretending steadiness. The moment she touched ground, her legs wobbled again.

He caught her, exhaled. "I should have woken you earlier. You're still drowsy. Or you're hypoglycemic again. You barely ate anything since we started this journey."

She didn't refute his explanations. Better to let him think it was all physical. She wouldn't tell him the truth. She couldn't. Not the general truth. Or the one behind her latest bout of chaos. That as soon as her feet touched the ground, she could almost swear the land pulled at her. And yelled at her.

Leave, the moment you can. Before you sustain an injury you won't survive this time.

They'd reached the limo awaiting them a dozen feet from the jet's stairs, where Emad had taken the driver's seat with Rose beside him, when she heard Fareed say, "We're going to my place, Ryan."

The words meant for Ryan skimmed her mind, leaving no impression. Then they slowly sank. And detonated.

She swung to him as he held the door open for her. *"What?"*

He frowned his confusion. "What do you mean 'what'?"

"What do you mean *your* place?"

He smiled, a smile drenched in that overriding sensuality that was as integral to him as his DNA. "My place is the place where I live. And where you'll stay."

"We're going to stay in your center!"

He gave an adamant headshake as he prodded her to enter the limo, making her slide across the backseat by entering after her. "Only during the immediate pre- and postoperative period. And don't contest this again."

"I never contested it a first time...,"

"Which was much appreciated, so don't suddenly change—"

She cut him off in return, feeling her brain overheating. "Because this is the first time I've heard of this."

"Not true. I told you during the flight."

"Was I awake when you told me?"

He gave her a thoughtful glance, then his smile scalded her with its amusement. "Come to think of it, that you didn't contest it should have clued me in that you were sleep talking."

"And now that I'm awake…"

"You'll be my esteemed guest."

Before she could utter another protest, Ryan, who'd been getting louder demanding his attention, grabbed his face and tugged. Fareed turned to him and at once they got engaged in another game of fetch-and-explain.

Even though he had been paying Ryan every attention, she knew he relished that timely excuse to end their conversation. She knew there was no use trying to continue it. He had this infallible way of getting his way, of making his unilateral decisions the only ones that made sense. But his place?

She felt she was sinking in quicksand and any move was making her sink faster.

And there was nothing she could do about it.

She exhaled, sought distraction, looked outside the window, her eyes finally registering the splendor of Jizaan's sparkling capital rushing by.

In the first slivers of dawn, the magnificence of Al Zaaferah, or The Victorious, named after the centuries-old ruling house, seeped into her awareness. It felt as if it had been erected today to the most lavish standards. It also looked constantly evolving with extreme-concept projects rising among the soaring mirrored buildings—

everything felt futuristic yet with pervasive cultural influences making it feel steeped in history.

She was lost in recording every detail when she noticed
they'd gotten off the main roads and were now driving
through automatic, thirty-feet-high, wrought-iron gates.
Fareed's "place," no doubt.

The limo winded through ingeniously landscaped
grounds, approaching a sprawling stone mansion crouch-
ing in the distance. Painted in sweeps of shadow and mys-
ticism, it had the feel of a fortress from a Middle Eastern
fable, the abode of someone who craved solitude, yet in
having to house those his rank dictated, expanded his
domain to give them space, and himself distance.

She hadn't thought what his place would be like. If she
had, she would have imagined he lived in either the royal
palace, or as imposing an edifice. But even though this
place spoke of affluence, it didn't reek of excess. It was
amazing how everything was permeated with the privileges of the prince, yet possessed the austerity of the surgeon.

All through their journey to the main door, she felt
invisible eyes monitoring their progress, relaying it to
forward stations. Even though she'd experienced many aspects of Fareed's status, that seamlessly orchestrated sur-
veillance solidified everything in her mind. Who Fareed
was. Where she was now.

He handed her out of the limo feet from stone steps
leading to the patio. Footmen appeared as if from nowhere
and rushed to open the massive brass-work doors.

She entered beside him with trepidation expanding in
her heart into a columned hall that spread under a thirty-
foot mosaic dome. The doors closed with a soft click. To
Gwen, it felt as if iron prison doors were slammed shut
behind her.

Her gaze darted around the indirectly lit space, got impressions of a sweeping floor plan extending on both sides, understated colors, a male influence in decor—his virile influence permeating the place. Her inspection ended where thirty-foot-wide stairs climbed to a spacious platform before winding away to each side of the upper floor.

Fareed led them up one side to a guest apartment triple the size of her condo, faithfully displaying the amalgam of modernity and Arabian Nights feel of the rest of the mansion. If she were in a condition to appreciate anything, she would have found it amazing to walk through doors that looked like they'd been transported through millennia intact only to swing open soundlessly with a proximity sensor. She was sure even Scheherazade's imagination couldn't have created anything like this place.

"Let me take him."

Gwen stirred from her reverie at Rose's words. She found her taking a now sound-asleep Ryan from Fareed.

"We're both done for." Rose stifled a yawn as she gave Gwen a kiss on the cheek. She grinned at Emad as she took Ryan's bag from him. "I'll find us the nearest beds and it might be night when you see either of us again."

In a minute everyone had left her alone with Fareed.

She turned blindly, pretending to inspect the sitting area. She ran a hand along the perfect smoothness of a hand-carved chair before turning to a spherical, fenestrated brass lantern hanging from the ceiling with spectacular chains. She made the mistake of transferring her gaze to him and the hypnotic play of light and shadows over his face and figure only deepened his influence.

He stared back at her for long, long moments, winding up the coil of tension inside her tighter until she felt she'd shatter.

Before she begged him to just stop, he finally exhaled.

"I apologize for not staying to show you around, but I have to go to work, catch up on everything I hadn't been able to attend to long-distance. Use the place as you would your own—and *don't* argue. Just explore, relax, rest. Then tomorrow we go the center."

Her heart almost knocked her off her feet. "You—you'll operate tomorrow?"

He simply said, "Yes."

After losing all of her family, one after the other, Gwen had thought she'd known all kinds of anguish and desperation. All forms of loss.

But now she knew there was more. There was worse. And there was one injury, one loss, she wouldn't survive.

If anything happened to Ryan...

"Everything will be fine."

She chafed at Rose's reassurance. What she'd reiterated over and over since Fareed had taken Ryan and disappeared into the depths of his staggeringly advanced medical center.

It didn't work now as it hadn't worked before. Fareed had come out once, fourteen hours ago, telling them Ryan had been prepared and was already in the O.R. He'd said he'd come out to reassure them as soon as he was done with the surgery.

That had lasted *eight* hours. Two hours longer than his longest estimate. Every second of the extra time, she'd known a worse hell than any she'd known before.

Guilt had consumed her. She'd sought inferior help initially, hoping it would suffice, save her from making contact with Fareed. What if she'd left it too late? What if she'd be punished for considering anything, no matter how momentous, ahead of Ryan's health?

Rose hugged her, sensing her thoughts. "Stop it, Gwen. Everything is fine. Fareed's assistant assured us it is."

"But *he* didn't."

Fareed hadn't come out to reassure her as he'd promised! What if that meant he couldn't face her with what had happened yet?

Rose tsked. "You did see the mass casualty situation that hit the center like a tornado, didn't you? With his being the chief around here and with God knows how many lives to save, I'm sure putting your mind to rest personally plunged to the bottom of his priorities."

Logic droned that Rose was right. But hysteria was drowning it out. They wouldn't let her see Ryan in Recovery or ICU. Fareed's orders. That was six mutilating hours ago.

Suddenly, Fareed appeared at the other end of the expansive waiting area.

She rose, could barely stand erect as his long strides ate the maddening distance between them. Then out of the blue, he was swamped by people. Other patients' frantic families.

He stopped his advance, turned to them with calm, patient and what must have been very detailed reassurance because it defused their tension. By the time he at last excused himself with utmost courteousness and resumed his path to her, she was at screaming pitch.

As he stopped before her, those fiery eyes piercing her, she felt he'd trodden on the heart that had crashed at his feet.

"It all went wrong."

Six

Gwen's lifeless statement barely scratched the surface of the terror in her heart.

Fareed hadn't smiled at her. He'd smiled at the others. She could only interpret his intensity as bad news. The worst…

He smiled. Her knees buckled.

"*Nothing* went wrong." His smile broadened as he caught her by the waist, stopped her from folding to the ground. "I *already* told you that—well, I sent Akram to tell you that everything went perfectly right."

"Oh, you magnificent man, thank you!" Rose charged him, made him relinquish his hold on Gwen and squeezed him in an exuberant hug.

Gwen felt the life force that had felt extracted from her slowly begin to reenter her body. Then he put Rose at arm's length, smiled down at her. "But I can't take much credit. Ryan did most of the work. From the pre-op preps to what my team told me felt like ordering his very tissues to assist me, he was the most interactive patient I ever had. I've never had a surgery go so smoothly."

Rose laughed her delight. "That's our Ryan! But we'll just pretend that you did have an equal role in this, and you'll accept our thanks like a good sport."

"As long as you realize the extent of my contribution, I'm happy to accept."

Their elation hammered at Gwen, demanding to breach her numbness. But the tidal wave hovered at the periphery of her mind, scared to crash and sweep her fears away.

"So why won't you let me see him?"

He turned to her, eyes flaring with sympathy. "Because children look heartrending when they're in ICU and I wanted to spare you the sight."

"*That* was why you left me to go insane out here for six hours? Didn't you realize I'd prefer having my heart rent by seeing him over going mad by not seeing him?"

His eyes widened with her every word, before they narrowed again with self-derision. "My concern was evidently misplaced. Guess I can't put myself in a mother's shoes after all."

Her frustration turned inward, a flame that burned her blood with mortification. "God, no…I didn't mean to imply that…"

"Don't apologize for loving Ryan too much. But even after you blasted me for being so blithely insensitive to your needs, I am still unable to meet them. I have to be this infuriating professional and insist on my position. For now. I promise you he's in perfect condition and that you'll see him in a few hours."

"Please, let me see him now. A look is all I want!"

"What you *don't* want is the image of him sedated and inert and hooked to tubes and monitors burned into your memory. You may know what you'll see, but seeing it for real is something totally different. And I refuse to let you inflict another mental scar on yourself. I've seen parents suffer debilitating anxiety long after their children are cured, and you've suffered enough of that. So even though you probably want to kill me right now, you might want to thank me later."

"But I don't want…" She paused, groaned. "Are—are you doing this on purpose?"

He chuckled, winked at Rose who joined him in chuckling. "Of course, I am. One of my PhDs is in distraction. But while it must feel like eternity now, the hours will pass, then I'll transfer him to a private suite and you'll be with him from then on." His logic was putting out the fires of dread and desperation. But the clamoring of her heart wouldn't subside. He silenced her turmoil. "Until then, how about you ladies join me for a meal? I've long passed starving, and knowing you, Gwen, I'm sure we were on that same path together."

Rose waved her hand. "Oh, you two go ahead. Emad told me to call him as soon as you made an appearance, and to meet him in the center's restaurant. He promised a meal to top the Cordon Bleu he treated me to in L.A., and I sure want to see how this can be achieved." Rose hugged her. "See? You should always listen to me. Now listen to me and take care of yourself. You won't do Ryan any good if you collapse. You're even allowed to smile without sinning against motherhood."

"I'll take care of her." Fareed took Gwen's elbow. "I'll even brave the impossible chore of making her smile." He tilted his head at her from his prodigious height. "Shall we?"

Gwen didn't even nod. She could do nothing but stare

after Rose, as she walked away with her phone at her ear, and let Fareed steer her wherever he wished.

She registered glimpses of their journey down the halls and corridors spread in reflective granite. She barely noticed the people whose eyes held deference for Fareed and curiosity for her on their way to an elevator straight out of a sci-fi movie. She didn't feel it move, but when its brushed-steel doors slid open moments later, it was into a room the size of a tennis court, with twenty-foot, floor-to-ceiling windows spanning its arched side.

It was like looking out of a plane, with Al Zaaferah and its skyscrapers sprawling below and into the horizon, lighting up the clear night sky like a network of blazing jewels. She dimly realized they must be in the top floors of the steel-and-glass tower that formed the main portion of the center.

She'd barely recovered from the breathtaking elevation when the opulence and austerity of the place hit her. This must be his office.

His hand burned its mark into her arm as he escorted her across a gleaming hardwood floor covered in what felt like acres of Persian silk carpet to a deepest-green leather couch ensemble around a unique worked-wood centerpiece table.

When she remained standing, he gave her the gentlest of tugs. She collapsed where he indicated. He stood before her for a long moment, his gaze storming through her. Then his lips spread.

Her heart tried its best to leap out of her throat.

"Even though I know asking your preference in food is an exercise of futility, it seems I like butting my head against a wall. So, again, any favorite cuisine?"

"Anything...with calories."

She was stunned she'd produced the words. She was only sure she had when he laughed.

Her hand pressed the painful, thudding lump that had replaced her heart. There should be a law against such hazardous behavior.

He phoned in his order of food before he turned his attention back to her. Beside that watchfulness that made her feel he was listening to her thoughts, and that supreme assurance that was integral to him, she saw satisfaction.

From what she knew of him from years of following his career, this was a man who knew his handiwork, never exaggerated his results. He really believed Ryan's surgery had been successful beyond even what he'd promised her.

And the floodgates of relief finally burst.

She shook under its enormity, and this time when he reached for her, she surrendered to the potent comfort he offered.

Fareed stroked Gwen's shining head, absorbed her softness and ebbing fear, inhaled her freshness and dissipating distress and told his burning hands that that was as far as it went—for now.

When he'd come out of the O.R., he'd seen no one but her. She'd looked so lost, those eyes that wreaked havoc with his control pleading for reassurance. He'd forced himself to answer the other families first or he would have crushed her in his arms. As it were, he'd been aware of the curious glances when he'd taken her to his private elevator.

Not that he cared. He did his absolute best for all his patients. If he chose to give his personal time and attention afterward to her, it was no one's business.

But holding her like that, having her burrow into him like a kitten seeking protection, was wrecking his reason.

His body had hardened beyond arousal, and that was with her wrapped in those shapeless clothes and only seeking comfort. What effect would she have if she sought him with hunger in her touch and eyes?

He shuddered with expectation. What he'd give to carry her to bed *now* and to hell with his professional code.

But he'd already strained that code for her. All he could do now was keep his passion under a tight leash until Ryan was no longer in his care. Afterward…

Afterward, he expected an even fiercer impediment than the dictates of his professional honor. His father.

He knew he'd wage a more ferocious war with him than when he'd chosen to go into medicine and not into politics or business.

Not that it mattered. He wasn't Hesham, young and vulnerable. He would fight anything and anyone, starting with his father, to have her. He'd face the whole world for her.

And he knew that, beyond a doubt, she wanted him as fiercely. That was what fueled her struggle to keep her distance, what she believed the circumstances dictated. But when her worry for her son and his obligations ended, he would plumb the depth of her answering need.

Feeling he was peeling off a layer of skin, he let her go as soon as her tremors subsided. She pulled away at the same instant.

Embarrassment blazed on her cheeks as she slid to the end of the couch. "You must be so sick of soothing frantic relatives."

"It's part of the job description."

He nearly laughed at his exaggeration. She'd seen how he'd dealt with his patients' relatives. While he'd been courteous and accommodating, he hadn't dissolved their fears in his embrace.

A knock on the door roused him. "Our calories are here." A smile wobbled on her lips. He sighed. "Next time, I'll manage to make that smile last longer than a nanosecond."

He went to the door, returned with a trolley laden with food and beverages. Everything smelled mouth-watering. But the hunger that rose inside him was for her. He could almost taste the grace and femininity in her every line. His body tightened even more.

He should be exhausted. He was. It made no difference when she was around. He remained alert, unable to waste one moment when he could...experience her. Even when she'd slept on the plane, he'd stayed awake to check on her. She aroused not only his passion but his protectiveness, too, to unreasoning levels.

Bowled over. That was what he was. And to think that before he'd seen her, he'd sighed in pity at those who used that expression. Reveling in his condition, he sat down beside her, started uncovering hot plates.

He whistled. "Seems they got us *everything* with calories. Are you up to the challenge?"

Fareed's question distracted her from drooling at the distressing scent. Not the food's. His.

She could only murmur, "No promises."

His fire-tinged eyes turned more enigmatic before he turned to serve the food. Her senses reeled with his closeness, her thoughts tangling at his inconsistencies.

Even though he was known to be most accessible professionally, on a personal level, he was considered inapproachable. Yet from her own experience, he was only too approachable, and she...

She *had* to stop fantasizing about him. He was the one

man she should never want, the one man who was off-limits.

But what if he is the one man you can *want?*

She crushed the insidious voice as she accepted a steaming plate piled with mouth-watering grilled salmon and vegetables, careful not to touch him again. Touching him had infused a dangerous narcotic into her bloodstream. She should be careful not to end up addicted. Or was she already?

Was this how it happened? Inadvertent exposure, moments of surrender to temptation and suddenly you were irrevocably lost....

"Eat, Gwen, and I'll reward you. I'll discuss Ryan's postoperative period and rehabilitation."

This brought her back to earth with a thud.

"Yes, please."

His eyes ignited. She shied away from their heat and her interpretation of it. It had to be her feverish mind superimposing her preposterous cravings on his glances and actions.

She cleared her throat. "Wh-what do you expect?"

"How about a deal?" he countered. "One mouthful a sentence."

"Oh, all right." She loaded a fork, forced it into her mouth.

He tutted. "A bigger mouthful won't get you a longer sentence, and I won't talk any faster if you choke."

She swallowed the lump and almost did just that.

"For God's sake, just tell me!" she spluttered.

"I expect a full recovery." At her evident frustration with his brevity, his eyebrows rose. "You expected more for that forkful? I already had Akram tell you everything. You just want me to repeat myself to see if I'll slip up."

Heat surged to her head. "I realize I'm being obsessive…"

"And I'm totally ribbing you, as you say in the States." His eyes laughed at her, coaxing her to ease up. "But as a scientist, too, I realize you won't be satisfied until you have all the details. So let's start with my findings during surgery."

Her heart jumped. He understood. That she needed to know what he'd seen with his own eyes, fixed with his own hands. That only specifics would make it all real.

"The defect was long and the tethering was more than I'd hoped. The meninges were also prolapsed. But I corrected it all with a procedure I have been developing. It takes double the time of any other procedure—yes, that's why I took longer than projected—but it ensures no scarring and no future retethering. The nerve roots were minimally damaged, but with Ryan's fast growth, and the sites of the tethering, progressive damage would have occurred within the next months. So your persistence couldn't have been more warranted, and the timing of the surgery couldn't have proved more critical. Now, with physiotherapy and a four-month course of your drug, Ryan should regain his legs' full power and sensation, and I don't expect there to be any problems with toilet training."

Tears welled up again as the certainty she'd needed seeped into her bones. "I—I can't find words to thank you."

He grimaced. "Then don't go in search of any." He tapped her plate with his fork. "Now eat. You need to be stocked up on as many calories as you can to be there for Ryan in the coming time."

She ended up finishing a three-course meal.

But taking a leaf from his repertoire, she specified

a reward in return. Letting her see Ryan as soon as she was done.

He'd finally succumbed, telling her she drove a hard bargain.

She'd been standing for what felt like hours behind the glass partition in pediatric ICU, gowned for the sterile zone, watching Ryan sleeping in a cot that looked like a space pod, her tears streaming. Ones of pure relief.

Even though it drove a hot lance through her heart to see Ryan's little body hooked to leads and invaded by drips and tubes, she knew one thing beyond a doubt: he was all right.

Fareed had been sharing the poignant vigil in silence.

He finally inhaled. "And Ryan invalidates my worries again. He looks as if he's sleeping in complete contentment."

"H-he probably is," she whispered. "He must feel how much care he's receiving, must have felt how much you've done for him. He might be relieved for the first time in his life now you've corrected h-his problem."

"Everything's possible, especially with a child as sensitive as Ryan." He turned her to him, wiped a tear that was trembling on her chin. "Now go say welcome back to your baby."

She gasped. "Oh, God…really?"

He nodded, his smile a ray of delight illuminating her world.

She streaked into the ICU. He followed at a slower pace.

He stood back patiently, let her fondle and coo to the sedated Ryan until she turned to him with tears mixing with unbridled smiles. Then he checked Ryan, discussed his management with his ICU staff, before escorting her out.

He took her to a suite on the same level as his office.

The sitting room overlooked the same view that had stunned her from his windows, from a different viewpoint, with the magic of the capital now shrouded in another dawn. She could barely believe it had been just a day since she'd set foot in Jizaan.

He took her by the shoulders. "I recommend another fourteen-hour sleep marathon. Or at least eight. Don't wake up sooner on Ryan's account. I'm keeping him in ICU for twelve more hours."

"But you said you'd let him out in a few hours!"

"And the concrete numerical value of 'a few' is?"

He was teasing her again. But now she knew in her bones Ryan would be all right, she found herself attempting to tease back.

"The world doesn't know how lucky it is that you decided to use your inexorableness for good. But even though you've benevolently steam-rolled me on every decision and I'm now forever in your debt, this—" her gesture encompassed the superbly decorated, all-amenities, expansive suite "—is going too far. Between here and the guest apartment at your place, you'll spoil Ryan and Rose so much that I might have to find us a new place when we return home."

Interest flared in his eyes. "Where *is* home? We never got around to talking about that."

She almost kicked herself. She'd just given him an opening to delve deeper into her life and everything she wanted kept hidden at all costs.

Panic surged. If she told the truth, he'd put things together sooner rather than later. If she lied, rather than omitted the truth, as she had done so far, apart from when she'd had to lie about Ryan's father, those same powers of observation would see through her. But she had no choice.

A lie was potentially less catastrophic than the truth,

Feeling it would corrode her on the way out, she opened her mouth to deliver it…and his pager went off.

She almost sagged when he released her from his focus. Then her breath caught. He was frowning at his pager. "Is it Ryan?"

He raised his eyes at her question, gave a lock of her hair a playful tug. "*No,* Gwen. Ryan is fine and will remain fine. It's just another emergency. Now have mercy on me and sleep. I'm exhausted already and it'll be a while before I get any rest. Don't add to my burdens. I'll *know* if you're not sleeping."

Without waiting for an answer, he turned away.

The door closed behind him in seconds. But she still felt his presence surrounding her, making her world secure, and life no longer a setting for anguish and struggles.

She could offer him nothing in return for the gifts he'd showered on her and her own. A chunk of her life wouldn't suffice. But he'd asked her to make his easier by taking herself off his endless list of worries. Complying with his request was all she had to offer for now.

She found the bedroom, and with a moan, sank into the bed's luxury, into the depths of thankfulness. For him, for Ryan's cure. And for being saved by the pager.

She prayed she'd never be forced to lie to him outright again, until he discharged Ryan.

Once he did, she'd run, disappear, and he'd never know.

And she'd never see him again.

The joy that had begun to take root inside her drained. Tears flowed again as she prayed.

Let his obligations keep him away for as long as she had to remain in Jizaan. Let his loss start now.

Only that would save her from sustaining further injuries.

Seven

She should have known.

That anything she hoped for would happen in reverse. With the record of the past years, how had she hoped otherwise?

Apart from Ryan's healing at a breathtaking rate, blossoming under Fareed's comprehensive care, everything else was going wrong. Terribly wrong.

For the week they stayed in the center, Fareed was constantly present. She knew this wasn't true, that he disappeared for hours but he came back so often, in her amplified awareness of him, it felt like he was always there, giving her no respite.

After dreading being in his place, where everything echoed with his feel and was soaked in his presence, she couldn't wait to go back there. She hoped that with him at work during the day, and hopefully returning home exhausted, she'd see less of him. But for the following four weeks, the opposite again happened. He came home too often, too unpredictably, so she couldn't brace for his appearance, worsening her condition at every exposure.

Everyone in the center had told her he made them feel he *was* omnipresent. She could well believe it. After the endless hours in the O.R., consultations, follow-ups and administrative chores, not to mention his duties as a prince, which he said he'd lately limited to steering the kingdom's health system, as if that wasn't huge enough, she couldn't figure out how he had time for her. Not to mention had a life. A private life…

Her throat tightened as it did each time that thought forced its reality on her. It was ridiculous to feel that way, but still…contemplating the horde of glamorous women who no doubt pursued him, of whom he took the most voluptuous and beautiful to bed…

Peals of laughter, masculine and childish, wrenched her mind away from the images, only for different ones to superimpose themselves. The images that would be engraved in her mind, seared into her soul forever. The sight of Fareed and Ryan together, bonding, reveling in each other.

But as painful as the sight was, it was also incredible. And worth any future suffering to live through.

Fareed was sitting with Ryan on the floor, in the middle of his mansion's family room, wrapped up in their game, caressed by the warm, golden lights of polished brass sconces that illuminated the expansive space. The French doors leading to the massive terrace were wide open and the gauzy cream curtains were billowing in the desert's cool evening breeze. The unpolished sand-colored marble floor was spread in hand-woven kilims and scattered in huge cushions covered with the same designs and vivid hues. Fareed had said those were the Aal Zaafers' tribal patterns and colors, intricate combinations of stripes and rhomboids, in vibrant crimsons, gold and greens. He'd also said the room had never been used. Until them.

As if she needed more heartache, to know he'd been welcoming them in the place reserved for his future family.

Before they'd settled down for the evening here, they'd finished another physiotherapy session with Ryan. He'd turned another of the mansion's rooms into a rehabilitation center, and had turned those uncomfortable, exhausting and sometimes painful sessions into Ryan's most anticipated playtime.

Now he was playing catch with Ryan. After giving Ryan easy catches to get him excited and motivated, he'd throw one out of reach and have him eagerly crawling to fetch.

He was always thinking of another exercise for Ryan, another method to gauge his improvement. He'd made an art of helping Ryan enjoy it, participate wholeheartedly, and subsequently heal faster, develop more power and better coordination.

He now threw the soft red ball on the huge square table that paralleled the couch she sat on. Ryan hurtled after it, reached the table, then stopped, an absorbed expression painting his face as he contemplated his dilemma.

She transferred her gaze to Fareed. "Seems you've given him a challenge he's not up to…yet."

Fareed shrugged, his face spread in the warmth that messed her up inside. "He hasn't given up yet. Let's see what he'll do."

She nodded even as her heart constricted. Every cell in her longed to end Ryan's frustration, give him the ball. But Fareed had been teaching her not to coddle him, to drive him to achieve his potential, and be as loving or even more so while at it.

Ryan finally approached one of the table's corners. Then after some internal debate, pulled himself up in degrees until he unfolded to his feet, stood braced at its edge. Her heart boomed.

It was the first time he'd ever stood up!

Her eyes flew to Fareed. He looked as moved, his smile as proud as hers. But when she moved to get the ball for Ryan, he gave her an imperative "wait" gesture.

She waited. And under her disbelieving, delighted eyes, Ryan hooked his right leg, the one that had always been weaker, over the edge of the table and pulled himself on top of it.

Once there, he weaved through worked-silver plates, gleaming copper candleholders and glass planters like a cat, knocking nothing over. Once he reached his quarry, he grabbed it, waved it at her in delighted victory.

"You did it, darling," she said, forcing back tears, her smile so wide that it hurt. "You got the ball because you're brilliant and strong and determined and the most wonderful boy on earth."

After a satisfactory dose of adulation, he remembered his playmate, the one he wanted to impress most.

Ryan reversed his way across the table, backed off its edge carefully. Once his feet touched ground, he plopped back down, catching his breath after the unprecedented endeavor.

Then he turned to Fareed, shrieking his triumph and throwing his trophy back to him.

He caught it, stuffed it beneath his arm and treated Ryan to a boisterous round of applause. Ryan zoomed to him, sought the haven of his arms. After having enough of

Fareed's validation, Ryan wriggled off and crawled away as if eager to resume their game.

Before following, Fareed spared her a glance, eyes twinkling with pride. "See? Nothing is beyond him. He's creative and problem-solving and ambitious and he'll always surpass your expectations."

She barely stifled the cry. *Stop surpassing mine! Stop making me want you more when I can't even dream of you.*

But it was already too late.

She'd come to depend on him when it was the worst thing she could have done. She couldn't think of a time when he wouldn't be in her life, their lives, when it was inevitable.

She'd fallen in love with him when it would mean destruction.

Yes, she loved him.

And she would have preferred it if he didn't realize she was alive. But she could no longer escape what she'd known from the moment he'd captured her gaze at that conference. He'd made it clear, in a hundred nuances, what he wanted from her, that he was only waiting until any doctor/patient's parent trace of their relationship had faded, to act on his desire.

His desire to have her in his bed.

And even though guilt and dread haunted her, this was the only place she wanted to be.

But it didn't matter what she wanted. She couldn't act on her desire. She wouldn't.

"I'm surprised he hasn't melted yet."

Rose. Sitting right beside her and she hadn't even noticed her come in.

Rose elaborated, "I've seen hunger blazing in eyes before, but the solar flares in yours...yowza!"

Her gaze moved nervously to Fareed, who was far

enough away not to catch Rose's comments. Thank goodness. If Rose had seen it, had he…?

Who was she kidding? He had. He knew he had her on the brink of mindlessness. And he'd been letting her know, subtly, inexorably, how he'd leave her no place to run when he made his move, how earth-shattering it would be when he claimed her.

She let out a resigned exhalation. "Don't start, Rose."

Rose repaid her with a fed up look. "Then why don't *you* stop? Jumping away as if he scalds you each time he comes near?"

"What do you expect? The man has a magnetic field that could upset a planet's orbit." After a moment's hesitation, she admitted, "He does scald me."

Rose nudged her. "Then help yourself to his inferno, girl."

She squeezed her eyes. "I can't, and you know it."

"So you've been mourning. Now enough." Rose turned fully to her, scowling. "Let the dead rest and get on with your life."

Gwen bit her lip, memories a shard embedded in her heart. "It's not only mourning."

"What else is it? Can't be Ryan because Fareed is the best thing that has ever happened to him, present company included."

"You're talking as if Fareed is in Ryan's life in anything more than a temporary way, when you know he's just his surgeon…."

"He's not just his surgeon, and *you* know it."

For a heart-wrenching moment, Gwen thought Rose knew. Who Fareed really was to Ryan.

But there was no way that she did. She hadn't been in her life for the past five years, had missed all the developments and upheavals that had ripped through her life.

Rose knew only what she'd told her once everything had been over. She didn't know about Ryan's parentage. And she must never know.

Rose turned her eyes to the man and baby who possessed Gwen's heart. "I mean…just look at them." Gwen didn't *want* to look. It hurt too much. "Look at *you*. You're burning for him." Gwen averted her eyes, damned being so transparent. "Then look at *him*. He would devour you whole if you didn't flit around like a hummingbird on speed."

A chuckle burst out of Gwen. Only Rose could cut to the truth, yet make it somehow bearable, even light-hearted. "And you recognize the symptoms because you and Emad are suffering from the same condition?"

Rose wouldn't be distracted. "Emad and I have *nothing* like the same condition. *I* don't have melodramatic tendencies and I'm not letting self-perpetuated worries stop me from taking whatever happiness I can now. We're free grown-ups with nothing to stop us from having whatever we want together. Apart from your baffling reluctance, I can say the same about you and Fareed."

Gwen exhaled dejectedly "I'm not free."

"Because you're a single mother? And I can't fathom your position because I'm not? So enlighten me, what are women in your situation supposed to do? Sacrifice your personal lives at the altar of your children's upbringing?"

Gwen stared sightlessly at the mansion's gardens. She wished with all her heart that she could share her burden with Rose, that everything wasn't so complicated, so impossible.

Why had Fareed of all men turned out to be the one who awakened the woman in her? And so completely, so violently?

To add to her heartache, Rose added, "And anyway,

don't knock temporary. You of all people know that nothing, starting with life itself, is permanent. Think about that and make up your mind."

She swallowed a lump at another impending and permanent loss. "My mind is made up, Rose."

Before Rose could counterattack, Fareed's rich baritone curled around Gwen's sensitized nerves, filling her with regret for what would never be.

He was walking toward them, with Ryan in his arms. He'd said, "I have an announcement to make."

Her heart pounded so fast that she felt the beats merging like the wings of the hummingbird Rose had compared her to.

Fareed stopped before them, so beautiful and vital that a fist of longing squeezed her heart, stilled it into its grip.

"I've done and redone every test there is. And the verdict is in. This magnificent boy is on his way to a full recovery. I expect he'll walk in a few months' time."

Gwen's hands shot to her lips, stifled her soundless cry.

She'd been monitoring Ryan's every notch of improvement obsessively, and from her experience with neurological progress, she'd been hoping for the best. But to have Fareed spell out such concrete conviction, put a time frame on it, made it all real.

Ryan *would* walk!

She raced with Rose to Fareed to drown him in thanks, to pluck Ryan from his arms, then from each other's to deluge him in kisses. Ryan thought this was a new game and threw himself from one set of arms to another, giggling his delight.

But as Emad joined them and dinner followed, Gwen's euphoria drained gradually.

She'd known the day when Fareed would announce the completion of his role in Ryan's care was fast-approaching.

She couldn't have hoped for a better outcome. There *was* no better outcome. For Ryan.

For her...

It was clear from everything Fareed said and did that he thought this day would mark the beginning of that temporary inferno Rose had urged her to hurtle into. *She* knew it would only herald the end. She'd thought she'd be ready for it. She wasn't.

As their "family" evening continued, Fareed's nearness only made it harder. She couldn't stop herself from feasting on his presence like it was her last meal.

And he made it worse still by no longer tempering the desire in his eyes, by barely touching his food, too, showing her that the only thing he hungered for was her.

For the rest of the evening, as she escaped his unspoken intentions, she struggled to convince herself that walking away would be survivable.

Gwen was suffocating.

Tentacles were tightening around her throat, cutting off air and blood, holding her back. Her arms reached out, but the tentacles jerked her tighter, immobilized her. The shadow she was reaching for tumbled in macabre slow-motion down the abyss....

"No!"

She heard the shout ring out even as she felt it tear out of her depths...and her eyes shot open.

She jerked up, her hands tearing at the nonexistent noose.

It had been another nightmare.

Knowing that didn't help. She still gasped, trembled, feeling like the day of the accident all over again. Crushed, torn, strangled by panic and helplessness.

In the months since, night terrors had plagued whatever

sleep she'd succumbed to. During the day, anxiety attacks had dismantled her psyche. It hadn't helped that she knew there had been nothing she could have done.

She stumbled out of the bed. It was 2:00 a.m. She'd barely slept an hour. No use thinking she'd sleep again tonight. She was afraid to, anyway.

She went to Ryan's room, checked on him even though she'd heard his steady breathing over the baby monitor. She found him on his back, which he hadn't done since the surgery, his arms flung over his head in abandon. She kissed him and he murmured something satisfied, melting her heart with thankfulness.

She went downstairs, roamed the seemingly deserted mansion, her steps as restless as her mind.

She felt Fareed all over, his scent clinging to her lungs, caressing her senses. And it wasn't because this was his domain. She'd feel him across the world. And she would, for the rest of her life.

And now, it was over. There was no more reason to stay here. She'd take her tiny family and leave Jizaan in the morning.

And he'd never know how she really felt. But that mattered nothing. What mattered was that he never knew who she really was....

"Do you know what you are?"

Fareed's hypnotic tones hit her with the force of a quake.

She jerked around, her gaze slamming to the top of the stairs, the side leading to his quarters.

He wasn't there. Had she imagined hearing him? Were her dread and guilt playing tricks on her?

Then his voice hit her again. "What I thought when I first saw you? A magical being from another realm."

She almost sagged. He was here. And he hadn't meant what she'd feared.

"And do you have any idea about the extent of my craving for you? How long it has gone unfulfilled? How much it has cost me to suppress it, to stay away from you?"

Each beat of her heart rocked her as a shadow detached itself from the depth of darkness engulfing the upper floor, taking his form. His body solidified, his influence intensified with every step. Then his face emerged from the shadows and she gasped.

Even from this distance, there was no mistake.

The ultra-efficient surgeon, the indulgent benefactor, the teasing, patient playmate was gone. A man of tempestuous passion had emerged in his place.

Making it worse was seeing him for the first time in what he'd been born to wear, an *abaya* that looked tailored of Jizaan's moonless skies themselves.

And she had no right to his passion. She'd lose even the bittersweet torment of his nearness tomorrow. She'd never again feel as alive.

"You sensed me." His voice reverberated inside her as he descended the stairs. "You knew I was coming to you, came to meet me halfway. You knew that I would no longer wait."

Something snapped inside her. Her paralysis shattered.

She needed to tell him…something, anything of the truth, if only that of her feelings, her needs. To have something, anything of him. Just this once.

He quickened his descent as she moved toward him, the *abaya* billowing around him like a shroud of darkest magic. Her feet felt as if they were gaining momentum from his power, his purpose, that force that had entered her life to change the face of her world forever.

Then he stopped. At the platform where the stairs diverged, as if giving her a last chance to retreat.

She stopped, too, three steps beneath him, momentum lost, confessions fled. She looked up at him, overwhelmed. He was even more than she'd ever dreamed.

The obsidian silk *abaya* draped over his endless shoulders, pleated for miles to his bare feet, falling open over the perfection of his chiseled, raven hair-dusted chest and abdomen. The low-riding drawstring pants of the same color and material hugged his thighs, hiding none of the power of his muscles, or that of his arousal.

He seemed as if he'd stepped out from another time, a force of nature and of the supernatural, poured into solid form. But it was the fever radiating from him, the same one that raged through her, that shook her most—setting free the one confession she could make.

"I don't want you to wait."

Eight

Something unbridled flared in Fareed's eyes.

Gwen's breathing stopped. She stood mesmerized by the ferocity that ate her up, finished her. Now...now he'd descend the last steps separating them, sweep her up in his arms....

But what he did stopped her heart. With shock.

She would have never expected that he would...*laugh*.

But he did. Peal after peal of pure male amusement.

His laughter mortified her even as it inflamed her.

What had she said or done that he found so funny?

Maybe it was her braid, mommy robe and fluffy slippers? And the cartoon character pajamas beneath?

God, *of course* it was. He must have gotten a good look at her and rethought his intentions. No wonder he was laughing.

All thoughts scattered as he moved, still laughing, until he was on the same step, bearing down on her with his heat and virility. Then he leaned down, put his lips to her ear.

"I just have one question—" each syllable, each feathering of his lips shot arousal right to her core "—will you ever stop surprising me?"

She raised confused eyes up to his, found fire simmering just below the mirth.

"You exhausted me at every turn," he whispered, intimate, maddening, "contesting my every declaration, my every decision, the minor before the major. Then I tell you I'm taking you to my bed and you just…agree?"

Her gaze wavered as his eyes lost their lightness, flames rising higher. She shivered as her own fever spiked in answer.

Then to her amazement, she heard her voice, husky with hunger and provocation. "I didn't exactly say I agree."

He caught her around the waist, slammed her against his hard length. Her breath and heartbeats emptied against his chest.

Twisting her braid around his wrist, harnessing her by it, ferocity barely leashed with gentleness, he tilted up her face, his eyes now a predator's excited by his mate's unexpected challenge.

His next words poured almost in her gasping mouth. "You said better. You commanded me not to wait. Now I'll obey you, *ya fatenati*. No more waiting, ever again."

Then he bent and swept her feet from beneath her, cut her every tie to gravity and sanity.

She went limp in his hold, becoming weightless, timeless, directionless, as she lay ensconced in his arms. She burrowed into him as the world moved in hard, hurried thuds, each one hitting her with vertigo, the pressure of emotion almost snuffing out her consciousness, like that day lifetimes ago.

And that was before he pressed his lips to her forehead

in a branding kiss. "Never stop surprising me, *ya sahe-rati.*"

She almost blurted out that *he* was the enchanter, the sorcerer. She choked on the words. She hadn't let on that she knew Arabic, couldn't bear lying if he asked why she did.

Every anxiety vanished as he relinquished his hold on her and she sank in the depths of soft dark beddings, was shrouded by the golden warmth of gaslight and the intoxication of incense and craving.

Then he came down over her.

She moaned with the blast of stimulation, emotional and sensual, of her first exposure to the reality of him, his weight and bulk and hunger, the physicality of his passion.

He rose off her, slid her robe off. She felt a blush creeping up from her toes to her hairline as he exposed her pajamas.

"Bugs Bunny." He shook his head in disbelief. "And if I find you arousing beyond endurance in this, I might not survive seeing you in something made to worship your beauty."

She crossed her hands over her chest, burning with self-consciousness. "I know how I look in this thing. I picked it to match one of Ryan's…"

"Answer me this other question, Gwen." His hand unlocked hers, before imprisoning them over her head in one of his. "Will I always have to say something over and over before you consider believing me? Will you ever believe I only ever say what I mean?"

She felt her flush deepening. "It's not you I'm doubting."

"Then how can you doubt your own beauty, your effect on me? If anything, I'm holding back, not telling you what you really make me feel, what I really want to do to you."

His eyes flared with mock-threat and too-real lust. "I don't want to scare you."

She shook her head against the sheets. "You won't ever scare me. Show me everything you feel."

Her ragged words elicited a smile that was sheer male triumph and assurance. "*Amrek, ya rohi*—command me."

Yet his hands trembled in her hair as they undid her braid, spread its thickness around her. Then he buried his face in it, breathed her in hard, let her hear in his ragged groans that he was at the mercy of his need for her as she was for him.

"I've wanted you, I've needed this…" He bore down on her harder, pressed all of him into all of her. "Your flesh and desire, you scent and feel, since the first moment I saw you all those years ago. I craved you until I was hollow. Now you're here and you'll be mine, at last, Gwen…*at last*."

She whimpered her agreement, her eagerness. He swooped up to capture the sound, his lips taking hers in a hot, moist seal, enveloping, dissolving, his tongue thrusting into her recesses, in total tasting, in thorough possession.

She'd imagined this until she'd felt *she'd* be forever empty, too, if she never experienced it. But this far surpassed the imaginings that had tormented her. The power and profundity of his kiss, his feel and scent, and his taste…his *taste*…

He bit into her lower lip, stilled its tremors in a nip so leashed, so carnal that it had her opening wider, deepening his invasion.

Just as she felt she'd come apart, he severed their meld, groaned, "Gwen, *habibati, hayaati, abghaaki, ahtaajek*."

She sobbed again as she pulled him back. He'd called her his love, his life, said he coveted her, *needed* her.

She knew those were the exaggerated endearments his culture indulged in. They didn't have to be literally meant, and in those moments, were likely driven by arousal.

It didn't matter. Just hearing him say those things was enough. And if it were possible to give him of her life to fill his needs, she would have surrendered it.

She surrendered what she could now, all of herself.

He swept her pajama top over her head, his arm beneath her melting her into his length, circling her waist, raising her against the headboard to bury his face into her confined breasts.

She moaned at seeing the dark majesty of his head against her, let her hands fulfill what she'd thought would remain a fantasy, burying them in the luxury of his silken, raven mane, pressing his head harder to her aching flesh.

He groaned something deep and driven, the sound spearing from his lips into her heart as his hands went to her back. She arched, helping him release breasts now peaked with arousal, throbbing for his ownership.

He gathered her hands again above her head, drew back to gaze at her. Naked to the waist, the image of abandon, on wanton offer. She turned her face into the sheets, unable to withstand his burning scrutiny.

"Look at me, *ya galbi*." His demand overrode her will, drew her eyes to his. "See what your sight does to me." He let one of her hands go, took it to his heart, let her feel the power of its thundering, then to his erection. "Feel it."

Her hand trembled as it fulfilled the ultimate privilege of feeling his potency. She stroked his daunting length and hardness through the heavy silk of his pants.

He undid the drawstring, slowly, maddeningly, holding her eyes as he guided her hand underneath. Her hand shook at touching him without barriers, couldn't close around him. But even with the nip of awe and alarm, knowing all this would soon dominate her, she reveled in his amazing heat, his satin over steel, the edge of anxiety making her readiness flow heavier, soaking her panties.

He came down over her again, thrust his tongue inside her mouth to her stroking rhythm, groaned inside her, "Your touch is a far better heaven than any I imagined."

She was lost in his feel when he suddenly drew back, spread her again, closed trembling hands on her breasts. She arched off the bed, in a shock of pleasure, making a fuller offering of her flesh. He kneaded her, pinched her nipples, had her writhing, begging, before he coaxed and caressed the rest of her clothes off her burning flesh.

The spike of ferocity in his eyes as they touched her full nakedness should have been alarming. It only sent her heart almost racing to a standstill with shyness, with anticipation. With pride that her sight affected him that intensely.

He tore his *abaya* off, finally exposing the body she'd known would make the gods of old fade into nothing. *"Ya Ullah ya Gwen, koll shai ma'ak afdal menn ahlami. Anti ajmal shai ra'aytoh fi hayati...anti rao'ah."*

Her awed hands shook over his burnished, sculpted perfection, barely biting back the protest that everything with *him* was better than *her* dreams, that it was he who was the most beautiful thing she'd ever seen in her life, he who was the wonder.

"Habibati..." His groan roughened to a growl as he rubbed his chest against her breasts until she thrashed beneath him. He bent, opened his mouth over her breasts as if he'd devour her.

Pleasure jackknifed through her with each nip of his teeth, each long, hard draw of his lips, had her shuddering all over.

"Fareed, just take me...all of me..."

He told her he wanted exactly that. All of her now. *Now.*
"Bareedek kollek, daheenah, habibati. Daheenah."

She lay powerless under the avalanche of need, her
moans becoming keens as his surgeon's hand glided over
her, taking every liberty and creating erogenous zones
wherever they fondled and owned, before settling between
her thighs. His strong, sensitive fingers slid up to her intimate flesh, now molten, throbbing its demand for his
touch, his invasion. They opened the lips of her femininity, slid between her folds, soaked in her readiness.

It took only a few strokes of those virtuoso fingers to
spill her over the edge. She convulsed with pleasure, hazy
with it, failing to imagine what union with him would
bring if just a few touches unraveled her body and mind.

Among her stifled cries of release she heard something
primal rumble in his gut, knew it was the sound of his control snapping.

He came over her and her hands fumbled with his to
remove his pants, the last barrier between them. She went
nerveless as his lips spilled worship into hers, proclaiming
her soul of his heart, his need to be inside her.

"Roh galbi, mehtaj akoon jow'wuuki."

She couldn't bear not having him filling her, couldn't
bear the emptiness he'd created inside her, couldn't...
couldn't...

She *couldn't* let him take her when she hadn't told
him...

No. She *couldn't* tell him. And she couldn't not have
him. Just this once. She needed this once. It wasn't too
much to ask, to take. She'd live in deprivation for the rest
of her life.

And she sobbed her need, her desperation. "Come
inside me, Fareed, now. Don't wait...just take me."

"Aih, ya hayat galbi...take me inside you, take all of me."

He bore down into her, as blinded, as lost. She cried out, in relief, in anguish, spread her legs wider for his demand, contained him, her heels digging into his buttocks, her nails into his back, demanding him, urging him.

His pained chuckle detailed his enjoyment of her frenzy as his muscled hips flexed, positioning himself at her entrance, prostrating her for his domination. Then in one burning plunge, he was there, inside her. Flesh in flesh.

The shock to her system was total.

Paralyzed, mute, she stared up at him, everything swollen and invaded and complete. He rested deep within her, stretching her beyond capacity, as incapacitated. Blackness frothed from the periphery of her vision, a storm front of pleasure advancing from her core. Fareed...at last.

It was he who broke the panting silence, his voice a feral growl now. "Gwen, the pleasure of you...*ya Ullah*..."

He rose on his palms, started to withdraw from her depths. She clung blindly, crazed for his branding pain and pleasure.

He withdrew all the way out, dragged a shriek of stimulation and loss from her. Before she cried out again for his return, he drove all the way back inside her.

On his next withdrawal, she lost what was left of her mind. She thrust her hips up, seeking his impalement. He bunched her hair in his fist, tugged her down to the bed, exposing her throat, latching his teeth into her flesh as if he'd consume her.

Then he plowed back into her, showed her that those first plunges had just been preparations. He fed her core more, then more of him with every thrust, causing an unknown, unbelievably pleasurable expansion within her, until she felt him hit the epicenter of her very essence.

She was destroyed, blind, mad, screaming, clinging to

him, biting him, convulsing, the ecstasy rending in intensity.

He withdrew, and she saw his magnificent face seize with ferocity, with his greed for every sensation he plumbed her body for, had ripping through her. Tension shot up in his eyes, as if he was judging when to let go.

She begged him, for him. "Give me—give me..."

And he gave. She felt each surge of his jetting climax inside her. It hit her at her peak, had her thrashing, weeping, unable to endure the spike in pleasure. Everything dimmed, faded...

She had no idea when awareness started trickling between the numb layers of satisfaction. She was still lying beneath Fareed. Then she realized what had roused her. He was leaving her body.

Before she could whimper with his loss, he pressed back over her, his weight sublime pleasure. She moaned her contentment. More bliss settled into her bones as he swept her around, draped her over his expansive body, mingling their sweat and satisfaction.

She closed her eyes, let his feel and those precious moments integrate into her cells. She'd need the memories to tide her through the rest of her life.

But this wasn't over yet. She had hours with him still. She wouldn't waste a second.

"And I thought it would be unprecedented with you."

Everything inside her stilled.

Would his next words elaborate on the disappointment of his expectations? Had he given her her life's most transfiguring experience, but she'd proved no more than a barely adequate one?

Suddenly, she wanted to bolt. She wanted to hold on

to what she'd experienced. It would be all she had of him.
And if it turned out to be a one-sided illusion…

"If I'd known how it would be between us, that it would
far exceed even my perfectionist fantasies, I would have
carried you off to my bed weeks ago."

She raised a wobbling head, trembling with relief. She
marveled anew at his beauty, and at how magical their
bodies looked entwined.

And she wanted more of him. Of them. All she could
get.

She bent to taste the powerful pulse in his neck, drag-
ging her teeth down his shoulder and chest to his nipple,
nipping it before she moved her head up, stroking his flesh
with her hair.

"I hope you know what you're inviting with this act of
extreme provocation."

Feeling all-powerful with his desire, reckless with
having nothing to lose and everything to win, before it
was too late, she squeezed his steel buttock even as she
slid her leg between his muscled, hair-roughened ones, her
knee pressing an erection that felt even harder and more
daunting than before.

"Which act are you referring to?" she purred, nipping
his lips, adding more fuel to his reignited passion.

He grabbed her around the waist, brought her straddling
him, menacing lust flaring in his eyes, filling his lips. "I
have a list now. Each with a consequence all its own."

Her hunger, now she knew what ecstasy awaited her
in his possession, was a hundred-fold that of her previous
ignorance.

She rocked against him, bathing him in her arousal and
their pleasure. "Terrible consequences all, I hope."

"Unspeakable." His hands convulsed in her flesh, raised her to scale his length. He dragged her down at the same moment he thrust upward, impaling her.

She screamed his name, body and mind unraveling at the unbearable expansion, the excruciating pleasure.

She melted into him, felt the world receding with only him left in existence. Along with one thought.

She'd had him. She'd been his.

Tomorrow, when she lost him, nothing could erase the experience from her body and soul.

Gwen had returned to her bedroom in the guest apartment as soon as Fareed had left her in bed. She'd hoped he'd stay away all day until she'd made her escape.

He hadn't stayed away an hour.

He'd just entered the bedroom, was walking to her in strides laden with urgency, something fierce blasting off him.

Before she could say anything, he hauled her into his arms and drowned her in the deepest kiss he'd claimed yet.

She felt his turmoil collide with hers, until she couldn't bear it, think of nothing but easing him.

She tugged at his hair gently, bringing his head up. And what she saw in his eyes almost brought tears to hers.

She'd seen this in his eyes off and on since they'd come here. This despair. Every time, being with her and Ryan had managed to erase the darkness that seemed to grip him heart and soul.

She'd never asked about the reason behind his anguish. Not only because she didn't feel she had the right to, but also because she thought she knew the answer. But what if she was wrong and there was some other reason? Something she could help with, at least by lending a sympathetic ear and heart?

"What is it, Fareed?"

He pulled her back, hugged her tighter, pressing her head to his chest, which heaved on a shuddering exhalation.

He spoke. And she wished she hadn't asked. For he told her, in mutilating detail, about his dead brother and the depth of futility and frustration he'd been suffering in his ongoing, fruitless quest to find his family.

"Then, a week after you came here, Emad found a lead that looked the most promising we've had yet. He's just told me it turned out to be another false hope."

Even had she had anything to say, the pain clamping her throat would have made it impossible to speak.

This was all her fault. And no fault of her own. She wished she could tell him to stop looking, to have mercy on himself, that he had nothing to blame himself for, had already done more than anyone would have dreamed. But she couldn't.

She could only leave and pray that in time, he'd end his search, come to terms with his failure, so that it would stop tearing at him.

Now all she could hope was that he'd go away again, give her a chance to leave without further heartache.

Before she pushed away, his hands were all over her, over himself, ridding them of their clothes. She knew the moment her flesh touched his, all would be lost. She had to act now.

She struggled out of his arms, hating herself and the whole world for having to say this, now of all times.

"I'm leaving Jizaan today."

He froze in mid-motion as he'd reached back for her, stared at her for a long, long moment.

Then his lips spread. In another moment a chuckle escaped him and intensified until he was laughing outright.

He at last wiped a tear of mirth. "Ah, Gwen, I needed that." He caught her back to him. "I love it when you let your wicked humor show, loved it when you teased me in bed. Teasing me out of it—if not for long—is even better."

He thought she was joking! And who could blame him, after the nightlong marathon of passion and abandonment?

He pulled her back into his arms and she gasped, "I'm serious, Fareed."

That made him loosen his arms enough so he could pull back, look at her, the humor in his eyes wavering.

She tried to maximize on her advantage, injected her expression and voice with all the firmness and finality she could muster. "With your follow-up of Ryan over, there's no reason to stay in Jizaan anymore. In fact, we should have left long before now. We've taken advantage of your generosity for far too long."

Devilry and desire ignited his eyes. "If last night has been your taking advantage of my...generosity, as you can *feel* " he pulled her back against his hard length, his arousal living steel pressing into her abdomen "—I am in dire need for your exploitation to continue."

"What happened between us doesn't change a thing."

"Not *a* thing, no. *Every*thing."

She tried to turn her face away. "No! Nothing has changed or will ever change. We have to leave, Fareed. Please, don't make this hard. I have to—"

"I have to, too." He latched his lips on the frantic pulse in her neck, suckled her until she felt her heart pouring its beats and love into him. "I have to take you again, Gwen. I have to pleasure you again and again."

Then as she struggled to hold on to her sanity and re-solve, he defeated her, practiced every spell of seduction on her viciously awakened body and starving heart.

She found herself naked, delirious with arousal and pleasure, straddling his powerful hips, her palms anchored on his chest as he dug his hands in her buttocks.

He held her by them, had her riding up and down his shaft, showing her the exact force and speed and angle to drive them both beyond insanity, egging her on.

"Ride me, Gwen, ride me."

Lost, mad, she obeyed him, rising and falling in a fever, milking his potency with her inner muscles, mines of plea-sure detonating in her every cell.

It built and built. She rode and rode, faster, harder, her hands bunching in his muscles, her eyes feverish on his, her mouth open on harsh inhalations vented in frenzied cries.

When it became too much, she wailed, *"Fareed!"*

"Aih ya galbi, take your pleasure all over me. Take it." He crashed her down on him, forged to her womb.

She imploded around him for long, still moments, shaking uncontrollably as the tidal wave hovered. Then it crashed, splintered and reformed her around him, over and over.

He took over when she lost her rhythm, a convulsing mess of sensation, changed the angle of his thrusts, hit-ting a bundle of nerves that triggered a fiercer explosion. It wracked her, drained her to her last nerve ending.

Yet she needed more, him, joining her in ecstasy, begged for it.

This time when the world vanished and nothing but him remained, around her, inside her, she promised herself.

This *would* be the last time.

Or maybe another time when next they woke up. Or maybe just one more day. Yes, one more day wouldn't hurt. But after that, there would be no more. Never again…

Nine

Fareed gazed down on Gwen and thought this was what sunlight would be like made flesh, made woman.

Her hair gleamed and her skin glowed in the flickering light of a dozen oil lamps. He'd placed them around this bedroom with only her in mind. This bedroom that wasn't his.

After all the time he'd fantasized about having her in his bed, he'd picked her up that first night, and his feet had taken him here. A guest suite that had never been used before. He'd wanted them to have a place all their own, a place he hadn't been before, where all the memories would be of her, of them.

He leaned over her, his heart in a constant state of expansion. Her lips, slightly parted in sleep, were crimson and swollen from his possession. Just their sight scorched him with the memories of the past days. He bent and took them, unable to have enough. She moaned, opening for him, her tongue first accepting the caress of his own, then dueling with it, in that never-ending quest for tasting, taking, surrendering. Even in the depth of sleep, she couldn't have enough either.

He'd lost track of how many times he'd possessed her, how many times she'd claimed him back.

He pulled back, filled his sight and senses and memory with her, beyond his fantasies, lush and vital and glittering in the dimness, naked and vulnerable and the most overwhelming power he'd ever known. Her hold over him was absolute.

His love for her was as infinite.

He groaned as emotions welled inside him, debilitating and empowering, even as his body hardened beyond agony. He needed to plunge into her depths again, mingle with her body and soul.

His hand glided over her, absorbing her softness and resilience, the pleasure that hummed inside her at his touch, the craving echoing his. He caressed her from breast to the concavity of her waist, over the swell of her hips and the curve of her thigh. His hand hooked beneath her knee, opening her over him.

He savored her every jerk betraying her enjoyment, her torment, even as she still dreamed. He bent and took more suckles of the breasts that had rewhetted his appetite for life. She moaned as she spread her thighs for him, cradled him in the only place he'd ever call home, where the fluid heat of her welcome was unraveling his sanity all over again.

Her eyes half opened, heavy with sleep and lust, endless, insatiable skies. "Come inside me, Fareed...*now*."

He felt he now lived to hear her say this, to know how much she needed him, to join them in unbridled intimacy and abandon, to take every liberty and give every ecstasy.

He pressed into her, reveling in the music of her gasps, the intoxication of her undulations, the urgency of the hands that clamped his head to her engorged-with-need flesh, begging him to devour her. The scent of her arousal sent blood crashing in his head, thundering in his loins.

He raised his head to take her vocal confessions, poured his own. "Every moment with you, *ya roh galbi* is magic. I want everything with you, every contradiction. Right now, I want to be giving and tender and I want to be greedy and ferocious, all at once."

She clung to him, wrapped her legs around him, her lips feverish over his face and shoulders and chest. "You almost wrecked my sanity with your last session of giving tenderness. Give me greedy and ferocious, please. Please, Fareed, please!"

He'd never known there was such pride, such pleasure, as that her desire could engender. Now her urgency hit a chord of blind lust inside him, reverberated it until it snapped.

He snatched her beneath him, rose above her, his senses ricocheting within a body that felt hollowed. Every breath electrocuted him. Every heartbeat felt like a wrecking ball inside his chest. He wanted to tear into her, pound her until there were no more barriers between their bodies. And she wanted him to do it, to plunder her, was shaking apart for his domination.

But he'd give her even better. He'd give it all to her.

He unlocked her convulsive limbs from around his body, ignored her cries of protest, swept her around on her stomach.

She whimpered as he held her down, captured her mound. His fingers delved between her soaking folds to her trigger. She climaxed with the first strokes, bucking and shuddering beneath him.

He showed her no mercy, fingers gliding, spreading the moistness from her core, made her shred her body and throat on pleasure.

He kept stroking her, raggedly encouraging her to have her fill of pleasure, until she slumped beneath him. Then he plunged his fingers inside her, his thumb echoing the action on the outside. She writhed under the renewed stimulation; the need for release a rising crest of incoherence. She thrust against his hand until his *"Marrah kaman, ya galbi"* hurled her convulsing into another orgasm.

She subsided beneath him, a mute mass of tremors. His fingers remained deep inside her, started preparing her for the next peak.

"I swear, Fareed, if you don't take me now…I won't let you take me for…for…" She stopped, panting.

"Not finding a suitable length of deprivation?" He chuckled, removing his hand. "Because you'll also be depriving yourself?"

She threw him a smoldering glance over her shoulder, one that almost caused his already-overheated system to vapor lock. Then she purred, "Maybe there is another way out of this predicament."

She thrust the perfection of her smooth, slick bottom back into his erection. Sensation ripped through him on a beast's growl, making him lunge over her, snap his teeth into her shoulder, making her grind harder into him.

He ground back, whispered hotly in her ear, "I'm finding demonstrations far more effective than threats. Go on, give me examples of what you need me to do."

The look she gave him this time, the sight of her as she trembled up to her knees, her waterfall of sunshine and ripe golden breasts swaying gently, blanked his sanity, almost made him slam into her. But the need to have her seek him, relinquish yet another notch of inhibition, over-powered even the insanity.

She lowered her head and upper body to the mattress. The total submission in her position, the devouring in her gaze as she rested her face against the dark sheets and silently demanded his domination, sent his breath hissing in his throat like steam, his erection filling with what felt like molten lead.

He still needed more. "A superlative demonstration. Now I need accompanying directions of what's required of me."

And she gave him what he needed. "I want you to bury yourself all the way inside me, holding nothing back, until you finish me, send us both into oblivion."

The last tether of his restraint snapped so hard, he rammed into her with all the violence of its recoil, bottoming out in one thrust. A shout burned its way from both their depths.

"Nothing ever felt like this, Gwen," he growled as he thrust deeper, harder into her, feeling as if he'd delved into an inferno of pure ecstasy. "Being inside you, this fit, this intensity, this perfection. Nothing could possibly be this pleasurable. But it is, you are, more pleasure than is possible. You sate me and craze me with insatiability. You burn me, Gwen, body and reason."

She sobbed with every thrust. "You *burn* me, too…you fill me beyond my ability to withstand…or my ability to have enough. Oh, Fareed…the pain and pleasure of you… do it all to me…*do* it."

Feeling his body hurtling into the danger zone, he put all his power behind each plunge. She writhed beneath him, thrusting back, letting him forge new depths inside her, panting more confessions, more proddings. Pressure built in his loins with each slide and thrust, each word, spread from the point inside her he was hitting deepest.

He rode her ever harder, insane for her release, for his.

Then like shock waves heralding a detonation too far to be felt yet, it started. Ripples spread from the outside in, pushing everything to his center, compacting where he was buried in her. He took her, in one more perfect fusion, and it came. The spike of shearing pleasure, his body all but charring with its intensity, slam after slam after slam of spreading satisfaction.

He pitched her forward, filled her with his white-hot release as they melted into one being, replete, complete.

An eternity passed before his senses rebooted. He heard a hum, felt it, pure contentment rising from her as she received his full weight over her back. It made him wish he could remain like this forever, containing her, covering her.

It was beyond incredible, what they shared. Every time had the exhilaration, the voracity, the surprise of a first time, yet had the practiced certainty of a long-established relationship.

After moments, with utmost regret, he had to obey the fact that he was twice her size and weight, and that no matter how much she insisted she craved feeling his weight, practical issues like blood circulation and breathing still existed.

He slid off her slippery, satin flesh, turned her limp, sated body around, gathered her into the curve of his body, locked her into his limbs. She burrowed into him, opened her lips on his pulse, her breathing settling back from chaos to serenity as she sank back into contented sleep.

He sighed in bone-deep bliss. Having her pressed to his side, having her in his life was nirvana.

He couldn't believe it had been only a week since

they'd first made love. It felt as if he'd always gone to sleep wrapped around her and woken up to her filling his arms.

Yet one thing marred the perfection.

Even though he felt their connection deepening, she was only vocal, only demonstrative when it came to physical passion. And only when he aroused her beyond inhibition.

When he'd thought he'd resolved her withdrawal the day after their first magical night, he hadn't.

She'd woken up the next day with renewed desire to leave. He'd had to use every trick in the book of unrepentant seduction to make her relinquish her intentions.

He had, but only until the next day had dawned. She'd pulled back every morning, forcing him to recapture her each night. Then today, he'd come home running when Emad had informed him she'd been trying to arrange her departure from Jizaan.

That had driven it home that something serious was behind her persistence. But chiding her for trying to depart behind his back hadn't shed any light on that motivation, or obtained a promise that she wouldn't repeat her efforts. He'd given up trying, taken her in his arms, and everything had been burned away in their mutual abandon.

He still knew passion-induced amnesia would lift and she'd wake up pinched and troubled, and it would be déjà vu all over again.

But he wasn't worried anymore.

He'd finally figured out why she tried to limit their involvement to a passion with a daily-extended expiration date.

His lifelong experience had been with women who'd wanted him for his status and wealth. But for Gwen, the reverse was true. Even though she appreciated everything that he was, the man and the surgeon, the very things that attracted other women repelled her. She'd made it clear how vital to her equality in a relationship was. How deeply disturbed she must be at what she perceived as the imbalance of power between them.

But now that he knew the source of her agitation and aversion, he had the perfect solution in mind.

Feeling secure next morning would break the cycle of her daily withdrawal, he snuggled with her and closed his eyes, contentment blanketing him.

"You can't mean that!"

Fareed watched Gwen bolt up in bed, sighed. "Here we go again."

Gwen groaned. "Don't *you* start again, you know what I mean. But you still *can't* mean that!"

He stroked the gleaming tresses that rained over the peaked perfection of her breasts. "I can and I do."

She moaned as she caught his hands. "Don't, Fareed. This is out of the question."

"No, it's not. You're ideal, to say the least."

Exasperation rose in her eyes again. "You're just saying that because…"

And he turned serious. "Because I'm lucky beyond measure that the woman who blinds me with lust also arouses my utmost professional respect and satisfies my most demanding scientific standards."

She gaped at him, then groaned, "Don't exaggerate, please."

He sighed again. "Do credit me with *some* professional integrity, *ya roh galbi.*"

"Don't tell me you can't find anyone better to be the head of R & D in your new multibillion-dollar pharmaceutical department. A job that seems to have just become available now."

He shrugged. "It's been available for a while and no one satisfied all my criteria. You do. Your narrow field of expertise, your body of work and future research plans, all which made me attend your presentation those years ago, fit the closest with my own practice's best interests, and the center's overall focus." He ran a finger down her neck, between her breasts and lower. "What would you have me do? Look for someone less well-suited because you happen to be my specific libido trigger, too?"

She fidgeted in response to his words and touch. "Many would consider that a conflict of interest."

"I'd consider it a *conflagration* of interest. Beside this…" He caught her against his chest, groaned his delight as her lush breasts flattened against him, as her breath caught and her body heated again. "*I'd* get the most innovative and intrepid researcher in the field I'm interested in, while *you* fulfill your professional aspirations. Think what you can achieve, for your own career, for me and the center, for the world, with all the resources I'll put at your fingertips."

She still shook her head. "I—I can't stay here, Fareed."

He chalked one point up to his cause. She was no longer contesting the position itself, was down to the next worry.

"I know some aspects of the kingdom and culture are alien to you, maybe even disturbing. But many aspects delight you, too, and you've assimilated into much of your surroundings. And then I will never let anything negative affect you, or Ryan or Rose, in any way."

She bit her lip. He restrained his desire to replace them with his—he had to let her air her doubts so he could pulverize them.

She finally exhaled. "Nothing is really negative as much as it's different. But you and your family… I just can't get my head around how much power you wield here."

He'd been right. She was disturbed by the extent of his and his family's influence. She had seen the evidence of their almost absolute power in every aspect of life in the kingdom. "No one, including me and my family, will ever wield any power over you. You'll always be free to make your own decisions, personally and professionally."

"As evidenced by how I ended up doing everything you unilaterally thought was the only thing to be done?"

He cocked one eyebrow at her. "You're saying I coerced you?"

"I'm saying free will and you are mutually exclusive."

"I had to take charge of Ryan's care. Then I had to make you act on our shared desire. But if I ever feel that being with me is no longer your priority or good for Ryan, if you ever have a better offer professionally, I won't try to make you stay. This I promise you. On my honor."

She looked as if she'd burst into tears.

Before he rushed to add something, anything, she choked out, "Oh, God, Fareed…you're being so unfair. You're…deluging me with so much. But I have to say no. I never dreamed it would go this far, but if you're too blinded to care about your best interest, and ours, to end it *now,* I have to do it."

He wanted to kick himself. He hadn't considered those reasons for her reticence. That she believed he was compromising himself, and her, for something that would end. She was calculating the damages, to him, to her and Ryan, after such a finite, even if prolonged and powerful, interlude ended.

But he couldn't make it clear he had no intention of ending this. Before he discussed permanence, he had to first resolve all her issues, about her and Ryan's future here, give her more than offers and promises, show her how it would work in practice.

His cell phone rang. He ignored it, began, "Gwen, *galbi*..."

She grabbed his forearm. "Won't you answer?"

"No." He glared his annoyance at the phone on the dresser, tugged her nearer. "Now, Gwen..."

Her grip tightened. "That's Emad's ringtone."

He shrugged. "He'll call later. Gwen..."

"But he's not hanging up," she persisted. "It might be Ryan or Rose and my own phone is dead or something."

She scrambled to get out of bed, and he stopped her, resigned that the moment was ruined.

"I'll answer him." He jumped out of bed, reveling in her hungry eyes on his aroused nakedness, despite her alarm. "And it's *not* about Ryan or Rose, I'm sure, so you stay right there. I'm coming back as soon as I blast Emad to the farthest kingdom in the region."

He felt steam rising from his skin as he snatched up the phone and put it to his ear.

Emad preempted his frustration. "I need to speak to you."

"You couldn't have picked a worse time," he hissed.

Emad's exhalation was weary. "That's true, if not for the reason you mean. I am waiting downstairs in your office."

"I'll come down in an hour. Maybe two."

"No, *Somow'wak*." Emad sounded like never before. Blunt, brooking no arguments. "You'll come down *now*."

"Now" turned out to be twenty minutes later, the shortest time it took Fareed to dress and to take his leave of Gwen.

He strode into his office, displeasure roiling inside him.

"You'd better have some unprecedented reason for this, Emad…"

Suddenly, Fareed's blood froze in his arteries. The look on Emad's face. This was momentous.

This was about Hesham's family.

A lead had finally led somewhere. He could think of nothing else that would make Emad ask his presence so imperatively, or look so…so…

"You found them?" he rasped.

Emad gave a difficult nod.

Fareed's heart crashed. "Something happened to them?"

Emad leveled grim eyes on him. "No, but it's not much less terrible than if something had."

"*B'Ellahi,* Emad, just tell me," he roared.

Emad winced at his loss of control.

Then with regret heavy in his voice, he said, "I've found proof that Hesham's woman is…Gwen."

Ten

"You're insane."

That was all Fareed could say, could think. That was the only explanation for what Emad had just uttered.

"Her given name was Gwendo*lyn*. She changed it to Gwen in official documents since her college days."

A dizzying mixture of relief and rage churned inside Fareed's chest. "*That's* your 'proof'?"

Regret deepened in Emad's eyes. "That's just the tip of the iceberg. The doubts that made me investigate Gwen began when I became convinced she knew Arabic. She responded appropriately to things said in Arabic too many times, if only in that inimitable glint of understanding in her eyes, that I thought it strange she wouldn't mention it. So I tested my theory by speaking Arabic on purpose when she was within earshot and observing her reaction. She was careful not to show that she understood, but I could see that she did. I became absolutely certain when

I once calmly told a servant to walk out of the room naturally, then run like the wind to investigate the silent alarm I received from the southern guard post. Her alarm was unmistakable, and she tried to indirectly find out if anything was wrong. Because I spoke fast and idiomatically, I became certain she has knowledge of not only Arabic but our specific dialect."

Fareed rejected Emad's words as they exited his lips.

But another voice rose inside his mind, borne of the observations he'd never heeded. How she'd never asked what the things he said in Arabic meant, especially the endearments he deluged her in, how she seemed to respond appropriately...

No. She'd only understood his tone. He wasn't letting Emad poison his mind with his crazy theory.

Emad continued. "I couldn't find a reason why she'd hide her knowledge, but because I don't believe in inexplicable, yet innocent, behavior, I tried to get more information from Rose."

"*That's* what you've been doing with Rose?" Fareed growled. "Leading her on so she'd supply you with possible dirt on Gwen? You went too far in your efforts to 'protect' me this time, Emad."

"I was getting close to Rose for real, and I hope to get closer. Although I don't know how I will, with the truth revealed..."

"This is *not* the truth. All you have to support this insane theory is circumstantial evidence."

Pain etched deeper on Emad's face. "I have new evidence that the places where Gwen lived are also where Hesham lived, at the same time, that she now lives in the same town he did when he died. She seemed to be living alone in all these places, but then so did Hesham. They must have kept separate residences in Hesham's obsession to keep their relationship a secret. She became a free-lance researcher for the past four years so she wouldn't have a base. Then she left the job scene around the time she would have been in her last months of pregnancy and during Ryan's first months. She went back to work only when Rose became Ryan's nanny.

"And I didn't get any of that from Rose. She might be shockingly open, but only with her own opinions. She wouldn't have shared anything about Gwen. But she doesn't know much anyway because she lived across the continent with her late ex-husband for the last five years. They divorced years ago, but when he had a stroke that paralyzed him, Rose went back to take care of him. He died two months before Gwen contacted her and asked her to become Ryan's live-in nanny. Two weeks after Hesham died."

Fareed shook his head, repeated what looped in his mind under the barrage of information. "Circumstantial evidence, all of it."

Emad closed yet another escape route. "The one thing Rose mentioned was that a tragedy befell Gwen around the same time her ex-husband died. She wouldn't elaborate and I couldn't probe more than I did and have her suspect my motives."

"Good thing you couldn't afford to alienate the first woman to move your heart since your late wife."

"I couldn't afford to alert her to my suspicions and have her relay them to Gwen. If Gwen felt danger, we might lose Ryan."

"Now I *know* you're insane."

"I would give anything to be wrong, but with you being who you are, with what's at stake, I have to consider the worst possible explanation for her actions, until proven otherwise."

Fareed gritted his teeth. "Just to see what kind of twisted ideas you can come up with, what would said explanation be?"

"The ideas I have are courtesy of the twisted fortune hunters who've pursued you since you turned eighteen."

Outrage, on Gwen's behalf, boiled his blood. "And you somehow suspect Gwen is one of those, among everything else?"

"It's a theory, but it answers every question. She met Hesham in that conference…" At Fareed's stunned glance, Emad grunted. "Yes, I realized why I felt inclined to give her a chance. Seemed I recognized her but failed to place her. Until I remembered that you spent a whole evening staring at her across that ballroom."

So Emad had seen Gwen's effect on him that day. And Hesham *had* come to see him during the end-of-conference party.

He still refused to sanction any of the accumulating evidence. "So they were in the same place once…"

"And my theory goes that she realized you were related. Once you left, she might have approached him to ask about you and their relationship began."

Fareed groped for air. "That's preposterous."

"If you have a better explanation to fill the spaces in Hesham's story, I'd be the first to grab at it. But we can't afford to blind ourselves to what might be the truth. But if you find Gwen irresistible, Hesham, your closest brother in nature, would have found her so, too. It might have developed naturally between them, with the reason they met, you, unknown by him, and forgotten by her. Then everything went wrong and the king made his ultimatum, and Hesham went into hiding with her. Then he died and she walked away from the accident unscathed. Everything till that point could have been innocent and aboveboard. But

I hit a wall trying to find any good reason why she didn't come forward when you searched for her.

"With Hesham dead, from her perspective, the king's threat to her was no more. Without a legal marriage, or the possibility of one, making her and Ryan legitimate heirs of a member of the royal family, she must have realized she'd be beneath his notice, therefore safe. *But* she was also in no position to demand anything from the Aal Zaafers, apart from your own voluntary support. As lavish as that would have been had she gotten it, she might have wanted more. And she had the perfect plan to get it.

"She must have known how she affected you all those years ago, so she approached you incognito through Ryan's crisis. She could have used Hesham's knowledge of you to make you fall under her spell, to have not only all you can provide, for Hesham's and Ryan's sake, but all that you *are,* for hers. And she succeeded, didn't she?"

Fareed pulled at his hair, trying to counteract the pressure building inside his skull. "You're sick, Emad. I thought you liked her, thought...thought..." He stopped, suffocating. "You're *wrong,* about everything. She's not Hesham's woman."

Emad eyed him bleakly. "And if she is? Will you consider the rest of my explanations?"

"No," Fareed shouted. "Even if she is—and she *isn't*—she'd have a reason, a good, even noble reason for hiding the truth."

"You haven't asked her to marry you yet, have you?"

Fareed blinked. "What does that have to do with anything?"

"It explains her sudden persistence to leave. I know you've become...intimate, and she might have feared you might cool down. Threatening you with leaving might have been to push you to offer her what would make her stay forever."

"No. *No way*. She doesn't have one exploitative cell in her body. I don't need to know facts. I know *her*. And I reject your evidence." He bunched his fists, tried to bring his turmoil under control. "That will be all, Emad."

"Forgive me, *Somow'wak,* but I *have* to voice my worst fears."

Fareed barely contained his fury. "And you have. I will ask her. She will refute it all. I will believe her and *that* will be that."

"But we can't afford for you to confront her, *Somow'wak.*"

"Why wouldn't you want her to defend herself against your delusional deductions, except if you suspect they are just that?"

"Because if I'm right, confronting her would cost us Ryan."

"There you go again with this…*absurdity.*"

"It's anything but absurd, *Somow'wak*. I've marveled at the bond you forge deeper by the hour. Now I know you've both recognized the same blood running through your veins, the legacy of your most beloved sibling and his father. I'm certain part of your desire to have her is to have him, too. But she has full rights to him, and if any of the intentions I assigned to her were true, if she's exposed you might enter an ugly fight over him. One you're certain to lose."

Fareed felt he was watching an explosion, played in reverse.

Emad's revelations were the shrapnel hurtling back into place to re-form the bomb. Which might be the truth.

Not his macabre rationalization of Gwen's motives and methods. But that she could be...be...

He couldn't even think it. It would be beyond endurance.

But it would explain so much. Her wariness and resistance from the first moment, her distress when he'd asked her about Ryan's father, his reaction to Ryan—which had the texture of what he'd felt for Hesham, the many similarities that *did* exist between the child Hesham had been and Ryan.

Then came Gwen's continued emotional reticence, her persistent efforts to stop their intimacies, to leave...

The doubt Emad had sown felt like a virus replicating at cancerous speed, infecting his every cell and thought.

He couldn't survive knowing. He wouldn't survive not knowing.

He stopped again. He didn't want his steps to take him back to her. He'd always rushed to her as if every step separating him from her dimmed his life force. Now...now...

Now those remaining steps were his last refuge. They could be what separated him from finding out that he couldn't love her.

Emad had tried his best to dissuade him from taking those steps. His parting advice still cut into his mind, paring away every belief in anything good and pure, painting his world with the ugliness of manipulation and deceit.

Marry her. Without confronting her. Make her give you all rights to Ryan, secure Hesham's son. Then *deal with her, according to her innocence or guilt.*

His steps ran out. They'd taken him where he'd experienced his life's first true happiness, the consummation of his most profound bond. Where he might now end it all.

He opened the door, stepped inside. She wasn't there.

He'd have the respite of ignorance, of hope, a bit longer.

A vase swayed as he bumped into it. It crashed, broke into countless, useless shards. Just like his heart might moments from now.

A door slammed and footsteps spilled onto the hardwood floor.

She emerged from the chamber leading to the bathroom, half-running, the face of all his hopes and dreams, alarmed, concerned, sublime in beauty. "Fareed, what…"

She faltered as she saw the ruins at his feet, took in his frozen stance.

Then it was there in her eyes. The realization. The desperation. The fear. Of exposure.

Certainty flooded him, drowned anything else inside him.

She *was* Hesham's woman.

Gwen stared at the stranger who looked back at her out of Fareed's eyes, desperation detonating in her heart.

He'd somehow found out.

"Laish?"

"Fareed, please…"

They'd spoken at the same moment. But he'd finished even as she stumbled to find words to implore him with.

He'd said all he was going to say.

He'd only asked, *"Why?"*

Why she'd lied. Why she'd kept lying.

She could only ask her own burning question, "How?"

The stranger who now inhabited Fareed's body said, "Emad."

She had no idea how Emad had found out, where she'd gone wrong. He couldn't have gotten it out of Rose. She didn't know.

"This is why you kept pushing me away, insisting on leaving."

Statements. She could do nothing but nod.

She'd trapped herself the day she'd withheld the truth from him. And only sealed her fate when she'd grabbed at that one night with him and hadn't left right afterward, when she'd kept telling herself, just one more night.

"Ryan lahmi w'dammi. Laish khabbaiti?"

Ryan is my flesh and blood. Why did you hide it?

The way he said that, that haunted look in his eyes crushed her. She'd seen him in that videotaped request for her to come forward. He'd looked and sounded wrecked over his brother's death. He looked like that again, as if he'd lost him all over again.

She still couldn't tell him why.

But his eyes weren't only deadened with that grief she'd experienced for as long and as intensely. In them still lay his inexorableness. He'd have an answer.

She gave him all she could. "I was abiding by Hesham's will."

The moment she uttered Hesham's name, Fareed swayed like a building in a massive earthquake.

And if she'd thought his eyes had gone dead before, she knew how wrong she'd been. He now looked at her as someone would at his own murderer.

She couldn't survive his pain and disillusion. She had to try to alleviate them, with what she could reveal.

"I had to keep on doing what he did. You know the lengths he went to to hide his family's whereabouts and identity."

In that same deep-as-death voice, he asked, *"Gallek laish?"*

He'd always spoken Arabic unintentionally, to express his hunger and appreciation with the spontaneity and accuracy he could only achieve in his mother tongue. He'd usually been too submerged in passion to explain.

Now he spoke Arabic as if he was convinced she understood, wanted more proof of the depth of her deception.

Her heart twisted until it felt it would tear out its tethers. "He—he was convinced it would ruin his family to have…*your* family know of…our existence. This is why he hid. This is why I did, too. I—I only sought you out because of Ryan's problem, thought I'd get your opinion and leave. But things kept snowballing, then things between us…ignited, turning my position from difficult to impossible and I kept wanting to leave, to disappear, so you'd never know, never feel like this…"

"Too late now."

Silence crashed after his monotone statement.

She waited for him to add something, to restart her heart or still it forever.

He only said, "Tell me everything about the last years since I lost my brother. Tell me about your life with Hesham."

Gwen looked as if he'd asked her to take a scalpel to her own neck.

Fareed felt he'd be doing the same. Worse. That he'd be cutting out his heart. But he had to know. Even if it killed him.

He no longer recognized that dreadful drone that issued from him. "You met him in that conference?"

She cast her eyes downward. It was an unbearable moment before she nodded.

He felt as if a bullet had ripped through his heart, stilling its last jerking attempts at a beat.

He'd thought she'd recognized him that day, had ended her engagement because she couldn't be with anyone else.

All that time, it had been Hesham.

"Did you love him?"

She collapsed on the bed, dropped her face in her hands.

She *had* loved him. The grief he felt from her now was the same he'd felt at first. Her anguish for Ryan seemed an insufficient explanation, if that could be said. It had been due to the loss of Hesham, the father of her son.

And even though it shredded his heart, he had to tell her. "He loved you. He lived for you, and when he was dying, his only thoughts were of you. Even though he gave up his name and family and whole life to be with you, he thought you deserved more. His dying words were that he was sorry he couldn't give it to you."

Tears came then. Hers. He wished he could shed any.

He bled instead, dark torrents of loss.

Two things had been sustaining him. The hope of finding Hesham's family. And finding her and Ryan.

But they were one and the same, and his hopes for a blissful future for all were doomed to be forever tainted by the past.

It wasn't because he believed the ulterior motives Emad had assigned her secrecy. He wished he could. It would have been a far lesser blow to believe her a self-serving manipulator. He would have been relieved Hesham had died clinging to his false belief in her and at peace. As for his agony at losing his faith in her, it would have been ameliorated if he could have coveted her knowing what she truly was.

But she was everything he could love and respect, the answer to all his fantasies and needs. And that she'd been the same to his brother, had been his in such an abiding love that she'd become a fugitive to be with him...*that* was despair.

For even if he could survive the guilt—and may Ullah forgive him, the jealousy—how could he survive knowing she might never feel the same for him? What *did* she feel for him? Beyond physical hunger? Had he been unable to fathom her emotions because they didn't exist? Had she been unable to deny her body's needs, while her heart remained buried with Hesham?

If it had, had everything she'd had with *him* been an attempt to resurrect what she'd had with Hesham? Had she found solace in their minor resemblances, taken comfort in sensing the love he had for him?

Had she ever felt anything that was purely for him?

He had to get away from her before whatever held him together disintegrated.

He found himself at the door, heard himself saying, "I'll be at the center. Don't try to leave."

He couldn't make this a request. It could no longer be one.

Even if it would kill him, she was staying. Forever.

Gwen raised swollen eyes to the door that had closed behind Fareed. Heartbeats fractured inside her chest as she expected him to walk back, take her with him where he could keep an eye on her.

After moments of frozen dread, she tried to rise.

She sagged back to the bed. The bed she'd never share with Fareed again. In the apartment she'd realized wasn't his.

He hadn't taken her to his private domain, had kept her in what was to him, for all its wonders, an impersonal space.

Relief had trumped the pain of knowing he hadn't thought her worthy of sharing his own bed. She didn't wish the depth of her involvement on him, wished him only the mildness of fond memories when she left his life, not the harshness of unquenchable longing she'd live with.

But as he'd said, it was too late. Whatever he'd felt for her had now been forever soiled and soured.

It wasn't too late to escape. This time, she wouldn't let anything stop her. She'd at least spirit Ryan and Rose away.

Panic finally got her legs working. At the door, her hand slipped on the handle…then she stumbled back.

The door was opening. Fareed. He'd come back as she'd feared….

Next moment, she stood gaping at the stranger…*strangers* on the other side of the door.

The dark, imposing man who looked like the highest-ranking among them, advanced on her, said without preamble, "You will come with us. The king has summoned you."

The ride to the royal palace passed in harrowing silence.

Her escorts wouldn't answer her questions. They'd said the king had summoned her, but in reality, she was being abducted.

Even if she hadn't heard enough from Hesham about his father, this act of blatant disregard for her most basic rights made her expect the worst.

She'd long dreaded this man. Her fear only deepened with every step through his palace's impossible opulence and extravagance.

Then she was ushered into his state room.

As the door closed behind her, she felt engulfed by malice.

It didn't matter. She'd fight him, king or not….

"Harlots always had the intelligence and self-preservation to try to entrap my sons outside my domain."

The voice was pure wrath and mercilessness, short-circuiting her resolve. It issued from the deep shadows at the far end of the gigantic room.

The owner of the voice rose from a throne-like seat and advanced to the relatively illuminated part where she stood. She almost cringed. Almost. She wouldn't give him the satisfaction.

"But you're here to steal Fareed under my very nose. You're either recklessly stupid or unbelievably cunning. I'd go with the second interpretation because you managed to have my most-level-headed son eating out of your hand."

This was about Fareed? He didn't know who she was?

Relief almost burst out of her, but she couldn't give any outward sign of it. She stood staring ahead, face blank.

This provoked him even more. She felt his rage encompassing her as he stormed toward her. Then she saw him clearly for the first time. It took all that remained of her tattered control not to recoil.

The man was an older version of Fareed, as tall but bulkier, must have been as blessed by nature once upon a time, but ruthlessness had degraded his looks, turning him forbidding, almost sinister. And he was incensed.

"You think I'll lose another son to another American hussy? One who wants to foist her bastard child on him, too?" He snatched at her. Her heart hit her throat as she stumbled out of reach. He brought himself under control. "But I'll give you the choice I would have given the trash who deprived me of my youngest son. Leave, disappear, and I'll leave you alone. If you don't, what happens to you and yours will be your fault."

And she knew. That the lengths Hesham had gone to, to hide from that man, what she'd always suspected had been at least a little exaggerated, had been warranted, and then some.

But ironically, because of the king's ignorance of her

true identity, he was giving her a way out of this horrific mess. He'd even provided the means for her to leave against Fareed's will, what she might have never secured on her own.

"What will it be?" the king rumbled, a predator about to pounce and to hell with giving his opponent a running chance.

She looked him in the eyes, made her answer a solemn pledge. "I'll leave. And I'll disappear. Fareed will never find me again."

The king had believed her.

But knowing that Fareed wouldn't just let her go, he'd said he would give her every assistance in her disappearance efforts.

His men had delivered her to Fareed's mansion to collect Rose and Ryan on her way to the king's private airstrip. She'd phoned Rose ahead, told her to be ready, wouldn't answer her confusion.

She now ran into the mansion, had reached the bottom of the stairs when his voice came out of nowhere.

"If you're still trying to leave, Gwen, don't bother."

She stumbled with the force of the déjà vu.

Fareed was separating from the shadows at the top of the stairs like that first night he'd made her his.

God, *no*. Now this wouldn't be the clean surgical amputation she'd hoped it would be.

He was coming down the stairs now, as deliberate, as determined as that other night. But instead of the passion that had buffeted her then, the void emanating from him did now.

"I'm not letting you and Ryan go, Gwen. And that's final."

She took one step back for each he took closer. But

nothing stopped his advance. He was now mere feet away....

Then two things happened at once.

Rose appeared at the top of the stairs with Ryan. And the king's men, all six of them, who'd been waiting for her outside, entered the mansion in force.

Fareed swerved to advance on them in steps loaded with danger, putting himself between her and them, his expression thunderous.

"What's the meaning of this, Zayed?"

The man who'd led the task force that had taken her to the king gave him a curt bow.

"Forgive me for the intrusion, Prince Fareed, but the king has changed our orders. Only this woman and her female companion will leave the kingdom. The child, Prince Hesham's son, will remain—will be taken to him."

Eleven

"This woman and her child are in my protection."

At Fareed's arctic outrage, her gaze slammed from Rose and Ryan—frozen like her at the top of the stairs—back to him.

"My father is never coming near either of them. As for all of you, you will leave my house, right now, or suffer the consequences."

She'd never dreamed Fareed could look so lethal. And she knew. He would fulfill his threat without a second's hesitation. He was ready to fight, go to any lengths, inflict or sustain any injury, in their defense.

A chill of dread ran down her spine. She'd tried everything she could so that it would never come to that. But— No, she could have left sooner, prevented this. Now it was too late.

The king had discovered Ryan's identity.

The man called Zayed, what Gwen imagined desert

raiders must have looked like, harsh and weathered and unbending, stood his ground. "*Somow'wak,* by the authority vested in me by the king, I order you to stand aside."

Fareed barked a laugh that must have sent every hair in the place standing on end like it did hers. "Or what? You'll tell my father on me? Do so, and take this message back to that uncompromising fossil while you're at it, word for word. I'm not Hesham, and not only won't he intimidate me, but he also wouldn't want to make me his enemy. I will be if he even thinks of Gwen or Ryan again. And that's his first and final warning."

Zayed's face clenched in a conflict of reluctance and determination. It was apparent he liked and respected his prince, wouldn't want to fight him. But his allegiance, even if he didn't appear to relish it, was to the king, and it was unswerving.

He finally said, "My orders were clear, *Somow'wak.* I can't back down. *Arjook,* I beg of you, don't force a confrontation."

"That's exactly what I'll do, with anyone who dares threaten Gwen or Ryan." Fareed advanced on Zayed, a warrior who had the same steel-nerved precision and efficiency of the surgeon. "I'll go to war for them. Will you? Will he?"

She could feel Zayed hesitating as her mind churned, trying to work out how to exploit this standoff, take Ryan and Rose and escape them all.

But there was no way out. Either the king won, and she was thrown out of the country, or Fareed won, and he kept her here.

Either way, Ryan would end up being lost to her.

Suddenly, the simmering scene fractured.

Zayed made up his mind and gestured to his men. They advanced instantaneously, a highly organized strike force.

Two men ran past her and Fareed, targeting the stairs. She heard Rose's shouted protests and Ryan's alarmed crying as they advanced. Fareed intercepted Zayed and three of his men as they made a grab for her. She gaped in horror as violence erupted.

She cried out as a fist connected with Fareed's face, as she heard the sickening impact of knuckles with flesh and bone. And she threw herself into the fight, blind now but to one thing: defending him, preventing any injury to him at any cost.

Fareed took the man who'd hit him down with one blow to the throat and Zayed with another to the solar plexus. The third man he took down with one roundhouse kick to the temple. He was fighting with the economy of the surgeon who knew the anatomy of incapacitation. She hit and kicked the man she'd attacked, but he finally managed to restrain her.

Fareed turned on him, rumbling like an enraged tiger. "Take your hands off her, Mohsen, or have them torn off."

"*Assef, Somow'wak*—sorry, but you will stand aside now and let me complete my mission." Mohsen produced his gun from his holster.

She drove her elbow into his gut with all her strength.

He gasped, staggered, but he tightened his hold on her neck. She choked, the world wavered and receded. She heard Fareed's roar as if from a distance, saw his contorted face as he charged toward her and her captor, saw a gun pointing at him, from a hand beside her face. Dread for him swelled as she fought to sink her teeth into that hand...

"That's enough!"

A roar reverberated in her bones, then she was snatched from the vise imprisoning her, and swept into the arms she'd thought she'd never feel again in this life. Fareed's.

Her wavering gaze panned around. Emad was at the top of the stairs standing between Rose and Ryan and the men who'd gone after them, protecting them with his own body, like Fareed had done for her minutes ago. Fareed's guards were cordoning the scene, four or five to each of Zayed's men, pinning them at gunpoint.

"Took you long enough, Emad," Fareed snarled as he took her deeper into his embrace, beckoned to Emad to get Rose and Ryan down and into his protection.

"My apologies, *Somow'wak*." Emad led the shaken Rose who was clutching the bawling Ryan in a feverish embrace down the stairs, encompassing her by his side. Gwen bolted from Fareed's arms, reaching out to Ryan who threw himself in her trembling ones.

Fareed's footsteps almost overlapped hers, and the moment Ryan filled her arms, he took them both back into his own.

Ryan's sobs subsided as soon as he found himself nestled between their bodies, his arms around her neck but his face buried into Fareed's chest, recognizing him as their protector.

Emad went on. "I was on the road when I got your emergency signal. I had to investigate the situation and organize enough men and the plan to end this farce with minimum fuss."

"With *no* further fuss." Fareed turned his wrathful glance to Zayed. "Isn't that right, Zayed?"

Zayed, still trying to recover from the vicious blow Fareed had dealt him, looked at him with grudging consent, acknowledging that he'd outmaneuvered him, had won. This round. He gestured for his men to stand down, retreat.

In minutes, all armed men, the king's and Fareed's, had left the mansion.

Rose was the first one to break the silence that expanded after their departure. "Holy James Bond! What was all that about? And what do they mean Ryan is some prince's son?" Rose put her hand on Gwen's arm. "Is this true?"

Gwen gave a difficult nod, unable to meet anyone's eyes, hugging Ryan tighter, the fright still cascading through her in intensifying shudders.

Fareed tightened his arm around her, as if to absorb her chaos, squeezing the restless Ryan between them, crooning to him, "It's over, *ya sugheeri,* you're safe. I'm here and I'll always be here. No one is ever coming near you again."

A whimper caught in Gwen's throat at the protectiveness and promise in Fareed's voice, at the way Ryan responded. As if he understood and totally believed him, he transferred his arms from her neck to Fareed's, burrowing deep into him, his whimpers silenced.

She almost snatched him back into her arms, cried to Fareed not to promise Ryan what he wouldn't be able to deliver.

Before she could say anything, Fareed turned his eyes to her. "I'm sorry about what happened. My father will pay for this."

She shook her head. "It doesn't matter."

"Of course, it does. And it's partially my fault, *our* fault, my siblings' and mine. We've long become too involved in our lives and projects, we've left his council to work unopposed. He's always been old-school, and has grown more rigid with age. That had once proven effective in matters of state, but when his inflexibility started causing problems, we just fixed them, instead of fixing his views and policies. And we've been paying bigger prices for treating the symptoms instead of the disease. His last unforgivable action was what he'd done to Hesham. But today he's gone too far."

Her headshake was more despondent this time. "I meant it doesn't matter what you, or I, do now. He's found out about Ryan, and everything that Hesham feared has come to pass."

Fareed frowned down at her, the intense pain that seemed to assail him when she mentioned Hesham gripping his face.

He turned to Emad, his frown deepening. "What I want to know is how my father found out about Ryan." The accusation was there in Fareed's voice. But when the confession surfaced with equal clarity on Emad's face, it still seemed to shock Fareed to his core. "*B'Ellahi,* why?"

Emad exhaled heavily. "I had no idea he'd react that way, but…I'd do it again, *Somow'wak.*"

Fury overcame confusion in Fareed's eyes as he ground out, "And you have a sane reason for this?"

Emad held his eyes, his grim but unwavering. "Because I've known the king longer than you have, have seen different sides to him than what he shows his children. But you are pragmatic and emotional at once and have never given your status or its dictates precedence over your decisions, so you never try to understand his position. There are worlds between being a prince who's not in line to the throne and being a king. That is the loneliest place to be."

"And is this analysis of my father's character and position and your view of both supposed to make any difference to me right now?" Fareed growled.

Emad shook his head. "I'm not asking that you forgive, just that you try to understand."

Sarcastic disgust coated Fareed's voice. "*Shukran,* Emad. I can't fault my father for playing true to type, but

I have *you* to thank for this impasse. You're a sentimental fool and you romanticized that heartless relic."

Emad cast his eyes downward, as if realizing anything he said now would incense Fareed further.

But Fareed wasn't done. "Because you've run to him with your discovery almost the moment you made it, have you also been keeping him updated on my efforts to find Gwen and Ryan?" Emad just nodded. Fareed snorted. "I can't tell you how great it is to find out that my most trusted ally is also a double agent. And for what? The most misguided sentimental *crap* for someone who's never shown anyone the least sympathy." He stopped, his fingers digging into Gwen's shoulder, his arm tightening over Ryan, as if he was intensifying his protection. "And among all those fond memories of my father, didn't you store the one when he forced Hesham into exile? Apart from the vile threats to the woman he loved, you do remember what he thought of the 'inferior union' that would soil our venerable line? So, because you're the expert on my father's deepest emotions and motives, *b'haggej'jaheem*—what by hell's name does he suddenly want with Hesham's son, the child he disowned before he came into being?"

Emad looked as if he wouldn't answer that, at the risk of enraging Fareed even more.

Then he did, his eyes heavy, solemn. "I know you think the king cared nothing about Hesham, and I might never be able to convince you otherwise. But he cared too much. He never stopped looking for him either, and in the last year or so, I believe it was to call him home, find a resolution that Hesham would accept. Then Hesham died and remorse and agony almost drove him to the brink of insanity. Only knowing Hesham had a son, and the hope of finding him, has been holding him together. Once I found out who that son was, I couldn't hide Ryan's existence and presence in Jizaan from him."

Fareed looked at Emad as if he was seeing him for the first time, his eyes gone totally cold for the first time since she'd seen him. "And I hope you're happy with the results of your catastrophic misjudgment."

And even though Emad had caused irreparable damage, she couldn't help squirming, as she felt Rose did, too, at the intensity of Fareed's disappointment in him, at Emad's mortification.

After a moment of heavy silence, without looking at Emad anymore, Fareed said a curt, "Ready the helicopter."

Emad only gave one of his deferential nods and strode out of the mansion. Rose ran out in his wake.

Gwen clutched Fareed's forearm. "Where are we going?"

"Where my father can't find us."

She clung harder, implored, "He will find us, sooner or later, Fareed. If you want to help me, help Ryan, you'll help us disappear. If you don't, your father will take Ryan away from me."

His face turned to stone. "No, he won't."

Her desperation mounted as she felt his finality trapping her, dooming Ryan. "If I don't disappear, he will."

His eyes bore into her as he put Ryan down on the floor, gave him a few things to play with. "So you're proposing to do what Hesham did? But Hesham could only do that because he gave up his Jizaanian nationality, changed his name and was a freelancer who could continue to be an artist wherever he lived. You won't be able to do any of that and remain yourself or sustain your career. *You* won't be able to wipe out your existence. Now that Emad has enlightened me about my father's obsession with finding Ryan, I know he would only trace you and kidnap him.

I also realize that was why Hesham begged me with his dying breaths to protect you. He must have known our father was still looking for him, was afraid he would find you and take Ryan from you. But it doesn't matter that he has now. I *will* protect you, but I can't do that long distance. You have to stay with me."

She was shaking all over now, feeling her world slip through her fingers like water, and there was nothing she could do to hang on to it.

"But you won't always be around," she pleaded. "You can't. I stand a better chance of keeping Ryan from him if I'm on the other side of the world, not here, where he rules absolute. You didn't see how he treated me. I wouldn't be surprised if he had me…"

Fareed's dug his fingers into her shoulder, stopping her projection in its track. "Gwen, you have nothing to fear, I swear it. I will fulfill my oath to Hesham. I will protect you, with my life. As for my father, he won't even think of coming near you once you're my wife."

Twelve

Gwen didn't know what happened after Fareed declared that she'd be his wife.

Everything blurred before her as he led her to a helipad behind the mansion where a sleek metal monster awaited them with Rose and Emad already inside. He buckled her in the passenger seat and took the pilot seat after securing Ryan in the back with Rose.

She barely noticed that he flew them over the desert, then out to sea. It could have been minutes or hours later when they came upon an island. He landed in front of a house in the same style as his mansion, only much smaller, steps away from darkening emerald waters and a golden beach glowing with the last rays of sunset.

Emad took Rose and a sound-asleep Ryan upstairs, leaving her and Fareed alone. Fareed gestured for her to wait for him as he walked away to get engaged in a marathon of phone calls.

He now walked back to her, tall and broad and indescribable, everything she could love, his fists clenched in the depths of his tailored pants pockets, his eyes cast downward, his brow knotted, his face cast in the harshness of dark thoughts.

Had she imagined hearing him say she'd be his wife? Or was this why he looked so troubled? Because he was regretting it, was preparing to tell her that he hadn't meant it?

He raised his eyes. Her heart clenched at what filled them. Nothing she could understand. He'd been always near, clear. Now he was as far, as unfathomable as the stars that twinkled in the sky framing him through the open veranda doors.

He exhaled. "I've arranged everything. The cleric and the lawyers will be here in a couple of hours."

Her heart stumbled through many false starts as she waited for him to elaborate. He just kept his heavy gaze fixed on her, as if he expected her to be the one with something to contribute. An answer. An opinion. An acceptance.

But of what?

She finally asked, "What…what do you intend to do?"

His jaw muscles bunched. "Whatever will keep my father at bay. Now I know his true inclinations, we will need every weapon to stop him. In our culture, a paternal grandfather's claim to a child, especially if he's an elder or a man of status and wealth, can trump even a mother's. My father's claim as king would be absolute without any foul play. I now understand that when Hesham begged me to find you, he hoped I'd find you *first*, so I would do this."

"This? You mean…"

"Marry you," he completed when she couldn't. "A mother can only gain power against a grandfather's claim if she's married to a man of equal status and wealth. My status might not be as lofty as his here, but my international status and assets are weightier. When I adopt Ryan, we'll have enough rights among us to outweigh my father's claim to him."

This was a dream come true.

And the worst nightmare she could have imagined.

Fareed was offering her marriage. But only because he thought Hesham had meant him to, to keep his child out of their father's clutches.

She'd already known she'd been just a lover to him. As intense as it had been, had she stayed at his insistence, he would have ended it sooner or later. He would have never offered her anything permanent. He would have never loved her.

She'd been grateful for that. She should be grateful now. For this proposal that would secure Ryan's future.

Even if it destroyed hers.

Fareed had thought he'd already hit rock bottom.

He'd thought he'd never know deeper misery than when he'd found out Gwen had been Hesham's worshipped lover, the mother of his child. Now he knew there were more depths to sink to. It seemed as long as Gwen was in his life, and that was now going to be forever, he'd never stop spiraling down.

He hadn't expected her to jump for joy when he'd mentioned marriage. But he'd thought even if her emotions weren't involved, that she wanted him, might welcome the idea of marrying him, at least see the benefit to her and to Ryan.

But it seemed nothing worse could have happened to her.

It seemed she'd suspended her grief in her gratitude

for him and relief over Ryan's cure. She'd plunged into sexual intimacies with him, but must have thought she'd been betraying Hesham's memory, and with his brother of all people. To ameliorate her guilt, she'd been promising herself she'd leave, and he'd never know. She might have thought that by disappearing and putting up with any subsequent hardship to protect her child and Hesham's, she'd atone for succumbing to her need to feel alive and desired again. It had all been bearable, as long as it remained temporary.

But now she'd found out it would turn permanent. She'd realized that the only way to protect Ryan was to marry him, Hesham's brother, when she'd been unable to marry Hesham himself. This looked as welcome to her as a dull knife through her heart.

He had to stop her punishing herself, assure her that he wouldn't be compounding her guilt.

His voice was as dead as he felt inside as he said, "I want you to know that I will never ask anything of you again. This is to give Ryan, and you as his mother, the Aal Zaafer name, what Hesham should have been able to give you, with all the privileges that you're both entitled to. This is also to give Ryan the father he needs, the only man on earth who'll love him like a true son."

He'd thought he'd seen her distraught before. But now, she looked as if her heart were fracturing, as if his every word crushed it.

He knew this pact would sentence him to a lifetime of deprivation, but he had to finish detailing it. "I'll give you the *essmuh*. In our culture, this means that you'll control the marriage. You'd be able to end it, if you so wish, without my consent. I'll also give you full power of attorney, giving you control of my assets. In case anything happens to me, I'll make a provision to circumvent our inheritance laws, so you'd inherit everything. If we're both gone, everything will be Ryan's. If he's not of age, anyone you choose would be his guardian until he is. This will make you as powerful as I am, will give my father no way to attack you even if I'm gone. As for our daily life, I'll be in Ryan's life however you choose me to be."

And he was done. Finished. She looked as annihilated.

He watched her sag to the couch, then turned around.

He heard a helicopter.

It was time to make this terrible pact securing Gwen and Ryan forever binding.

"Zawaj'toka nafsi."
I give you myself in marriage.

Gwen droned the words, her eyes glued to the pristine white handkerchief. Her hand was clasped with Fareed's beneath it. The cleric had his hand on top of theirs as he recited the Jizaanian marriage vows and prompted their repetition.

Emad and a guard were their witnesses. Rose and Ryan were present, one crying rivers, the other giggling a storm.

Soon the brief ritual was concluded and the cleric documented their marriage. She watched him drawing intricate script that looked as if he was casting spells, in a huge, ancient edition, the royal book of matrimony. Then he invited them to sign their vows and the details of the holy bargain they'd struck.

Fareed looked as if he was signing away his life.

Sinking deeper in misery, she signed, wishing she could sign her own. If only he'd take it, she would have.

One of the female servants let out a *zaghrootah,* a shrill, festive ululation. Rose—who thought this was all real in spite of the irregular circumstances she was just beginning to understand—was highly intrigued and tried to replicate the sound. Ryan was delighted and did his own ear-piercing imitations. Gwen felt her head might split open at any moment.

Fareed looked as pained at the unbridled mood as *sharbaat ward*—rose essence nectar—was distributed to those present in celebration of the happy marriage. But he endured it all with a stiff smile. He was the one who'd organized it after all.

She wondered why? It couldn't be because he was treating this as a real marriage. He'd told her in mutilating detail not to expect anything from him. Except everything she didn't want, that was. His status, his name, his wealth, in life and death. His heart had never been on offer. His passion, his ease and humor were things of the past. She wouldn't even have his companionship. She could only expect his presence where Ryan was involved.

She would have preferred it if he'd been enraged and outraged that she'd lied to him all this time. At least those would have been emotions, something to make her hope anything he'd felt for her survived, even if wounded. But he'd just turned off, as if he'd never felt a thing, not even on a physical level.

He hadn't even suspected her motives for hiding the truth. Didn't doubt she could be hiding even more. He'd just accepted her announced reasons, then proceeded to trust her with the sum total of his life and achievements.

But that wasn't for her, as he kept pointing out. That was for Hesham's woman, for Ryan's mother.

He was now probably putting on a show for those present, so they'd spread news of their marriage's authenticity. All for Hesham's memory, for Ryan's future.

None of it was for her.

And if he knew the whole truth, she'd lose even the crumbs he'd been forced to give her.

* * *

Tranquil waves frothed on the shore, erasing the names Fareed kept inscribing in the sand.

Gwen. Ryan. Gwen. Ryan.

He felt as if his world had emptied of anything but them.

It had been a week since they'd come here. He'd been away only to go the center for a few hours a day. When he returned, he hadn't been able to stay away from either of them all their waking hours. He had nothing but those. Longing for her kept him up nights, his mind and body on fire. He'd only slake it inside her, in her passion. And that was forever gone, too.

He might have survived it if he hadn't known what it was like with her, the pleasures that had enslaved his brother before him....

His thoughts convulsed on a torrent of regret. Jealousy and guilt were slowly poisoning him. And he could do nothing but let the emotions corrode him.

But at least his objective had been secured. He'd called every favor he was owed worldwide, had thrown money and influence at every obstacle in his path, and he'd gotten Ryan's adoption finalized. Gwen had been stunned when he'd told her in the morning.

Then this afternoon, she'd come out of the villa for the first time with Ryan, followed him as he'd paced the beach.

What had followed had been an unexpected torment, a simulation of the times they'd spent together as the family he'd thought they'd been forging. A glimpse of what might never, probably *would never* be. But then, whatever spontaneity and warmth he'd thought they'd shared had had probably been both of them responding to Ryan's delighted discovery of his surroundings, his tireless demand that they join him in frolicking in the sand and sea. Left to her own devices, she'd probably avoid him for life.

She would have.

Suddenly her scent carried to him even over the tanginess of the open sea. He braced himself, hating his weakness, the molten steel of ever-present desire that poured into his heart and loins.

"Ryan is finally sand-free."

He turned at her breathless declaration. She seemed to be floating to him in a full-length dress the sunlit color of her hair. It molded to her, accentuating her willowy splendor as if made for her. Seemed he *could* translate his obsessive knowledge of her every dip and curve and swell to ultra-precise fit. It was one of the dresses he'd had delivered for her because she'd left her belongings in his mansion. He'd never thought he could buy a woman clothes. Visualizing, fitting and buying them for *her* could turn into an addiction. As everything concerning her had.

She stopped before him, her skin and hair reflecting the radiance of the setting sun, her eyes the endlessness of the sky. Her warmth enveloped him, her hesitant smile pierced his vitals.

Then she reached out, almost touched him.

He wouldn't be able to resist such a brutal test. If she touched him, he'd drag her to the sand and take her. And she'd beg him to do everything to her. Then after the mindlessness of abandon, she'd sink into that misery that had so baffled him, that he now understood. He couldn't survive that of all things.

He caught her hand in midair, his jaw, his whole being rigid fighting the need to drag her by that supple hand, crush her beneath his aching flesh, ride her.

He hurt. Inside and out.

She pulled her hand away, her smile as shaky. "You have sand in your hair. Ryan bathed us both in it."

He gestured to her glowing cleanliness. "You're sand-free."

"Took a lot of heavy-duty scrubbing. The sand here is incredibly fine, like powdered gold."

He bit back a groan as the images and sensation bombarded him. He could almost feel his hands running down the smoothness of her slippery body as he lathered her, kneaded her under a steady jet of warm wetness, as he drove inside her tight, fluid heat, over and over until she climaxed around him, singed him with her pleasure. Then he would rinse her, caress and fondle her, whisper to her how she felt around him, what more he'd do to her as he brought her down from the pinnacle of pleasure, had her simmering for the next ride....

He exhaled forcibly, trying to expel the encroaching madness. "I'm glad Ryan enjoys the beach. Activities on the sand and in the sea are the best natural form of physiotherapy for him."

She bit her lower lip, made him feel she'd sunk those white teeth in his own, in his heart. "I never even took him to the pool. I was afraid to expose him to physical stress because I had no way of knowing if I'd be harming him. So it was his first exposure to the sea, and as you saw, he went berserk with delight."

He had been as thrilled as he could be in his condition with Ryan's joy. "We'll come here as often as possible, then."

She gave him such a look, hesitant, anxious, as if asking him what was to become of them, what kind of life they'd have.

What *did* she expect? They'd come here, they'd be together everywhere, where he'd be Ryan's father and her parenting partner, but never again her lover. They'd never be a real husband and wife and just a simulation of a family.

B'Ellahi, why was she here? Trying to smile and make small talk and shake sand out of his hair? Did she think he could be her easy companion now as he shared Ryan's upbringing?

Or *was* she considering resuming their intimacies because they were now married, for worse or worst?

Would he want this, if this were what she was after?

No. He'd either have all or none of her, couldn't share…

"Fareed, there's something I need…I *have* to confess to you."

His focus sharpened on her. Her incandescent beauty was now gilded by the lights emanating from the villa. The spasm of sheer love he felt for her, the enormity of it, suddenly crystallized one irrefutable fact.

He was wrong. He had been wrong. About everything he'd felt or thought since he'd found out she'd been Hesham's woman.

What she had been didn't matter. What she was did.

She was the woman he'd loved on sight, the only one who'd ever aroused his unadulterated desire, possessed his unqualified trust and admiration. She had been a selfless lover to his brother, then as sacrificing a mother to Ryan. She'd been the best thing that had ever happened to him, too, his life's first absolute intimacy. And he had been willing to give up anything, risk anything for her. His assets, his peace of mind, his hopes, his life. He now realized he could give up even more. He would.

He'd give up his jealousy, that Hesham had loved her first. His guilt over loving her when Hesham no longer could. His anguish over surviving when Hesham was no longer there.

But maybe she was already meeting him halfway. With this confession she wanted to make. He gestured for her to go ahead.

"You didn't question the reasons I stated for hiding Ryan's paternity..." She stopped, her agitation mounting.

He had to spare her. "There was nothing to question. You were doing what Hesham would have wanted you to do. He lived in fear of our father finding him and spoiling his life and yours. He clearly knew what Emad did, that our father *was* looking for him, not in the way I thought, out of anger. When he knew he'd die, he knew if he ever found you, you could lose Ryan to the man who almost destroyed him. My siblings and I were lucky because we had our mothers, whom everyone called the lioness, the Amazon and the harpy, to fend for us. But Hesham didn't. His mother died giving birth to him."

Her gaze wavered. "Hesham said your father never let anyone mention her to him as he grew up."

Fareed exhaled another of his frustrations with his father. "It *was* whispered around the kingdom that she couldn't withstand him, being this artistic, ethereal creature. It did seem that our father was so furious with her for being different from what he'd wanted, then for dying, that he banned any mention of her. When he realized Hesham was turning out like her, he did everything to force him into the mold he thought acceptable for a son of his. Hesham was right to fear our father and to instill that fear in you. If Ryan had fallen into his hands, he would have suffered an even worse fate because Hesham at least had us, older siblings who'd done all we could to temper his autocratic upbringing. So I understand that you had to hide the truth with all you had. I only wish you'd trusted me. At least, trusted Hesham's decision to entrust your and Ryan's futures to me."

She grabbed his forearm, urgency emanating from her. "I trusted you with Ryan's *life,* with *both* our lives when I came to the land I feared most on the strength of nothing but my belief in you. But it's more complicated than you think. And when we...we..."

"Became lovers?" He placed his hand on top of hers before she could retract it. "I *can* see how this made you feel more trapped. But after I was furious with Emad when he revealed the truth, then told my father, I can't be more thankful to him now. Like we say here, *assa an takraho shai wa hwa khayronn lakom*."

She nodded. *"You may hate something and it's for your best."*

He smiled. "I'll never stop being impressed by how good your Arabic is. Hesham taught you well."

She blushed. *Blushed.* With pleasure at his praise. And at the ease with which he now referred to Hesham, and the beauty of the relationship she'd shared with him?

Then her color deepened to distress again. "But Emad didn't find out the full truth. And when you know it, you won't find acceptable excuses for my half truths."

He took her by the shoulders. "No, Gwen, whatever you hid, I'm on your side, and only on your side, always."

The tears gathered in her eyes slipped down the velvet of her cheeks as she nodded. "Hesham said your father told him his life story when he was fifteen. He said he married three women, one after the other for political and tribal obligations, had children from each, sometimes almost simultaneously." Fareed knew well the story of his father and his four wives and ten children. He had a feeling she'd tell him things he didn't know. "But he didn't love any of them."

"It was mutual, I assure you."

Gwen winced. "Yes. Then he met Hesham's mother and

they fell in love on sight." Fareed's jaw dropped. *That* he surely didn't know. He believed his father was love-proof, let alone to the on-sight variety. "But even if his marriages were to serve the kingdom, she wouldn't be a fourth wife. So he divorced his wives wholesale, and dealt with the catastrophic political fallout."

He was only six when this happened. He still remembered the upheavals. "My mother and the other two women say it was the best day of their lives when they finally got rid of him."

She nodded. "It was how he convinced Hesham's mother to marry him. She feared if he could divorce the mothers of his children so easily, that she couldn't trust him. So he let her interview them and they told her it was what they longed for, how they, like him, had felt trapped in the marriages, that he'd never loved anyone but her in his life. He pledged only death would part *them*.

"Their marriage was deliriously happy, and when she got pregnant, he told her he'd love her child the most of his children. But she died, and he almost went insane. He at first hated the son he blamed for killing his love. Then as Hesham grew up and he saw her in him, he transferred all his love and expectations and obsessions to him. He ordered no one to mention her because it made him crazy with grief."

Fareed felt more disoriented than when his father's guard had struck him. "And it seems I will keep finding that I know nothing about those I considered my closest people."

She shut her eyes. "Th-there's more. Much more."

"Then *arjooki,* please, tell me everything."

She drew in a shaky breath. "What nobody knew is that a few years after Hesham's mother's death, her tribe, the royal family of Durrah, invoked an ancient Jizaanian law.

That if a king married more than one woman, the sons of his highest-ranking wife would succeed him to the throne, with no respect to age. Since Hesham's mother was a pure-blood princess, that made Hesham the crown prince."

He stared at her, beyond flabbergasted.

This…this…explained so much. Yet was totally inexplicable.

Not that he considered disbelieving her for a second.

But he had to ask. "*Kaif?* How could my father hide something like this? How is that not common knowledge?"

"Your father pledged to Hesham's maternal relatives that Hesham would be his crown prince. On one condition—that they reveal this to no one until he prepared his kingdom and his other sons, especially the one who lived his life believing he was his heir, for the change in succession. But most important, until he prepared Hesham for the role he'd be required to fill. They agreed, in a binding blood oath. The king told Hesham when he turned fifteen and your oldest brother, although still in confidence. Hesham said Abbas was sorry for him, if relieved for himself. He didn't relish being crown prince."

Fareed could believe that. Abbas was a swashbuckling, extreme-sport-loving, corporate-raiding daredevil. He dreaded the day he'd have to give up the wildness and freedom of his existence to step into their father's shoes. He always said, only half-jokingly, that the day of his *joloos* on the throne he'd turn the kingdom into a democracy and be on his way.

But it was making more sense by the second, explaining the infuriating enigma of his father.

"So this was why Father pressured Hesham to that extent. He was trying to turn him into the crown prince he knew he wasn't equipped to become."

"Yes, and this was why he so objected to…to…"

"To his choosing you. He must have had some pure-blood royal bride lined up for him, too. This does explain why he reacted so viciously to Hesham's news that he was marrying you."

"But even with Hesham gone, Ryan…"

"Wait, Hesham meant Ryan's name the way I pronounce it, the Arabic version, didn't he? But he picked it because it worked in your culture, too, with a different meaning."

She nodded, her urgency heightening at what she considered unimportant now. "What I was saying is that Ryan might still be considered the king's first-in-line heir. And this is why he might never give up trying to get custody of him."

He ran his hands down his face. "*Ya Ullah.* I see how your fear of our father is a thousand times what I believed it should be. But you no longer have to worry. Even a king's claim to his rightful heir wouldn't trump our combined custody."

"You might be wrong…"

His raised hand silenced her. Ominous thunder was approaching from the darkness that had engulfed the sea.

A helicopter. He would bet his center it was carrying his father. This had to be Emad's doing.

His fury crested as he turned to Gwen. "Go inside, please. I'll deal with this."

"Fareed, let me tell you first…"

But he was already running to meet the helicopter as it landed, needing to end this before it started. And to end Gwen's worries once and for all.

The moment his father stepped out of the helicopter that, to Fareed's fury, Emad was piloting, Fareed blocked his way.

"Father, go back where you came from. Gwen told me

everything. And it's over. Ryan will never be in your custody."

Challenge flared in his father's eyes. "I'm surprised you even think your 'adoption' is a deterrent. Our laws don't sanction adoption, just fostering, and adopting him according to another culture's laws means nothing."

"The deterrent is not only that Ryan has the Aal Zaafer name through me, not Hesham. It is that I'll give up my Jizaanian nationality if it will make my adoption binding anywhere in the world, starting with here. But most of all it is that I, a man of equal status to you and superior wealth, am married to Ryan's mother."

The king only transferred his gaze behind him. Gwen had followed him, was almost plastered to his back.

Then, without taking his eyes off her, his father said, "That is not your greatest weapon but your greatest weakness, Fareed. Gwen isn't Ryan's mother. She's his aunt."

Thirteen

Fareed heard his father's declaration. He understood the words. He couldn't make any sense of them.

Still looking at Gwen, his father addressed her this time, "It was your sister, Marilyn, who was Hesham's woman."

After all these months, Fareed had a full name for Hesham's Lyn. Marilyn. Not Gwendolyn.

He turned, no longer of his own volition, but under her agitation's compulsion.

She was looking at him, and only at him, her eyes flooded with imploring. Certainty was instantaneous, absolute.

She wasn't Hesham's woman. Wasn't Ryan's mother.

They would register. The import and impact of this knowledge. They would crash on him and rewrite his existence. But not now.

Now only one thing mattered.

He turned to his father. "It makes no difference. Ryan is Gwen's and you're not getting him."

His father's expression was one he well knew. A "you dare?" and a "dream on" rolled into one eyebrow raise.

Before he did something irretrievable, his father said, "I won't continue this discussion standing by a helicopter on a beach. Anyone would get the impression I'm not welcome."

"You're not," Fareed growled, aborting his father's stride. "And this discussion is over. There is nothing to discuss. And don't try to pull rank. You're not king here. I am."

His father ignored him, looked at Gwen. "And you're queen here. You won't invite your father-in-law into your home, even if your husband is rude enough not to?"

"Leave Gwen out of this, Father. I'm warning you…"

Gwen's hand on his arm stopped his tirade.

Then she stepped in front of him. "It would be an honor and a pleasure to receive you in o-our home, Your Majesty."

Fareed wanted to hug the breath right out of her, emotions colliding inside him. Pride and delight, at how she held herself, addressed his father, the effect her graciousness and classiness had on the old goat. Delight that she'd said *our* home. Oppression that she'd hesitated while saying it. But mostly, dread of letting his father deeper into their lives under any pretext.

He watched his father take Gwen's elbow as she led the way back into the villa. He walked a step behind, felt Emad fall into step with him. He only spared him a gritted "Later."

His father tossed him a glance. "Later, I might take him off your hands. It appears I've been remiss in estimating his worth."

"I'll make you a gift of him. It appears I've overestimated it."

Emad grunted something, the very sound of politeness. To Fareed's versed-in-his-noises ears, it sounded like a grown-up groaning at the posturing antics of two juvenile charges.

Once inside the villa, Gwen turned to his father. "We were about to have dinner. I hope you'll be able to join us. If you don't like seafood, I'll get something else prepared right away."

"The only time we met, I insulted and threatened you." The king's regard turned thoughtful. "Even if I abhorred seafood, it would still be better than crow."

Fareed blinked. Had his father just cracked a joke?

He could think of only one explanation for this aberration. He got his confirmation in Gwen's crimson discomfiture.

"Oh, no, you don't, Father. I'm damned if I let you play on Gwen's sympathies. You're not some kind, bereaved old man, so you can quit trying to blindside us into lowering our guard right now. We're not letting you get your hands on Ryan."

His father gave him a considering glance. "What have you told her I'd do when this comes to pass?"

"No 'when' here. And it was Hesham who told her—" he tried again to adjust to the fact that it hadn't been her Hesham had told, had loved "—told her *sister* that you almost loved him to death, pressuring and coercing and hounding him into becoming the heir you would find acceptable." Suddenly he couldn't stand not knowing. He swung his gaze to Gwen. "What happened to your sister?"

He knew the answer. If not from the fact that she had Ryan, then from the grief that he'd felt dimming her spirit. She'd been mourning her sister. How had she died?

He hated to resurrect her pain, her loss. But he needed knowledge to stop his father's incursion, especially now that he was using unexpected weapons.

He still almost retracted his question when mention of her sister reopened her wounds right before his eyes.

But she was already answering. "After the accident, they gave her only a preliminary exam. M-Marilyn was told she was fine. They discharged her to make room for those with obvious injuries. Hesham had already…" Her tears ran faster. "By the time I got to her she was deteriorating. I rushed her to another hospital, but she hung on only long enough to start my adoption of Ryan and give me her and Hesham's last will. I knew everything already because I more or less shared their lives, moving everywhere when they did. I stayed even closer after I realized something was wrong with Ryan…"

"So you *were* the one who diagnosed him."

A tear splashed on his hand, burning him through to his soul. "When he was four months old. But Hesham feared seeking you out."

He rounded on his father, snarling, "*That's* why you're not coming near Ryan, Father. Because Hesham feared you so much he wouldn't seek my help for his son, his own brother, the best-equipped to offer that help, until he was on his deathbed."

His father ignored his wrath, addressing Gwen directly. "But your adoption of Ryan hasn't been concluded yet."

Fareed felt his head about to explode.

It almost did when Gwen said, "It's still pending." That imploring that compromised his sanity intensified. "That's what I was trying to tell you. I expected you to find out when your legal team discovered I'm not the birth mother, and my adoption hasn't been finalized. But they somehow got *your* adoption approved without this coming to light."

His daze deepened. "I told them not to bother me with details, to just do *anything* to get my adoption through."

His father tsked. "Seems *anything* included falsifying data. Once a discrepancy is found, the adoption might be invalidated."

He erupted. "No, it won't. Go ahead. Do your worst, Father. I'm getting this fixed, and Ryan will be Gwen's and mine, legally, anywhere in the world, no matter what you do. I'll fight you, I'll fight Jizaan and Durrah and the whole world for him, for Gwen's right to be his mother. And I'll win. Ryan will never be anyone's but Gwen's, the one who loves him, who sacrificed all for him."

His father only sighed. "Have I ever told you how much I wish *you* were my heir?"

"You know better than to try to appeal to my ego, Father."

"No, you're right. What I wish is irrelevant. In matters of state, it always is. I hope Abbas will come around when it's time for him to take my place. He might not think so, but he'd make a formidable king. While you are more ben-eficial to Jizaan and the world being who you are, where you are."

"We're not talking matters of state here. I mean it, Father. I won't let you near Ryan."

"But it's not up to you." He turned to Gwen. "I would see my grandson now, *ya marat ebni*."

At hearing his father calling her "my son's wife," Gwen's eyes filled.

Fareed stopped her as she moved. "You don't have to."

Those eyes that were his world glittered with too much that they took his breath away. "He has more right to Ryan than I do."

"That's not true," he gritted. "You *are* his mother."

Twin tears slithered down her face as she tore her gaze away and hurried out of the room.

He stood glaring at his father as they waited for her to come back. She did in minutes, hugging a flushed-with-sleep Ryan.

At the sight of him, Ryan perked up with the smiles and sounds he bestowed on no one else. He was endlessly thankful for that, for he did love Ryan as if he were his own.

Then Ryan realized Gwen was taking him elsewhere and turned to investigate his new destination.

Ryan blinked and looked back at Fareed as if to make sure he hadn't teleported.

Fareed's jaw bunched. Surely Ryan didn't think he resembled his father *that* much? And even if they did share much of their looks, he couldn't possibly feel the same vibes from him!

Next moment, Ryan buried his face into Gwen's bosom. *That* was more like it.

Before satisfaction seethed inside Fareed's chest, he saw Ryan peeking shyly, inquisitively, *interestedly* at his father from the depths of Gwen's chest, and his tension roared back.

His father spoke, his voice rough with emotion, "*Ya Ullah,* this is Hesham as an infant all over again."

"That's not true," Fareed hissed. "Ryan is a replica of Gwen…of her sister, his mother."

His father turned to him with dazed eyes shimmering with what suspiciously looked like tears. "His coloring is throwing you off and that dimpled chin. But I am the one who hung on Hesham's every detail from birth. He has his same bone structure, the shape of his features. And wait until his hair grows out. It will be the exact color and curl as Hesham's. He'll also be like his father in many other ways. Isn't that right, *ya ebni?*"

Ryan squirmed excitedly in Gwen's arms as if he understood what the king was saying, and that he'd called him "my son." Then the king reached out to him, and with one last look at Gwen and Fareed, as if he was asking their permission, Ryan reached back.

Fareed's mind almost snapped when a tiny whimper escaped Gwen as she let Ryan go. He was about to snatch him back when her hand on his arm stopped him. He wouldn't have stopped if he'd seen dread filling her eyes. But what he saw there…it was something truly feminine, knowing, almost…serene.

He stood beside her, confounded, watched his father caress Ryan, murmur things for his ears only, what Ryan clearly liked.

When the introduction between child and grandfather seemed concluded, and they seemed to have come to an understanding, Ryan made his wish to be held by Fareed clear.

Fareed took him, feeling as if he was returning his own heart to his chest.

Silence reigned for endless moments.

His father finally let out a shuddering exhalation. "I have been more than half-mad since I lost my Kareemah." He looked at Fareed. "You might now realize how it was for me."

Fareed grudgingly had to concede that. If he lost Gwen…

He couldn't even think of it.

"Is that your excuse for what you did to her son and yours?"

"I thought I was honoring her memory, making her son my heir. But I wasn't sane most of the time. Not when it came to Hesham. He had too much of her, inspired in me the same overwhelming emotions." Suddenly his father seemed to let go of the invincibility he cloaked himself in, seemed to age twenty years over his sixty-five. "Now it's too late to right my wrongs. I'm the reason he's lost."

Gwen took an urgent step toward him, her eyes anxious, adamant. "You may be the reason for many things, but not that, Your Majesty. *Never* blame yourself for that. The accident that cost you your son, cost Fareed his brother and me my sister, was an act of blind fate. But I want you to know Hesham and Lyn *didn't* live in fear. While Hesham took hiding to unbelievable lengths, he and Lyn soon approached it all as an adventure, one they included me in. I never saw anyone more in love or delighted with every second they had together. The shadow of separation only made them appreciate every breath they had of each other. So in a way, you were to thank for the extraordinary relationship they had."

His father swayed and reached for the nearest chair, only to collapse in it, dropping his head into his hands.

Fareed stood frozen, watching this unprecedented sign that his father was human.

He finally raised reddened eyes, looking at Gwen. "I wish I could have met your mother, *ya bnayti*." Gwen started at hearing him call her "my daughter." "She must have been a remarkable woman to raise not only you, a woman who possesses such generosity, you'd offer me this absolution, this solace, after the injustices I dealt you and yours, but to raise *two* women who had my most fastidious sons think their lives are a small price to pay to have them. That was the kind of woman my Kareemah was. I hope she had a man worship her as she deserved, as I worshiped my Kareemah."

Gwen shook her head, her eyes as red. "Regretfully,

no. Our father took off while she was still pregnant with Marilyn. She raised us alone until an accident in the factory she worked in left her paralyzed from the waist down. She died from the complications of a spinal surgery years later, with only me and Marilyn with her. We changed our names to McNeal, her maiden name, because she was our only parent, our whole family."

Those were more shocking revelations to Fareed. More insights illuminating Gwen's life and character and choices.

"Your father had better be dead, too, or I will avenge her," his father rumbled as he rose.

Gwen started in alarm. "Oh, no. He's not worth it." Then she gave him a tremulous smile. "And then Mom always said it was the best thing that happened to all of us that he walked. She was happy without him. We were happy together. What happened afterward…blind fate was again to blame."

Fareed hugged her into him, unable to bear her losses, the gratitude that she'd survived it all, that he'd found her.

His father approached, his steps not completely steady. "I was only stating facts when I mentioned your pending adoption…."

Fareed cut him off. "Adoption or not, I will fight you, and I will win."

His father looked at Gwen. "Will you hold your dragon of a husband back?"

Gwen stared at him. Fareed did, too. A shaken king was unbelievable enough. An indulgent one had to be a hallucination.

His father exhaled. "I came here to negotiate, and that's why Emad let me come. But I won't now. Not because I believe you would triumph over me in any fight, Fareed. And not because I've learned a lesson I'll never recover from with Hesham. It's because seeing you together, talking to Gwen and meeting Ryan has changed everything. Gwen has given me a reason to live again with her forgiveness, on her own behalf and that of Hesham and her sister. I'm not losing this reason or more of my flesh and blood to the demands of duty and pride." He placed a hand on each of their shoulders. "You are Ryan's mother, Gwen. I will swear to that to the world, starting with the Aal Durrah. Ryan will be your heir, Fareed. While I only want to remain part of your lives, if you would have me."

Fareed gaped at him. He'd never…ever…

His stupefaction was interrupted by another surprise.

Gwen threw herself at his father, clung around his neck, reiterating, "Thank you, thank you."

His father was as taken aback. It took him long moments before he brought his shock under control and hugged her back.

At last he put her at arm's length, looked down at her. "You are all heart, aren't you? But you don't have to accept me. Your husband *can* get me off your backs permanently if he so wishes."

Her smile trembled up at him. "I don't want him to. And Ryan doesn't either. He wants his grandfather. He… recognized you, like he recognized Fareed."

"He was *far* more eager with me," Fareed protested.

His father *dared* placate him. "Of course he was. He knows his priorities, recognized you'd be the one who would be constantly present in his life and therefore in need of more intensive…humoring."

Fareed harrumphed. "With all due respect, Father…"

His father suddenly laughed. "I think you left it too late to even mention respect where I'm concerned, Fareed."

"Fine, we won't mention it. But even though I am thankful for your change of heart—make that flabbergasted by it, not to mention distressed that I have to revise my opinion of you, and of my whole life, and we do have to discuss the past, present and future down to the last detail later—please, *go away now.*"

The king went away. Eventually. After the dinner Gwen had invited him to.

She was sorry she had. Not because it didn't turn out to be beyond her wildest expectations. It was because Fareed constantly looked about to explode with wanting him gone.

He didn't, thankfully, but he kept prodding him with demands to eat faster. He even cut up his food so he'd finish it sooner.

Now everyone was gone. She was alone with Fareed.

She wanted to do one thing. Beg. His forgiveness.

Before she found the words, he said, "Tell me. Everything."

Everything was made of one simple statement. "Lyn was with me during that conference party."

He looked at her as if he was revisualizing the past. It was as intense a gaze as what had mesmerized her during that conference. And changed her life forever.

"And Hesham was with me. I walked out, but he stayed behind, approached her."

She nodded. "I didn't notice much that night, but she told me later it was love at first sight."

"And the rest is history."

She had nothing to add. Not about this. But she had so much to say about everything else.

Words rushed under pressure. "I never dreamed your father could be this way. Hesham and Lyn made me dread him so much I…"

He waved away her explanations. "You had every right to expect the worst. I myself can't believe what happened still, am wondering if he's biding his time until he can pull something."

"I *know* he won't. But I wanted to be the one to tell you the whole truth, and…I left it too late."

The weight of his gaze increased. "Why *didn't* you tell me?"

She'd probably lose everything answering him. She probably had already. But whatever happened, she owed him a full confession. "I believed I'd just pass through your life, and I'd be risking losing Ryan by revealing my weaker claim to him, weaker than yours, let alone your father's. I *did* trust you, but I thought if you knew, your father eventually would. But I should have told you. You married me because I didn't. I was still hoping that my adoption would come through and the marriage would serve its purpose. But we now know Ryan will be safe, so the marriage no longer serves any purpose. Now you can…end it."

His eyes had been flaring and subsiding like fanned coals. Now they went almost black. "I gave you the *essmuh*."

"Then…take it back."

"It doesn't work that way. Only you can end it now."

So this was it. Moment of truth. He would have never chosen to be her husband. But he would remain in this non-marriage for Ryan's sake or if she didn't release him.

"H-how do I do that?"

"You just tell me. The rest is just paperwork. It's the words, the intention, that are binding."

She looked at him. The only man she'd ever or would ever love. She'd be forever empty when he left her life. But she'd be destroyed if she clung to him when he didn't reciprocate.

And she let go. "I…end it."

* * *

Gwen closed Ryan's nursery door lost in dark musings.

Would he miss her if she left? Did he even need her anymore? Now that he had Fareed, his grandfather and an extensive family to love and cherish him? Or was she the one who needed him? He who was everything she had left to live for?

Fareed was probably realizing this now. That her role in Ryan's life had been as temporary as it had been in his. She'd protected him until she'd delivered him into the hands of those capable of giving him the love and life he deserved.

But knowing Fareed, out of kindness, he wouldn't say anything. He hadn't said anything as she'd given him back his freedom. But he must have welcomed it. Chivalry and honor aside, he'd probably welcome her disappearance from his life completely, would prefer not to have her in it through their connection to Ryan.

She approached the bedroom he'd given her. The one farthest from his. She'd hoped he'd cut her off from his passion because he'd thought she was his brother's woman, that when she confessed, his desire would be reignited.

But it had just been extinguished. The bad taste of her duplicity, however he mentally rationalized and accepted it, must have put out the lust that would have burned itself out sooner rather than later.

God, what was she still doing here? He no longer wanted her. Ryan no longer needed her. She had to go away now. She'd solve all their problems this way. She'd unburden Fareed of her presence, and Ryan was too young, he'd forget her in a month.

As for her, she might be less miserable without them, than with them and unwanted and unneeded. She might even survive.

She wouldn't if she stayed.

She opened the door, hesitated on the threshold.

What was she doing here anyway? She didn't need to gather her stuff. It wasn't hers in the first place. Nothing here had ever been hers.

She'd leave like she'd come, with nothing.

And this time, Fareed wouldn't come running to stop her. He'd stand by and would be relieved to see her go. He might even help...

"Do you know what I wanted to do when I saw you standing on that podium?"

Goose bumps stormed through her. The deep purr, like a coiled predator's, issued from the bed.

Fareed.

She grabbed at the light switch, her hand hitting and missing it many times before soft, indirect light illuminated him.

He was wearing an *abaya* again, both it and the loose pants beneath, white and gold trimmed this time. His hair gleamed wet and sooty from a shower, his skin glowed with the same bronze of the headboard he was propped against, with his legs stretched out almost to the end of the bed, crossed at the ankles.

He hurt her with his beauty.

What was he doing here? What did he mean when he asked...

His voice drowned everything again, answering his own question. "I wanted to walk up to you, gather your papers, tell you that you didn't need to solicit the world's approval or endorsement anymore, that you have mine, that I would put everything that I have at your disposal. Then I wanted to haul you over my shoulder and take you where I can ravish you."

She'd walked up to the bed. Was looking down at him. Was she dreaming this?

But he was saying things she hadn't even dreamed he'd say.

And he was saying more, infinitely better than any dream. "Then I discovered you were engaged. I was enraged, stunned. How could you not wait for me? I was also noble, *stupid* and I walked away. Four years of stoic deprivation later, you tell me you walked out of that conference and on that fiancé I fantasized about exiling to some undiscovered island."

His hand clasped hers, tugged her down. She fell over him, disbelief and debilitating relief racing through her. He melted her softness and longing into his hardness and demand. She shook, gasped, resuscitation surging from his every word and touch.

"Then instead of our siblings paving the way for our being together, everything they did kept us apart and it took a string of tragedies to unite us as we should have been from that first day."

He dissolved clothes that felt like thorns off her inflamed flesh as he spoke. She writhed in his arms, a flame igniting higher as he tore off his own clothes, the feel of his flesh her fuel.

He crushed her lips under his, breached her in a tongue-thrusting kiss that had her begging for his invasion now, no buildup, just total, instant possession.

He rolled her over, pressed his flesh onto her every exposed inch, driving her into the bed. "Then you were mine, then you were not, then you were my wife, but not really, then you set me free, when my freedom lies in making you mine, in being yours."

"You mean…you really wanted…this?" she gasped.

"Want is a flimsy, insubstantial emotion. Does it feel

like this to you?" He pressed the red-hot length of his erection, of every cabled muscle and sinew into her. Nothing flimsy or insubstantial there; everything invincible, enduring.

"I meant…you told me the marriage was only for Ryan, and to fulfill Hesham's last request."

"What would *you* tell the woman you were disintegrating for, if she looked like she was breaking up inside with grief and guilt, if you thought it was over your dead brother, and that she was hating you and herself for succumbing to your seduction and her needs? And when you're buried under misconceptions, would you tell her, and yourself, to get over that trivial matter of a beloved dead lover and brother, demand she be your wife for real?"

She gaped at him. And gaped some more. What he was saying…

Everything she hadn't been creative enough, daring enough, to hope for. His own version of her own misconceptions.

But one thing she couldn't get her head around yet. "You mean…you would have asked me to marry you… anyway?"

"Why so disbelieving? You wanted me from the moment you saw me, too. And you wanted me forever because it was how I wanted you. But I wasn't going to propose yet because I thought I first had to battle your issues with my family's clout and your fear of being a kept woman. Little did I know that, although those might have been considerations under other circumstances, you were only bound on sacrificing your heart for Ryan's safety."

She shook a head spinning with the revelations and realizations. "Fareed...I—I...can't..."

"Yes, you can, Gwen. Like you let me go, to be noble and self-sacrificing again, you can take me back. I'm giving you all that I am again, this time when you know it's all for you. Because I fell in love with you from that first moment, thought I'd be alone forever if I didn't have you."

"Fareed, oh, my love..."

He captured her hot gasp. "Say this again."

"I might never say anything else ever again. I've loved you from that first moment, too, knew that if I can't have you, I'd never want anyone else. Then..."

"Then everything happened. But we found each other again, and this, what we share, is worth every heartache we endured getting here, earning it. And even though Hesham and Lyn are gone, they left us Ryan, the most beautiful part of them. We'll continue to love them both in him, and he'll have us both to love."

"He...uh...might soon have more...people to love," she mumbled.

He stared at her. "You mean..."

She felt a flush spreading over her. "Too early to be sure, but...most probably." She hid her face into his chest, burning. "That's why I never mentioned protection. I wanted to have your baby, thought it would be all I had of you."

He turned her face up to his, his smile delight itself. "Same here." Then whimsy quirked his lips. "I shudder to think what more complications we could have had if we weren't already on the same wavelength."

She pulled his head down to hers, took his lips in a kiss that pledged him everything, melded them for life. "I'll tell you all I can think of. You. All of you. Your flesh in mine, your pleasure, your happiness, your existence."

And he joined them, took her, gave her, pledged back, "Then take all of me, for life, *ya hayati*. For you *are* my life."

* * * * *

"I will always appreciate our time together, and if you ever need me for anything, you know how to reach me. Don't ever hesitate to call, all right?"

Farrah nodded. "All right. Thanks."

He cupped her chin in his hand before leaning down and capturing her mouth in a kiss that she felt all the way to her toes. His tongue tangled with hers, eliciting all kinds of lust that began rushing through her veins in a matter of seconds.

When he finally released her mouth and stepped back, she eased back down to the edge of the bed to watch him get dressed. He slid his jeans back over his muscular thighs before readjusting his briefs. She studied the bulge in his crotch, the object that had given her so much pleasure over the past year. It was still hard, thick and so engorged it practically seemed ready to explode.

Desire thrummed through her body as she remembered how good he felt inside of her, how good he tasted, and she quickly decided there was no use letting a good opportunity go to waste.

"Xavier?"

He glanced over at her as he buttoned his jeans. "Yes?"

"How about one more for the road?"

Dear Reader,

When I first introduced Xavier Kane in *Risky Pleasures* (Vanessa Steele and Cameron Cody's love story), I was already imagining the kind of love interest he would have. Then, while writing *Intimate Seduction* (Donovan's story) and introducing Farrah (Natalie's best friend), I knew I had found the woman for Xavier.

Bachelor Unleashed is Xavier and Farrah's story. It's a love affair started in *Intimate Seduction*, where hints were given as to where things were headed in *Bachelor Untamed*. Both have reasons for not wanting to become involved in a serious relationship, but when it comes to true love, this couple finds out that they can only follow their hearts.

And don't worry if you haven't read any of the previous books—this is a wonderful stand-alone story, as well.

I hope you enjoy reading Xavier and Farrah's story as much as I enjoyed writing it.

Happy reading!

Brenda Jackson

BACHELOR UNLEASHED

BY
BRENDA JACKSON

Brenda Jackson is a die "heart" romantic who married her childhood sweetheart and still proudly wears the "going steady" ring he gave her when she was fifteen. Because she's always believed in the power of love, Brenda's stories always have happy endings. In her real-life love story, Brenda and Gerald, her husband of thirty-eight years, live in Jacksonville, Florida, and have two sons.

A *New York Times* bestselling author of more than seventy-five romance titles, Brenda is a retiree from a major insurance company and now divides her time between family, writing and traveling with Gerald. You may write to Brenda at PO Box 28267, Jacksonville, Florida 32226, USA or her e-mail address, WriterBJackson@aol.com, or visit her website at www.brendajackson.net.

To the love of my life,
Gerald Jackson, Snr.

Acknowledgements
Special thanks to Sharon Beaner, who took the time to
enlighten me about the job of a mediator.
This one is especially for you.

Give, and it will be given to you. A good measure,
pressed down, shaken together and running over, will
be poured into your lap.
—*Luke 6:38*

Prologue

There was nothing a woman was left wanting before, during and after making love with Xavier Kane. And Farrah Langley was caught now in the throes of one of those heated, satisfying moments.

She had known she was in for a sensual treat the minute she'd opened the door to him earlier. With a bottle of wine in his hand, he'd stood there looking sexier than any man had a right to look, arriving for what had become known as one of his infamous booty calls. Now with three orgasms behind her in less than an hour and her body climbing greedily toward a fourth, she reached the conclusion that Xavier Kane was a pleasure-producing maniac.

They were in the middle of her bed, on top of the covers, naked, soaked in perspiration, their limbs entwined, their bodies connected, making out like sex-deprived addicts who couldn't get enough of each other. It was always this endless need that drove them out of control and over the edge. Something about the feel of his hot, sweaty flesh rubbing against hers as he thrust in and out of her body made her g-spot literally weep.

The room exuded the scent of raw sex, the aroma of a virile man, and she was drenched in the fragrance of a deeply satisfied woman. A woman who was his most willing partner and was doing everything to keep up with him. The man's sexual appetite was voracious, and he delivered just as much as he procured. She had no complaints, just compliments. Xavier definitely knew how to conduct business in the bedroom.

It was storming outside, and they were having their own monsoon inside. Only with him did she experience such a downpour of torrential sensations, such a deluge of emotions...some she knew were best kept under wraps. But he had a way of pulling them out of her anyway. He had the ability to make her want things she was better off not having. More than once with him she'd let her guard down, allowed her body's own greedy wants and needs to betray her, which was a transgression that could cost her.

It was nearly two years since her divorce from Dustin Holloway had become final. Dustin, her college sweetheart, a man she had vowed to always love. A man who'd vowed to love her forever as well. But four years into their marriage she'd begun noticing things. Like him wearing a scent that wasn't hers. Him moaning out a strange name during sex, and him sneaking out of bed in the wee hours of the night to make private calls on his cell phone.

She had finally confronted him, and without any remorse, he'd confessed that for the past two years he'd been living a double life. He not only had a mistress but also a child, and he wanted a divorce to marry the other woman and be a father to his daughter.

It had taken a full year for the hurt to go away, and she would admit remnants of it still lingered, making her cautious, wary and adamant even at twenty-seven years of age never to give her heart to another man again.

"Let your pleasure rip for me now, Farrah."

Xavier's deep, husky command struck a delicious chord, sent sensuous shivers up her spine, sank deep into her sensitive flesh and touched her everywhere, especially at the juncture of her thighs where their bodies were joined.

She forgot everything except how he was making her feel. Her body fragmented into a cascade of gratifying prisms that ran from the top of her head to the soles of her feet. She was flooded with more sensations than she could sink her teeth into…so she sank them into him, biting his shoulder as she found herself drowning in total and complete sensual abandonment.

It was then that he skillfully lifted her hips in order to thrust deeper into a spot he always reserved for last. Her legs tightened around his waist, and she released one hellacious scream as pleasure tore through her.

Farrah was convinced his ear drums were damage-proof, just as she figured the power and strength of his erection should be patented. While she let go and continued to take one merciless fall into ecstatic oblivion, she knew the moment the sexual tension that had been building inside him popped, and with it went his control. His body responded to hers, and following her lead, he went off the deep end. His thrusts became harder, stronger, went deeper, and his hold on her tightened as she locked him between her thighs. And then came the Xavier Kane growl that pierced the air and only made her want him even more.

"Xavier, please. More."

And he continued to give her more, giving in to her shameless plea. Heat built as he stroked her while pushing her thighs apart with his knee to go even deeper. His thrusts were the strokes of rapture, and the skill with which he was delivering them was the pinnacle of pure sensual delight. They were what continued to spark that foolishness in her head that whispered what they were sharing was more than just great sex. It was about a man and woman so in tune to each other's wants and needs, so in harmony to each other's desires that practically anything—a touch, a lick, a breathless groan—nipped at their nerve endings and pushed them to this.

As she continued to tumble over the edge, she didn't want to be reminded that he'd become her weakness, nor that she'd made a decision as to how she would handle it. As much as she preferred not taking such drastic actions, her decision was one that couldn't be helped. Not if she wanted to retain her sanity and peace of mind. And she couldn't put it off any longer.

Tonight she would end things between them.

She pushed the thought to the back of her mind. She didn't want to dwell on all the pleasurable lovemaking hours she would be giving up. She would just have to learn to deal with it.

For now she wanted nothing more than to keep falling into the most sensuous waters a woman's body could plunge.

Xavier reluctantly eased out of Farrah's body, sighed deeply and then slid out of bed. The first thing he noticed was that it was no longer storming outside. Calm had settled over the earth.

The second thing he noticed was the absence of Farrah's even breathing, which meant even after all those powerful orgasms she was still awake. Usually she would have fallen into an exhausted sleep.

He glanced over his shoulder and met her hazy gaze and thought he saw two things in the dark depths of her eyes—regret and resolve.

"We need to talk, Xavier," she said softly.

For some reason he didn't like the sound of that. Usually when a woman informed a man they needed to talk right after they'd made love it meant she had a bomb to drop. The first crazy notion that ran through his mind was that she was going to tell him that somehow, although she was on the pill and he always wore a condom, she'd gotten pregnant. The chances of that happening were probably less than one percent, but it was the one percent that had him feeling kind of nervous right now.

He studied her features and thought, as he always had, that she was an utterly beautiful woman who wore that "just made love to" look well. And just the thought that he'd given her that look, dressed her in it real good, sent primitive shivers of male pride and possessiveness down his spine. Hell, if he was a cave man, he would be beating on his damn chest about now.

"Let me take care of things in the bathroom first and then I'll be right back," he said. And with every step toward the bathroom he couldn't help wondering what this discussion would be about.

If she was going to inform him that he was going to be a daddy, the thought didn't send him into panic for some reason. He was thirty-two, closer to thirty-three if you wanted to be more specific, and he was pretty well-off, so he could handle child support payments without breaking a sweat, just as long as a woman didn't try taking him to the cleaners. He knew, after being Farrah's lover for almost a year, that she was not the greedy type.

Except for when they were in bed. Between the sheets, her sexual appetite could just about rival his. But he had no complaints. And he knew that, like him, she had this thing about commitments. They'd both gotten burned once, he with an ex-girlfriend and she an ex-husband, so a no-strings affair was all they'd ever wanted from each other.

They hadn't meant for things to last as long as they had. He'd been with her longer than any other woman... except Dionne Witherspoon. However, he refused to go there tonight. He would not think about the woman he'd fallen in love with while attending law school at Harvard. Dionne had only sought out his affections so he could provide the help she needed for her law exams. Once she aced them all, she had dropped him like a hot potato.

Xavier returned from the bathroom a short while later accepting there was a strong possibility that, regardless of whether he and Farrah wanted to play the commitment game or not, they would be forced to do so if she was pregnant. After all, he much preferred being a real father to his child rather than just a child support check. He wanted to be the type of parent to his child that his father had been to him. Benjamin Kane had been a top-notch dad. He still was.

Instead of getting back in bed, Xavier picked up his jeans and slid into them, then he eased down in the wingback chair across the room from the bed. He had followed Farrah's lead. She was no longer naked but was wearing a robe. It was short and showed a lot of thigh. He thought she had luscious thighs, the kind a man loved to hold on to and ride. Farrah Langley made any man with red hot testosterone appreciate being a man. Hell, he was getting another hard-on just looking at her.

"Tonight was it for us, Xavier."

He pulled his gaze from her thighs to her face, not sure he had heard her correctly. He stared at her for a long, silent moment, and when he saw the regret and resolve he'd caught a glimpse of earlier, he asked, "What did you say?"

She sat down on the side of her bed to face him. "I said, tonight was it."

He fought to keep back the shock from his face. "It?"

"Yes. We started this thing between us almost a year ago, longer than either of us intended. It was never meant to last more than a couple of months, if even that."

He nodded, knowing that much was true. For him the practice of self-preservation was a way of life. He abhorred emotional involvements of any kind. He and Farrah had established the boundaries up front, basically on that first night.

And he could recall that first night well…

They had met at the Racetrack Café, a popular hangout here in Charlotte. He'd been there with a close friend by the name of Donovan Steele, and Farrah had been with her best friend, Natalie Ford. Before the night was over, Donovan and Natalie had paired off and so had he and Farrah. He'd thought she was ultrabeautiful, hot. There had been something about her that had immediately made his mouth water, his tongue tingle, and he'd known from the jump that he wanted some of her. And he had been able to tell from her body language that the feeling was mutual.

A few nights later he had shown up at her front door with a bottle of wine in his hand and a hard-on in his pants. She had opened the door and let him in, fully aware of the nature of his visit. And things had been that way between them since. No commitment, just great sex.

And now she wanted to end things.

Before he could fix his mouth to ask why, she said in a teasing voice that he really didn't find amusing, "I wouldn't want to threaten your standing as a member of that club."

He knew exactly what club she was referring to. It was one he and his five godbrothers had formed a few years ago—the Bachelors in Demand Club. They were men who enjoyed their single lives with no plans of settling down. All six of them had their own issues with commitment and were basically guarding their hearts. Now there were only five of them left, since one of his godbrothers, Uriel Lassiter, had gotten married last year.

"Donovan and Natalie's wedding reminded me of all the reasons why I don't want to be seriously involved with anyone again," she went on to add.

He drew in a deep breath. As much as he preferred things continuing between them for a little while longer, the decision to split now was hers to make, and he respected that. And then maybe she was right. Things had lasted longer than either of them had planned, and things were beginning to get too complacent between them. Hell, he could recall speeding away from Uriel's wedding reception like a mad man trying to make it to her place. And wasn't it just last weekend they had literally burned the sheets off the bed at the Ritz-Carlton in New York after Donovan and Natalie's wedding reception?

He didn't need a rocket scientist to see that things could start getting serious between them if they weren't careful. She had the ability to unleash feelings within him he preferred staying locked away. So maybe they should make a clean break before things got messy and complicated. Those were two words he didn't like having in his vocabulary.

He eased out of the chair and stood. "Hey, no problem. It was nice while it lasted, sweetheart." He not only meant that from the bottom of his heart, but also from the head of his penis that was already swelling in protest with his words. He was definitely going to miss sharing all those bedroom hours with her.

"You do understand, right?"

"Of course I do," he said, ignoring the tightening in his chest. He slowly crossed the room and reached out and pulled her into his arms. "I will always appreciate our time together and if you ever need me for anything, you know how to reach me. Don't ever hesitate to call, all right?"

Farrah nodded. "All right. Thanks."

He cupped her chin in his hand before leaning down and capturing her mouth in a kiss that she felt all the way to her toes. She thought being a good kisser was just another quality he possessed. His tongue tangling with hers elicited all kinds of lust that began rushing through her veins in a matter of seconds. It didn't take much to get her wet again.

When he finally released her mouth to step back, she eased back down on the edge of the bed to watch him dress. He slid his jeans back down his tight, muscular thighs before grabbing his briefs to put them on. Her gaze studied his erection, the object that had given her so much pleasure over the past year. It was still hard, thick and so engorged its veins seemed ready to explode.

Desire thrummed through her, and she began remembering how his shaft felt inside of her, how good it tasted, and she quickly decided there was no use letting a good hard-on go to waste. Especially since it was one she wouldn't be seeing again. "Xavier?"

He glanced over at her as he reached for his jeans. "Yes?"

"How about one more for the road?"

A slow smiled tugged at the corners of what she thought was a pair of ultrasexy lips. She watch him slide underwear back down his legs and toss them aside before walking back over to her. He then said in a deep, husky voice, "Baby, I'll give you something better than one more for the road. Get ready because we're about to take flight. I'm about to take you on the ride of your life on the interstate."

And with that said, he tumbled her back onto the rumpled bedcovers.

Chapter 1

Six months later

"So, what are your plans for the holidays, X?"

Xavier leaned back in the leather chair and propped his legs up on his desk while glancing out the window at New York City's skyline. The Empire State Building was in his direct line of vision and looked massive against the dark blue sky overhead.

He had arrived in New York a few days ago to wrap up a business deal between the Northeast Division of Cody Enterprises and Oxley Financial Services. Cameron Cody's takeover of the investment firm was a done deal, and as the executive attorney for all Cameron's affairs, Xavier needed to be in place to make sure everything was handled as it should be. Not only was he considered

Cameron's right-hand man, they were very close friends. That friendship had begun back at Harvard when the two had been struggling students, determined to become successful in life.

And now, just like then, they looked out for each other, so he wasn't surprised by Cameron's question. Cameron knew that Xavier's parents had left for their annual six-month missionary crusade—this year to Haiti—and wouldn't be returning back to the States until sometime in the spring. "I'm not sure yet, Cam. I have a number of invitations out there."

Cameron's deep chuckle sounded over the speaker-phone. "Hey, don't brag about it. Not everyone is blessed to have five sets of godparents."

A frown settled on Xavier's face that was best not seen by anyone. "That could be a blessing or a curse," he said, shaking his head pensively. "Currently it might be the latter. Now that Uriel has married, some of the godparents are eyeing the remaining five of us. I'm not sure I want to be included in any of their get-togethers for the holidays. Thanksgiving was hard enough."

"I bet."

Everyone had been invited to Uriel and Ellie's place on Cavanaugh Lake. Former neighbors on the lake, the two had remodeled both their homes once married, combining them into one with an enclosed walkway. That meant plenty of space for sleepovers.

And it was nice having all six godfathers present as they retold the story of how they'd met at Morehouse and become close friends, and how on graduation day they'd promised to stay in touch by becoming godfathers to each of their children, and that the firstborn sons' names would carry the letters of the alphabet from U to Z. And that was how Uriel Lassiter, Virgil Bougard, Winston Coltrane, Xavier Kane, York Ellis and Zion Blackstone had come into existence.

"Well, you know you can add me and Vanessa to your list," Cam was saying. "You're always welcome to our place. We're doing Christmas in Jamaica this year."

Xavier couldn't help but smile. His friend sounded happy and contented. What man wouldn't be once he'd finally gotten the woman of his dreams? The former Vanessa Steele had been determined not to become involved with Cameron after his attempt to take over her family's business. Cameron, on the other hand, had been just as determined to win her over. Not surprisingly, Cam had succeeded and was a happily married man with a baby on the way.

"Thanks, Cam, but I think I'm going to use the two weeks I'll have off during the holidays to chill and relax. I'm even thinking about going someplace quiet. I might decide to visit Zion in Rome," he said.

Moments later after hanging up the phone with Cameron, Xavier stood to stretch, ignoring the pile of work sitting on his desk. Not only was he executive attorney to Cameron Cody, he also managed the legal affairs for several well-known Hollywood celebrities, which was the reason he had an office in Los Angeles as well.

Of all his clients, Cam kept him the busiest, which

accounted for Xavier's additional offices in London, Jamaica and Paris. And since Cameron's newest brother-in-law, Quade Westmoreland, had a first cousin who was married to a sheikh, Cameron and Sheikh Jamal Yasir were anticipating a business venture that could now take Xavier to parts of the Middle East.

"Mr. Kane, those reports you ordered are ready."

He glanced over at the intercom on his desk before leaning over to press a button. "Thanks, Vicki. Please bring them in."

"With pleasure, sir."

Xavier shook his head. Vicki Connell, the woman who'd replaced Christine James, his New York administrative assistant, while she was out on an extended maternity leave, was determined to get inside his pants one way or the other. He knew the signs and had read those hidden seductive looks in her pretty dark eyes plenty of times whenever he came to town. All of that would be fine and dandy if he was interested, but he wasn't. And he downright hated admitting that he hadn't been gung ho about any woman getting into his pants since splitting with Farrah almost a half a year ago.

He didn't know what the hell was wrong with him since, typically, he wasn't the brooding type. He'd certainly never given a woman any lasting thoughts once things between them had ended. So why was he doing so now?

He walked over to the window and glanced out again. If the forecaster's predictions held true, a snowstorm would be hitting the city by Sunday, and Xavier wished he could return to Charlotte before that happened. He could kiss that wish goodbye since he was due to remain in New York for another week or so.

He heard the door opening behind him and then an ultra sexy feminine voice said, "Here are the reports, Mr. Kane. Will there be anything else?"

He slowly turned around at the same time Vicki was smoothing her short skirt down her thighs, at least as much of them that could be covered. He was convinced if she were to bend over he would find out what color her panties were.

He had to admit her outfit looked fine on her, but did nothing for him, other than reminding him how inappropriate it was for the workplace. But then the same thing held true for the outfit she'd worn yesterday. One of his godbrothers, York, who lived in New York, had dropped by the office to take him to lunch and had mentioned a number of times during their meal how good he thought Vicki had looked. Apparently he was impressed with her attire.

"Yes, there will be something else," Xavier replied to Vicki. As he spoke he watched lust flare in her eyes.

"Yes?" she asked, with anticipation flowing in her voice.

"Please have a seat."

She lifted a brow. "A seat?"

"Yes."

"In the chair?"

He inwardly smiled. Evidently she'd been hoping he

meant spread-eagle on the desk. "Yes, Vicki, please sit in the chair."

When she did so, the hem of her skirt barely covered her thighs. "Yes, Mr. Kane?"

"How old are you, Vicki?"

After probably trying to figure out why he was asking, she said, "I'm twenty."

He nodded as he leaned against his desk. "And I understand you're attending classes at the university at night and working for a temp agency part-time."

She shifted in her seat to deliberately show more of a bare thigh. "Yes, that's right. I'm hoping to get hired here full-time during the summer so I can qualify for an internship next fall."

He wasn't surprised to hear that. Cody Enterprises had several internship programs available. Going to college had been a financial hardship for Cameron, so he was a firm believer in assisting college students whatever way he could. The internship program he had in place was just one way of doing so.

"I see no reason why that can't happen for you, other than for one."

She looked surprised. "And what reason is that?"

"You need to improve your attire in the workplace."

She actually looked offended. "I was told there wasn't a dress code here."

"There isn't one per se. However, a person trying to move up in a company needs to care about the image she projects."

She lifted her chin. "And just what kind of image am I projecting?"

"An image of someone who enjoys getting a lot of attention. You've become a distraction. Deliberately so. Every man in this building finds some excuse to come to this floor every day and your work is suffering because you're spending more time entertaining than taking care of business matters. I've yet to get that report that was due yesterday."

"It's not my fault those guys drop by and take up my time."

Xavier's gaze roamed up and down her outfit. "Isn't it?"

He didn't say anything, wanting to give her time to consider everything he'd said. "That will be all for now, Vicki," he finally said. "I hope we don't have to discuss this issue again and I hope to have that report on my desk before I leave today."

He took his seat behind his desk and watched her quickly leave the room. Moments later, while sitting staring into space, the truth hit him right between the eyes as to why he wasn't attracted to other women. He hadn't gotten Farrah out of his system.

Considering everything they'd shared for close to a year, that was understandable. Usually his affairs with women rarely lasted a couple of months. That was when the women began to get possessive, and Xavier had no interest in being tied down to one woman.

With Farrah things had been quite different. She'd never stamped a claim to any kind of ownership on him. He'd liked that. He'd liked her. And dammit, he missed her. He still wasn't sure why she had ended things between them, but he did have a hunch.

They had started getting too comfortable with each other, had fallen into one of those relationship routines where they just couldn't get enough of each other. That sort of addiction between two people was kind of scary since there was no telling where it could lead. Straight to their hearts was out of the question since falling in love was in neither of their plans. Still, the thought of doing something as drastic as ending things between them hadn't crossed his mind.

He'd been perfectly satisfied with how things had been going. She didn't ask for anything but gave everything. Hell, no woman could compare to her in the bedroom. And she had never questioned his activities when they weren't together. But then in his mind she'd had exclusive rights as his bed partner, although he'd never given them to her verbally. It had been something understood between them. He'd known she hadn't dated anyone else during the time he'd been her lover, and neither had he.

He reached for the report Vicki had delivered to him and, after flipping through a few pages, decided his concentration level wasn't where it needed to be today. This was New York. There was no reason he couldn't get back in the groove and begin enjoying life again. He had the phone number of a few ladies living here who were laid back and easy. The latter was the key word. He should give one a call, invite her to meet him somewhere for a drink. And then afterward, they could go to her place for a roll between the sheets. Hell, skip the drink, he would just go for the roll between the sheets. He hadn't had sex with a woman since Farrah. What was he waiting on? Christmas?

He glanced over at his calendar. And speaking of Christmas…it was only three weeks away, so if he was waiting on Christmas, he didn't have long, but he doubted his testosterone could last until then.

Xavier shrugged off the feeling that something was missing in his life. Instead, he thought about the woman he would pay a visit later tonight. Beth Logan was a flight attendant he'd met a couple of years ago and was a sure bet if she was in town. It wouldn't bother her in the least that they hadn't connected in over a year. She was known to be hot and ready whenever they got together in one of their uninhibited passionate romps.

He smiled. Yes, making a booty call tonight was definitely in order. All he needed was to stop somewhere to grab a bottle of wine, and he would be all set.

"So there you have it, Farrah," Frank McGraw said, handing the file to her. "The judge recommended the women seek mediation before officially going to court."

Farrah nodded as she scanned the file. She'd reviewed it already while on the plane from Charlotte since Frank's secretary had faxed a copy to her that morning before her flight. The case was interesting. Two best friends from high school, Kerrie Shaw and Lori Byers, had started a line of cosmetics right after college, investing equally in the start-up. Lori had eventually lost interest when she married and became a mother. Kerrie, still single, had continued to make the business prosper and, with Lori's blessings, had even moved things in another direction when she created an antiaging cream. Though Lori hadn't been actively involved in the company in over ten years, her new husband wanted Kerrie to buy out Lori's share at a percentage Kerrie felt was unreasonable, considering she was the one who'd made CL cosmetics into the mega-company it was today.

"So what do you think?" Frank broke into Farrah's concentration to ask.

She glanced up. "Like all the others, I find this case interesting."

"Well, you're the best damn mediator this firm has. I'm just glad you were able to change your schedule to accommodate us."

Farrah smiled. "What woman would turn down a chance to come to New York, especially in December? I plan to do some major holiday shopping while I'm here."

Frank chuckled. "Good luck. Forecasters predict a snowstorm by Sunday. Personally, I think it might be before then. If that happens, you won't get much shopping done."

Farrah stood, stuffing the file into her messenger case. "Hey, no problem. If that happens, then I'll stay in my hotel room with a bottle of wine and a good mystery novel and be just as happy. Then I'll fly out as planned and return next week to wrap up things when the weather is more cooperative. When I return I'll just tack on a few additional days for shopping and a Broadway show."

Frank smiled. "That sounds nice." He leaned back in his chair. The look in his eyes shifted from professional to predatory. "How about dinner tonight, Farrah?"

Farrah shook her head. She should have known the moment she mouthed the word *bed* that Frank wouldn't waste time trying to get her into one. He'd been trying for a few years now and hadn't given up yet. The man just didn't get it, although she'd tried explaining it to him several times—and not even mincing her words while doing so. She thought her ex-husband had been scum, but Frank—who'd divorced his wife for the younger woman hired to nurse his wife after a near-fatal car accident—was no bargain either. Professionally, he was a skilled negotiator who deserved every penny of the six figures he made. As a man, he was as low on the totem pole as you could get. The only satisfaction she took was in knowing that eventually Frank's second wife had dumped him for a younger man, but not before cleaning out his bank account.

"Thanks, Frank, but I don't think so."

"Not this time?"

"Not ever."

"I won't give up."

"I wish you would," she threw over her shoulder as she moved toward the door. She was determined to prove she was just as stubborn as he was persistent.

"Will you continue to hate all men because of what your ex-husband did to you, Farrah?"

She continued walking, thinking his question didn't even deserve a response. She didn't hate all men because of Dustin. She just knew what she did or didn't want out of a relationship these days. Where she had once been the happily-ever-after kind of girl, the one who believed in white picket fences and everything that went along with it, she now knew that nothing was forever, especially a man's love. She refused to look at things through rose-colored glasses ever again.

A few moments later Farrah caught the elevator down to the lobby and exited the Stillwell Building to step out onto the busy sidewalk. She loved New York and thought there was no place quite like it. She tilted her head back to look up at all the tall buildings. Being here was always so invigorating.

Times Square. This was the heart of Manhattan. She could pick up the scent of fresh baked breads, see all the digital billboards flashing bright lights and watch people move so fast that if you didn't keep pace they would practically knock you over. For the few times a year she had to come here on business, she not only put up with it, she loved it.

Deciding not to take a cab since she wasn't too far from the hotel, she looked forward to a brisk walk. One of her coworkers had taken her out for a prime rib lunch. It was so scrumptious she'd even loaded the baked potato with butter and sour cream. She pushed guilt aside because this was December, the one month she ate whatever she wanted. She'd jump on the weight loss train like everyone else the first of the year. This was the season to be merry, so what were some extra calories now?

She thought about the case she would be working this week. She loved her job as a mediator at Holland and Bradford and couldn't imagine doing anything else. And as long as there were disputes to be ironed out, she would always be employed.

The reason her profession would remain in demand was because mediation was definitely less expensive than litigation, and in addition to the financial advantage, there was also the time saved. You didn't have to wait on court time, the worry of witnesses disappearing on you, or people not remembering facts occurring years before. Also, the sooner you could resolve a dispute, the sooner people's lives could get back to normal.

Lives getting back to normal...

A lot could be said for that, including hers. It had been six months since she and Xavier had ended things, and she was still trying to work him out of her system. It was as if she'd become addicted to the man. No matter how many times she'd washed her sheets, she couldn't get his scent out of them. After a while, she'd stopped trying and just went to bed each night breathing him in.

But that wasn't good because his scent reminded her of what they'd done between those sheets. She often dreamed about him, and in her dreams he did every single thing to her that he'd done while they'd been together and then some. More than once she had awakened the next morning with the covers tossed haphazardly on her bed and feeling like someone had ridden her all night. But that had only made her crave the real thing even more.

Breaking things off had been the right thing to do. She had begun anticipating his visits, wondering what he was up to during those days and nights he wasn't with her, getting antsy when he didn't call or acting like a bubbly sixteen-year-old when he did. Bottom line was that she had begun getting attached, and she'd sworn after Dustin that she would never get attached to another man again.

She tightened her coat around her, glad she'd worn boots because her toes were beginning to freeze. Seeing a wine shop ahead, she decided to stop in and make a purchase. There was nothing like a glass of wine to take the chill off. Besides, if it got too cold to venture out tomorrow, she would make good on what she'd told Frank. She'd stay in bed and enjoy the wine and the book she'd already purchased from a bookstore at the airport.

Farrah quickly opened the door to the wine shop and bumped into the person who was walking out. "Excuse me."

"No problem."

She snatched her head up. The sound of his voice and the scent of his cologne sent shock waves through her body. She gazed up into the man's dark eyes, recognizing them immediately. "Xavier!"

Chapter 2

It was quite obvious to Farrah that Xavier was as surprised to see her as she was to see him. Had it been six months since they'd last communicated? Six months since she'd had the best sex of her life?

She could remember, just as if it had been yesterday, the last time he had taken her—hard. And how the mouth she was staring at now had inflamed every single inch between her legs while she'd held on to his wide shoulders and cried out her pleasure.

She forced that thought from her mind, not wanting to go there, although her body was defying her and doing so anyway. As if on cue, the tips of her nipples felt sensitive against her blouse and a telltale ache was making itself known between her legs.

"What are you doing in New York?" she asked, and

then felt silly for doing so when she quickly recalled that Cody Enterprises had one of their offices here. Damn, he looked good, and seeing him again unnerved her, had her remembering just how he looked naked. He was wearing a full-length coat, but he didn't have to remove the coat for her to know the suit he wore looked as if it had been tailored just for him, and probably had been.

And there was his masculine physique—tall, well-built with a broad chest, massive shoulders and tapered thighs. Yes, she especially remembered those thighs. He worked out regularly at the gym which accounted for him being in such great shape. He was a man who took care of himself. He certainly had taken care of her.

"I'm here working. What about you?" he asked, as a smile touched his lips.

She wished he wouldn't smile. Seeing his mouth stretched wide was doing things to her. Making her remember other times he'd smiled at her and the reasons he'd done so. Like right after she'd licked him all over before taking him into her mouth.

"I'm working as a mediator for a case I've been assigned." She glanced down at the wine bottle in the bag he was carrying in his hand, and immediately knew what it meant. He was on his way to make a booty call. Whenever he'd done so with her, he'd always showed up with a bottle of wine. She remembered that oh, so well.

"How have you been?" she heard herself asking, glancing back up at him while fighting off anger at the thought he had probably reverted back to his old ways fairly easily, when she'd found it difficult to get back to hers. She hadn't slept with another man since him. The thought of doing so had turned her body off for some reason.

"I've been doing fine," he replied. "What about you?"

"Great. Just busy."

"Same here. How long will you be in New York?" he asked.

She wondered why he wanted to know. Did he not think this city was big enough for the both of them? That thought annoyed her. In fact, if she were to be honest with herself, she would admit to being annoyed with the whole split, although it had been her idea. A part of her hadn't expected him to agree to it so easily. When he'd left that night, not once had he looked back. She knew that for certain because she had watched him from her bedroom window until he'd gotten into his car and driven off.

According to her best friend, Natalie, who was married to Xavier's good friend Donovan, Xavier hadn't asked about her once. He could have, even if for no other reason than to inquire how she was doing. For all he'd known, she could have fallen off the face of the planet.

"I'm scheduled to fly out on Friday, but if the parties involved in the case don't reach a resolution by then, I'll be returning to New York sometime next week. At least I hope to return, but that will depend on the weather.

A snowstorm is supposed to be headed this way on Sunday," she said.

"So I heard, but I'll be here for another week, so if it does come, I'll be here with it."

Farrah nodded. "Well, I guess I'd better let you go. I wouldn't want you late for your date."

Too late she wished she could bite off her tongue. Had she just sounded like a jealous ex? She hoped not because it shouldn't matter one way or the other if he was on his way to see another woman.

"Who said I had a date?"

He asked the question in a deep, husky voice, which stirred something within her. She found the tone just as mesmerizing as his scent, which was all male. His signature cologne certainly knew how to make a woman hot and bothered. And then there was the way he was looking at her, with those gorgeous dark eyes of his, as if he knew he was making her panties wet.

She shrugged as she glanced back down at the wine bottle in the bag he was holding. "I just assumed you had one."

"I will if you'll have dinner with me."

She lifted a brow. "Dinner?"

"Yes. There are several restaurants around here. We can get caught up. I'd like to know how you've been doing since the last time I saw you."

He really didn't want to know, Farrah thought. He didn't need to know. It was best if they didn't go there. But, heaven help her, she would like to know what he'd been doing since the last time she saw him. "You sure you want to do that?"

"Why not? I see no reason why we shouldn't. I'd like to think, although we're no longer lovers, we're still friends."

Friends? Could two people go from being lovers to friends? After all, they'd shared a bed off and on for close to a year, longer than some people remained married.

She met his gaze, and the eyes looking deep into hers were robbing her of the ability to think straight. Instead she was overcome with memories of a satisfied woman, stretched out naked on a bed. And that woman was her. At least it had been her when they'd been together.

"So, since we're here in New York together, the least we can do is share dinner," he added in that resonant voice that could make her want to toss her panties to the wind any time and any place.

But then she knew that wasn't all he could make her toss to the wind. Her ability to resist his potent male charm topped the list. He already had the wine, so all he needed was a willing woman to share his bed...or for him to share hers.

Farrah drew in a deep breath as she thought about his invitation. Didn't she turn down Frank's invitation to dinner less than an hour ago? Why shouldn't she turn down this one as well? She really should, but for some reason, she couldn't fix her mouth to do that.

Going to dinner with him wouldn't be a big deal unless she made it one. And she wouldn't. She could handle it. And there was no reason why she couldn't handle him. He was just a man who'd been a past lover. And it was only dinner, and it didn't necessarily mean she would do anything foolish like sleep with him again. No way. No how.

"I'd love to join you for dinner, Xavier, but I'd like to go back to the hotel and change first."

"All right. What's the name of your hotel? I'll swing by and pick you up later. Let's say within the hour."

"I'm staying at the Waldorf Astoria."

She tried to ignore the flutter in her stomach when he smiled and said, "It's right up the street. Why don't I walk you there now and hang in the lobby while you change."

Farrah shook her head. "I can't ask you to do that. I'm sure you—"

"I don't mind waiting. I have some work I need to look over anyway," he said, lifting up his briefcase. "That would be easier than for me to go all the way to my home on Long Island and then come back," he added.

She knew in addition to the home he owned in Charlotte, he also had residences here in New York, Los Angeles and Florida. "You sure?" she asked.

"Positive."

"Okay, then, give me a minute to buy my wine."

"Sure."

At least he hadn't said anything about her sharing his, which meant after dinner there was still that possibility he would make one of his infamous booty calls to some woman. Why did she care? And why did the thought irk her?

She figured he would wait to the side for her to make her purchase. She hadn't counted on him following her when she walked up to the counter. And when he stood directly behind her, she could actually feel heat emanating from his body to hers. She was sure she'd felt it...or was she just imagining things?

She shook off the thought. Just the very idea that she had run into him—in New York of all places—was enough to torment her in one way and make her giddy in another. It wouldn't be so bad if she hadn't thought of him often. She had missed him, and although she would never admit such a thing to him, she would and could admit it to herself.

After making her purchase, she turned around to Xavier and smiled. "Thanks for waiting."

"No problem."

As they left the wine shop to head over to her hotel, she silently kept reminding herself that her days of lusting after Xavier had ended six months ago. Still, every time she felt his gaze on her she couldn't help but wonder if accepting his invitation to dinner had been a smart move after all.

Chapter 3

"I won't be long," Farrah said, giving Xavier a smile as she stepped on the elevator.

"Take your time. I'll be waiting down here in the lobby."

The elevator door slid shut, and it was only then that Xavier allowed himself a chance to breathe deeply. What were the odds of him running into the one woman he just couldn't seem to forget? And in New York of all places. A place that held memories for them both. At least they weren't back at the same hotel they'd been in for Donovan's wedding, he thought, settling down on one of the sofas in the lobby. Had that happened, it would have been one hell of a coincidence.

Still, just the thought of her going up to her room and taking off her clothes was doing all kinds of things to his libido…as if it wasn't out of whack already. The moment she'd bumped into him at that wine store and their bodies had touched, he had felt a frisson of heat consume him that could only be ignited by one woman. He'd known before looking into her face it was Farrah.

He settled back against the cushions of the sofa and recalled the last time they'd been in New York together, the first week in June for Donovan and Natalie's wedding. After the wedding he'd been invited to join Donovan's six cousins from Phoenix, his godbrothers as well as another good friend, Bronson Scott, for a night on the town. But the only night he'd wanted was in Farrah's bed, and as soon as the wedding reception had ended, he hadn't wasted any time going to her hotel room. And then a week later she had ended things between them.

Now they were both back in New York, and he would give anything for a repeat performance of what they'd shared the last time, although he knew doing so would be asking for trouble. And speaking of trouble, he pulled the cell phone from his pocket to call Beth to cancel his late night visit. He really didn't consider his time with Beth a "date," so he really hadn't lied to Farrah when she'd asked about it. As far as his mind and body were concerned, there was only one woman who had total control of his thoughts right now.

He leaned back and glanced around. This was a nice hotel, drenched in all kinds of history and decorated to the nines in elegance. He bet a lot of romantic trysts took place within these walls. He could see himself spending the night in one of those rooms upstairs if Farrah was so inclined. They would make love all night. He would make damn sure of it.

He reached down for his briefcase, and after placing it across his lap, he opened it up and pulled out a file. He might as well try to concentrate on something other than getting into Farrah's body and then hearing her scream after pumping her into an orgasm.

Moments later, after reading over several reports, he glanced beyond the huge glass doors and saw it had gotten dark outside already. He had a private car at his disposal twenty-four hours a day, but since the restaurant was just a block away there was no reason for them not to walk.

He closed his files, deciding to think about the eleven months he and Farrah had spent together after all, since his concentration was at an all-time low. She hadn't wanted a big deal made about their affair, so they hadn't made one. Although neither had announced it or flaunted it, he had been aware that his friends and hers suspected they were involved. But not at first.

Of course her best friend, Natalie, had known, which meant Donovan hadn't been clueless. And Cameron had known he was seeing some woman on a regular basis. His friend had never inquired as to whom, and Xavier had never openly shared the information.

His godbrothers—although they'd known he was sniffing real bad behind some woman—hadn't officially met her until Donovan's wedding. After that, they'd grilled him about why he'd gone to such pains to keep her a secret. And then he'd had to quickly spread the word at the wedding among the single men that she was taken after one of Donovan's cousins from Phoenix had tried hitting on her.

What he couldn't explain to anyone, least of all to himself, was the degree of possessiveness he felt toward Farrah. He'd felt the need to keep her all to himself and not share her or her time with anyone. Whenever he'd traveled on business, he'd found himself looking forward to returning to Charlotte to spend time with her. They had developed a routine and rarely ventured out beyond the walls of her house, preferring to remain inside—namely in the bedroom. That was the way they'd both wanted it. For some reason they'd enjoyed being detached from the outside world whenever they were together.

Showing up at her place, usually after eight at night, with his bottle of wine, had become the norm whenever he was in town, and they would often joke about it. He knew the wine was the reason she'd figured he was about to make a booty call tonight, and she had been right.

But what Farrah didn't know was that he hadn't been sexually involved with a woman since her, and Beth would have only been a substitute for the one woman he truly wanted. The woman he was sitting in the lobby waiting for at that very moment.

As if he conjured her, the elevator door opened, and Farrah stepped out. He blinked as he stared at her. She was wearing a long coat so he couldn't see her outfit, but just seeing her made his erection spring to life. He was grateful his briefcase was still placed across his lap, and he kept it strategically placed in front of him when he stood, trying to get control of his mind and body.

"You look nice, Farrah," he said, reaching for his coat on the sofa beside him.

"Thanks. If you'd like, you can leave your briefcase and wine at the front desk until we return, or I can take it back up to my room," she said sliding her hands into a pair of black leather gloves.

He preferred her taking it back up to her room so he'd have an excuse to go up there when they got back. Or he could go back up to her room with her now to leave the items. But if he were to follow her up to her hotel room, that would be asking for trouble. Seeing Farrah made him realize just how much he'd missed her. How much he still wanted her.

"I can leave them at the front desk. That's no problem," he heard himself saying, knowing that was the best option.

"You sure?"

Yes, he was sure—if she wanted to keep her clothes on for the rest of the night. "Yes, I'm sure. Ready to go?"

She nodded. "Yes."

Together they strolled over to the front desk, and he completed a claim slip for his belongings. Moments later they were walking through the hotel's glass door to exit the building. The temperature had dropped dramatically, and the cold air seemed to blast down on them the moment they stepped onto the sidewalk.

"Wow, it's freezing out here," Farrah said, tightening her leather coat around her.

Instead of responding, on instinct Xavier wrapped his arms around her waist to bring her closer to his side. The moment he touched her, a shot of something akin to hot liquid fire exploded through his veins and he nearly groaned out loud. But he kept his arms around her to share his heat, grateful for his own wool coat. However, nothing could stop his reaction to the feel of her being plastered to his body.

That made him remember how it was being skin to skin with her while they made love, sliding in and out of her body, feeling her moist heat clench him in a way that could make him moan out her name.

She didn't look over at him. Instead she stared straight ahead. He didn't have a problem with that; in fact, he much preferred it. If their gazes were to connect now, he would be tempted to take her mouth and to tongue her right in the middle of the sidewalk.

He decided talking would be much safer, so he asked, "Warmer now?"

She nodded. "Yes and thanks. We have cold weather back in Charlotte, but this seems to be a different kind of cold. I'm even wearing an extra layer of clothing."

Telling him what she had on her body wasn't helping matters, he thought, especially when he was having visions of her not wearing anything at all. He always enjoyed seeing her naked. But then her clothing was known to be sexy as well. He recalled arriving one night when she'd worked late at the office and she'd been wearing a two-piece suit. She'd looked professional as well as sensual.

Even now he couldn't help wondering what she was wearing underneath her long coat. All he could see was a nice pair of chocolate-colored suede boots.

"Is the restaurant far?" she interrupted his thoughts to ask.

He smiled, hearing the shiver in her voice. His woman was cold. He frowned. He'd never thought of any female as "his woman" before. That had definitely been a slip of the senses.

"No, in fact it's right on the corner. Otherwise, I would have called for a car. However, I did call ahead and make reservations while you were upstairs getting dressed."

"Good. I could eat a horse about now."

And he could eat her. Pushing that thought out of his mind, he tried dwelling on what she said. One of the things he'd always liked about Farrah was that she had no problems filling her plate with the takeout he'd bring with him to her place. How she managed to stay in such fantastic shape was beyond him. She had the kind of curves that would make any man take a second look and moan, then take another look and wish.

"Here we are," he said, opening the door to the Chinese restaurant. He knew how much she enjoyed Asian foods and had immediately remembered this place. He had eaten here a few months ago while in New York on business and had thought of her then. But to be honest, he'd thought of her a lot since they'd ended things between them.

"Nice place," she said, glancing around.

He followed her gaze. Like them, several couples had braved the cold temperatures to eat out this evening.

After providing the hostess their names, they followed the woman to an area in the back where a fireplace had a blaze roaring, emitting plenty of heat. He assisted Farrah in removing her coat to hang it up on a nearby rack. When he saw her outfit, his heart began pounding in his chest and his body tightened in ways only she could make it do.

She was wearing a short tan-colored wool skirt, brown tights and a multicolor V-neck cardigan sweater. The way the sweater draped over her skirt emphasized her small waist and those nice curves he'd been thinking about earlier. His gaze traveled the full length of her physique, from the curly shoulder length hair, past a well-endowed chest, down her thighs and to shapely legs encased in a pair of knee-high boots.

While removing her gloves, she seemed not to notice the way he was staring at her. A muscle jerked in his jaw as he watched her slide into her chair. He felt sort of off balance, and he realized the depth of his desires for this particular woman was…well, getting exposed. Trying to get a grip, he moved away slightly to remove his own coat and proceeded to place it on the rack next to Farrah's before taking the chair across from her.

"How did you find out about this place?" she asked,

smiling, while picking up the menu a waitress placed in front of them.

He met her gaze, and a sensual shiver ran through him. He had been attracted to her from the first time they met, and over a year later he was still very much attracted to her now. "Cameron and I came here for a business meeting in September. Like you, he enjoys Chinese food, and not surprisingly, he knew about this place."

She nodded. "And how is Mr. Cody doing these days? Natalie mentioned Vanessa's pregnant and they're expecting a baby in the spring."

Since Vanessa was Donovan's cousin, Xavier was aware Farrah had met Vanessa at a bridal shower given for Natalie last spring, but Farrah hadn't met Cameron until the wedding.

"Cameron is fine, and yes, Vanessa is due in April, and they already know it's going to be a little girl. He's excited about that. I can see her wrapping her dad around her little finger."

During one of their pillow talk sessions, he'd told her a lot about Cameron, and how their friendship began back at Harvard. He'd even shared with her how determined his friend had been to win Vanessa Steele's love.

"It seems strange," Farrah said, taking a sip of her water.

He arched a brow. "What does?"

"Being here with you. This is the first time we've ever gone out on a real date."

She was right. By mutual consent, they hadn't had that kind of relationship. From the beginning, they'd only wanted one thing from each other—a good time in bed.

"First time for everything," he said, studying his own menu and dismissing her observation as nothing more than that and not a complaint.

"I know, but it just seems strange."

He decided not to tell her what really seemed strange was them *sitting* at a table, instead of him having her naked body spread across it and eager to have her for his meal, or getting ready to thrust into her. Xavier shifted in his seat at the memories of both and felt his persistent erection press hard against his zipper.

He would be the first to admit he'd considered asking her out on a number of occasions but had changed his mind. He'd known from the get-go that she had a problem with any type of serious involvement, and although she'd never really gone into details as to what her ex-husband had done that had resulted in the breakup of her marriage, he'd gotten the lowdown anyway from Donovan, who'd gotten it from Natalie. And just thinking about what the man had done to her filled him with anger. No man should hurt a woman the way her ex had hurt her, and on that same note, no woman should intentionally use a man the way Dionne had used him.

"See anything you like?"

He glanced over at her. It was on the tip of his tongue to tell her that yes, he saw what he liked and she was sitting across from him. There was so much about her he'd enjoyed during the months they'd shared a relationship. Even now he would love to go back to her place or take her to his and make love to her like he used to do, all night long.

There was something about being inside of her that would often make him pound into her almost nonstop, never to cause pain, only intense pleasure for the both of them. And during those times when she'd locked her hot lips around his shaft, gently scraping her teeth across his most sensitive flesh, his pleasure had been almost unbearable.

He picked up his cold glass of water and took a huge gulp, appreciating how good it felt flowing down his throat to cool his heated insides. But that only lasted for a little while. All it took was a glance over at her, to see the creamy brown texture of her skin, the long lashes fanning her dark brown eyes, the high cheekbones with a dimple in each and the shape of her mouth to know even after their separation, he was still very much in lust with her.

"Xavier?"

He then realized that he hadn't answered. "Yes. I think I'm going to try the pepper steak with onions and white rice. I had it the last time I was here and thought it was good." *But not as good as you,* he thought to himself. *Nothing is as good as you.*

"That sounds like a winner and I think I'll have that, too."

Moments later, after placing their order with the waitress, Farrah settled back in her chair recalling what had filled her mind when Xavier had removed his coat. His tall, muscular frame always excited her whether he was in a suit or a pair of jeans. Business or casual wear, it didn't matter. He exuded an air of total masculinity in anything he put on his body.

And then there were his facial features—definite eye candy of the sweetest kind. His strong, sensuous jaw, full lips, sculpted nose and chocolate brown eyes. And the dimple in his left cheek, she thought, added the finishing touch.

What she'd told Xavier earlier was true. Being with him, sitting across from each other in a restaurant, felt strange mainly because they'd never actually gone out on a date before. Their relationship had been defined from the beginning. She'd told him the night they'd met at the Racetrack Café that the last thing she wanted was an involvement in a serious relationship. She'd been there and done that with her marriage and had no intentions of doing so again.

She had explained, and quite specifically, that all she wanted was an occasional bed partner, a lover who wouldn't get underfoot and become possessive and be a nuisance. She wanted a man who would know and understand the only rights he was entitled to were the ones she gave him.

Xavier had agreed to her terms without batting an eye because his wants and desires from a relationship had been identical to hers. She didn't know the whole story, since it hadn't been her business to ask him. But out of curiosity she had asked Natalie, who had heard what had happened from Donovan. It seemed some chick in college, whom he'd fallen in love with, had done him in, and as a result he'd erected a stone wall around his heart. Probably similar to the stone wall she had around her own.

From the first, they'd gotten along marvelously. Since they both traveled a lot in their professions, there had been times when they hadn't seen each other for weeks. That hadn't bothered her since she appreciated her space and didn't like overcrowding of any kind. He had, however, on occasion given her a call during those times to see how she was doing. She merely took those as him being thoughtful and nothing more. She had never returned the gesture, although he had given her his business card with all his contact information.

For some reason, she'd never felt inclined to hold a conversation with him outside of their pillow talk. It was only then, while her body had been recuperating from the effects of mind-blowing orgasms, that he had shared things about himself. He'd never said a whole lot, just enough to let her know he was an okay guy who didn't have a lot of the issues that some men did. He had learned from his past mistakes the same way she had learned from hers. Emotional involvements weren't what they were cracked up to be and were best left alone.

He had told her about his five godbrothers and the story of how their fathers had made a pact upon graduating from college. She'd met them at Donovan and Natalie's wedding and thought they were really nice guys and admired their close friendship.

"So tell me about the case you're here working on, Farrah."

The sound of his sexy voice made her glance up, and immediately she wished she hadn't. Intentional or not, he had a look in his eyes that stirred desire she hadn't felt since the last time she'd seen him. The last time she'd shared a bed with a man. Just remembering made the area between her thighs ache like crazy.

She shifted in her seat before saying, "What I have are best friends from high school who started a cosmetics company together after college." She filled him in on the details of the case, then explained, "The new husband wants her to sell her share at what the other partner sees as an outlandish amount since she hadn't been involved in the day-to-day operations of the business."

Xavier nodded. "Doesn't matter. If she's still listed as a partner, whether she contributed to the success of the company or not, she's entitled to her share, usually a fifty-fifty split, unless it can be proven that such an oral agreement was made."

Farrah couldn't stop the smile that touched her lips. "Everything you've said might be true from a legal standpoint, but I'm a mediator and not an attorney. My concern is not who is right or wrong in this case. My job is to facilitate a process of resolution, to help them work through the issue and resolve it."

"You enjoy your work?" He realized he'd never asked her that before.

"Um, I find it rewarding. The people I deal with

usually can come to an amicable decision on most issues and I like helping them get there," she said.

At that moment the waitress returned with their food, which Xavier felt was timely since it gave him a chance to ponder all the things he didn't know about her, despite having been involved in an affair with her for almost a year. He'd known the basics—like what she did for a living, her marital status and that her parents were divorced and she'd been an only child. He'd also known from observation that she was an extremely neat person, which he could appreciate since he was as well.

"What about you, Xavier? Do you enjoy your work?"

He glanced over at her. Just as he'd never inquired about her work, she'd never inquired about his until now. Once in a while after making love, he would share things with her, just for conversational purposes, nothing more. "Pretty much, although some days are more hectic than others. Cam keeps me busier than any of my other clients, but he's pretty good to work for."

"I'd think being a counselor for someone who is also a close friend would be hard."

He chuckled. "It's not hard because we try and keep it real. My job is to protect his interests and he knows I have his back and will give him the best advice. It's all about trust."

They didn't say anything for a while as they ate their food, but he couldn't help wondering what she was thinking. Was she thinking that going on a date with him wasn't so bad and perhaps they should do it again? He didn't have a problem with it if she didn't.

"This is good."

He glanced over at her and saw the smile on her face. "I'm glad you think so."

Xavier resumed eating and tried to get out of his mind how good she looked. She'd always looked good before, but today she looked even better. It might just be his mind messing with him since he hadn't seen or talked to her in a while.

"So what have you been up to lately?" she asked.

He glanced up again and watched as she put food in her mouth and began chewing. Damn, she even turned him on just by chewing her food.

He dropped his gaze to his plate to gain control of his senses before lifting them again to her. "I've been doing a lot of international traveling, mostly to the Middle East."

"The Middle East?"

"Yes, a country call Mowaiti. Natalie might have mentioned that one of her cousin in-laws, Quade West-moreland, has a cousin who is married to a sheikh."

"She did. I met Cheyenne at one of Natalie's bridal showers and got to meet Quade at the wedding. They have adorable triplets."

He smiled. "Quade introduced Cameron to Sheikh Jamal Yasir, and they're discussing a possible joint business venture in Dubai. I had to be on hand during those talks."

Farrah flashed him another smile. "Cameron is definitely a mover and a shaker, isn't he?"

"Yes, he is."

She would probably be surprised to know that Xavier thought she was a mover and a shaker as well. She had certainly moved his libido up a monumental notch since knowing her, and she was shaking his common sense right out of his head, making him think of all kinds of naughty things he'd like to do to her. He wondered what her response would be if he were to ask to share her bed tonight. For old times' sake.

He drew in a deep breath, knowing that doing something like that wasn't a good idea. Their relationship had ended months ago, the decision mutually accepted by both, and they'd moved on. Or had they? She seemed to have handled the split well, and on his good days, he thought so had he. But now he wasn't so sure.

He was definitely due for a cold shower when he got home. But as he continued to watch her eat, getting turned on every time she took a bite of her food, he knew that a cold shower wouldn't put an end to what he was feeling or the raw, primitive need growing inside of him.

And he would be the first to admit that that wasn't good.

Xavier Kane will not break down my defenses to-night!

Those words echoed in Farrah's head while she buttoned her coat after dinner. The meal had been more than delicious, and the conversation between them enjoyable. Her misgivings regarding the breaking down of her defenses could have been put to rest if sometime during the course of dinner, she could have stopped remembering certain things.

Every time Xavier had picked up his wine glass to take a sip and planted his mouth on the rim of the glass, she could recall him planting his mouth on certain parts of her body just that way. Xavier had a way with his mouth that surpassed that of any man she'd ever known. And now that they were about to leave the toasty warm haven of the restaurant, she needed the strength not to succumb to those memories and give him the idea that she wanted more than the dinner they'd just shared.

"Ready?" he asked after she worked her hand into the remaining glove.

She glanced up at him and met his gaze, saw the look that flashed in the dark depths of his eyes and had to compose herself quickly. He wanted her. She had seen that look many times before, and although it had flared to life in his gaze just for an instant, it had been there. The impact of that sudden and unexpected look had her pulling in a deep breath.

She was well aware that Xavier would follow her lead. He was a man who only took what was offered. There was no doubt in her mind if she gave him even the slightest indication that she reciprocated that desire, he would pounce on it. Pounce on her. Umm, the thought of him pouncing, especially on her, wasn't a bad one.

She smiled, fighting back the urge to ask if he was interested in going back to her hotel and making love to her all night long. "Yes, I'm ready to leave, although I'm not ready for what I know is awaiting me outside that door," she finally said. "I feel a chill in my bones already, just thinking about how cold it is. And I'm sure the temperature has dropped some more since we got here."

He chuckled. "It probably has. Would it make you feel better if I promise to keep you warm?"

Depends on how you go about accomplishing it, she quickly thought. It wasn't an impossible feat where he was concerned, especially since he had the ability to set her on fire whenever and however he chose to do so. "Yes, that will certainly make me feel better," she said.

"Then I'll make you that promise," he said engulfing her gloved hand in his. The glove was no buffer from the power of his touch, and automatically, sensations began swirling around in the pit of her stomach and sliding down to the lower part of her body. They were invading her feminine core and making her crave things she was better off not having—especially from the man standing in front of her looking like he could eat her alive if given the chance.

And it was a chance she refused to give him, no matter how much she was tempted. She knew now the same thing she'd known six months ago, the same thing she'd discovered the night of Natalie and Donovan's wedding reception when he'd given her the best sex of her life. Four orgasms later—or had it been five?—she'd finally reached the conclusion that after sharing his bed for nearly a year, he was the one man who could make her think of losing her heart again. And it was a heart she'd guarded, protected and shielded since being dumped by Dustin.

She decided now not to comment on his promise. Since she'd learned from experience never to trust a promise from a man, she merely smiled as he led her out of the restaurant. The moment they exited the door, a cold blast of winter air smacked her face, and she couldn't help but grin when she saw a private car waiting at the curb.

She glanced up at Xavier. "Your car and driver, right?"

"Yes."

"But how did he know to come here?" she asked.

"I called him while you were in the ladies room. He had to come pick me up anyway, so I figured he could very well do it here. It would save us the bother of walking back to your hotel in the cold. I promised to keep you warm."

And then before she could catch her next breath, she was swept off her feet into a pair of strong arms. "Xavier! What are you doing?"

"Carrying you to the car to make sure you don't slip."

She couldn't resist burying her nose for a quick second in his chest. Her face may have touched wool material, but her nose inhaled the scent of a man. A man who used to be the best lover she'd ever had.

His driver opened the door, and Xavier deposited her on the backseat of the car with the ease of a man who knew just how to take care of a woman, and she knew that he did.

She scooted over when he slid in beside her, but not for long. The moment the driver closed the door, he pulled her against his side.

"Thanks, Xavier. You didn't have to do that," she said removing her gloves and placing them in the pocket of her coat.

"Yes, I did," he said, reaching out and letting his fingertips stroke the side of her face. "I like taking care of you, Farrah."

His words oozed liquid heat that sizzled along her nerve endings. She tilted her head to look up at him, and he stared back, watching her with an expression that turned the sizzle into a flame and sent shudders racing through her. How had he managed to do that with just a look?

She knew the answer before the question fully blossomed in her mind. It was there in the darkness of his gaze, a red-hot hunger that had the ability to strip her control, eradicate her resistance and make her crave the kind of pleasure that only Xavier Kane could deliver.

"Xavier." She heard herself moan his name, unable to hold it back any longer. And while she continued to watch him, taking in how his lashes fanned over the intensity of his dark gaze and how his lips formed a curve like they always did right before he got ready to devour her mouth, she felt a deep need spiral between her thighs.

She was tumbling into forbidden territory and

couldn't stop herself. He was there, but he wouldn't lift one finger to keep her from falling. She knew that. In fact, he was poised, ready to push her over the edge if he had to. But she couldn't let that happen, not for her peace of mind and her survival.

However, what she could do and what she would allow was a way to satisfy them both for a little while. A kiss. They could even turn their kiss into a full make-out session. It would be a quick moment of satisfaction, but it would be well worth it, she told herself. No harm, right?

How could tangling her tongue with his cause any harm as long as it didn't lead to anything? She convinced herself that it wouldn't as she eased her body closer to his on the leather seat. She felt his finger move from her face to the back of her neck and begin stroking her there. Her body automatically responded to his touch.

When he lowered his head and met her lips, she heard herself groan in a way that only he could make her do. And she knew before it was over she would do more than moan.

Chapter 4

Xavier felt as if he'd come home the moment his tongue invaded Farrah's mouth. It was as if he had been away from his favorite place and was returning to a hometown welcome of the most sensuous kind.

He relished the taste of her with a primitive longing and with an urgency he couldn't deny. Not that he was thinking about denying it. He didn't intend to leave any part of her mouth untouched, untapped or unstroked. He loved her taste. He had missed it. And he was damn near starving for it.

He was kissing her with an intensity he felt in every part of his body, including the erection that nearly burst his zipper. Only Farrah had the ability to make him want to toss caution to the wind, say the hell with it and take her as he pleased. There had been so many times he had ached to take her without wearing a condom, wanting the feel of her flesh clenching him instead of the latex separating them.

And now it wouldn't take much for him to take her right here. His driver, Jules, had had the good sense to use the privacy shield and was probably driving around Manhattan at his leisure since he was certain they would have been back to Farrah's hotel by now.

The backseat of the car was dark and intimate and had the scent of pure woman. She was kissing him back with an intensity that matched his own, and the way she was sucking deep on his tongue was bringing to life every erotic bone in his body. She tasted hot, untamed, and he knew they were both on the verge of unleashing sensations they had kept bottled up for too long.

She pulled her mouth away and drew in a deep breath, evidently needing to breathe. Personally, he needed more of her taste, but would give her a moment. He watched as she glanced out of the car window. Although they could see out of it, no one could see them inside because of the window's darkened tint. "Where are we?" she asked.

Xavier smiled, refusing to remove his hand from her neck, liking the feel of the soft skin his fingertips were stroking. He curved his hand around her neck even more, making sure she didn't try easing away from him. "Driving around the city."

She glanced back at him and smiled. "On a sightseeing tour?"

He returned her smile. "If that's what *Jules* wants to think, but I think we know better, don't we?"

"Yes."

And then he reached out and lifted her out of the seat and into his lap and captured her mouth once again.

Farrah wrapped her arms around Xavier's neck while he continued to plunder her mouth with a hunger that had her moaning again. She wasn't sure how long the ride would last, but she planned to take advantage of every tormenting and satisfying minute.

Even through his coat she could feel the hardness of his erection poking her in the backside, but she didn't mind. In fact, she relished the feel and regretted that clothing separated their bodies.

Evidently he felt the same way when he released the back of her neck, and his fingers went to the buttons of her coat while his tongue was still inside her mouth. She wanted him so bad she was almost consumed by the mere idea of being here, in the backseat of a car in his lap while he kissed her senseless. His tongue was teasing and tormenting her into sweet oblivion, and there was nothing she could do about it. There was nothing she wanted to do about it.

She felt him spread open her coat before his fingers went about tackling the buttons of her cardigan. She knew this was lust of the most potent kind, and it was probably time for her to rein him back in, but when he eased free a button and touched a spot above her bra, she could do nothing but moan.

He knew what touching her breasts did to her, and she had a feeling he was about to get downright naughty.

And when he eased open the next button, she knew she was right.

She pulled her mouth away from his. "Xavier?"

"Umm?" he asked, taking the tip of his tongue and licking the area around her chin.

"What are you doing?" She knew it was a stupid question, but she asked it anyway. It was quite obvious that he was seducing her.

"Letting you know how much I've missed you."

That was definitely the wrong answer because she knew, although she would never admit it, that she'd missed him, too.

"I think I've gotten the message," she said in a soft tone when he released yet another button.

He tilted his head and met her gaze. "Not sure you have yet and not to the degree that I want you to know," he said in a deep, husky voice. "By the time you get back to your hotel room tonight, there will be no doubt in your mind just how much I've truly missed you, Farrah."

That meant he planned to torture her some more, probably a whole lot more, before it was all over. How far would he go? How far would she let him? Those questions slipped from her mind when her cardigan opened, exposing her lace bra to his view. She knew blue was his favorite color. Had she worn a blue bra for that reason tonight? And one with a front clasp?

He released the front hook, and her body began vibrating in pleasure when he lowered his head to take a hardened nipple into his mouth. "Xavier." She whimpered his name on a breathless sigh and grabbed ahold of his head. Not to push him away but to keep his mouth right there to feast on her.

Shudders tore into her, touching every part of her body, tearing at nerve endings with every stroke of his tongue on her nipple. She tightened her legs, feeling a throb between them so deep she wanted to scream. She was on the verge of one hell of an explosion. She knew it, and from her past history, he had to know it as well.

It didn't take penetration to make her come. Xavier's mouth anywhere on her was known to do the trick. She had a feeling this would be one of those times, because tonight he was being generous *and* naughty, a combination that could cost her. At that moment, though, nothing seemed more important than having him suck her nipples like he was doing now.

Unless he decided he wanted to…

The thought of his tongue sliding between her womanly folds had her releasing a trembling breath, and when she felt his hand work its way under her skirt to touch a thigh, she couldn't help but groan out loud. She needed to get laid and bad. The hot ache between her thighs was all but demanding it, and the mouth planted firmly on her breast seconded that motion.

"We've reached the Waldorf Astoria, Mr. Kane."

The sound of the driver's voice was a colder blast than the one she'd felt when they'd walked out of the restaurant. Why now, when she'd been so close to her body fragmenting in one sensuous explosion? Talk about lousy timing.

She looked up and met Xavier's gaze and knew he was thinking the same thing. She also knew what else he was thinking...

Farrah drew in a deep breath and watched as he palmed delicately over her breasts before he began refastening her bra. "Circle the block one more time, Jules," he said.

"Just one block, sir?"

"Yes."

By the time the vehicle began moving again, a semblance of Farrah's common sense had returned. But the part still lurking out there in Blissville had her worried because she was fully aware just what an orgasm at the hands and mouth of Xavier Kane could mean. She would sleep well tonight and wake up tomorrow probably craving even more.

She knew she had to regain control and not succumb to a weakness of the body nor a deep addiction for him. When he had buttoned her sweater and pulled the lapels of her coat together, he met her gaze. And then while she was still nestled snugly in his lap, he lowered his head and kissed her again.

This kiss had all the intensity of the last, probably more so, and she could only kiss him back while shudders shook her from head to toe. When he finally released her mouth moments later, it was on the tip of that same tongue he'd just ravished to ask him up to her room for a nightcap, although they would both know the true intent of the invitation.

But a part of her kept from doing so. It was the part

that couldn't forget or let go of the pain she'd felt the day Dustin had asked for a divorce to marry another woman.

"I got my bottle of wine and you have yours," Xavier said softly close to her moist lips. "How about if we…"

"Drink them separately," she finished for him.

He leaned back, lifted a brow and was probably as surprised as she that she wasn't inviting him up to her room. She would probably hate herself later, and the area between her legs would probably protest something awful, but that area of her chest where her heart was planted would eventually thank her for sparing it from further damage. It had finally gotten repaired, and she refused to let it get broken again.

"You sure you want that, Farrah?"

She decided to answer him the only way she knew how. Honestly. "No, that's not what I want, but I know that's what I need to happen, Xavier. For my sake, you're going to have to trust me on this."

He opened his mouth to say something, and then as if he thought better of it, he clamped his mouth shut. He brought her hand to his face and gently rubbed against it. "Leaving you alone tonight isn't going to be easy, Farrah," he said in a low, sexy voice.

"And having you leave me alone won't be easy, Xavier. But for my peace of mind, I don't have a choice. Please say you understand, or please try to."

He met her gaze and held it for a long moment. And then a slow smile of understanding tugged at his sensuous lips. "I'll try, but only if you agree to see me again while you're here."

"What's the point?" she couldn't help but ask.

He cupped her chin in his hand. "To prove I'm not a bad guy."

She shook her head. "I never thought you were a bad guy, Xavier. If I had thought that, you would not have shared my bed. In fact, I think you're too good to be true and that's what scares me."

"Too good to be true?"

"Yes, both physically and emotionally. I could end up getting hurt. You wouldn't hurt me intentionally, but I could get hurt just the same and I can't let that happen."

She knew she had said too much, had let her feelings become raw and exposed, but he needed to understand and accept what she was saying. He was becoming the one weakness she had to do without.

When Jules opened the car door for them, he slid out, and before her leg could touch the sidewalk, he had whisked her into his arms again. "Xavier!"

Jules raced ahead to open the glass door to the hotel, and Xavier didn't place her back on her feet until they stood in the hotel's lobby.

"I need to get my items from the front desk," he said. "But first I'll walk you to the elevator."

He tucked her hand in his and they walked toward the elevator. "I'll call you tomorrow, Farrah. I'd like to take you to a Broadway play while you're here."

"Xavier, I—"

He placed a finger to her lips. "At least think about it. It will be just two friends going out. No big deal."

She drew in a deep breath. *No big deal? Yeah, right.* She'd assumed going to dinner with him tonight would not be a big deal either, but it turned out to be one anyway. "I'll see if I'm available."

"All right."

He leaned down and brushed a kiss across her lips when the elevator door opened. She stepped inside and glanced over her shoulder at him. "Good night, Xavier."

"Good night, Farrah."

And as the elevator carried her from the lobby up to her room, she couldn't help wondering how she was going to turn him down when he called her tomorrow.

Chapter 5

"Good morning, Mr. Kane."

"Good morning, Vicki. Hold my calls for a while. By the way, you look nice this morning."

Xavier entered his office thinking his secretary's attire, a beige pantsuit, looked more appropriate for the office than those sexy outfits she'd been wearing. He was glad she'd taken his advice.

He eased out of his jacket and then sat down in the chair behind his desk. He was ready to roll his sleeves up and get some work done. He hadn't been sure he would ever get to sleep last night, but when he had finally done so, he had basically slept like a baby. But that hadn't kept visions of a hot and ready Farrah out of his mind. At least that's how she used to be. This overly cautious Farrah would take some getting used to.

His cell phone rang and he leaned forward to pull it off his belt. "Yes?"

"When are you returning to Charlotte, X?"

He smiled at the sound of Uriel Lassiter's voice. Since he and his five godbrothers had been kids, they'd shortened each other's names to just the first letter. "Why you want to know? You miss me, U?"

"No. It's Ellie."

Xavier chuckled. "Your wife misses me?"

"No, and stop being a smart ass. Ellie's having a New Year's Eve party and wants to make sure you're coming, especially since no one knows your schedule for the holidays."

He leaned back in his chair. "I still haven't decided where I'll be for Christmas but I'm game for New Year's. And as far as when I'll be returning to Charlotte, it will depend on how soon we can close the deal here. I hope to be back in Charlotte in a week."

"And then you're taking the rest of the month off, right?"

"That's right."

"Good. Z is coming home."

Xavier sat up straight in his chair, surprised. "He is?"

"Yes. I talked to him last night." Uriel chuckled. "He couldn't tell Ellie no, so he'll be here for Christmas and New Year's."

Xavier nodded. Of his five godbrothers, Zion was the youngest, at twenty-eight, and the most well-known because of the jewelry he designed. And he was the one who at the moment was going through some major issues. Before she died four years ago, his mother had revealed to him that she wasn't sure that the man Zion thought was his father really was since she'd taken a lover during the earlier part of her marriage.

It was Zion's secret, one he'd only shared with his godbrothers. Xavier figured it would be an easy enough thing to prove or disprove, but Zion didn't want to risk his father ever finding out that the woman he'd loved so much had once been unfaithful to him. So instead of hanging around and letting something slip, Zion had escaped to Rome and built a home and an empire there. Xavier couldn't help wondering if Z had finally figured you can't run away from your problems and was now thinking about moving back to the States.

Moments later, Xavier was hanging up the phone and pulling a file off the huge stack of papers on his desk. His thoughts, however, shifted to Farrah, and he couldn't help but remember what she'd said about not wanting to get hurt again. He knew how she felt. Wasn't that the same reason he'd avoided serious involvement with women?

What he needed to do was prove they could enjoy themselves without getting all that serious. They had done so for close to a year, so there was no reason they couldn't continue. After such a long separation, he was certain if they rekindled their affair, they would be mindful of the mistakes they had begun making the last time by getting too attached.

The thought of them falling in love was scary stuff.

He knew that better than anyone. But he was just as certain it wouldn't happen. There wasn't a woman alive he would give his heart to. He had no intention of getting great sex confused with any emotions of the heart. Things didn't work that way for him, and he was sure things wouldn't work that way for her either.

Her ex had damaged her emotionally on the institution of marriage, so what was the problem? Why couldn't two people who only wanted to enjoy off-the-chain sex do so without worrying about their hearts getting in the way?

It would be up to him to convince her that they could resume their no-strings-attached affair with no entanglements, and he intended to do just that.

"Mrs. Byers and Ms. Shaw, we're here to bring about an acceptable resolution to the case pending before Judge Lewis Braille. Hopefully, we'll reach an agreeable resolution so that we can avoid a costly court battle and—"

"Not unless that woman gives my wife her fair share of what is due to her."

Farrah frowned at Mr. Byers's outburst. She'd known the moment he'd walked into the room with his wife that he was bad news. For some reason, he thought he was calling the shots. He might very well do so in his marriage, but she had no intention of letting him take control of these proceedings.

"Mr. Byers, I need you to refrain from speaking out of turn. Doing so will not get us anywhere."

"Please calm down, Rudolph," Lori Byers whispered to her husband in a calm voice. "Please let Ms. Langley do her job so we won't have to go to court."

Other than a roll of her eyes, Kerrie Shaw didn't say anything, although it was evident she was angry at what Rudolph Byers had said.

When the parties had entered the room, Farrah's keen sense of observation had picked up on several points. Even with all this legal mess going on, it was plain to see that the two women had shared a very close friendship at one time, and if given the chance, without any outside interference, that friendship could be restored.

It was also quite obvious they still cared for each other. That was probably the reason Kerrie Shaw had refrained from speaking her mind a few moments ago when Mr. Byers had spoken out of line. Farrah figured she'd kept her mouth closed to spare Lori Byers's feelings. That meant during the time they'd been friends, Kerrie had had the role of protector, and Lori had been the one more vulnerable and easily swayed and misled.

Farrah glanced over at Rudolph and quickly decided that was exactly what was taking place now. Lori allowed the man she had fallen in love with to come between her and her friend. Their close relationship had started in high school and continued in college and through Lori's first marriage and birth of her two little girls. Lori had even named Kerrie as godmother for her two girls.

Both women were now thirty-four. Kerrie was engaged to be married and Lori's first husband had been killed in a car accident a few years ago. She had met Rudolph on the internet, which didn't say a whole lot to some, but definitely spoke volumes to Farrah. Not that all pickups from cyberspace were bad, but the one Farrah had landed a couple of years ago, Alvin Cornell, had made her want to toss him right back. He'd been such a jerk. She could only wonder if Alvin had an older brother by the name of Rudolph.

How two women who had been such good friends could let a man come between them was beyond Farrah. She couldn't imagine any man or woman coming in and destroying her and Natalie's friendship, which had been in existence since high school as well. After her breakup with Dustin, it had been Natalie who'd been there for her, to help her get through the worst time in her life. Natalie had known she would wallow in self-pity her first Christmas as a divorced woman and had flown into Charlotte from New Jersey to spend time with her so she wouldn't be alone, and to make her see there was life after divorce.

"Yes, let's continue," Farrah said in an authoritative voice, more so for Rudolph Byers's benefit than for the two women. "As I was saying, my goal is to resolve the complaint and conflict informally. I'm impartial. I don't know either of you, and have no ties, previous or present, to your company."

Farrah paused and then looked back and forth at the women. "My concern is not who is right. It doesn't matter to me. I'm here to work you through this, and in doing that you need to talk to me about why you think you were wronged and how we can resolve things and move forward. Are there any questions?"

"No," both women said simultaneously.

Farrah noted Rudolph had clenched down on his lips to keep from answering, but the glare he gave her let her know he wanted to say something. Probably something he had no business saying.

"I hope we can work things out," Lori said softly. "I don't want anger between me and Kerrie."

"Who cares if there's anger between the two of you?" Rudolph butted in to say, evidently not able to keep quiet any longer. "I won't let her sell that company without giving you every penny you deserve."

Farrah drew in a deep breath and shifted her gaze to Kerrie. She could tell it was taking all Kerrie's control to not lash out against Rudolph, and she knew why Kerrie was remaining silent. It was her way of protecting Lori's feelings. These two women still cared for each other, and if Rudolph dropped off the face of the earth, Farrah had a feeling there would be no need for her services here today.

But Rudolph was alive and well and sitting across from her being a total jerk. Was greed the only factor motivating him? Farrah thought. Little did he know Farrah would be successful with this case because, whether they realized it or not, the two women's friendship had always been solid as a rock. Now it was time for Farrah to remind them of that.

"So tell me, Ms. Byers. When did your friendship with Ms. Shaw begin?" Though the woman seemed surprised, Farrah knew why she'd asked the question. She intended to make them recall why they'd become friends in the first place, in hopes they'd realize their relationship was too important to give up.

Lori glanced over at Kerrie and smiled as if remembering. "It was my first year of high school. I was thirteen and the new kid in town since my parents had moved to the city over the summer. Kerrie lived on my block and invited me to walk home with her. We became best friends immediately, and—"

"Why are we rehashing all of that stuff?" Rudolph said in a snarl. "We need to be discussing the money and—"

"Rudolph, if you're not happy with the way things are going here, you can leave!" Lori spoke up and said to her husband. It was apparent the man was surprised by his wife's sharp statement, and like a spoiled child, he pushed his chair back and stormed from the room, slamming the door behind him.

Farrah waited a beat to see if Lori would run after him. Instead, the woman seemed to remain calm, and then after a few moments she continued the story of how she and Kerrie had met.

Farrah fought to hide her smile. Now she felt they would finally get somewhere.

Xavier glanced at his watch. It was close to three in the afternoon, and he hadn't received a response yet from the text message he'd sent to Farrah earlier inviting her to a Broadway play tonight. He had decided against calling her since he hadn't known the hours she would be tied up with the case she was mediating.

When his cell phone rang, he quickly picked it up and smiled when he saw the caller was Farrah. "Yes?"

"Xavier, it's Farrah. Sorry I didn't have time to text you back earlier, but I was in mediation sessions all day."

"How did it go?"

"Rather well, actually. At least it did once the husband left. He was determined to cause problems. I spent most of the day reminding the two women why they became friends in the first place. I think another session will resolve things. That is if the wife doesn't go home and let her husband's manipulations undo all we've achieved today. He seems to have a lot of influence on her."

Xavier nodded. "Are you still at work?"

"No, I just got back to the hotel and am about to take a long, leisurely bubble bath. I'm running the water as hot as I can stand it to unfreeze my bones. It's still extremely cold outside."

Xavier paused a moment and then asked, "Have you given any thought to joining me tonight for a Broadway play? The one I thought you'd enjoy is *Hair*. And I promise to keep you warm again if you do venture out."

That's what I'm afraid of, Farrah thought, sitting on the edge of her bed. The only reason she hadn't swooned each and every time she'd thought of the kiss they'd shared in the car last night was because it had taken all of her time and energy getting Kerrie and Lori to stroll back down memory lane.

"Umm, I've always wanted to see *Hair*," she said softly.

"Here's your chance."

Yes, here was her chance. Should she take it or should she let the opportunity drift in the wind because she didn't trust herself around one particular man? Would he try kissing her again? She drew in a deep breath knowing he would and knowing she would be disappointed if he didn't.

She had gone to bed last night with that hot and sizzling kiss on her mind and too many warm, touchy-feely emotions stirring in her heart. And she knew why. During the year she and Xavier had been bed partners, he'd had a way of making her feel special and had taken whatever time was needed to bring her as much pleasure as any one woman could possibly handle. He had been more attentive to her in that one year than Dustin had been during the four years of their marriage. She had missed Xavier's attentiveness, his presence, his lovemaking and every single thing about him.

Now he was back, not in her life on a routine basis but just for the period of time she would be here in New York. When they returned to Charlotte, things would go back to normal, with him having his life and her having hers. Their paths would rarely cross, and on those occasions when they might run into each other, she was satisfied they'd know they could never become lovers again.

Sharing a kiss wasn't so bad, and the way he'd given attention to her breasts wasn't a sin and a shame either. But she couldn't share a bed with him. That would be her ultimate downfall. If he ever went inside her body again she would be tempted to never, ever let him out. She could possibly get hooked back on what it had taken six months to wean herself from.

Could she handle his presence, his closeness and his heat without temptation pushing her on her back with him on top of her? She nibbled on her bottom lip while thinking, yes, she would handle it, even if it almost killed her. All she would have to do was close her eyes and see Dustin's face to remember why such a thing was necessary.

"Farrah?"

She drew in a deep breath. "Yes, I'd love to go see *Hair* with you. What time does the show begin?"

"Eight. I'll be there to pick you up around seven if that's okay with you."

"That's fine. I'll be waiting for you in the lobby."

She hung up the phone knowing she needed to build up her resolve that no matter what, she would not be sharing a bed with Xavier while she was in New York.

Chapter 6

"Circle around the block a few times, Jules. I should be back out in a few minutes."

"Yes, Mr. Kane."

Xavier tightened the coat around him as he made his way toward the hotel's entrance. He was early, intentionally so, and that meant Farrah would not be in the lobby waiting on him, ready to go. He would let her know he'd arrived and ask if he could come up to her hotel room.

He was a man who usually didn't like playing games; however, under these circumstances, he wasn't averse to having a game plan. He couldn't help but smile when he thought of all the things Cameron had done to win Vanessa over. For Xavier, it wasn't that kind of party, definitely not one that serious. All he wanted was his bed partner back, not a woman to make his wife. So he wouldn't go to the extremes as Cam had done.

However, he knew the key to winning a woman over was to discover her weakness and use it against her. He had no problem doing that if it meant getting his libido back on track. He needed to use the same tactic Farrah had mentioned she'd used on the two women with whom she was holding mediation sessions. He would force Farrah to remember what they once had and why it was way too good to give up.

He glanced around the lobby before pulling out his cell phone. He swiped his finger across Farrah's name that was already programmed in his iPhone. She picked up immediately. "Yes?"

"I arrived a little early. If you're not ready I can come up and wait."

"No need. I'm ready."

He was surprised. "You are?"

"Yes," she said, and he could swear he heard a smile in her voice. "For some reason I figured you might be early."

He lifted a brow. "Did you?"

"Yes."

He didn't like the sound of that. Was she on to him and his game plan? Hell, he hoped not. "Well, I'm here."

"And I'll be right down, Xavier."

She clicked off the phone, and Xavier was about to return the phone to his pocket when it rang. He hoped it was Farrah saying she'd changed her mind, and he could come up to her room anyway. Instead, it was York.

"Yes, Y?"

"What are you doing tonight? How about coming over for a beer and to shoot some pool?"

York, a former officer for the NYPD who now owned his own security firm in Queens, loved to play pool and was pretty damn good at it. There was a time he used to participate in tournaments around the country.

"Sorry, I have a date."

He could hear York's chuckle. "Hell, you don't go out on dates, X. All you do is make booty calls. That's been your M.O. for years."

Xavier frowned. Had it? Come to think of it, yes, it had been. After Dionne, he'd made sure no other woman got close to his heart, although they'd been more than welcome to share a bed with him, preferably theirs. What he would do was select a woman, get to know her well enough to suit him and then begin showing up at her place with a bottle of wine determined to get just one thing. He'd operated that way with every woman he'd slept with.

Including Farrah.

Why did the thought of grouping Farrah with all his other bed partners leave a bad taste in his mouth? Probably for the same reason he'd stayed with her longer than the others. For him, eleven months was a long time to sleep with the same woman. Hell, normally something like that could get downright boring. But there hadn't been a damn boring thing about Farrah. She had made her bed one of the most exciting places to be. But, like the others, he'd never invited her over to his place to share his bed. Umm, he would have to remedy that one day.

"So, who is she, X?"

He couldn't very well say she wasn't someone York knew since Xavier had introduced Farrah to all five of his godbrothers at Donovan and Natalie's wedding in June. But what he could do was be evasive as hell, which wouldn't be the first time. "Why do you want to know? And aren't you supposed to be checking out Ellie's friend Darcy?"

He smiled as he could actually hear York growling through the cell phone. "Hell, don't mess with me like that, X. The woman and I don't get along. I'm convinced she hates my guts."

Xavier laughed. Bad blood had developed between the two when, during Darcy's first week of moving to New York, she'd encountered a burglar who'd broken into her home while she slept. By the time the police had arrived, Darcy Owens had already administered her own brand of punishment to the unsuspecting criminal, who hadn't known she had a black belt in karate.

Ellie had gotten York out of bed to go across town to check on her friend. When he'd gotten there and discovered what had happened, he'd raked Darcy over the coals for placing her life in danger instead of letting the NYPD handle it. Darcy evidently hadn't appreciated York's attitude, and the two hadn't been exactly bosom buddies since. Frankly, Xavier had a feeling York liked Darcy more than he was letting on.

"You still haven't told me who's your date, X."

At that moment the bell over the elevator sounded, the door opened and Farrah waked out. Xavier smiled. *Saved by the bell.* "And I won't. Goodbye, Y."

He quickly disconnected the call and stuffed the phone in his coat pocket. His smile widened when Farrah came to a stop in front of him. She was wearing her full-length coat again, but he couldn't wait to see the outfit she had on underneath it. "Ready?"

She smiled up at him. "Yes, I'm ready."

Xavier doubted very seriously that Farrah Langley was ready for what he had in store for her tonight.

"The play was wonderful, Xavier. Thanks for taking me," Farrah said, glancing across the length of the rear car seat. She really hadn't been surprised when he'd swept her off her feet again to put her in the car at the hotel, and again when they'd arrived and left the theater. But she was surprised he had kept distance between them in the car now.

Although he'd ordered the privacy shield drawn and the lights dimmed, things were a lot different tonight than they had been last night when she'd practically sat in his lap during the car ride back to the hotel, and he'd kissed her so fervently her panties got wet.

"I thought so, too," he agreed. "And I'm glad you enjoyed it."

She glanced out the window and saw they were

headed in the opposite direction from her hotel. "Where are we going?"

"I thought I'd take you for a ride across the river on a ferry boat."

"A ferry boat? In this weather?"

He chuckled. "It's a private barge and we won't have to get out of the car. I thought you'd like seeing the Statue of Liberty up close."

"You were able to arrange something like that tonight? At this hour?"

"Yes, as much as security would allow, which is understandable."

She nodded, knowing it was. She looked out the window and saw they were at the New York harbor. Several huge cruise ships were docked, and glass lanterns that were hanging from light fixtures brightened up the entire area.

"Everything is ready, Mr. Kane. Should we proceed?" the driver asked over the intercom.

"Yes, Jules, and you can darken the lights back here."

On cue, the lights in the panel of both doors went out, drenching the rear of the car in total blackness. The only illumination came from the light reflecting off the tall buildings of the Manhattan skyline.

Farrah knew the exact moment the car drove onto the huge barge, and moments later she heard the sound of the car door opening and closing. She glanced questioningly over at Xavier.

"Jules is leaving," he said. "He's joining the captain of the barge in the wheelhouse. They're old friends."

"Oh." She knew that meant that she and Xavier would be in the car alone.

Moments later she could actually feel the swish and sway of the water beneath them when the barge began moving. She had ridden a ferry once before while visiting a friend in Florida. It had been a passenger ferry, and it had been during daylight hours. However, this ferry ride provided a beautiful view of New York City at night.

She glanced over at Xavier. He was still sitting across from her and was looking at her. Although the lights reflected off his features, she couldn't see his entire face. However, knowing his eyes were on her was enough to send a luscious shiver up her spine.

Why did he have to be so mind-bogglingly handsome? Why did being here with him and sharing this space with him remind her of other times she'd shared more than space with him? She couldn't help but recall when she had shared her body, given it to him whenever and however he'd wanted it.

She decided the best thing to do was strike up a conversation to ease the heated tension flowing between them, although she doubted it would do a single thing to douse the hot-blooded desire flowing through her veins.

"We won't be running into the passenger ferry that runs twenty-four hours a day, will we?" she asked.

"No, we're taking a different route so we're safe."

She wondered just how safe she was alone with him in the darkened backseat of a car while rolling down the Hudson. There was the scent of a predatory male circulating in the air, but she was determined to stay in her corner. If anyone made the first move it would be him…although he didn't seem in a rush to do so.

Silence hovered between them for a few moments, and then he asked, "Would you like some wine, Farrah?"

She lifted a brow. "You have wine in here?"

"Yes."

He proceeded to press a button, and a compartment opened that transformed into a minibar.

"Wow, I'm impressed," she said.

He chuckled. "Are you?"

"Yes."

He uncorked the wine bottle and poured two glasses. He then leaned over and handed one to her. "Umm, you smell good," he said in a deep, throaty voice.

They were passing beneath a brightly lit building that illuminated his features. Heated lust was definitely shining in the dark depths of his eyes.

"Thanks. I think."

He smiled. "You aren't sure?"

She took a sip of her wine, liking how it tasted on her tongue. She looked at her wine in the glass and then at him. "Yes, I'm sure. I think you smell good, too. I guess our noses are in rare form tonight."

"That's not the only thing. Slide over here for a moment."

Farrah met his gaze and decided she was either a

glutton for punishment or eager for pleasure. Ignoring the voice inside her head advising her to stay put, she slid over the warm leather seat toward him. What she'd told him earlier was the truth. He smelled good. Good enough to lick all over.

When she was basically plastered to his side, he stretched his arm across the back of the seat. "Now," he said when she was snuggled close to him, "this is where you belong."

"Is it?"

"Yes."

She would have thought such a statement—a bold proclamation made by him or any man about where she belonged—was out of order and deserved a blistering retort, but she didn't have time to do so when he eased the glass from her hand and placed it in the holder next to his seat.

Then he turned toward her. "You have on too many clothes," he whispered in a deep, husky voice.

"Mainly to stay warm I get cold easily," was her response.

"I promised to keep you warm, didn't I?"

"Yes, but that was last night."

He began unbuttoning her coat. "That promise stands whenever we're together."

Farrah drew in a deep breath as she studied his face. His gaze was focused on every button he was opening as if what he was doing was a very important task. She knew she should probably tell him that when it came to promises from men, she found they didn't hold water, so he didn't have to waste his time making one that he expected her to believe. But for some reason she couldn't say it. Not when he had kept her warm last night. And not when he was taking his time now, handling her like she was a piece of fine china. He was opening each button slowly, with painstaking deliberateness, as if he was about to expose something beneath her coat other than the short blue dress she was wearing.

The dress might be short, true enough, but her black leather boots were long, stopping at her knees. Did he intend to remove them as well? Would she let him? Before she could think further on that question, he whispered, "Now scoot up a bit so I can work your arms out of the sleeves."

Like a dutiful child, she did what she was told. When she leaned forward, she placed her hand on his thigh and almost snatched it back when she felt his hard erection. Her eyes flew to his face and there was nothing apologetic about the look staring back at her. Instead it was a look that almost made her regret they were no longer bed partners.

And she didn't want to have any regrets. Although she'd found it extremely difficult to forget him and get beyond everything they'd shared, she was convinced she had done the right thing when she'd made up in her mind not to fall back in bed with him.

Fate, it seemed, was working against her now. It was as if some fragment of her brain was trying to convince her that getting back with him would be a fantasy come true and that her sex-deprived body would thank her for the chance to get laid again. But a part of her, the part that had endured pain of the worst kind at the hands of a man she'd once loved, was holding back, keeping that guardrail around her heart firmly in place. She doubted that even Xavier could knock it down.

She knew she should remove her hand from his thigh, but the feel of his erection beneath her palm was doing something to her, reminding her how it had been a vital part of her life at one time. And how it had given her so much pleasure.

She felt his erection begin to throb beneath her fingertips, a slow, steady pulsating thump that was causing her hand to tremble while causing certain parts of her body to vibrate. She was so in tune to this part of him and remembered well how once it was inside of her, it could stroke her into a frenzy of the sweetest kind. She felt the inner muscles of her feminine core clench just thinking about it.

Farrah glanced up and met his gaze when he pushed the coat off her shoulders. There was a look in his eyes that sent a delicious warmth through her body. She couldn't help wondering how she had endured a half year without this. Without him.

When her coat was off, he tossed it to the other side of the backseat and his gaze slid down the length of her outfit, which wasn't much. What little it was seemed to have his attention.

"I like blue," he said, running his fingers along the hem of her dress.

"Do you?"

"Yes. It's my favorite color. And these boots look good on you."

She smiled. "Thanks."

"So tell me," he said, easing closer to her after removing his own coat and lowering his head to whisper huskily in her ear. "What does a man like me have to do to get you out of a dress like this?"

She grinned and looked at him. "Umm, I don't know, Mr. Kane. You've always seemed to be a very innovative kind of guy. What do you have in mind?"

She couldn't help but take note that her hand was still on his thigh, still in contact with his throbbing erection. For some reason she couldn't let go just yet.

"What I have in mind is stripping you out of every stitch of clothing you have on. Here and now. What do you think about that?"

She couldn't help but chuckle. "Umm, not sure that's a good idea."

"But you would consider it?"

She smiled upon seeing the challenging glean in his eyes. "Let's just say I don't have a problem with you trying to convince me that I should consider it."

He didn't say anything for a minute, as if giving her words some thought. "I hope you know I can be very convincing when I want to be."

"I'm very much aware of that."

She knew Xavier well enough to understand her words were like a carrot dangling in his face. A carrot he intended to devour. This was the most fun she'd had lately. The summer months had been a complete bore to her and autumn hadn't been much better. When Natalie and Donovan had returned from their honeymoon, the amorous newlyweds hadn't socialized a lot, preferring to stay inside behind closed doors, probably burning the sheets. So with no lover to sleep with, no best friend to talk to, Farrah had had a lot of free time on her hands and had wondered if she'd done the right thing in breaking things off with Xavier.

But then, all it had taken was running into Dustin, his wife and daughter at the mall one Sunday evening in mid-October to recall why it had been the only thing she could do in order to protect herself and not get hurt by any man again.

"So what do you think about the view?"

She looked past Xavier to glance out the window. It was hard to believe they were in a car, riding down the Hudson on a barge. If he had deliberately set out to impress her, he had achieved that goal. "The view is beautiful. You definitely know how to wow a girl. I'm impressed."

"Are you?"

"Yes."

"Enough to let me take this dress off you?"

She shook her head smiling. "You won't give up, will you?"

"Not until I have you naked."

There was a determination in his tone that made shivers run up and down her spine. Heat began spreading through her stomach, and she felt a tingling sensation take life between her legs. She wondered if he had any idea just what was happening to her, how much she was fighting the temptation of giving him everything he was asking for. And then some.

She looked past him out the window again. Only Xavier would go to this trouble to impress a woman. And it was working.

Farrah glanced back at him, and the look he was giving her sent a burst of desire exploding through her. She found herself leaning toward him and his masculine mouth that was so sexy it should be declared illegal.

"And once you have me naked, what's next?"

The erection beneath her hand seemed to get larger. "Then I plan to taste you all over."

With his words, blatant and hot, her thighs seem to automatically spread apart, and she couldn't help but remember how it felt to have his tongue between them, licking her with hungry strokes to sweet oblivion, fueling not one orgasm but several.

"So what do you think of that, Farrah?"

She swallowed, not wanting to think at all. Her body was pushing her to feel instead. Making her crave things she was better off not having, but making those damn hot memories invade her mind anyway. They were just too delicious to ignore.

She met his gaze, felt the heat emanating from the dark depths. And it was heat that was generating a slow yet intense sizzle within her. "Why are you doing this to me, Xavier?"

Without responding, his gaze seemed to say it all. The heat from his eyes nearly burned off her remaining

clothes. Lust flowed up her spine as a fierce degree of
need filled her all over. He continued to look at her,
saying nothing, yet saying everything.

"I think you know the answer to that, Farrah," he
finally said in a deep, throaty voice. "But in case there's
a possibility that you don't, the reason is simple. I never
got over you. Our split was your idea, not mine."

She lifted a brow. "But you didn't disagree."

"Because I knew it was what you wanted."

"And now?"

"And now I plan to convince you that decision was
a mistake."

She saw the determination in his gaze. "What if I
said you can't do that?"

A smile touched his lips. "Then I would say I intend
to die trying. I want you back, Farrah."

Farrah knew he was dead serious. She forced herself
to breathe in before asking, "And you think wanting me
back is simple?"

A smile touched the corners of his lips. "Yes, wanting
you back is simple, but *getting* you back will be the
hard part." He paused and then said, "And speaking of
hard..."

She held his gaze as the throb beneath her hand increased, and she could feel his erection grow and harden
even more. "Yes, what about it?" she asked, not even
trying to ignore the burning sensation in the pit of her
stomach.

He placed his hand over hers. "For the past six
months, I've been working hard, Farrah, harder than

I wanted to. But I had to do it as a way to try to forget you. And I failed at doing that."

She nibbled on her bottom lip, surprised that Xavier would admit something like that. It would have been just as easy, less messy and a whole lot simpler for her to think he had moved on without any passing thoughts of her and what they'd shared. But to know he had thought of her, had worked doubly hard to forget her, yet failed, made something inside her swell to gigantic proportions, and that wasn't good.

"And can you honestly say you didn't think of me, Farrah?" he then asked.

That question was a no-brainer. Of course she had thought about him. Constantly. Every day. In the middle of the night. When she woke up in the morning. And she'd definitely thought of him during those times her body went through a physical meltdown when it needed the kind of toss between the sheets only he could give her.

She could admit such a thing now, while sitting here with him alone, in the privacy of a car where they had a spacious backseat. She had no qualms saying it because regardless of all of that, she believed she had done the right thing in ending their affair.

And she would be doing the right thing in not letting him talk her into starting things back up again between them.

"Yes, I thought about you, Xavier, but I *had* to end things between us for all the right reasons," she said quietly.

"And what are these right reasons?"

Now that would be a little harder to explain. How could she eloquently break it down so he would understand that she had to end things to keep her sanity? That with him, for the first time since breaking up with Dustin, she had begun to feel things, want things and need things that she knew could only cause her heartbreak.

How could she explain to him that every time he showed up at her place, looked at her, touched her, tasted her and made love to her until she screamed her throat raw, her heart swelled? That was the part she wouldn't try explaining since there were some things about a woman's emotions that a man didn't need to know or understand.

She had gotten a lot smarter since her Dustin days, but because of Xavier, the part of her heart that had hardened had begun to soften each time she saw him, each time he held her in his arms and kissed her with that sinful tongue of his.

"Tell me, Farrah."

Gathering her control, she removed her hand from his thigh and shifted in her seat, placing her hand into her own lap. For this she needed some semblance of detachment and distance…as much as she could get. But she was well aware that no matter how much space she put between them, she would still be able to feel his heat, the same heat that could succeed in melting the ice encasing her heart. But he needed to hear what she had to say.

"You know my history with Dustin."

He nodded. "Yes."

She drew in a deep breath. Discussing her ex-husband had never been on the agenda. But one night when Xavier had come over she'd been caught in one of her melancholy moods. She had run into Dustin earlier that day in a department store, and he'd tried of all things to flirt with her. The bastard who'd left her for another woman had actually tried coming on to her, tried to entice her to leave the department store and have an evening of sex with him in a hotel across the street. He'd said his wife would never find out and that they would be doing it for old times' sake.

Dustin had claimed his problem with her had never been in the bedroom, but said her constant travels for her job were to blame for the loneliness that had forced him to seek out other women. He had actually tried to make her feel responsible for his adulterous behavior.

Any other woman probably would have fallen for his pitiful spiel, but she had stopped being Dustin's fool the day he'd asked her for a divorce. She doubted she would ever forgive him for the hurt and humiliation that he'd caused her.

"I don't ever want to go through anything like that again," she heard herself saying.

Xavier's mouth drew in a tight line. "I can respect that, but what does that have to do with me?"

"A good question," she murmured softly to herself. He probably didn't see the connection because, for him, there truly wasn't one. Nothing about his purpose in seeking her out then and now had changed. He was footloose and fancy-free and intended to stay that way. He shied away from serious relationships, preferring to make his booty calls whenever, wherever and to whomever he desired with no strings attached. He was a man, and he could go through that type of program without any emotional attachments. She'd tried the same but found that she just couldn't do it. Especially with Xavier.

"What it has to do with you, Xavier, is that I felt the time had come for me to take a step back from our little affair. Eleven months was way too long for me. We were getting too complacent."

She wanted to express herself in a way where she didn't come off sounding like a needy woman. God knows she didn't want that. Since her divorce she had tried not to depend on anyone—especially a man—for her happiness. But with Xavier she had found herself slipping.

When he didn't say anything, she continued. "That first night you came over we agreed to have a no-strings-attached affair, and I felt we had run our course."

He nodded. "Have there been any men since me, Farrah?"

His question surprised her. It would be so easy to say it wasn't any of his business and let him assume there had been others. After all, he'd probably slept with other women since her. Something kept the lie from forming on her lips, however. Instead she said, "No, I've been too busy." That really wasn't a total lie.

"And I haven't had another woman since you," he said in a throaty tone.

His words shocked her; in fact, they left her speechless. He hadn't had another woman since her? Xavier, the man with a sex drive that never quit? At that moment she couldn't explain the satisfied pleasure she felt blooming inside of her. Why had he denied himself?

"Seems like we have the same problem, Farrah."

She pulled herself back into the conversation, trying to tread lightly while all kinds of wicked thoughts flowed through her. "And what problem is that?"

He reached out and rubbed his thumb over her bottom lip. "We need to get unleashed. You need a man to make love to you like I need to make love to a woman. Bad. But I don't need to make love to any woman, Farrah. I need to make love to you. I so miss hearing you scream."

More sensations washed over her, wetting her panties, causing every nerve ending in her body to respond to the sensuality in his voice and the heat in his words. She had definitely missed him making her scream as well.

"So you think we need to get unleashed, huh?" she asked in a low tone, while her heartbeat throbbed in her chest.

"Yes, but due to schedule restraints, I'll just have time to prime you for now."

Oh, she knew all about his priming methods and just what setting up for that stage of seduction could do to her. They'd never made out in a car before, and just the thought of doing so was downright naughty. But she felt like being naughty tonight. She had been a good girl for a long time and felt the need to sexually unwind. But more than anything, she wanted to scream. She shuddered at the thought of all he was offering her on a sensual platter.

"So what do you think about that plan, Farrah?"

At the moment she didn't want to think. She didn't want to talk.

Instead she leaned close to him, deciding she needed to respond to him this way. She intended to start off by initiating a game they'd often played when he'd come over to her place. She leaned close and offered him the tip of her tongue. Just as expected, he swooped down quickly and all but sucked her tongue into his mouth.

She moaned deep in her throat as familiar sensations burned in her soul. The strength of the passion he was evoking within her was the same as it had been from the first. Xavier could make a woman want things she was better off not having.

As she proceeded to melt under the force of his kiss, she knew that somehow she would take whatever he was offering for now and then find the strength to walk away and not look back when their time together in New York ended.

Chapter 7

Xavier knew the moment Farrah surrendered.

He was practically on his back with her draped all over him while she took his mouth with a hunger that he was more than willing to reciprocate.

God, he wanted her with a vengeance. It wouldn't take much to zip down his pants, pull out his shaft and ease right into her. She had made it easy to do so with the way her thighs were positioned over his. He remembered—not that he could ever forget—that she preferred wearing skimpy panties, thongs or the barely-there kind. He'd bet nothing had changed in that area. Hell, he was hoping as much.

She pulled back, breaking off the kiss, and he drew in a deep breath as he gazed up into her face. She was the spitting image of a woman unleashed, a woman who knew what she wanted and planned on getting it. A woman who had gone long enough without a lover. He intended to change that. Right here. Right now.

He drew in a deep breath and swallowed hard when, not bothering to unbuckle his belt, she jerked his shirt from the waistband of his pants before proceeding to ease down his zipper. He didn't have to ask what she was about to do; he just hoped he would be able to survive the experience.

When she smiled at him while licking her lips, his heart began beating frantically in his chest. She had effectively turned the tables on him. He was supposed to be seducing her and not the other way around. What about that control he was known for? Hell, it was slipping, and there was nothing he could do about it now. At the moment he couldn't deny her anything, especially the piece of him she obviously wanted.

And when he felt her warm fingers probing inside his pants, anticipation sizzled up his spine, and it took all he could do not to moan out loud. After she pulled his erection free, he watched through lowered lashes as she studied his shaft, as if she was savoring the thought of tasting him and trying to decide the best way to go about it.

Then her fingers started moving as she began to stroke it, palmed him in her hand, pumped him with her fingers. His body shuddered, and heat surged through him, especially in his groin.

She glanced up at him and smiled as his belly clenched with the look he saw in her eyes. The fire he saw there not only sharpened his senses but had his erection expanding right in her hands.

"I'm about to show you, Xavier Kane, that you're not the only one who knows about priming. And don't you dare think about pulling my mouth away until I'm ready to let go."

She didn't give him a chance to think, let alone respond, when her mouth lowered and took him in.

"Heaven help me." He murmured the words in a heated rush of breath, closed his eyes and released a deep, guttural groan.

Her mouth seemed to expand to encompass his erection all the way from the head to the root, and when she began using her tongue in full earnest, pleasure—which he hadn't felt in six months—shot through every part of his body.

With slow thoroughness, she took her time torturing him, letting him see that she was the one in control of this, and when her mouth deliberately began exerting pressure to the head of his erection, he clenched his jaw, and his body rumbled into one hell of an explosion.

When he gripped the side of her head and tried pulling her away, she planted her teeth on him with enough pressure to remind him of her earlier order. She was in control.

When his turn came, she was going to be sorry, he thought as his jaw clenched tight and the climax shook him. He wondered if he was still breathing. Surely he had died, gotten buried and gone to heaven.

Then before he could recover from that first explosion, another one hit; this one even stronger, and he felt all kinds of sensations tear up the length of his body and back.

"Farrah!"

If he thought she was ready to let go, then evidently he was out of his mind. The latter was true anyway. He was definitely out of his mind with all the scintillating excitement thrown in the mix. And he saw that she was determined not to release him until the last shudder eased from his body.

It was then that he slowly forced open his eyes and stared at her. It took every ounce of energy he possessed to reach out his hand to caress her cheek. He wasn't sure if he was imagining things or not, but her entire face took on an ethereal beauty that was more vibrant, more soul-touchingly exquisite than ever before.

And when she tilted her lips in a smile, he dragged in a staggering breath and felt his body getting hard all over again as desire once again enflamed him, filled him to capacity. But something else happened at that moment, too. He wasn't sure just what it was, since it was something he couldn't put a name to at that moment. But he was convinced it was something he'd never felt before, and he suddenly felt totally consumed by it.

"So what do you think, Xavier?"

Instead of answering, he moved quickly, and, ignoring her shriek of surprise, he eased her back and loomed over her. He caught her chin in his hand as his mouth came down on hers, effectively absorbing whatever words she was about to say. He intended to show her just what he thought.

* * *

His kiss tried taking control of her mouth, but Farrah refused to let it. She enjoyed sharing his heat, participating in such a sensual duel as their tongues tangled. Electricity flowed through her body.

And she still wanted more.

She intended to get it, and it seemed he was just as determined to give it to her. Okay, she could handle this, she thought. Then she wasn't all that sure when she felt his hands under her dress. When he finally released her mouth, she was breathless, left in a state of pure enthrallment. Totally awestruck. Mesmerized.

"You should never have pushed me over the edge, Farrah."

She met his gaze. Had she actually done that?

"You do know what that means, don't you?"

She nodded. Yes, she knew exactly what that meant. She'd had him in her mouth, and now he intended to have her in his. He didn't waste time pushing her dress up and out of his way before pulling her barely-there panties down past her thighs.

"Xavier, don't we need to talk about this?"

"No."

And that was the last word he said before lifting her hips with his hand and lowering his head between her legs. The moment the tip of his tongue eased between her feminine folds, she cried out, closed her eyes and reached out to grab hold of his shoulders.

How had she gone without this for so long? How had she survived without the feel of his mouth on her, in her, his tongue lapping her up before delving deeper and deeper. He was feasting on her, pushing her legs apart to treat himself to more of her.

A soft moan flowed from her lips. Then another. Pleasure began rolling over her in melodious waves, pushing her over the edge while at the same time taking her under. No inner part of her was left untouched. If his tongue could reach it, it was stroked. Mercilessly so.

Farrah suddenly cried out when she couldn't take any more, and rapture struck every inch of her body. He continued to devour her, as she quivered from an orgasm that would have topped the Richter scale. When he pulled back and captured her mouth, his tongue was still hot and hungry.

And she knew he wasn't through with her yet when she heard him tear open a condom package.

Then there it was. The head of his erection probing where his mouth had been. He lifted her hips up in his hands the moment he thrust into her. The surge of pleasure that ripped through her with this coming together made her scream. That only pushed him to go deeper, made his strokes stronger.

"Xavier!"

He lifted his head to stare down at her, and the primal look in his eyes almost made her lose her breath while at the same time it triggered another explosion within her. She had wanted to be naughty, but he was making her crazy.

And then he bucked, thrust harder, went deeper and her boot-clad legs tightened around him, greedy for everything he wanted to give and ready to take it. She didn't have long to wait for his release. Hot molten liquid shot everywhere inside of her, lubricating her inner walls with the very essence of him.

"Farrah!"

He had thrown his head back and her name came out as a deep growl from his throat, and he then lowered his head to take her mouth, to feed greedily off of it, as his body continued to thrust insatiably inside of her. Harder.

She screamed again as spasms shook her. When had making love to any man been this good? And she knew at that moment it could only be this way with Xavier.

He broke off the kiss, and his forehead came to rest against hers when their bodies slowed. She breathed in a deep, trembling breath as she stared up at him.

"Satisfied?" he asked, staring down at her. His shirt was unbuttoned to his waist and he was still wearing his pants. She could just imagine how erotic things would have gotten if they'd been naked.

"Very," she said, smiling up at him and meaning every word. He was still inside of her. Still hard. The man had more staying power than anyone she knew.

"Good." He paused a minute then asked, "So what do *you* think, Farrah?" It took her a moment to follow him. He was deliberately countering the question she'd asked him earlier.

She released a deep breath. "I can't think at the moment. Ask me again later."

He chuckled as he slowly eased out of her and

proceeded to pull her panties back up and pull her dress down. He then buttoned his shirt.

"I can just imagine what your driver is probably thinking, though," she said, sitting up.

Xavier chuckled. "Jules is probably grateful he got to spend time with his old Navy buddy. He's worked for me for a while and knows—"

"How you operate?"

He glanced over at her while tucking his shirt back inside his pants. For some reason, that statement bothered him. "And how do you think I operate, Farrah?"

She leaned back against the seat of the car and closed her eyes. "Ask me later. I told you, I can't think now. I just want to savor the moment."

And he thought he wouldn't mind savoring some more of her. Not understanding why he needed to do so, what exactly was driving him, he caught her off guard when he leaned over and kissed her with the same degree of passion he'd demonstrated earlier but with far less desperation. He wanted this to be slow pleasure that was meant to be savored, relished and enjoyed. And from the unhurried and leisurely way her tongue was mating with his, he knew that it was.

When he released her mouth, her head fell back against the seat cushions, and she stared at him as if she was incapable of saying anything. He couldn't help but smile, pleased he'd kissed any words from her lips for the time being.

"What was that for?" she finally was able to ask.

"Ask me later. I can't think now," he said rezipping his pants.

She laughed and playfully punched him in the arm. "Funny. You're a regular comedian who happens to be a damn good kisser."

"Earned brownie points, did I?"

"Yes, you most certainly did. I don't know many guys like you."

"I'm glad to hear it," he said, pulling his cell phone out of the pocket of his jacket and punching a lone number. "Jules, how far are we from port?" he asked, glancing out the window while working his arms into the sleeves of his jacket. He nodded and then said, "Good."

He clicked off the phone and replaced it in his jacket and glanced over at Farrah. "When we get back to your hotel, do I get invited up for a nightcap?"

"After what we did just now do you really think you need an invitation? Better yet, do you have the energy for more?"

He couldn't help but smile at that.

She frowned at him. "Forget I asked. Silly me. How could I forget your endless amount of energy? You know, this was the first time we did it some place other than my house," she said, reaching for her purse. He watched her pull out her makeup compact.

"First time for everything. I plan for us to start being adventurous," he said, working his tie back around his neck.

She clicked the compact closed and glanced over

at him. Surprise lit her eyes. "You do understand that nothing between us has changed."

Something fluttered in his chest. "What do you mean?" he asked.

She shrugged as if she assumed they were in one accord with what she was about to say. "Going back to our conversation earlier about restarting our affair… Spending time with you like this, here in New York, is wonderful, but when we return to Charlotte we won't be seeing each other again."

The hell we won't! He fought to keep the frown off his face while wondering just how she figured that. "I don't see why not. You've missed me. I've missed you. So there."

"Yes, which is the reason we're spending time together now. A holiday fling is just what we evidently need. It's the season to be jolly, and we can even act a little loony, out of character, even behave like sex addicts and all that good stuff. We're adults with needs. But when it's all said and done, eventually things have to get back to normal, and when they do, it will be life as we know it."

"And what kind of life is that?" he asked, trying to keep anger from burning the back of his throat.

"I can't speak for you, but mine will be one with no serious entanglements. I have too much baggage for any man to deal with."

Try me. He decided now was not the time to tell her that their entanglement was already as serious as it could get. He also decided not to break the news that he had all intentions of resuming what they had shared before. The only kind of life he planned on having was one with her in it.

He opened his mouth to speak but closed it when he heard them docking back at the port. A short time later the car door opened, and he knew Jules had returned. That gave him a chance to sit and ponder why he had this burning obsession with getting back with her. And he knew the reason had nothing to do with the off-the-chain sex they'd had tonight or all those other times before. It was way too deep for him to try and dissect at this moment. Especially when she thought she'd delivered the last word.

He fully understood why she intended to keep him at arm's length again once they returned to Charlotte. She'd been burned once and didn't intend for any man to light a match to her again. Well, he had news for her. He was not going to let her lump him in with that poor excuse for a husband any longer.

"You've gotten quiet on me, Xavier."

They were back on the road again. Bright lights were everywhere as the car headed back toward her hotel. "I was just thinking."

"About what?"

"What I need to do to convince you that we need to restart our affair on a long-term basis."

She shook her head. "Don't bother. I don't do long-term."

"You did me for one month shy of a year."

"I got carried away," she said simply. "*We* got carried

away. It was an abnormality for you as much as it was for me."

Yes, it had been, but he hadn't complained.

"And what about your status in the club?"

The question annoyed him. "Forget about the club."

"Why should I? And can you? You and your god-brothers are the ones who established it. What will they think?"

At the moment he didn't give a royal damn.

What had he been thinking when he'd conceived of the Bachelors in Demand Club, he wondered now. And at the time, his five godbrothers, for various reasons, had been more than happy to be a part of it.

"Xavier?"

He glanced over at her. "I'm still thinking."

She smiled. "Yes, you do that and pretty soon you'll see I'm right. What you're asking for is not what you really want. You just got caught up in the moment. You even admitted yourself that because of work you hadn't slept with another woman since me. The way I see it, you've been suffering from a bad case of horniness. Don't get your heads mixed up, Xavier. You used to be pretty good knowing one from the other."

He looked away out the window. She sounded like she assumed she had all the answers. Well, he had news for her. If she thought—

"And I think considering everything, we should forget about that nightcap."

At her interruption, he looked at her. "Are you saying you don't want me to spend the night with you?"

"I don't recall issuing you an invitation."

He frowned. "Are we into playing games now, Farrah?"

"No." She didn't say anything for a moment and then, "Look, Xavier, I'll spend every moment that I can with you while we're here in New York. I really want that. There's nothing wrong with enjoying the fun while it lasts."

There was a momentary pause, and then he asked, "But when we return to Charlotte, I can't call you or drop by like before?"

"I prefer that you didn't."

Did she really mean that, he asked himself. She was returning his stare with a straight face, and her tone of voice sounded serious enough. But still...

She was the same woman who'd come apart in his arms moments ago. The same woman who'd admitted to missing him, to trying to forget him these past six months.

He studied her features and saw the determined look in her eyes. However, he took a minute to look beyond that, and he could swear he saw something else. Was she really that scared to admit that possibly those eleven months they'd been together had meant more than just sex?

His eyebrows knit in a tight frown. This was getting pretty damn confusing. He should be in agreement with how she was thinking. She definitely expected him to be, but he just wasn't feeling it, and he needed a reality check to figure out why.

"Let's do dinner tomorrow night," he heard himself suggesting.

"That's fine, if I'm in town."

He lifted a brow. "Where will you be if not here?"

"Heading back to Charlotte if I wrap things up with my clients tomorrow. Either way I hope to be leaving by Friday."

A sense of dread felt like a sword twisting in his chest. Friday was two days away. "I want to spend time with you again before you leave, Farrah, and I agree tonight might not be a good time."

"I'll call you tomorrow, Xavier. That's the best I can do."

She was deliberately giving him little to work with, but she didn't know that Xavier worked best under pressure. He would take tonight to go home and regroup, plan a new strategy and decide just what he intended to do about Farrah Langley.

One thing was for certain. He had no intentions of letting her go. If she thought things were over between them, then she definitely had another thought coming.

Chapter 8

Farrah wrapped the huge towel around her as she stepped out of the shower. From where she stood in the bathroom she could see her bed, and if anyone would have told her she would be sleeping in it alone tonight, without Xavier, she would not have believed them.

There was no reason for him not to have spent the night...at least there hadn't been a reason until he began spouting all that nonsense about them continuing their affair once they returned to Charlotte. What could he have been thinking to even suggest such a thing?

As she slipped into her nightgown, she shook her head, totally confused. Tonight had been an adventure, definitely something new and different. She smiled, thinking she liked the idea of being naughty. She liked the idea of a holiday affair, too.

A casual relationship was all she was interested in. With Xavier, however, what had started out as a strictly no-strings affair had slipped into a hot and heavy routine, a full-blown sexual habit they couldn't kick. Not that they'd tried. The more he'd shown up on her doorstep, the more she'd wanted him to keep coming.

And that wasn't good.

He could argue with her on that point all day long, and she would not change her mind and relent. As far as she was concerned, they either agreed to indulge in a New York affair or nothing.

Then why, she thought a short while later when she slipped between the sheets of her lonely bed, was she thinking of him and all they'd done that night? What they'd shared for eleven months, and more importantly, what she'd gone without the past six months and what she would continue to go without?

If tonight had been a calculated move on his part to stir up memories, then she would be the first to say he'd succeeded. As she lay staring up at the ceiling, she couldn't get out of her mind just how he'd felt inside of her, killing her softly with every sensual stroke.

So many memories began swirling around in her head, making sleep impossible. At least for now. Instead, she couldn't help but recall the first time he'd shown up on her doorstep and how quickly and easily she'd tumbled with him into her bed. She'd opened the door, and he'd stood there, wearing a pair of jeans and a white shirt and looking as sexy as any man had a right to look. There had been something about him that had wowed her from the first time she'd seen him that night at the Racetrack Café. She'd heard about him and the bachelor club he was affiliated with, but until she'd seen him for herself, she hadn't known how any man could have that effect on a woman.

She'd known she had wanted him from the start, passionately so, and hadn't intended to let something like protocol stand in her way. She'd seen him as a way to have fun and forget about all the hurt Dustin had caused her. She'd wanted to know how it felt to have a no-strings-attached affair and not care one iota if she saw the man again. She'd wanted an affair that was as casual as it could get.

And that's what she'd gotten in the beginning. But then she'd noticed things beginning to change, even if he hadn't. Probably because those changes had been one-sided. There was no reason to assume that he'd begun thinking about her in the wee hours of the night and anticipating the next time they would hook up. Or find himself smiling in the middle of the day after thinking of something that happened between them the night before. And she was pretty confident that when she did open the door for him, he didn't feel that funny feeling in the pit of his stomach.

Those had been the warning signs, and she'd had no reason not to heed them and put in place any and every preventive measure that she could. Nothing seemed to work. The situation seemed to get worse. And she'd known the best thing to do was to break things off with him completely.

And now he wanted to jump-start things again and had done a pretty good job giving her a reason to do so. But she couldn't. Bottom line was that she was dealing with something he couldn't understand. It was only about sex for him, but for her she was taking every memory as seriously as it could get.

She moved to another position, not that she thought that would help. It would be a sleepless night. Even after the workout Xavier had given her tonight, her feminine core was achy, in need of some intimate attention, Xavier Kane style.

Give in to him, a voice inside her head whispered. *You're a big girl. You can handle another affair with Xavier. It would be up to you to make sure it's an affair that leads nowhere. And if it did, what's another little broken heart? What's the big deal?*

The big deal was there in his eyes each and every time he looked at her. It was there on his tongue every time he kissed her. It was embedded in the fingers that touched her.

After a few tosses and turns, she discovered she still couldn't get to sleep and decided she needed to talk to someone, and there was no other person she could share her woes with than her best friend.

She glanced over at the clock and cringed when she saw it was almost one o'clock. She didn't know what kind of hours Natalie was keeping now, but before she was married, Dr. Natalie Ford Steele, esteemed chemistry professor at Princeton University, used to be up at all hours of the night.

She grabbed her cell phone off the nightstand and punched in one number that automatically connected to Natalie. The phone was picked up on the first ring. "Hey, Farrah, what's going on?"

Farrah smiled, grateful to hear her friend's bubbly voice at a minute before one in the morning. "Evidently, you are. I take it you aren't sleep."

"Heavens, no. I just finished another chapter of this book I'm working on and was sitting here cuddled on the sofa enjoying a cup of hot chocolate."

She then remembered that Natalie was working on what would probably be another New York Times bestseller on global warming. "Where's Donovan?"

"Oh, he went to bed hours ago. I think the triplets wore him out. We kept them earlier while Cheyenne and Quade went shopping to play Santa. They are definitely three busy beavers. Donovan and I could barely keep up with them."

Farrah chuckled. "Are you two having second thoughts about having kids of your own now?"

"Never! I want Donovan's baby so bad."

Natalie's words made something twist in her heart when she remembered how she had wanted Dustin's baby, too. Instead of giving a child to her, he'd given one to someone else. That pain reminded her why she could never give her heart to another man.

"So what's up, Farrah?"

She swallowed. There was no reason to talk anything over with Natalie now. Not with the reminder she'd just gotten. The pain was still stabbing her chest. "Nothing."

"Um, I know you, girl. You would not have called me at one in the morning for nothing. Go on. Let it out. What's bothering you?"

Farrah nibbled on her bottom lip a minute before saying, "I ran into Xavier yesterday."

There was a pause on the other end, which Farrah understood. Natalie knew why she had broken things off with Xavier. "In that case, I'm sure cold New York is probably pretty hot by now."

Farrah threw her head back and laughed, especially when she remembered how hot things had gotten while riding across the Hudson in Xavier's private car. She then cleared her throat. "Hey, what can I say?"

"You can say the two of you have decided to get back together."

The smile on Farrah's face immediately became a frown. She'd known that Natalie liked Xavier. What was there not to like? Besides being good-looking as sin, he was also a downright nice person. She would attest to that. And of course he was one of Donovan's closest friends. But all of that had nothing to do with her heart.

"No, we're not getting back together, although he suggested such a thing. I told him I'd indulge in a holiday fling while we're here in New York. That was the best I could do."

Understandably there was another pause, which was

followed by a feminine snort. "I wish you would rethink that proposal, Farrah. Not all men are like Dustin."

Farrah changed positions in bed while she rolled her eyes. How many times had she heard that very thing—not only from Natalie, but from several others? "I don't want to try and weed the good from the bad. Casual affairs suit me just fine, but the one with Xavier was beginning to get too hot, heavy and addictive."

"That's not bad with the right guy, Farrah. Hey, let's run down a few things."

"A few things like what?"

"Why Xavier might be a keeper."

There was no doubt in Farrah's mind that he was a keeper. All she had to do was concentrate on the tingling between her legs to know just how much of a keeper he was. But he would be a keeper for some other woman, definitely not her. She frowned, wondering why the thought of that suddenly annoyed her.

Natalie began her checklist. "I don't have to ask if he's good in bed."

She couldn't help but laugh again. "No, please, don't bother."

"Okay, then. Is he someone you would want as a friend?"

A friend? Yes, she could see him being her friend once they put the bedroom behind them. But when she saw him, she didn't think of friendship, just sexual satisfaction. "Yes, he's someone I'd want as a friend."

"Okay, then. Do you consider yourself happy when you're with him?"

That was a no-brainer. Of course she was happy whenever she was with him. He could do things with his mouth, tongue and erection that could keep any woman delirious. "Definitely," she heard herself saying.

"Get your mind out of the bedroom, Langley, and provide responses on a purely plausible basis."

"Not sure I can do that with Xavier. Our relationship was one that started in the bedroom."

"That's not true. If anyone's relationship started in the bedroom, it was mine and Donovan's. Your relationship with Xavier started at Racetrack Café, Farrah. You were the one who was quick to carry it into the bedroom."

Farrah thought about Natalie's accusation and had to agree that she had been the one who'd instituted a sex-only relationship with Xavier from the first. Of course he had gone along with it. What man wouldn't have? She had known the moment she'd lit her gaze upon him that night that she'd wanted him.

"Sorry, but I've conditioned myself to only think one way when it comes to men. And please, please don't tell me again that all men aren't the same."

"Maybe if I keep saying it, one day you'll believe me."

"I believe that now, Nat, but like I said, I don't have the time to find out who's naughty and who's nice. I can't risk taking a chance and being wrong."

"I think deep down you want a man who's both naughty and nice and you have both with Xavier."

Farrah released a deep sigh. "What is this? Slapsome-sense-into-my-best-friend-where-Xavier-Kane-is-concerned Day?"

"I won't even try doing that. You'll have to see for yourself what a great guy he is."

"I hate to burst that romantic bubble floating around your heart, but all Xavier wants from me is sex, too. It's not that serious. Only problem with that is that I could fall in love with him, Nat, if I'm not careful and I can't let that happen. Thanks for listening." Not waiting for Natalie to reply, she quickly ended the call. "Love you. Bye."

Finding a more comfortable position in bed, she stared up at the ceiling again as she drew in a ragged breath. Sleep continued to elude her as one thought replayed in her head. A woman was entitled to make at least one mistake in her lifetime, but a smart woman wouldn't be a fool and make two.

Xavier slipped into his robe as he eased out of bed, unable to sleep. At this very moment he should have been in Farrah's bed making love to her again. When she'd ridden the elevator up to her room, he should have been on that elevator with her, kissing her every second of the ride.

Okay, so her refusal to jump-start their affair again had thrown him for a loop. He'd figured after tonight she would have seen the merit in them hooking back up. Evidently they weren't on the same page. Not even close.

Moving through the hallway, he walked down the

stairs to the kitchen. He had purchased this house on Long Island as investment property a few years ago and hadn't regretted doing so. He liked New York and whenever he came to town he much preferred staying here than in a hotel.

Grabbing a beer from the refrigerator, he slid onto a bar stool. The night was quiet, understandably so. Most sane people were in bed getting a good night's sleep. But not him. He was letting a woman tie him in knots.

He was in a bad way. Pretty messed up. Royally.

He took a huge gulp of his beer, acknowledging that he'd been delivered a setback. It wasn't the first time with a woman, but he'd never been this interested in one before. And to think that all she wanted was a holiday fling.

He took another swig of his beer while memories of their night together came tearing into him, and he couldn't help but recall when she'd gone down on him. And then later when his body had slid into hers, he'd felt as if he was someplace he could stay forever. Even stretched out as best she could on the car's backseat, she had used their limited space effectively and met him stroke for stroke. And as much as he wanted to chalk her up as a lost cause and move on with his life, he knew that he couldn't.

He knew it wasn't just about sex with Farrah, although that part of their relationship was always off the chart. But now when he took the time to think about it, it had always been more than just two bodies mating, at least in his book. She had a way of touching him everywhere and not just below the belt. From the first, he'd always felt in sync with her. Whenever she would smile, something inside of him would light up. And then there were those feelings of loneliness whenever he wasn't with her. For the past six months it had felt as if something was missing from his life. She was the only woman since Dionne who could fill him with emotions. Emotions he thought had died a hard death a long time ago.

He held his beer bottle to his lips, ready to take another healthy sip, when he was hit with a realization that had his heart pounding, his pulse racing and his esophagus tightening. This couldn't be happening to him. No way. But as he stared into space for a few seconds, he knew that it had already happened. He had fallen for Farrah and hard.

Damn.

What had happened to that strong resolve to guard his heart? What had happened to all those instilled and painful memories of what Dionne had done to him? He wasn't sure what had happened, but he knew, just as surely as he knew Diana Ross was once a Supreme, that he was in love with Farrah Langley.

He set his beer bottle down, thinking that definitely put a whole new spin on things. It hadn't been his intent to fall in love, but it had happened and now he planned to do something about it, which didn't include running in the other direction. No, he'd confront the opposition head on. This was his heart they were talking about.

He knew without being told that if she got wind of

his feelings, she would make things even more difficult. But he had news for her. Not only was he going to have his fling with her in the Big Apple, but it would continue right to Charlotte and eventually lead into marriage.

Marriage?

Yeah, marriage.

He smiled, thinking he liked the sound of that. He knew the hell she would probably give him, but he was up for the battle. All was fair in love and war, and he would do whatever it took to win her over and make her realize that regardless of what had happened in her past, he was the man for her.

It was a good thing Farrah wasn't there to see the sly smile that had formed around his lips. She wouldn't know what hit her until it was too late for her to do a damn thing about it.

Chapter 9

Farrah wasn't so sure how today's session with Kerrie Shaw and Lori Byers would pan out when Rudolph Byers strolled in by his wife's side with a smirk on his face, as if he knew something they all didn't. She couldn't help wondering if all the progress she'd made with the two women would get flushed down the toilet by the man who was determined to keep a wedge between the friends.

"Good morning, everyone, and welcome back," she said when they were all seated at the conference table. "I think we made really good progress yesterday and would like to pick up where we left off if everyone is in agreement." She held her breath, almost certain that Rudolph Byers would step in and oppose. When he did not and sat there beside his wife with that silly smirk still on his face, she continued.

"Okay, then, yesterday we ended with you, Kerrie, telling us about the early years when you and Lori worked together. Kerrie, I believe you were sharing with me how things were that first year when the two of you finished college."

Kerrie nodded, glanced over at Lori and smiled. Lori smiled back, which in Farrah's book was still a good sign. "Lori came up with this idea of how we could raise money for our first batch of makeup by getting a group of friends of ours in a band to agree to do a concert…"

Farrah leaned back in her seat listening to what Kerrie was saying, while at the same time noticing there seemed to be a bit of tension between Lori and Rudolph. Being rude, he was doing annoying things to get his wife's attention as if to remind her that he was there. At first he'd been rubbing his finger up and down the sleeve of her blouse, and now he was entwining his fingers on the table with hers. It probably would have come off as a romantic gesture if he wasn't making it so obvious, so deliberate.

Moments later when Kerrie finished talking, Lori jumped in and said, "We used to have so much fun, although we operated in the red most of the time. I can recall when we finally were able to get out of Kerrie's parents' basement and into our own store in Queens."

"That was the store given to the two of you as a gift from your parents, right?"

"Yes, I guess they figured that was the least they could do after we bummed off the Shaws for almost two years," Lori said laughing.

Kerrie joined in the laughter, and she saw Rudolph Byers flinch as if the sound of the two women sharing memories of happier times bothered him. A half hour later Farrah called for a break and wasn't surprised when he pulled Lori off to the side. It wasn't hard to tell that whatever he was saying to her wasn't nice.

Moments later Lori frowned deeply before pulling away from him, and Farrah was grateful when the man stormed out of the conference room, slamming the door behind him.

Kerrie was on the other side of the room with her back to everyone while she talked on the phone, and the loud sound made her swirl around. An apologetic look appeared on Lori's face and she hunched her shoulders in disgust when she said, "Rudolph has an errand he needs to take care of and will be back after lunch."

The expression on Kerrie's face all but clearly said *good riddance*. Farrah refrained from saying anything, but she definitely agreed with Kerrie. She had the same opinion that she had yesterday. The man was bad news and a born manipulator.

Farrah glanced at her watch; it was still early. They had an hour and a half to go before they stopped for lunch. She couldn't help wondering what Xavier was doing. She had promised to call and let him know if she was free for dinner, and she would do so. She felt she needed to see him again since she knew their days together were numbered. She had thought about it, and to avoid being alone during the holidays, if he wanted to extend things until then, she would even consider that.

She began nibbling on her bottom lip wondering why she was doing this to herself. Why not make a clean break after she left here as she'd planned, instead of looking for any excuse to spend more time with him? Maybe one of the reasons was that she could remember the last holidays so well, and he had been a part of them.

It had been the best Christmas she had had in a long time, even better than the times when she'd been married to Dustin. But especially better than the year before when she'd been prepared to spend her holidays alone until Natalie had decided to come home.

The Steeles were a large family, and from talking to Natalie, she knew that this Christmas Donovan's parents, who traveled a lot since retiring, would be returning home for a huge family get-together. That meant, Farrah thought, that more than likely she would be spending the holidays alone.

If she were to suggest to Xavier that they continue their affair at least through the holidays, would he figure out why and grant her that request, or would he decide he didn't want to be used and tell her just where she could go? Besides, chances were he'd already made plans for the holidays.

She glanced across the room and noticed Kerrie had ended her phone call and was standing at the window looking out. Lori, standing on the other side of the room, appeared lost, and from her body language and expression, it was obvious she wanted to approach Kerrie but didn't know how to do so.

Farrah shook her head. Her heart truly went out to both women. Their relationship was badly in need of repair, and neither knew the best way of going about making it happen. "Ladies, I'm ready to resume things."

When both women sat down, she thought for a minute and then said, "You know I have a best friend, who, like the two of you, has been there for me since our high school years. There's nothing I wouldn't do for Natalie and there's nothing Natalie wouldn't do for me."

A smile touched the corners of Farrah's lips. "I know her secrets and she knows mine. She knows my weaknesses and my strengths and vice versa. We understand each other, which is why we've been friends for so long. We might not agree on everything, and I'm sure there have been times when she would have knocked my head off if she could have, but in the end, no matter what, I know our friendship is one that defies the test of time."

"I thought ours would, too," Lori said softly, looking at her when Farrah knew she wanted to glance over at Kerrie.

"I'm not going to ask what happened," Farrah said. "I just ask that no matter what, you remember what you had, what you still have and what will always be there no matter what."

At that moment, Lori did glance over at Kerrie. "You

think I'm only doing this because of Rudolph, don't you?"

Kerrie met her gaze and asked, "Why wouldn't I think it, Lori? Leaving the company in my hands was your idea. Saying that you would only want half up to the day you left was also yours. You also said that we keep things as they were to avoid any messy legal entanglements. It would be unnecessary, you said, since we fully trusted each other."

Kerrie shook her head and said softly, "The sad thing is that I believed you. Stupid me."

The room got quiet and Farrah spoke up. "Is this the first time your friendship has been tested?"

Both women glanced over at her with a bemused look on their faces, so much so that she couldn't help but smile. "You both know that's what this is, don't you?"

Neither woman made a comment, and Farrah figured she had given them something to think about. She glanced at her watch. "You know, I think now is a good time to break for lunch. It's a little early but I think we deserve it today."

Instead of responding, both women nodded as they stood. Kerrie was pulling out her cell phone while heading for the door. Lori watched her leave before turning to Farrah. She could see the tears in the woman's eyes.

"I didn't mean to hurt her," she said in a broken tone.

Farrah stood as she gathered her folders together. The last thing Lori needed was to be sent on a guilt trip, but in this case one was probably warranted. "Well, I hate to tell you this, Lori, but I think you did."

Xavier read the report spread across his desk and tried not to glance up at the clock on the wall. How many times had he done it already? He had to believe that eventually Farrah would call him. She'd said she would, hadn't she?

He threw the pencil he held in his hand down on his desk and leaned back in his chair as he squinted his eyes in thought, trying to recall exactly what she had said. *I'll call you tomorrow, Xavier. That's the best I can do.* Those had been her exact words. He recalled them clearly.

He was about to get up and pour another cup of coffee when his cell phone rang. If it was York, he was going to kill him. He'd called twice already. It seemed that York needed a life more than he did.

Xavier reached for the phone and exhaled a sigh of relief when he saw the caller was Farrah. He glanced at the clock. It was almost four. What had taken her so long? Of course he wouldn't ask her that. In fact, he intended to sound cool, calm and collected. "Hello."

"Xavier. Hi."

"And how are you, Farrah?"

"Fine. Sorry it took me so long to call but it turned out to be a long session today."

He nodded as he leaned back in his chair. "Did the women reach a resolution?"

"I wish."

"I take it that they didn't."

"You've got that right. But I can say I feel we're close. Hopefully tomorrow."

Not if it means you'll be catching the first plane out of here, he thought to himself.

"Anyway, I just wanted to let you know I'd love to have dinner with you."

He couldn't help the smile that touched his lips from corner to corner. "Good. Where are you now? Back at the hotel or still at work?"

"Still at work. I need to complete a few reports and then I'll head back to the hotel."

He glanced at the clock again. "Umm, how about around seven?"

"That's good."

"I'll send a car for you."

"A car?"

"Yes. I'm treating you to dinner at my place."

"In Long Island?"

"Yes."

There was a pause, and he waited, knowing she was rummaging through that gorgeous brain of hers for an excuse not to come. On cue she said, "You don't have to do that. I really don't want to put you through any trouble, Xavier. For me to come all the way to your place really isn't necessary."

Yes, it is, sweetheart. She had no idea just how necessary it truly was. "No trouble. Jules will be there to pick you up exactly at seven. I hope you're hungry."

She didn't say anything for a minute and then, "Yes, I'm hungry. I had a light lunch. But—"

"Good. I'll have something I know you'll like when you get here."

Another pause…and then, "Okay. Thanks."

"Don't mention it. I'll see you when you get here."

He closed his cell phone and placed it back on the desk where it had been since early morning, awaiting her call. Then he stood. It was time for him to go home and prepare dinner for the most lovable yet detached woman he knew. He planned to make things right for her or die trying.

He was well aware of why she assumed she didn't want another man in her life. His mission, which he fully intended to accept, was to convince her that she was worthy of everything life had to offer.

Especially his love.

Chapter 10

"Here we are, Ms. Langley."

"Thanks."

Jules offered Farrah his hand as she eased out of the car and glanced around. The huge triple-story house sat on what appeared to be a private lane, surrounded by a number of huge overhanging trees that formed a canopy over the impressive residence. If privacy was something Xavier was shooting for, then he had succeeded.

Pulling her coat tightly around her, she moved quickly toward the front door. She liked the sound of her booted heels as they clicked loudly against the stone pavers. She had lifted her hand to knock when the door opened.

Xavier was there, and she took a good look at him. He was eye candy of the most delicious kind. And dressed in a pullover sweater and low-riding jeans, he was the epitome of sexy. He moved out of her way as he invited her in. "Come on, I have a blaze roaring in the fireplace. I still intend to keep my promise to make sure you stay warm."

"I appreciate that."

As she followed him through his house, she noticed two things—the aroma of food cooking that made her mouth water, and the fact that he had a beautiful home. She knew this place was just one of many of his showplaces. He also had homes in Los Angeles, Miami and in the Palisades section of Charlotte, where houses went for millions. At least those were the ones he'd mentioned. There was no telling how many others he might own.

They passed a spiral staircase, and she couldn't help but glance up wondering if that was where his bedroom was and if she would find out for certain later. She shook her head. She needed to get her mind off sex, but that was definitely hard when, following him, she got an eyeful of the sexiest backside any man could possibly have.

By the time she'd reined in her wandering thoughts, she only caught his last word: *weather.*

"Excuse me, Xavier, what were you saying?"

He glanced over his shoulder, stopped walking and smiled. "I said it doesn't appear the weather is getting any better," he said, reaching for her hands. He removed her gloves and took her hands in his. As if he'd known they would be cold and stiff, he began massaging them.

Immediately, she felt heated sensations run through the tendons in her palms. The feelings were so strong she clenched her legs together when she felt an unexpected throbbing there.

No, the weather was not getting any better, which was quite obvious. The temperature had dropped, and depending on which news reports you were listening to, a snowstorm the likes of which New York hadn't seen in a long time was headed this way by Sunday. But Farrah knew that regardless of how cold it was outside, she would feel hot in here even if Xavier didn't have a fire roaring in the fireplace. Together, they could generate that kind of heat.

"Make yourself at home."

She broke eye contact with him and glanced around. They were in a room that he probably used as a den. It looked rustic with dark oak plank walls, the kind you'd find in a mountain cabin, and the fireplace was encased in whitewashed stone. The furniture looked sturdy and masculine, including the gigantic pool table in the middle of the room. He had mentioned that he enjoyed playing a game of pool every once in a while.

She glanced around the room again as she removed her coat, and as if he knew what she was thinking, he said, "No, I didn't decorate the place. It was bought as is. I figured the last owner wanted the feel of the Smoky Mountains in here, which is something I didn't have a problem with. In fact I think that's what enticed me to buy it."

She nodded as he came over and took the coat out of

her hands. She automatically eased down on the sofa, a little surprised she was still wearing clothes. She had really expected him to strip her naked the moment she had stepped over the threshold. It seemed he was going to take things slow. Slow was good. But if he started showing signs of wasting too much time, she knew how to take things into her own hands, literally. She inwardly smiled, thinking how she'd done that several times before.

"Here, you probably could use this to get your blood warm."

He handed her a glass filled with wine. When had he poured it? She took a sip, liking the sparkling taste, but then she'd always enjoyed his wine selections. She licked her lips and glanced across the room knowing he was watching her. That was good. Let him look. It would make things easier later when she threw her new idea out to him.

She cleared her throat. "Whatever you're cooking smells good, Xavier."

He chuckled. "Thanks, but I didn't cook it. Ms. Blackburn did it all."

She lifted a brow. "Ms. Blackburn?"

"Yes. My housekeeper, cook, gardener. You name it, she does it."

She lifted a brow again. "Umm, does she now?"

He laughed. "Except for that. For crying out loud, Farrah, she's old enough to be my mother. But I would admit to coming close to asking her to marry me one day after eating a slice of her apple pie."

"It was that delicious?"

"Honey, delicious doesn't come close."

She swallowed. No one could say the word delicious quite the way he could, and no one could do things deliciously quite like him. She'd bet no one could even come close.

"So, will you be meeting with those women again tomorrow since no closure came about today?"

She glanced over at him. He had moved to sit on a bar stool. His taut thighs strained tightly against the denim of his jeans, and his abs were outlined in his form-fitting sweater. Not an inch of flab anywhere. She knew in reality he much preferred beer to wine, but unlike some men, he didn't have a belly to show it.

And speaking of his belly…she thought he had a nice looking one, especially when it wasn't covered with clothes. She remembered quite well how a sprinkling of dark hair adorned it. And then there was that trail of hair that tapered off to his groin area. She felt her mouth watering again, and it wasn't for anything his housekeeper had left cooking on the stove.

She took a sip of her wine before saying, "Yes, I'll be meeting with them, but if everything continues in the same way as today, I'm hoping we'll wrap up by tomorrow. But that depends on—"

"One of the women's husband's involvement," he finished for her.

She nodded and smiled. "You remembered."

"Yes."

"And here I thought you were listening just to humor me and weren't really paying attention."

He met her gaze and held it. "I'm sure since we've met that you've made a number of assumptions about me that aren't true, Farrah."

She blinked, surprised he would say that. "Like what?"

"You'll find out soon enough."

She wondered what he meant by that. But then she would admit that maybe she had made a few assumptions. Being here in his home challenged one of them. She had always assumed his home, his domain, was off-limits to any woman. He'd never said that, but given the way he'd meticulously made his booty calls, she'd certainly thought so.

Xavier stood and placed his wine glass on the counter. She couldn't help the way her gaze followed his movement, especially the muscles in his thighs when they stretched. He was definitely a man who could wear a pair of jeans. But then he looked damn good in a business suit as well. And Lordy, she didn't want to think about how good he looked naked.

She blinked again, noticing his lips move. He was saying something. "Excuse me?"

He smiled, and she felt a tingle that seemed to take life in her stomach. Why did he have to have such a luscious mouth? And why did she have to remember all the things that mouth could do?

"I asked if you were ready for dinner."

She was ready for whatever he had in mind. Holding

back that thought, she cleared her throat and said instead, "Yes, just lead the way."

She followed him, appreciating another chance to check out his broad shoulders and the best backside a man could possess.

Xavier glanced across the table at Farrah and decided he was going to enjoy every single plan he put into action to win her over. They were almost finished with dinner, and just in case she planned to leave any time soon, he would suggest that she stick around to help with kitchen cleanup. He glanced back down at his plate thinking she didn't have to know Ms. Blackburn had instructed him to leave everything for her to take care of in the morning.

"You should have warned me, Xavier."

He glanced back up and met her gaze. The eyes staring back at him were a serious brown. He wondered if she'd figured out his action plan for tonight. "Warned you about what?"

"That I would be so full after this meal that you'd probably have to roll me out the door."

A relieved smile touched his lips. "I did warn you. I told you how I felt after eating her apple pie."

"I thought you were exaggerating. Now I see that you weren't. I've never eaten pork chops that all but melt in your mouth. They are so tender."

He had to agree, Ms. Blackburn had done a great job with dinner. And Farrah, he thought, had done a great job with dressing. She looked good tonight. When she'd taken off her coat, his tongue had almost wrapped around his head. That was one sexy purple dress she was wearing. It was short, which showed off her legs that were encased in tights and another pair of black leather knee-high boots. He had invited her over for dinner, not to give him heart failure.

"You look nice tonight, by the way."

She smiled at his compliment. "Thanks. You look good yourself."

He pushed his empty plate aside to lean back in his chair. "Glad you think so."

"I do. Always."

She was flirting with him, and as a man, he could only appreciate it. "Would you like some dessert now?" He watched her lick her lips, and he couldn't help but shift in the chair to ease the pressure behind his zipper.

"Sounds tempting but I'll wait for a while. I'd like to talk to you about something."

He wondered what she wanted to talk about. "Sure. Let's go in the family room and sit in front of the fireplace."

"But what about the dinner dishes?"

He smiled. "We can leave them for now and you can help me clean up the kitchen later."

"All right. That's the least I can do after such a wonderful meal."

No, that wasn't the least she could do, but he would keep that little tidbit to himself.

He rounded the table to pull the chair back for her. One thing he'd liked about Farrah from the first was that she never got offended when he did gentlemanly things for her. No matter how raw and raunchy they got in the bedroom, he totally enjoyed treating her like the lady he knew she was.

And she was a downright sexy lady at that, he thought as his gaze swept over her, up and down her body. Just looking at her almost derailed any thoughts about what was the best way to handle her. He wanted to get out of her the one thing he deemed most important. For her to return his love.

He knew that was a tall order, one that would take measured, strategic planning. His goal was to convince her that he was a viable candidate for her affections, and that he was more husband material than her ex ever was.

When she walked off swaying her hips, it took all of his control not to reach out and pull her into his arms and begin removing every stitch of clothing she had on her body before tearing off his. Then it would be on, all over the place. His erection throbbed just thinking about it.

He momentarily closed his eyes while telling himself to hold tight and keep a handle on his control. It would all be worth it in the end, even though not making love to her tonight was going to drive him insane, especially when she was intentionally trying to bait him.

Xavier reopened his eyes the moment she glanced over her shoulder at him with a teasing smile on her face. "Are you coming, Xavier?"

He gave her a warning frown. He would definitely

be coming if she kept it up, but he intended to resist her temptation, even if it killed him. And he had a feeling that if it did kill him, he would die an excruciating, slow death. "I'm right behind you."

And he was. As she led the way back to his family room, he was what he considered a safe distance behind her, which had its advantages if you were into ass-watching. He was, especially when that part of the anatomy was hers.

She slid down on his sofa in a movement so fluid, so damn enticing, he didn't even blink as he watched her. He waited until she was settled in her seat before crossing the room and taking the recliner across from her. He'd known resisting her wouldn't be easy, but he hadn't counted on it being such torture. The woman was almost too hot for his own good.

He cleared his throat. "So, what do you want to talk about?"

"Us."

Us? She'd never referred to them as an *us,* so in a way things sounded pretty good already. "I'm listening."

She began nibbling on her lower lips. He knew that sign. Whatever topic she wanted to broach wasn't easy for her. "I, um, I was thinking about what you said last night."

He'd said a lot of things. He'd done a lot of things, too. "And?"

"And you wanted us to continue the affair past New York."

Had she come around without much prodding from him? "Yes, I recall having said that."

She began nibbling on her lips again, and then she said, "I'd like to offer a proposal to you."

He lifted a brow. "A proposal?"

"Yes."

He leaned back in the chair as he rubbed his jaw. This had better be good, he thought. It'd better be what he wanted. "I'm listening."

"I don't have any plans for the holidays and I thought…"

She paused, but he was determined that she finish what she was saying. "You thought what, Farrah?'

She met his gaze while nibbling those luscious lips again. "That since you wanted to continue things between us for a while, that we could extend our affair at least through New Year's."

He didn't say anything. He had to make sure he fully understood what she was offering. "Are you saying that once you leave here it's okay for us to hook up in Charlotte again, with things being like they used to be with us?"

She nodded. "Yes, but only through the holidays."

He ignored the ache in his body that tried convincing him that something was better than nothing, and that he should take her up on her offer. But he wasn't in the market for just being involved in a holiday affair. He wanted the whole shebang. That meant he had no intention of letting her place limitations on their relationship.

"So, what do you think?"

He shrugged his shoulders and wondered if she was prepared for what he was about to say. "I think I'll pass."

Voices in his head were calling him all kinds of fool for not accepting her offer. One voice in particular was all but giving his brain a hard kick, screaming that if he thought he could convince her to consider a real relationship with him, he was crazy and wasting his time. Her ex had done too much of a number on her for that to happen. How many times had she told him that she would never, ever, become involved in a serious relationship again? How many times had she reiterated that fact for his benefit?

"You'll pass?" she asked, with a mixture of shock and confusion outlining what he thought were gorgeous features. "But why?"

He held her gaze. "Because I told you what I wanted."

"For us to pick up where we left off?"

"Yes, and continue from there without any limitations, Farrah."

She shook her head. "That's not going to work, Xavier. That's why I thought it was best if we ended things six months ago."

"Whatever hang-ups there were, Farrah, were yours, not mine. The only reason I gave into it at the time was because I convinced myself that perhaps you were right. After last night I decided you're dead wrong."

The flaring of fire in her eyes let him know she hadn't

appreciated what he'd just said. It didn't take a rocket scientist to know he'd pushed the wrong button, but at the moment he really didn't give a damn. It was time they had it out. He refused to go through another long spell without her.

She leaned forward in her seat. "This new attitude of yours is all because of last night? One good blow job got you all up in arms? Got you refusing a holiday fling with me because you want more than that?"

He slid out the chair to stand on his feet. "It's more than that, Farrah, and you know it. It's about the chemistry we stir whenever we're together. I see nothing wrong with wanting more. But after almost a year, you decided we should end things. Why? Because you had begun feeling something a lot deeper and more solid than mere orgasms."

"That's not true!" she said adamantly.

"Isn't it?"

"It was just sex, Xavier. You could have gotten the same from any woman."

"Hardly, which is why I haven't slept with another woman since you. And probably why you haven't, by your admission, been intimate with anyone since me."

He thought he'd hit a nerve, and she proved him right when she began pacing angrily. He decided to sit back in the chair and let her blow off steam, come to terms with being called out. Except he was getting more turned on by the second watching her, seeing how the hair was flying around her face with every livid step she took in boots that were definitely made for more than walking.

Her hips were not just swaying now, they were being brandished about under the sting of rejection. Something she evidently didn't care much for. Not for the first time, he noticed just how small her waist was, and how her hips flared out in an almost perfect womanly shape. And her breasts—heaven help him, they were the most luscious pair on any woman—were straining against the bodice of her dress.

While his gaze roamed all over her, she finally came to a stop mere inches from where he sat. She placed her hands on her hips. "So, what exactly is it that you want?"

He smiled and leaned forward in his chair and met her gaze without wavering. He fought the urge to tell her that what he wanted was marriage, until death do them part. Considering everything, he figured now was not a good time to share that with her.

"What I want is for us to resume our affair without limitations. That means we go for as long as we're mutually satisfied."

She rolled her eyes. "People only do long-term affairs when they want to get serious eventually. People who want more out of a relationship. People who might even contemplate marriage."

"Not necessarily. I think we know each other's position on marriage, so we don't have to worry about us wanting anything *that* serious. However, I'm at a point in my life where I prefer long-term exclusiveness. Not only do I want a satisfying bed partner, I also want to be with someone I can take out to dinner on occasion, to a movie, to those business functions that I'm oftentimes invited to attend. I don't like women coming on to me anymore. I want to emit an air that I'm taken…even if I'm truly not."

He paused, wanting her to digest what he'd just said. Then he continued. "You enjoy my company and I enjoy yours. I see no reason why we can't continue what we had unless…"

She tilted her head and looked at him, lifting a brow. "Unless what?"

"Unless you're afraid of falling in love with me."

He eased up from his seat, ignoring the burst of longing and love he felt for the woman standing in front of him. The woman he was determined to make fall in love with him to the same degree that he was with her.

He knew now that she wasn't as opposed to restarting their affair as she put on. But she was scared of letting her heart get broken again. So he knew he had to tread lightly but at the same time push harder…if that made sense.

"Are you afraid, Farrah? If you are, then I understand and totally agree that we should not pick up where we left off."

He immediately saw the effect his words had on her. After her jaw dropped to the floor, she went still. He was convinced she was barely breathing. And her gaze intensified, focused on him. Her eyes zeroed in on him like he was the only thing in their laser beam's target. From the distance separating them, he felt her anger, but he also felt her fear. He actually saw it in her eyes, and he knew at that moment what he'd assumed was right. She was falling in love with him, but was fighting it tooth and nail. She would never, ever admit such a thing.

So he stood there watching her, waiting to see how she planned on getting out of the neat little box he'd just placed her in.

Chapter 11

*T*hink, *Farrah!*

She nibbled on her bottom lip as she tried unscrambling her brain, refusing to admit Xavier had hit a nerve, which automatically put her on the defensive. "Me? Not being able to control my emotions and fall in love? Please. That is the last thing you, or any man, have to worry about, trust me."

He shrugged. "If you say so."

She didn't like the sound of that. Did he honestly think she'd fall in love with him? Okay, she would admit—although never to him—that she had ended things between them because she'd had feelings for him and had been uncomfortable with those newfound emotions. But she would never let any man suspect she was afraid of losing her heart.

She threw her head back, sending her hair flying over her shoulders. "I'm going to only say this once and I hope you're listening, Xavier. The last thing you have to worry about, and the one thing I am *not* afraid of, is falling in love with you or any man. I've been there, done that and you can believe I'll never go that way again."

"In that case, I see no reason for us not to continue our affair beyond the holidays. In other words, there is no reason not to go back to things being the way they were. And in addition, I see no reason why we can't bring our affair out of the bedroom and start going out more…unless there's a reason you prefer not being seen with me."

Farrah's head was spinning dizzily with everything Xavier was saying. But she was coherent enough to latch on to his last statement. "For what reason would I not want to be seen with you?"

"That you're still pining away for your ex-husband and you don't want him to know you're in a relationship with someone."

If Farrah hadn't been programmed to act in a dignified manner, especially when discussing such an important topic, she would have fallen to the floor and rolled over a few times in laughter. Anyone who knew her and Dustin's history knew there was no way that she was pining for her ex. In fact, whenever she saw him, she wondered why she'd fallen in love with him in the first place. It's not that he'd ever had anything going for him that was so spectacular. But while they'd been in college, he had convinced her he was the best thing since sliced bread and that he would be going places.

She had believed he loved her, wanted to spend the rest of his life with her and they would stay together forever. She didn't even mind during their first year when he couldn't get a job and she had supported the both of them, or the times she'd put up with his deadbeat parents whose way of life was calling for loans and not paying them back.

"So, did I hit it out of the ballpark, Farrah?"

She could only assume he figured that because she hadn't yet responded to his statement. "You didn't come close, Xavier. In fact, you struck out so bad they are replacing you in the game entirely. There is no way I'd ever get back with Dustin, nor do I want to."

She didn't like the look she saw in his eyes. Although he heard what she said, she couldn't tell if he believed her.

"*If* what you say is true, then there is no reason why we can't continue what we once had without limitations, right?"

Farrah's pulse began beating wildly, anxiously, and that cloak of protectiveness she used as a shield immediately went into place. There were lots of reasons why they couldn't continue what they once had. And not imposing limitations was simply out of the question.

Although she would never admit she had developed a weakness for him, the truth of the matter was that on more than one occasion she had lost control and lowered her guard, which was totally unacceptable behavior. When she was with Xavier she had a tendency to let loose, getting buck wild and crazy. Not just in the bedroom—that she could handle. But with her heart. Only with him did she care about the here and now and not worry about the outcome.

She lifted her chin. "There *is* a reason," she said, knowing what she was about to say was an absolute lie. "Have you ever considered that the only reason I don't want to take up where we left off in an affair, Xavier, is because I just don't want to be romantically involved with you any longer?"

Darn. Instead of frowning, he was smiling, which meant he hadn't believed a word she'd just said. Hadn't taken her seriously. She watched as he crossed his arms over his chest and braced his legs apart in a ready-for-combat stance. She hated thinking it, but his standing that way and looking at her with that "I know better" smirk on his face sent a rush of adrenaline up her spine.

"You expect me to believe that, Farrah? The same woman who I took on the backseat of a private car last night while cruising on a barge on an icy cold night down the Hudson."

She narrowed her eyes at him. "Why can't I convince you it was nothing but sex?"

He shrugged his shoulders. "I don't know, but here's your chance. Convince me. Prove you're not afraid of letting your emotions get in the way of an affair with me, and that your mind is not getting confused with the L-word. Prove to me, Farrah, that for us it's only about sex, which is the only thing we want anyway, and that we don't have to worry about anything else to the point that we establish limitations."

Her mind was spinning in confusion, and she wondered if he'd caused that to happen deliberately. All she knew at that moment was that she had a point to prove to him, several in fact. First, she was capable of keeping her emotions under wraps. Second, she was not still carrying a torch for Dustin. And last but not least, she was not afraid of falling in love with Xavier.

"Fine," she threw out heatedly. "You think you've got everything figured out, but I'm going to prove you wrong, Xavier. I'm going to give you your affair without limitations and then you're going to see just how wrong you are about everything."

Xavier couldn't ignore the burst of happiness that tore through him at that moment, and he had to fight hard to keep a smile off his lips. With some outright manipulation, which he wasn't all that thrilled about, he had moved Farrah into the spot where he wanted her for now.

She had agreed to an affair without limitations, and he doubted that she fully understood exactly what that meant, but she would find out soon enough. Although they would continue to make love just as before, they would not be spending one hundred percent of the time between the sheets. He would take her out on dates, to parties—there were always a number of them to attend this time of year—and she would get to spend time with him around people who meant a lot to him. They were family and friends who would come to love her as much as he did.

"Good, we're on the same page now," he heard himself saying as he crossed the room to her, needing to feel her in his arms, although he could tell she was still somewhat tiffed with him.

"Fine," she said, when he slid his arm around her waist and brought her body closer to his. She might not be happy with him now, but the moment he pulled her into his arms, she came willingly. And when he lowered his head to capture her mouth, there was not a single ounce of resistance in her body.

She leaned in, and he felt her warmth deep, all the way to the pit of his stomach. He wasn't surprised when he felt the shiver ease up his spine and his erection get harder. Desire sizzled through him, and he fought to push it back. This woman could set his body on fire, and at any other time he would take advantage of it. But not this time. He had his game plan tonight and didn't want to ruin it.

But there was no reason he couldn't make love to her mouth if not her body, was there? After all, when it came to kissing, they always indulged in the ultimate enjoyment. Then he remembered. The fact that he had managed to breathe six months without tasting her was a miracle, and he didn't intend to suffer through that agony again.

He finally pulled his mouth away, but their greedy tongues were still intent on doing a tangling dance, if not inside their mouths then out. They always enjoyed this type of play where they took licking and sucking to a whole new level.

And then his tongue was back inside her mouth again, and his arms tightened around her. It wouldn't take much to ease her down on the sofa, push her dress up, pull down those leggings and bury his head between her legs and do a lot of tongue play there. It wouldn't take much enticement for him to kiss every inch of her body. Unfortunately, he would save that specific activity for another day. Unknown her to, this kind of kissing was all they would be doing tonight.

Ah hell, he thought, when he felt her hands wiggle between them and her fingers tug on his zipper. He needed to stop her before she went down on him. There was no way he could resist that. With all the strength he could gather, all the control he could muster, he reached down and took hold of her hand to stop her from going further.

She pulled her mouth from his and looked up at him with a questioning gaze. "Why are you holding my hands, Xavier?"

Before answering her question, he leaned down and took another lick around her mouth. Hell, she tasted as good as she looked. "I want to give you time to be absolutely sure I'm what you want, Farrah."

He had worded the statement carefully. Instead of saying he wanted her to be sure that the *affair* was what she wanted, he had said he wanted her to be sure that *he* was what she wanted. There was a difference, and over the next few weeks he would show her what that difference was.

"But I already know you're what I want, Xavier."

Yes, she would want him sexually, that was a given. But he wanted her to want him in a way she'd never wanted another man, a way that went deeper than mere sex. He wanted to conquer her heart. For a man who just last week had thought he didn't need the love of a woman, in the last forty-eight hours he had been proven wrong.

"Yes, but I want you to be certain because now that you've agreed to an unlimited affair with me, Farrah, there's no turning back."

She lifted her brow, as if his comment gave her pause. "No turning back" sounded kind of final in his book, so he knew it sounded likewise in hers, but now he was talking for keeps.

She didn't say anything for a long moment and then, "Why are you trying to make things so complicated, Xavier?"

"Sorry if you think I'm doing that, sweetheart, but I just want to make sure a few weeks from now you don't try kicking me out of your life again. I have to know that we want the same thing out of this relationship."

He was trying to defuse any suspicions she had that things with him weren't on the up-and-up. He only hoped when she discovered they weren't she would be too far gone to care.

She nodded slowly. "Okay, I guess that makes sense."

"It does. Besides, another reason I need to make it an early night is because Cameron is flying in tomorrow and I need to have some papers ready for him to sign when he does."

He was deliberately giving her the impression that he was putting work before her. Although she didn't say anything, he could tell she was both surprised and disappointed.

"Oh, well, then I guess I need to go."

"Not before we share dessert and not before you help me with kitchen clean up."

She smiled. "All right."

He wanted to kiss her again, and he figured before she left to return to the hotel that he would, several times. But at least she would be leaving with the knowledge that for the first time, though they'd had the convenience and the privacy to make love, they hadn't.

"Is the car warm enough for you, Ms. Langley?"

Farrah glanced over the seat in front of her at Jules. Xavier had given the driver strict instructions to see to her every comfort, and to especially make sure she was kept warm.

"Yes, thank you for asking."

She settled back against the plush leather seat, determined to replay in her mind all that had transpired tonight and to make sure she hadn't imagined anything.

She'd gone to his house fully intending to convince

him to extend their affair through the holidays, after which, they would go their separate ways again.

For reasons she was still trying to figure out, he hadn't wanted any part of that suggestion. Instead, he wanted to resume the affair with no limitations. He'd even gone so far as to suggest her reluctance to do so was because she was afraid of falling in love with him and because she still harbored feelings for Dustin.

Okay, secretly she would agree the former did have some merit, but the latter did not. To prove him wrong on both counts, she had no choice but to agree to his terms. So technically, they were now involved in a long-term, no-strings relationship.

Even more confusing to her was how, once she'd agreed, their relationship had taken a definite turn. But to where she hadn't a clue. First, it had been the way he'd kissed her. It was greedy and hungry as usual, but it seemed like he was holding back, which didn't make sense. After all, she had agreed to what he'd wanted. And no matter what she'd done, she hadn't changed his mind about sleeping with her, although she knew without a doubt that he'd wanted her.

Men!

Now here she was, riding in the car alone as she returned to her hotel. Truly, what sense did that make? He could have easily asked that she stay the night and she would have. But he hadn't. He'd even suggested she take time to think her decision through. Now, drawing in a deep breath, she decided to do just what he'd suggested.

As the car sped along the Long Island Expressway, she closed her eyes. An unlimited affair with him meant essentially no more booty calls. At least they wouldn't be termed that anymore. She had agreed that she and Xavier would start doing things outside the bedroom. More than likely they would go out to dinner on occasion, to a movie, to business functions.

She felt a knot forming in the pit of her stomach at the thought of doing those things with him and knew the reason why. She might just begin to enjoy it too much. Her challenge was going to be keeping things in perspective. Though neither of them wanted to take things any further than they had previously, Xavier was now ready for more exclusiveness. At least she could rest assured he still wasn't the marrying kind. Good, she thought, because neither was she.

She opened her eyes and glanced down at her watch. It wasn't even midnight. Depending on how things turned out between Kerrie Shaw and Lori Byers, she could very well be back in Charlotte around this time tomorrow. Doing so would have her out of New York before the snowstorm hit on Sunday. Xavier had even offered to take her to the airport tomorrow. Getting back home might be a good thing. It would put distance between them for at least a week and would give her time to clear her head and decide on the best way to handle him.

Over ice cream and apple pie, Xavier had told her about his trip after the holidays to Los Angeles where he would be for a few days in January. Usually, she wouldn't know about his trips until he was packed and ready to go because that was the type of relationship they'd had. For him to keep her abreast of his plans was going to take some getting used to.

But for now she wanted just to concentrate on what had or hadn't happened tonight. Sex was one of the things that hadn't happened, and for a reason she didn't quite understand. A part of her believed it was intentional on Xavier's part.

She had come here fully expecting dinner followed by hot, mind-blowing sex. That was the only kind she'd ever shared with Xavier, and tonight she had been willing, but for some reason, he had held back.

After dessert he had kissed her a few times, and although she would admit the kisses had been long, drugging and delicious enough to tingle her toes and wet her panties, she had still felt him holding back on her. It was as if he was keeping himself in check, fearful of just what too many slow, deep kisses could do to them.

And then, after they'd cleaned up the kitchen together, he had helped her back into her coat and gloves, had picked her up in his arms and, instead of carrying her upstairs to a bedroom, he had carried her outside and placed her on the backseat of the private car.

He had told her that regardless of whether she stayed in New York over the weekend, he would be seeing her tomorrow and to expect his call. Why was she thinking already that, in addition to the feel of him easing back off sex, she was also losing control of the relationship? Now it seemed as if he had taken the lead role in managing just how things went between them.

And she wasn't sure if she particularly liked giving any man that much control over her.

"We'll be at your hotel in less than five minutes, Ms. Langley," the driver interrupted her thoughts to inform her.

"Thanks, Jules."

As they drove into the city, she wondered what would be the best way to take back that control she had somehow lost tonight. She didn't like any man calling the shots and had dispensed with that nonsense at the moment the ink had dried on her divorce papers from Dustin.

After the divorce she had been furious, even resentful, and at one point out for blood. In a fit of spite, she'd thought about suing the other woman. North Carolina was one of a few states that still enforced a century-old case law that said a wife could sue her husband's mistress for breaking up a marriage. Her attorney had been more than happy to do it, and Dustin's attorney had scared her ex-husband shitless by informing him of a recent suit in which the duped ex-wife had gotten nine million dollars richer. Natalie had talked her out of it, but still she'd felt good knowing she had made Dustin sweat for a while.

When the driver brought the car to a stop in front of her hotel, she gathered up her things. She had been so certain about tonight that she'd put her toothbrush in her purse. In a way, she was somewhat disappointed. But then she would be the first to admit engaging in the unknown was kind of exciting. She couldn't help wondering what Xavier had planned for tomorrow. Surely he wasn't going to push for another wasted night. If he did try going that route, she would have to do something about it.

Chapter 12

"Hey, man, you okay?"

Xavier glanced across the desk at Cameron thinking that if he looked like a man who'd had a sleepless night then that was definitely right on the money. After he'd put Farrah inside the car and sent her home, he had walked around his house with a hard-on that wouldn't go down. He'd called himself all kinds of fool. Although he'd known that in the long run he had done the right thing for them, he'd gone to bed with regrets of not having made love to her.

"No, not really," he said, deciding to be honest.

The necessary documents had been signed, and now Cameron Cody owned yet another company. The negotiations had gone well, better than expected. Sleep-deprived or not, when it came to business, Xavier knew he was on top of his game. But now that he and Cameron were alone, that adrenaline high from earlier was fizzling fast.

"What's your problem, Xavier?"

He couldn't help but smile at Cameron's question. For the first time since Dionne, he was actually having a problem with a woman. Before, he'd never considered a female significant enough to cause a problem in his life, but with Farrah things were different.

"I have a lot of decisions to make and I want to be absolutely sure I'm making the right ones."

Cameron leaned back in his seat and chuckled. "I assume these decisions are about Farrah Langley."

Xavier raised a brow. He'd never discussed Farrah with anyone, although he was certain after Donovan's wedding a number of his friends—his godbrothers in particular—had figured he and Farrah were involved in a hot and heavy affair. "How did you know?"

Cameron chuckled. "Because I know you. You started paying late-night visits to the same woman on a rather frequent basis. And since you never discussed these visits or the woman with me or anyone, that was the first sign."

"Sign?"

"Yes, a sign that this particular woman meant something to you and that you thought she was different from all the others."

Xavier nodded slowly. Yes, Farrah was different from the others. At first he'd just enjoyed being in her bed, but then something had begun happening to him, although at first he hadn't known exactly what. It had taken half a year of not being with her to make him realize Farrah was more than a woman he just wanted in his bed. Once he'd seen her again, spent time with her, he'd known she was the only woman he wanted in his life for always. "I'm crazy about her, Cam," he admitted.

"Does she know how you feel?"

Xavier shook his head. "Hell, I just figured it out myself a few days ago. We broke up a week after Donovan's wedding—her idea, not particularly mine. She thought our short-term affair had gone on longer than intended and it was time to move on. I didn't argue and will admit at the time I thought maybe she was right. And then a couple of days ago we ran into each other here in New York. She's in town on business like I am. We went out to dinner that first night and a Broadway play the next. I enjoyed her company and realized just how much I had missed her. Then I knew exactly what had been truly missing from my life for the past six months."

Cameron smiled. "Now you can understand why I wouldn't let up in my pursuit of Vanessa, although it didn't take me as long as it took you to figure out I was in love, and that Vanessa was the woman I wanted in my life."

"Um, that might be true, but I have a feeling I'm going to work just as hard to win her over," Xavier said. He paused, thinking of all the things Cameron had done during his pursuit of Vanessa, and then shook his head and laughed. "Hell, I hope not."

Cameron couldn't help laughing as well. "But in the end it was all worth it."

All Xavier had to do was to see them together to know what Cameron said was true. "I'm definitely in love with Farrah, Cam." Xavier wasn't surprised how easily the words flowed from his lips.

"Good. I like her, so what's the problem?" Cameron asked.

Xavier sighed deeply. After all Cameron had gone through for Vanessa, if anyone understood his plight, it would be him. "She can't seem to get over a bad marriage. Her husband cheated on her and ended up marrying the other woman. He even went so far as to have a child with her while married to Farrah."

Cameron shook his head sadly. "Some bastards really make it hard for the rest of us, don't they?"

Xavier nodded in agreement. Farrah's ex was making it nearly impossible for him. "Yes, it's going to be difficult for her to trust another man."

"Be patient. Some scars are harder to heal than others."

Xavier understood that. It had taken him years to get over the damage Dionne had done to him. But he truly believed in his heart that Farrah and Dionne were nothing alike, and now he had to prove that fact to Farrah.

"I'm sure you have a plan, Xavier."

Xavier chuckled. Cameron knew him well enough to know just how he operated. "Yes. Last night I got her to agree to resume our affair with no limitations. That in itself wasn't an easy task, so I feel good about it. The next thing I intend to do is prove to her that there's more between us than just great sex."

Farrah had expected to get carted off to his bed last night. He could tell. A part of him believed she was somewhat confused as to why he hadn't slept with her. She had tried more than once to tempt him, and he'd known exactly what she was doing. A few times his traitorous body had almost given in, but luckily his ironclad control had ruled.

"Thanks for listening to my woes, Cam."

"Hey, no problem. That's what friends are for. Now, I'm out of here. That snow storm they had predicted for Sunday is blowing in early, and I intend to be gone before then."

Xavier glanced out the window, noticing for the first time the weather had changed. The sky was white and heavy, the wind blustery. He needed to call Farrah to see if she planned to leave for Charlotte today. A smile touched his lips. Although he knew it would be a bad idea with all the temptation she would present, he kind of liked the idea of her getting snowed in, in the city. Of course he would invite her to move in with him until the worst of the storm passed. He could imagine how it would be if that were to happen.

"What are you smiling about, Xavier?"

He glanced up at Cameron. "Trust me, you don't want to know."

"I've made a decision about things, Ms. Langley."

Farrah glanced over at Lori. Her husband hadn't come

with her today, and as far as Farrah was concerned, that was a good sign. She wondered if today would entail another long, drawn out session. They had covered a lot of ground yesterday, revisited a lot of memories, and Farrah hoped doing so had worked.

"And what decision is that, Lori?"

"That I'm fine with a seventy-thirty split. Kerrie's right in thinking that I don't deserve fifty-fifty. Besides, I admit to telling her that years ago, and I won't go back on my word now. Our friendship means more to me than that."

Kerrie glanced over at Lori. "I think you deserve more than seventy-thirty Lori. I'm willing to go back to the original contract between us and honor that."

Lori shook her head. "I won't let you do that. I walked away from the business. You're the one who made it into what it is today, and I won't be greedy about it."

Kerrie then asked, "What about Rudolph? How will he feel about it?"

Lori shrugged. "I told him my decision this morning. He's not happy about it, but it was my decision to make. He'll just have to get over it since this doesn't really concern him. These past few days have made me realize that the business was based on our friendship, our trust and love for each other. I can't let anyone destroy those things."

Farrah couldn't help but admire Lori for the decision she'd made and for standing up to her husband. She wondered if it was the first time Lori had defied him. "Well, I'm glad we've resolved the matter, and I'll get the papers ready to be signed so we can all leave before the weather worsens. It looks like it's about to start snowing any minute."

"It does," Lori said in agreement. "And I want to thank you for reminding me that true friendship will outlast anything, and that's what Kerrie and I have always had."

Kerrie nodded in agreement before reaching across the table and taking Lori's hand in hers.

Farrah drew in a deep breath, feeling good about the resolution and happy about how things had worked out in the end. She glanced at her watch, wondering if she would be able to get a flight out today before the storm hit.

An hour or so later she checked her phone and saw she'd received a text message from Xavier. All it said was—Cold outside. Car will pick you up.

Moments later when she exited the building, she saw his private car parked at the curb waiting for her. Jules smiled when he saw her and quickly opened the car door. "Mr. Kane sent me with instructions to take you wherever you want to go, Ms. Langley."

Farrah smiled as she slid onto the backseat. It was cold, and she couldn't help but appreciate the vehicle's warmth. "Please take me to my hotel. I want to get a flight out before the storm arrives."

At that minute her phone rang. She smiled when she saw it was Xavier and immediately clicked on the call. "Xavier, thanks for sending the car."

"I promised to keep you warm, didn't I?"

Her smile widened. "Yes."

"So did things get resolved today?"

"Yes," she said excitedly. "I feel good in not only resolving another case, but with this particular one, renewing a friendship. Now I'm headed back to the hotel to pack. The storm's coming and I'm afraid if I don't get a flight out today, I might get stranded here."

"I hate to tell you this but you might already be stranded. I heard on the news that they've already started canceling flights headed to New York, which means that flights leaving the city are being impacted."

Farrah frowned, disappointed. "The last thing I want is to get stranded here."

"In that case you might be in luck. Cameron is here and will be flying out in his private plane in a few hours. If you're ready to leave, then you can fly back to Charlotte with him."

Farrah blinked. "I can't impose on Mr. Cody like that, Xavier. He doesn't know me that well."

Xavier laughed. "Cam knows you're a close friend of mine. I'll make the necessary arrangements with him. You just get packed. I'll touch base with you in an hour."

Farrah clicked off the phone, thinking just how appreciative she would be if Xavier could arrange for her to leave New York before the storm hit. But to accompany Cameron Cody in his private plane, she thought, was asking too much. Although he and his wife were Natalie's cousins-in-law, as she'd told Xavier, she didn't want to impose on the man.

She shook her head, somewhat disappointed. If she left the hotel and went straight to the airport, that would mean she wouldn't see Xavier before leaving. Nor had he said anything about wanting to see her again before she left.

"We're here, Ms. Langley."

Farrah pushed her disappointment aside. This had turned out to be a happy day, and she refused to let thoughts of Xavier put a damper on it.

Xavier couldn't ignore the shiver of pleasure that ran down his spine when Jules pulled the car up in front of Farrah's hotel. And then moments later he watched the woman he loved come through the revolving glass doors pulling luggage behind her.

She looked all bundled up in her leather coat, gloves, boots and a furry-looking hat that covered her head. It was cold outside, and according to the weather reports, it was the coldest it had been in New York all year. If the forecasters were right, the following days would get even more frigid with record-breaking temperatures. Combine that with snow and it was a recipe for disaster.

Jules opened the car door for her, and the wide-eyed look of surprise and the warm smile that lit her face caused a sensual jolt to his midsection. "Xavier! I didn't think I'd see you before I—"

He didn't give her a chance to finish what she was saying. In fact he barely gave her time to get settled in the backseat before he leaned over and captured her mouth with his. Damn, he needed her taste. He needed her. And at that moment there was no doubt in his mind that he loved her.

Their mouths mated hungrily and fused passionately as their tongues tangled in a wild and frenzied exchange that had him groaning. Thankfully, Jules drew the privacy shield closed without being told, and Xavier proceeded to pull Farrah into his lap. At that moment he couldn't fight the rush of desire that suddenly consumed him, making him hot, almost causing him to overload. She was returning his kiss measure for measure while sensation after glorious earth-shattering sensation tore into him.

They finally ended the kiss, but he kept his mouth close to hers, a breath away from her moist lips. The look in her eyes almost sent him over the edge. If he were to spread her out on the seat, strip her naked and take her, she wouldn't resist. There was no doubt in his mind that she wanted him as much as he wanted her.

But he wanted her to do more than just need him. He wanted her to love him as much as he loved her. To reach that goal he had to prove to her there was more between them than just the physical. That didn't mean he would stop making love to her. He just needed to find a balance between the physical and the emotional so that she would see she was not only desired but also loved.

"Now what were you about to say?" he asked, pulling her close to him while wrapping his arms around the back of the seat.

His gaze went immediately to her lips when they

began moving again. He liked kissing them, nibbling on them, licking them and doing all kinds of naughty things to them.

"I said I didn't think I would see you before I left," Farrah said.

Unable to resist any longer, Xavier leaned down and swiped a slow lick off her lips. "Did you honestly think I would let you leave without seeing you again and saying goodbye?"

"After last night I wasn't so sure."

Xavier pulled her closer to him. "Well, I am here, and in fact I intend to go back to Charlotte with you and Cam."

She blinked as if she wasn't certain she'd heard him correctly. "You're going back to Charlotte?"

"Yes, there's no reason for me to get stranded here, too. Besides, if the storm is as bad as the forecasters predict, the office will be closed anyway. I can fly back sometime next week to finalize things."

"Oh."

"I've got a favor to ask of you," he said, pulling off her gloves, needing to feel his skin enmeshed with hers.

"What?"

He entwined their fingers and felt the warmth of her flesh. He looked down at their joined hands in her lap. "I've been invited to several holiday parties and I want you to go as my date."

He felt her flinch but chose to ignore her reaction. "I had originally planned not to accept the invitations, but since we've decided to remove the limitations on our affair, I think it would be nice for us to share the holiday spirit, don't you?" Xavier figured those parties would be perfect for him and Farrah to be officially seen out together as a couple.

Farrah wasn't sure if what he was proposing would be nice or not. She certainly hadn't expected him to ask her out on a date so soon. And from what he'd said, it sounded as if it would be several dates. She knew it might sound pretty sleazy to some, but she much preferred sharing her time with him in the bedroom in a strictly physical and nonemotional affair. However, it had nothing to do with the reasons he had accused her of last night. To get him to believe that would be close to impossible.

Instead of answering his question, she posed one of her own. "How many parties are we talking about, Xavier?"

He leaned over and began nibbling on her neck, ears and the corners of her mouth. "Um, I think we're talking about three or four. And then there's the New Year's Eve party that Uriel and his wife, Ellie, are hosting at the lake."

She gazed up at him. "And you want me to attend all those parties with you?"

"Yes. Is there a reason why you can't? Have you made other plans for the holidays?"

Farrah inwardly sighed. Unfortunately, she hadn't made other plans. She figured on it being a low-key time for her. Her company was closed for ten days, and she had planned to buy a number of books and to stay in, relax and have a read-a-thon.

"Farrah?"

Why did he have to say her name in such a way that waylaid her senses and sent a ripple of desire through her? "Yes?"

"Have you made plans for the holidays already?"

"No, but—but—"

He lifted his head and stared down at her. "But what?"

How could she tell him that she wasn't comfortable dating the way normal couples did? How could she explain that she equated dating with establishing the foundation for something more serious, and she didn't do serious?

Instead of wasting her time explaining anything, she said, "Nothing. Going to all those events will be fine. Just let me know when and where and I'll meet you there."

Xavier threw his head back and laughed. "Sorry, sweetheart, but it doesn't quite work that way. I'll let you know when and where, but I'll pick you up. We won't show up in separate cars."

She nibbled on her bottom lip wondering why it mattered if they both ended up at the same place. But she didn't want to argue with him about it. She glanced out the window and noticed they had passed the exit for the airport. "Where are we going?"

"Back to my place to get luggage. When I talked

to you earlier I was at the office finishing up a few things."

She nodded. "And where's Mr. Cody?"

"Cameron has his own private car and will join us at the airport at the designated time."

"Okay."

She settled back against his chest, and when he shifted positions, she could feel his hard erection pressing against her backside. What she felt was a sure sign that he wanted her, so why wasn't he taking her?

As the car sped toward Long Island, she sat cuddled in Xavier's lap, thinking and wondering just what was going on in that mind of his.

Chapter 13

A few hours later Farrah entered her home, and Xavier walked in behind her. He thought the flight from New York had gone well, with Cam and Farrah chatting amiably during most of the trip. More than once Cam had shot him a look that had clearly asked, *Why have you kept her hidden?*

He closed the door, leaned against it and watched as she moved across the room and switched on a lamp. Although it was late afternoon, it had already been dark when the plane had landed. Two private cars had sat waiting on the airstrip. One had whisked Cameron home, and Xavier had placed Farrah and her luggage with him in the other.

Swallowing thickly, he recalled how tempted he had been to take her directly to his place instead of bringing her here. In the end, his common sense had won out. He had to be patient in his handling of her.

When she moved to turn on another lamp he glanced around thinking how he had missed coming here.

"Thanks for everything, Xavier, especially for making the arrangements to get me back home."

His gaze returned to her. "You're welcome."

Xavier straightened from leaning against the door, and his stomach clenched when she walked slowly toward him. He wasn't sure what she planned to do, but from the look in her eyes, he had a feeling he was in trouble.

When she reached him, she wrapped her arms around his neck. And when she tilted her face up to him, he lowered his head to give her what she wanted. What he wanted. The moment their lips connected, he slid his tongue in her mouth and began mating hungrily with hers. She melted into him, and he deepened the kiss by widening his mouth over hers.

He needed this contact as much as he needed to breathe. And she clung to him as if she felt the same way. For him, that was a good sign, one he intended to cultivate any way that he could. He reluctantly broke the kiss and whispered against her moist lips. "Come home with me tonight."

He saw the indecisiveness in her arched brow and knew why. One of their unspoken agreements had been he would visit her here. She'd preferred things that way because it had given her a semblance of control. What she didn't know, and what she would eventually discover, was that no matter how many roadblocks she erected, he intended to rush right through each and every one of them.

When she didn't say anything, he leaned down to place kisses around her mouth. "I figure we could grab something to eat at the Racetrack Café and go to my place to watch a movie and then go to sleep."

"Sleep?" she asked in a deep, raspy tone.

"Yes, if that's what you want to do," he said in a husky voice. "But would you really want to?"

Farrah threw her head back and groaned deep in her throat when the tip of Xavier's tongue became naughty and began licking all around her mouth. The man was torturing her something awful. She tried pushing the thoughts from her mind that he was asking her to relinquish control by doing something atypical in their relationship.

However, she *had* agreed to an unlimited affair with him, hadn't she? And she did want to make love to him again, didn't she? Should it matter if it was his bed or hers? His home or hers?

"Farrah?"

She met his gaze. The look she saw in his eyes was enough to make her panties wet. "No, I don't want to sleep," she heard herself saying. "And yes, I want to spend the night at your place."

Farrah moved around her bedroom unpacking her things, while at the same time tossing a few items into an overnight bag. The private car had taken Xavier home where he would get his car and come back for her in an hour.

Snapping her overnight bag shut, she moved from her bedroom toward the living room, intent on making sure she was ready when he returned. Tremors of anticipation were racing through her at the thought that he would be taking her back to the place where they had met. A place where a number of his friends, as well as hers, hung out.

She nearly jumped when the doorbell sounded, and moved toward the door. She looked through the peephole, and sensations flooded her insides. It was Xavier, and as she had done, he had taken time to change clothes. Opening the door, she saw he was no longer wearing a suit but had changed into a pair of jeans and a shirt. And this was the first time he had appeared on her doorstep without his signature bottle of wine.

She felt his gaze roam over her, and when he smiled, she couldn't help but smile, too. "Ready?" he asked, taking her overnight bag from her hand.

"Yes."

He stepped back, and after she locked the door behind her, he took her hand and escorted her to his two-seater sports car.

"Did you enjoy your meal?" Xavier asked Farrah a short while later at the Racetrack Café.

The popular bar and grill in town was jointly owned by several drivers on the NASCAR circuit. Over the years it had become one of his favorite places to eat and to hang out, especially on the weekends.

Tonight the place was crowded, understandably so since there was a live band every Friday night. Couples were on the dance floor, and he couldn't wait to get out there himself. The need to hold Farrah in his arms was hitting him hard.

"Yes, everything was wonderful."

"Do you remember that we met here?" He wondered if she remembered that night like he did.

She smiled. "Yes, I know. It was girls night out for me and Natalie. She had her eyes on Donovan and my eyes were on you. I thought you were hot."

Xavier chuckled. One of the things he liked about Farrah was her honesty. She was up front with her responses. "You thought so?"

"Yes, I still do," she said softly at the same time one of her bare feet intentionally rubbed against his pants leg.

He held her gaze, fully aware of what she was trying to do. It wouldn't take much to push him over the edge. She was ready for them to leave and go to his place to be alone.

"Hey, you two, when did you get back?"

He glanced up to find Donovan Steele and his wife, Natalie, standing at their table. Immediately Farrah was out of her seat to give her best friend a hug, while likewise, he stood to shake Donovan's hand and invite him and Natalie to join them.

"We decided to head back before the snowstorm hit,"

he said, smiling over at Donovan. "Cameron made that possible since he was anxious to return to Charlotte anyway. We caught a ride back on his private plane."

Donovan chuckled. "I can just imagine Cam wanting to get back. Now that Vanessa is pregnant, he doesn't like being away from her for too long."

"So you didn't get any shopping in?" Natalie asked Farrah, grinning.

"Are you kidding?" Farrah laughed. "You know I don't do cold weather well. I was ready to come home the minute the temperatures dropped below twenty."

Xavier leaned back in his chair and noticed Farrah seemed comfortable with them being seen together as a couple tonight. During the course of their meal, several people they knew had stopped by their table to say hello.

"Since the two of you have finished eating, will you be leaving here soon?" Donovan asked.

Xavier glanced over at Farrah and saw the hopeful look in her eyes but chose to ignore it. "Not until we get a few dances in, starting now, so please excuse us," he said, standing up and extending his hand out to Farrah when he heard the band play a slow number. She took it and stood.

He was grateful she wasn't upset that he was stalling about leaving. But he wanted her to enjoy doing things with him other than making love. He pulled her into his arms the moment their feet touched the dance floor. Wrapping his arms around her waist, he drank in her luscious fragrance. "Do you remember the first time we danced here together?" he asked, angling his head and leaning his mouth close to her ear.

She nodded, tilting her head back to look up at him. "Yes, it was right after we spent an hour or so in the game room. You beat me at everything that night. Pool. Darts. Pinball."

He chuckled. "Yes, but you weren't so bad. In fact I thought you were pretty good."

She seemed pleased with his compliment. "Really?"

"Yes, really. I think we need to play a few of those games again sometime."

She studied his gaze. "But not tonight."

He chuckled. "No, definitely not tonight."

He pulled her tighter in his arms, and she rested her head against his chest. He felt his desire for her growing and his love right along with it. He tightened his arm around her even more, and glancing over at their table, he saw Donovan and Natalie watching them with curious eyes. But he didn't care. The only thing he cared about was the feel of her in his arms. The woman whose head was pressed against his heart. A heart that belonged to her whether she knew it or not.

They moved to the slow music, and luckily for him, when the song ended, another slow one began. And just like before, he held her close. At one point he rested his lips close to her ear and sang parts of the song to her. In between the lyrics, he whispered just what he wanted to do to her later. And he was as detailed and explicit as he could be.

When the song came to an end, before they parted, Farrah leaned closed to him and whispered, "Don't be all talk. Do it."

Xavier decided to accept her challenge. He took her hand in his and led her back over to their table. After quickly gathering their coats and her purse, they bid good-night to their friends and left.

They didn't share much conversation in the car. Instead, Farrah stared out the window at the moonless sky, although there were a number of bright stars overhead.

She figured there was nothing left to be said between them since they both knew what they wanted. But that didn't keep her from anticipating what was in store. She didn't have any regrets about them being together and couldn't help thinking how easy it had been to be out with him tonight. She had enjoyed herself before dinner, during dinner and after dinner.

They had discussed a number of topics, and when people who knew them had approached their table, it hadn't bothered her when she could tell they assumed she and Xavier were an item. Even when Donovan and Natalie had shown up and joined them, she hadn't been bothered by the knowing looks Natalie had given her.

Farrah's attention was pulled back to the present when they came to the entrance of Xavier's subdivision, and he pulled up to the security gate. Moments later he drove through. Most of the homes they passed were adorned with holiday decorations. It then dawned on her that she hadn't bothered putting up a tree since her divorce from Dustin. At one time she used to fully embrace the merriment of the season and would look forward to all the holiday festivities.

When Xavier's car pulled into the driveway to his home and the garage door went up, she felt an anxiousness in the pit of her stomach. She was here at the place he considered his primary home. After the garage door closed behind him and he'd brought the car to a stop, he killed the engine before glancing over at her and smiling. "Welcome to my home, Farrah."

There was something about what he said that sent a warm feeling through her. "Thanks for bringing me here."

And she truly meant it. There *was* something about being here, being a part of Xavier's element and sharing his personal space that had her feeling emotions she had never felt before.

He opened the car door and she watched as he moved around the front of the vehicle to open the door for her. He extended his hand to her, and she took it, and then, surprising her, he whisked her off her feet and into his arms.

"Xavier!"

He lowered his head and captured the squeal from her lips, effectively silencing her while mating his mouth hungrily and greedily with hers. His tongue was devouring her, escalating her desire and longing for him as he took her mouth with a mastery that made her groan.

Moments later he released her mouth and began walking with her toward his back door. Desire began spiraling through her when he opened the door. She didn't say a word. She just stared up at him while he continued to hold her in his arms.

He pushed the door open and carried her over the threshold. She could barely see her surroundings as he swiftly moved through his kitchen, dining room and living room and then carried her up the stairs.

Xavier walked down a hall before finally entering a dark bedroom. He placed her in the middle of the bed before turning on a lamp to bring light into the room. It was then that she looked at him and saw the heat within his gaze. Her eyes roamed all over every square inch of his muscular body after he removed his coat and tossed it aside. The muscles bulging beneath his shirt made her appreciate the fact he was a man with the ability to make her mind incapable of thought. With Xavier all she could do was feel.

He unbuttoned his shirt, then removed it to reveal one incredibly hot-looking chest dusted with hair she wouldn't mind running her fingers through or burying her nose in, while inhaling his masculine scent.

When her gaze moved from his chest to meet his eyes, he said, "In case you're wondering what I'm doing, I'm about to prove to you, Farrah Langley, that I am not all talk."

Chapter 14

No, he wasn't all talk, Farrah thought a short while later as his engorged erection pushed through her womanly folds to join their bodies as one.

Already she had climaxed from his mouth twice, and every single inch of her was still humming for more. How was he able to do that? He used his mouth in ways that should be outlawed.

Once he had stripped every stitch of clothing from her body and encased his huge erection into a condom, he had joined her in bed. A slow, sensual smile had touched his lips when he pulled her into his arms, and anticipation had rammed through her, making her want him that much more.

"At last," she whispered when she felt the strength of him continue to push through her. He lifted her hips in his big hands, holding her steady while he pushed inside of her to the hilt. And then he threw his head back and growled satisfaction. He began moving inside of her, sending sensations from where their bodies were joined to every part of her body, touching every single nerve ending and making breath whoosh from her lungs.

Each stroke, each tantalizing thrust, made her moan his name over and over. He lowered his head to her breasts and captured a nipple between his lips and began sucking on it like it was the best thing he'd ever tasted. She felt on the verge of total sensuous madness and ultimate fulfillment.

"Farrah!"

She knew the moment his body exploded, and she tightened her legs around his waist when she felt him driven to yet another orgasm. She screamed his name when she felt herself losing control, digging her fingers deep in his shoulders while doing so. He continued to thrust into her, over and over again.

It was only then he slumped off her, still keeping her in his arms and their bodies connected. Even now it seemed he wasn't ready to let her go. And for the moment, as he held her in his arms, there was no other place she'd rather be.

The sound of cabinet doors opening and closing downstairs made Xavier open his eyes to squint against the sunlight coming in through his window. He smiled, realizing he was in his bedroom. His bed. And he had made love to Farrah in it last night. To him that was a major accomplishment.

He gazed up at the ceiling remembering last night. Oh, what a night. After removing his own clothes he had proceeded to remove hers before tasting every single inch of her body. Her full sweet breasts had been heavenly, the dark nipples meant for sucking and licking.

The sounds she'd made when his mouth touched her body only made him want to do even more things to her. And they were things that had made his erection swell even more.

By the time he had eased between her legs, while she had clutched his shoulders tight and wrapped her long legs around his waist, he'd known they would be having orgasms all over the place. They had. The mere memory had his erection throbbing. He wanted her again, and he wanted her now.

Easing out of bed, he slipped into the jeans he had discarded last night. He went into the bathroom to quickly wash his face and brush his teeth and couldn't help but smile when he saw her toothbrush already in the holder beside his.

He moved slowly down the stairs, and when his nose picked up the aroma of coffee, he increased his pace. He rounded the corner to the kitchen and stopped dead in his tracks. Farrah was standing at the refrigerator, leaning over to look inside and wearing the shirt he'd worn last night. It barely covered her rear end and he could clearly see the luscious swell of her butt cheeks, which meant she wasn't wearing any panties.

It could have been his groan that made her aware he was behind her. She turned, and they stared at each other, not saying anything. It was as if time stood still.

He finally moved, crossed the room to her and, without saying a word, he lifted her into his arms, carried her over to the table and sat down in the chair with her straddling his lap. He wanted her. Now.

He took her mouth, mated with it voraciously while she took matters into her own hands by lowering his zipper to release his erection from bondage. Once free, his erection swelled in anticipation, and when he released her mouth, he whispered against her moist lips, "I want to come inside of you."

He knew just what he was saying, exactly what he was asking. They both were fully aware that since the night they'd met neither had indulged in sex with anyone else. And as far as he was concerned, they wouldn't be making love with anyone but each other from now on. They both had good health records, so as far as he was concerned, there was no reason they couldn't be skin-to-skin, flesh-to-flesh and make love with the purpose of giving each other the most primitive pleasure possible. He'd never released his semen inside a woman before but wanted to do so with her. He just hoped and prayed that she went along with it.

He watched her nervously nibble on her bottom lip, which meant she was considering his request. "Why?" she asked.

"Because every time I sank my body into yours," he whispered, "I wanted to know what it's like to feel you without any barriers and to know when I come I will fill you with the very essence of me. Not for the purpose of making a baby, but for the purpose of knowing how it feels to mingle my semen with your juices when we share pleasure."

His pulse throbbed painfully in his throat as he waited for her to make the next move. Her grip on his erection tightened, and she lifted her body off his lap so he could slide inside of her. As he began pushing forward, she groaned while her muscles clenched him all the way. And when he met her gaze he saw a mirror of desire so heated it almost took his breath away.

He pushed farther inside of her and knew the exact moment the physical and the emotional became one, merging in a way that robbed him of any coherent thought other than to be with her like this. And when he began moving, he felt her heated flesh consume him with every thrust. Unable to retain hold of his sanity, he leaned over and devoured her mouth as he gave her body and the chair one hell of a workout.

And then it happened. An explosion that nearly knocked the chair from under them. In a mad rush his semen filled her, triggering her climax. She screamed his name, and he gritted his teeth as he continued to pump into her. Hard. Fast. He was giving her all he had with no holding back. This was the way it was supposed to be, he thought. This was the way he wanted it. And from her deep, guttural scream this was the way she wanted it as well.

Little did she know that for them this was only the beginning.

Farrah sat at Xavier's kitchen table and glanced out the window that faced the majestic Palisades Golf Course. Already golfers were moving about. Luckily the curtains had been drawn when they'd made out in the very chair she was sitting in a short while ago. Xavier had assured her that even if the curtain had been open it would have been highly unlikely that anyone would have seen what they'd done in his kitchen. Still, the thought couldn't help but make her blush.

She took another sip of her coffee as she moved her gaze from the window to the man standing at the stove preparing pancakes. He hadn't bothered to snap up his jeans that hung low on lean hips, and they looked so darn good on his hard masculine thighs and fine-as-a-dime backside. Her gaze traveled upward and did a wide sweep of his hairy chest, tight abs, well-defined arm muscles and wide shoulders.

She moved her gaze upward, past his broad shoulders to his face. He had long lashes, the kind most women would kill for. And the shadow darkening his jaw indicated he hadn't bothered to shave. Then there were his lips, full and inviting. She felt heat flood her stomach when she remembered all the things those lips and his mouth had done to her.

She released a deep breath, suddenly feeling the

effect of the caffeine. The effect of Xavier Kane. The man had a gorgeous body, and he most certainly knew how to use it.

"You like what you see, Farrah?"

She blinked, wondering how he'd known she was staring at him when he was supposed to be concentrating on fixing breakfast. He looked up and smiled before turning around to face her while leaning his hip against the kitchen counter.

"How could I not like what I see? You're a straight guy, pretty well-off and you look pretty darn good in a pair of jeans. And you can make me purr in the bedroom. According to some women, a man with those qualities is a rarity these days."

He lifted a brow. "Some women?"

"Yes, those looking for a mate."

"Oh, I see." He didn't say anything for a minute and then asked, "What are you doing next Saturday night?"

She blinked. His question had caught her off guard. She hesitated for a second and then said, "I don't recall having any plans. Why?"

"I'd like you to go to a party with me."

She placed her coffee cup down, feeling anxiety set in. "A party?"

"Yes."

Her anxiety increased. Although he had mentioned attending parties with him, she wasn't prepared to do so this soon.

"It's being given by Donovan's brother Morgan and

his wife, Lena. A holiday fundraiser to benefit under-privileged kids."

Instead of saying anything, Farrah picked up her cup to take a sip of her coffee. She needed to think about that. She didn't know Morgan Steele that well, but she had known Lena for years. As a real estate agent, Lena had been the one to sell her and Dustin their first home, and four years later she had sought out Lena's services to find her another place after their divorce.

"Farrah?"

She glanced up and met Xavier's gaze. His expression didn't give anything away, but she had a feeling he fully expected her to turn him down, although she *had* agreed to the affair without limitations. In a way, she felt foolish for letting past pain dictate how she lived her life.

She forced her eyes away from his to glance out the window, knowing she couldn't hide behind her pain forever. Maybe it was time to take a stand and finally move on. Something she hadn't done and something it seemed Xavier was hell-bent on forcing her to do.

She glanced back at him and swallowed deeply before saying, "Yes. I'll go to the party with you."

Chapter 15

Farrah stared at herself in the full-length mirror. When was the last time she had dressed to please a man? And as much as she'd tried convincing herself she'd purchased this dress because she'd liked it, deep down she'd bought it because she figured Xavier would like it. It was blue, his favorite color, and the style of the dress showed off her figure. Even Natalie had said so when the two had gone shopping.

At least there would be people at the party she would know besides the host and hostess. Donovan and Natalie would be there, as well as other members of the Steele family. And Xavier had mentioned a couple of his godbrothers would be in attendance as well.

Last weekend, she had ended up spending the entire time at Xavier's home. On Saturday night he had brought her back home to get more clothes and to dress for a movie.

She laughed softly to herself when she thought how Xavier had threatened never to take her to a movie again if she had to cry through the entire feature. She hadn't been able to help it, convinced during most of the film the hero was going to lose his life and never return to the heroine.

When she heard the doorbell sound, she slowly inhaled a breath of air and gave herself time to release it. Xavier had returned to New York on Tuesday to finalize a few things and had called every night to see how she was doing. He'd returned to Charlotte late last night and had called her this morning to invite her to his place for breakfast. Unfortunately, she had been on her way out the door for her hair and nail appointment.

As she headed for the door, a part of her wondered what on earth she was doing by letting another man get under her skin. But in reality, he'd done more than get under her skin. He had licked every part of it at one time or another. She would be the first to admit that although she was still trying with all her might to keep her guard in place, the time she was beginning to spend with him outside of the bedroom was awakening something within her that she thought had long ago died a brutal death. She could actually say she enjoyed spending time with a man in something other than a sexual affair.

She stopped walking and squeezed her eyes shut for a second, remembering why she had broken things off

between them six months ago. Why wasn't the thought
of becoming too close not scaring her out of her wits
now?

A shiver ran down her spine as she opened her eyes
and resumed walking. It was hard to describe what she
was feeling these days. It was as if each and every time
Xavier touched her he was branding her for life. She
knew the idea of such a thing sounded absolutely crazy
and probably was, but she couldn't let go of the question
running through her head. Why was she comfortable
with how things were between them now?

She opened the door, and he stood there, leaning in
her doorway, and as usual, looking as sexy as ever. For
some reason, he seemed even more so today, dressed
in a pair of jeans, a white shirt and a chocolate brown
suede jacket. He smiled at her in a way that deepened
the lines around his lips and brought out a dimple she
rarely saw. And then she saw something flame to life
in his gaze, and her heart began pounding in her chest.
She felt sensual stirrings in the pit of her stomach.

"Xavier," she said in a raspy voice that she couldn't
hide. "Welcome back to Charlotte." She took a step back
to let him inside.

"It's good to be back. I missed you." And then he
reached out for her, pulled her into his arms and captured her mouth in his. A part of her understood his
craving since it mirrored her own hunger. He said he'd
missed her. She honestly didn't know what to make of
that. They had been together nearly a year before and

had gone weeks without seeing each other, and not once had he ever admitted to missing her.

But tonight he had.

He finally pulled his mouth away but rested his forehead against hers, drawing in a deep breath while she did likewise. He then whispered against her moist lips, "It wouldn't take much to strip you naked right now."

"What's stopping you?" she murmured, taking a quick lick of his lips and causing his erection to jump. She felt it and couldn't help but smile at his body's response to her words.

His gaze roamed over her before returning to her eyes. "It's tempting, sweetheart, but we have a party to attend."

She leaned forward and wrapped her arms around his neck. "You mean you'd rather go to a party tonight than stay here and spend some productive time with me?"

A smile spread across his lips. "No, but I plan for us to go to that damn party and when it's over I'll bring you back here and get a lot of productive time in."

"You might be too tired."

He threw his head back and laughed. "Not on your life, sweetheart, so come on and let's go. The sooner we can make an appearance at the party, the sooner we can get back here and get naughty."

She couldn't help but smile. "I'm holding you to that, Xavier Kane."

* * *

"Will you be withdrawing your membership from the club, X?"

Xavier glanced up at one of his godbrothers, Virgil Bougard. "What gives you that idea, V?" he asked, taking a sip of his wine.

"The way you're acting with Farrah Langley. Tonight's the first time I've seen you out with a woman in a long time and unless I'm seeing wrong, you're quite taken with her."

Xavier smiled. No, Virgil wasn't seeing wrong. But then, even if he were to explain how things were, Virgil wouldn't understand.

"And what do you think you see, V?" he couldn't help but ask. He could tell Virgil was getting annoyed with his evasiveness.

Virgil frowned. "I see you acting almost as bad as Uriel. At least he's married. Just look at you now. You're talking to me but not once have you taken your eyes off Farrah."

Xavier knew that much was true. He had pretty much hung by Farrah's side most of the evening. Only when Natalie and Vanessa had come and grabbed her had he sought out Virgil's company for a while.

"Xavier?"

He glanced back to Virgil. "Yes?"

"I said that—"

"Mind if I join you guys?"

He glanced over at the woman who walked up. Marti Goshay. They'd been involved in a sex-only affair a few years ago that hadn't even lasted a month. That was all of her he could take, especially when she'd begun hinting at a serious affair that she'd wanted to end in marriage.

"Would it matter if we said that we did mind?" Virgil asked the woman.

Xavier had to keep from smiling. He'd forgotten there was bad blood between Virgil and Marti. Some claimed she was the reason her sister had dumped Virgil a few years ago over some lie Marti had told.

Ignoring Virgil, Marti turned her attention to Xavier. "I thought I'd give you my business card. I hadn't heard from you in a while and figured you probably didn't know my phone number had changed."

He nodded as he accepted the card she handed him. Not that he would use it. He intended to toss it in the trash at the next opportunity. Of course, Marti would think the only reason he hadn't contacted her in almost two years was because he didn't have her new phone number. The woman really thought a lot of herself. She was attractive, true enough, but her beauty was only on the outside. Farrah's beauty, he thought, was both inside and out.

"How would you like to attend the Tina Turner concert with me next weekend, Xavier?" she asked him.

"I'll be busy next weekend."

Virgil decided not to be so subtle. "He's involved with someone, Marti. Move on."

The woman seemed amused by that bit of news.

"Who? Definitely not the woman you brought here tonight," she said smiling. "Everybody knows Farrah Langley couldn't hold on to her husband. He was involved in an affair, so what does that tell you?"

Xavier turned his dark, laser sharp eyes on Marti and said, "It tells me the man was a damn fool." He walked off, leaving Virgil to deal with her, knowing without a doubt that his godbrother could.

"I thought the party was nice, Xavier. Thanks for bringing me."

He glanced over at Farrah as they pulled out of Morgan's driveway. "Thank you for coming."

Farrah leaned back against the headrest and closed her eyes. The party had been nice, and she hadn't once felt awkward being seen out with him. In fact, she'd read a lot of envy in the gazes of a number of women. What she'd told Xavier earlier tonight was true. He would be a great catch for any woman.

Even her.

She snapped her eyes back open and glanced over at him. His full attention seemed to be on driving, but her full attention was on him. What made her put herself in the group with all those other women when she wasn't interested in a serious relationship? She didn't think of Xavier in terms of a good catch, but rather a perfect lover. What if she began seeing him in a whole new light?

She shook her head and then turned her attention to the objects outside the car window, refusing to go there. The only reason she was thinking such things was because of how good she felt. She had enjoyed a good party and now she was looking forward to an even better night. That had to be it. It couldn't be any other reason.

"What are you doing next weekend, Farrah?"

She glanced back over at Xavier. "Why do you want to know?"

"I have tickets to the *Nutcracker* and was wondering if you'd go with me?"

She drew in a deep breath. Now was the time to tell him that although she had enjoyed herself with him tonight, they shouldn't overdo it. But for some reason, she couldn't fix her mouth to say that. Especially when she enjoyed the *Nutcracker*.

"Yes, I'd love to go with you," she heard herself saying.

He smiled. "Good."

Farrah looked back out of the car's window, not sure if it was good or not.

Chapter 16

Farrah tried shifting to another position and discovered she couldn't, due to the masculine body still connected to hers. Ever since Xavier had stopped using a condom, he liked drifting off to sleep with his manhood still inside of her and one of his legs thrown over hers. More than once over the past few weeks, she had awakened from the feel of his erection stretching her inner muscles as it enlarged inside of her.

It was hard to believe that next week would be Christmas, and so far she had been Xavier's date to four parties and to the *Nutcracker*. Since they ran into most of the same people at all the events, she knew everyone thought they were having a hot and heavy love affair... and she would have to agree with them.

That thought no longer bothered her, and each and

every day she was beginning to feel more and more comfortable with him and how their relationship was going. Just last week he'd flown her to New York to spend a few days with him while he'd wrapped up business there. She had stayed with him at his home, spending her days shopping and her nights in his bed.

Needing to go to the bathroom, she tapped him on the shoulder and his sleep-laden sexy eyes stared into hers. "I have to go to the bathroom," she whispered.

He lifted his leg off hers and disconnected their bodies before flipping on his stomach. From the sound of his even breathing, he had gone back to sleep within seconds. She smiled as she eased out of the bed. Poor baby, she thought. Evidently she had worn him out.

The light shining from the bathroom showed their clothes were scattered all over the floor. They had begun stripping the moment they had entered her bedroom. How they'd made it up the stairs with their clothes on was beyond her.

After using the bathroom, she was returning to the bed and decided to gather up the scattered clothing along the way and toss them on a chair. She picked a business card off the floor that evidently had fallen out of Xavier's jacket. She was about to put it back inside the pocket when she read the words someone had scrawled on the back.

Call me. You won't regret it.

She frowned when she flipped the card over. Marti Goshay, Attorney-at-Law.

Her frown deepened. Although she didn't know Marti

Goshay personally, she knew of her. And she'd known from that night at the party that Morgan and Lena had guessed the woman had the hots for Xavier. Farrah had heard from Natalie that Xavier and Marti had dated a while back, and from the looks Marti had had in her eyes whenever she'd glanced at Xavier, the woman wanted him back.

Farrah had been talking to Natalie and Vanessa that particular night and had seen Marti hand Xavier her business card. He had taken it, and at the time Farrah had wondered why. Now she wanted to know why he'd kept it. That had been almost two weeks ago. Hadn't he claimed he wanted a long-term affair with her because he was tired of women coming on to him? So why hadn't he let Marti Goshay know he was already involved?

Not even bothering to fight back the anger and jealousy she suddenly felt, she quickly moved to the bed to tap Xavier on the shoulder. "Wake up, Xavier. You need to leave. Now."

She had to tap him a couple more times before he finally awoke. "Xavier, you need to leave."

He lifted his head and flipped on his back to stare up at her with sleep-filled eyes. "What's wrong?"

"Nothing other than this," she said, dropping the business card onto his naked chest.

He rubbed a hand down his face before picking up the card. He considered it for a moment and then tossed it on her nightstand. "Come back to bed, Farrah."

His command angered her even more. "I won't, and

I want you out of my bed. Now," she said, looming over him, in his face.

Instead of moving, he stretched out, placed his hands behind his head and stared up at her. "Why?"

She rolled angry eyes. "I just told you why."

"No, you didn't."

And before she could blink, he had reached out and grabbed her hands and tumbled her down in the bed with him. He shifted his position, and now she was the one on her back with him looming over her. "Now tell me why you're upset, Farrah."

"That business card fell out of your jacket."

He shrugged. "And?"

That one word seemed to make her angrier. "And that was enough."

He chuckled. "I care to differ. Marti Goshay gave me that business card at Morgan and Lena's party."

"But you kept it."

"Only because I'd forgotten about it. I had intended to throw it away." Now it was his eyes that darkened with anger. "And just what are you accusing me of?"

"What do you think?"

For a few seconds Xavier just stared down at her, and then a smile replaced his anger. "You're jealous."

That observation really riled her. "I am *not* jealous. I detest men who can't be trusted. Now get off of me."

Xavier released her and eased off the bed. He moved across the room and slumped down in the chair. "So you're saying I can't be trusted because you found a business card in my jacket?"

She sat up in bed. "A business card from an old girlfriend who said to call her."

"And you figured I would?"

"You kept the card, Xavier."

She fought back the tears. She wouldn't tell him that was the first sign she'd gotten that Dustin was cheating. It was the first one she'd gotten and the main one she'd overlooked, thinking there was nothing to it. She had been a fool not to catch the early warning signs. She wouldn't be a fool ever again.

"Does your mistrust of me have anything to do with that ass you were married to?"

"And if it does?"

He held her gaze. "Then I want you to stop."

"Stop?"

"Yes. Stop comparing me to him, Farrah." He slowly shook his head. "You still don't get it, do you?"

She crossed her arms over her chest. "And just what am I supposed to be getting?"

"The fact that no other woman interests me because I love you."

Her mouth dropped open. "Love me? That's crazy."

He eased to his feet. "Maybe. And what's even crazier is that I believe you love me back. You're just afraid to admit it. However, your overblown jealousy just proved I'm right."

She glared over at him. "You're not right. I don't love you."

He smiled. "Yes, you do and please don't say what we've been sharing was nothing but sex. Sex between us is good—hell, it's unbelievable, Farrah. But nothing can be that good unless there's some heavy-duty love thrown into the mix. For the past three weeks I've deliberately and painstakingly tried proving to you that we're good together, in or out of bed. Think about it." He then moved to walk away.

She floundered for a response and then asked, "And just where do you think you're going?"

"To take a shower," he called over his shoulder as he kept walking. He went into the bathroom and closed the door behind him.

A frustrated Farrah reclined on her back and stared up at the ceiling when she heard the shower going. How dare he insinuate that she loved him just because she'd gotten tiffed over finding that business card. Any woman would be upset. Wouldn't she?

She turned her head toward his pillow and breathed in deeply to inhale the scent he'd left behind. And then she closed her eyes, and memories began flooding her brain. The magic of everything she and Xavier had shared touched her deeply. Did he really mean it when he said that he loved her?

She considered the possibility for a second and knew it was true. What other man would have taken the time to deliberately take their affair out of the bedroom? And each and every time she'd gone out on a date with him, she had enjoyed it immensely. He'd been adept at balancing the physical part of their relationship with the emotional.

And she knew, believed in her heart, that he was

nothing like Dustin. Xavier could be trusted. He would never deliberately hurt her, use her or abuse what they had together. He would only love her.

Tears sprang into her eyes, and she wiped them away as she eased off the bed and headed toward the bathroom. He was so right. He wasn't Dustin, and her ex couldn't compare to Xavier in any way.

He was right about something else, too. She did love him, and it was about time she showed him how much.

A spray of water poured over Xavier's body as he stood underneath the showerhead. A part of him always regretted washing away Farrah's scent; he much preferred to wear it all day.

He hoped he'd given her something to think about, although that was not how he'd wanted to blurt out that he loved her. He'd pretty much envisioned a romantic candlelit dinner on Christmas night where he would pour his heart and soul out to her before asking her to marry him. But at least now she knew how he felt, and the way she'd gotten in a tiff about Marti's business card had sent hopeful chills up his spine.

If she thought for one minute he was going to let her end things between them again, she had another thought coming. He was in for the long haul, and the sooner she admitted to herself that she loved him, the better it would be for the both of them. Then they could get on with their lives. Together.

He reached up to turn off the water when the shower

door opened and she stood there. Naked. Beautiful. He leaned against the tile wall. His heart began doing jumping jacks in his chest when she stepped into the shower stall with him. "I didn't know you planned to take a shower with me," he said throatily, feeling every word torn deep in his lungs.

Instead of saying anything, she grabbed the soap and lathered her hands and then reached for his chest. He grabbed her hands to stop her. Whenever they showered together, she always lathered him all over. She was acting as if nothing had changed between them. But things had, and it was time for her to acknowledge that fact.

He held her hands tightly in his and met her gaze. "Tell me, Farrah. Don't show me anymore. Whether you wanted to or not, you've been showing me each and every time we made love. Now I want you to tell me."

She shook her head. "I can't."

He rubbed a finger gently across her cheek. "Yes, you can, baby. You're not the only one who's ever been hurt by love."

Her mouth pressed into a thin line, and for a minute he thought that maybe he had pushed her too far, had asked too much of her. But then she took a step toward him and reached up to wrap her arms around his neck while water sprayed down on them both. He reached behind him and turned off the water and turned back to her. "Tell me."

She inhaled deeply and met his gaze. "I love you, Xavier," she then said softly. "I've loved you for a long time. I've been too scared to admit it to myself. I tried denying it by sending you away. And then when I ran into you in New York, I convinced myself that a holiday fling was all I wanted. But I know now that would not have been the case. I will always love you and I want you."

He lowered his mouth to hers at the same time his hands spread across her backside to bring her closer to him. He fully understood what she'd been going through. It had taken him a while to recover from Dionne, so he knew why she'd been hesitant to give her love freely again. But each and every day he would show her, tell her, prove to her just how much she was loved, wanted and cherished.

He continued to take her mouth in agonizing pleasure, tasting her as their tongues tangled, mated in a dance of possession and non-restraint. He wasn't the only one coming unleashed. She was deliberately tempting him by rubbing her body against his, cradling his manhood between her open thighs. She moaned into his mouth, and the sound sent sensuous shivers all the way up his spine.

Xavier broke off the kiss and drew in a deep breath. He studied the face staring up at him, and it was all he could do to maintain his control and not sweep her into his arms and take her back to bed.

"I was determined to prove to you it wasn't just about sex with us, Farrah," he said, reaching out to brush back wet hair from her face.

"And you did." A smile touched her lips. "But the sex was still good."

He chuckled. "It will always be good between us. I love you."

"And I love you, too."

Xavier lowered his head, capturing her mouth again. He knew at that moment that their life together was just beginning.

Epilogue

Six months later

"I now pronounce you man and wife. You may kiss your bride, Xavier."

Xavier pulled Farrah into his arms and kissed her deeply. Moments later when he felt one of his godbrothers poke him in the side, he winced before releasing her mouth. He'd gotten carried away, but that was okay. It was his wedding day, and he intended to let everyone know just what a happy man he was.

A short while later at the wedding reception, he stood on the sidelines watching Farrah toss her bouquet to all the single ladies when one of the men standing by his side said, "You're officially out of the club now, X."

He glanced over to his godbrothers, the ones who

were still bachelors in demand—Virgil, Winston, York and Zion. "I know, but I have no regrets."

He glanced back to Farrah. In her wedding gown, she looked simply beautiful. She met his gaze and smiled. He hoped one day each of his godbrothers would have a reason to lose membership in the club as well. He was convinced that nothing could replace a good woman in a man's life. Nothing.

"It's time for our dance," Farrah said, walking straight into his outstretched arms.

Her small hands felt secure in his as he led her to the dance floor. He couldn't wait until later tonight when he had her alone. In the morning, they would leave for a two-week honeymoon in Hawaii.

Xavier caught the eye of his friend Galen Steele, who was also one of Donovan's cousins from Phoenix. Galen, who'd been a devout bachelor, had gotten married himself a few months ago. From the smile he still wore on his face, Galen, like Xavier, had no regrets about moving from a being single man to a truly happily married one.

Farrah smiled up at him when they reached the dance floor. "Are you happy, sweetheart?" he asked her.

"Yes, I am truly happy. What about you?"

Instead of answering he leaned down and kissed her. After hearing a number of catcalls and whistles he figured he would let her mouth go.

"Did that answer your question?" he asked, whispering against her moist lips.

She laughed softly as she looked up at him. "Oh, yes, that pretty much summed it up."

Xavier pulled her tighter into his arms, feeling all of the love in his heart. He would have to agree. That pretty much summed it up.

* * * * *

A sneaky peek at next month...

Desire™

PASSIONATE AND DRAMATIC LOVE STORIES

My wish list for next month's titles...

In stores from 20th July 2012:

☐ Tempted by Her Innocent Kiss — Maya Banks

& The Nanny Bombshell — Michelle Celmer

☐ A Tangled Affair — Fiona Brand

& Caught in the Spotlight — Jules Bennett

☐ Feeling the Heat — Brenda Jackson

& A Man of His Word — Sarah M. Anderson

☐ Into His Private Domain — Janice Maynard

& A Touch of Persuasion — Janice Maynard

Available at WHSmith, Tesco, Asda, Eason, Amazon and Apple

Just can't wait?

Special Offers

Every month we put together collections and longer reads written by your favourite authors.

Here are some of next month's highlights— and don't miss our fabulous discount online!

Nora Roberts

Over 400 million of her books in print worldwide.

Luring a Lady

On sale 3rd August

Hot nights with a SPANIARD

CAROLE MORTIMER   INDIA GREY   LYNN RAYE HARRIS

On sale 3rd August

AT HIS SERVICE HIS 9-5 SECRETARY

HELEN BROOKS   MICHELLE CELMER   JENNIE ADAMS

On sale 3rd August

Save 20% on all Special Releases

Find out more at
www.millsandboon.co.uk/specialreleases

Visit us Online

MILLS & BOON
Book Club

2 Free Books!

Join the Mills & Boon Book Club

Want to read more **Desire**™ books? We're offering you **2 more** absolutely **FREE!**

We'll also treat you to these fabulous extras:

- **Books up to 2 months ahead of shops**
- **FREE home delivery**
- **Bonus books with our special rewards scheme**
- **Exclusive offers and much more!**

Get your free books now!

Visit us Online

Find out more at
www.millsandboon.co.uk/freebookoffer

Have Your Say

You've just finished your book.
So what did you think?

We'd love to hear your thoughts on our
'Have your say' online panel
www.millsandboon.co.uk/haveyoursay

- Easy to use
- Short questionnaire
- Chance to win Mills & Boon® goodies

Visit us Online

Tell us what you thought of this book now at
www.millsandboon.co.uk/haveyoursay

YOUR_SAY